DON'T TRY THIS AT HOME

Also by Paul Reizin

Dumping Hilary?

DON'T TRY THIS AT HOME

Paul Reizin

review

Title courtesy of London Weekend Television.

First published in Great Britain in 2003
by Review
An imprint of Headline Book Publishing

10 9 8 7 6 5 4 3 2 1

ISBN 0 7472 7056 2

Typeset in Perpetua by
Palimpsest Book Production Limited, Polmont, Stirlingshire

Printed and bound in Great Britain by
Mackays of Chatham plc, Chatham, Kent

Headline Book Publishing
A division of Hodder Headline
338 Euston Road
London NW1 3BH

www.headline.co.uk
www.hodderheadline.com

For Rachel (eventually)

My thanks to my agent Clare Alexander for her usual sagacity; to my editor Sarah Keen for her many insightful contributions; and to Mark Smith for the Frank-out-the-back joke.

'It is delightful to be hidden, but a disaster not to be found.'

D. W. Winnicott

O N E

1

If she thinks I'm someone else, why disappoint her?

I'd been sitting in Café Rouge, killing an hour, so I noticed her immediately when she walked in. Thin as a rail, wearing a leather jacket and checked trousers, a curtain of black hair, high forehead, serious black glasses. She looked French. A French Philosophy student, at a guess. She'd have a copy of *Being and Nothingness* in her handbag, smoke Gitanes, and when she opened her mouth a lovely gravelly French voice would come out of it. She'd be called Claudine. Or Marcelle. Severine, maybe. Anyhow, she was obviously looking for someone, making a big show of casting her gaze round the bar. And then, to my surprise, she lighted on me, smiled slightly, and marched up to my table.

'Are you Matthew?'

Deep rather than gravelly. And not French. And maybe not a student of Philosophy either. But there is something in that smile, and the . . . *springy* sort of way she loped up to me that makes me very much regret that I am not Matthew. Well, not technically. Not yet.

Like I say, if she thinks I'm someone else . . .

'Yes, I am. You must be . . .'

'Kate. Hi.' She looks relieved. We shake hands – a long, thin, almost bony hand, but warm, and a confident, expressive squeeze, not the limp, dead bird that so many women offer as a handshake – and she sits. A waiter shimmers up. The curtain of hair swings across Kate's face as she studies the wine list. With a flick, it flies back again, an intelligence and intensity in her eyes as she says, 'I'll have a glass of the Californian Chardonnay, please.'

'Medium or large?' enquires the waiter.

She looks at my own (large) glass.

'Oh, large, I should think.' And she laughs. We both do. OK, she's not Zizi or Claudine, she's Kate; she's spoken not even a dozen words, but I tell you something I already know. I *like* this woman.

'You look a bit different from how I pictured you,' she says, not unpleasantly. Her legs are crossed. Her bony knee and dangling foot are both pointing at me – a good sign, I once read in a newspaper.

'Really? How did you picture me?'

'Well, I thought you said you wore glasses.'

'I do, but not always. To tell you the truth, I've never really got used to them.'

'Didn't you say you'd be wearing a suit?'

'Oh, I did, didn't I? Sorry about that.' I shoot her what I hope is a winning hey-I'm-hopeless-but-kinda-likeable grin. It seems to work.

'You sound a bit different too. Your voice on the phone sounded . . . older.'

'Yes, it's strange that. People have said that to me before.'

'Am I what you expected, then?'

I pause to consider this fascinating question. Take a reflective glug of the Chilean Merlot. Do further consideration type stuff. Glug once again.

'Well . . .'

'I mean, you must have met quite a few people like this. You're chatting away on the phone and you get a picture in your head, don't you? But when they turn up in the flesh . . . you know. Haven't you ever wanted to do a runner?'

'No. Not really. There was one . . .'

'Go on. What was she like?'

'She was probably . . . a very nice person. Deep down.'

'Oh dear. That's terribly damning, isn't it?'

'I mean, there's nothing wrong per se in being interested in astrology, is there? Well, obsessed really. She had the book in her handbag. It was a system where you cross your Western sign with your Chinese sign and you come out as a Libra Donkey or a Scorpio Mouse. She told me I was a Gemini Goat. I think it all went downhill from there.'

'Astrology is pretty unforgivable,' says Kate boldly, and my attraction to her ratchets up another few clicks.

'I remember she wore this ratty old coat.'

'Bag woman.'

'Exactly! She reminded me of a mad old bag woman with her battered bloody astrology book. *And* she rolled her own cigarettes. I think she even wore a piece of pottery on a string round her neck. God, it's all coming back to me now. I'd blanked her from my memory. You don't roll your own cigarettes, do you? Or wear pottery? Ever, at all?'

She laughs. Her drink arrives. She takes a sip of Chardonnay.

I realise I have been describing someone I used to go out with at university.

'Anyway,' I continue, 'to answer your question, I didn't know what to expect this evening. But I'm glad we've met, put it that way.'

Kate cocks her head at an interesting angle. 'So what's it like working for Tony Blair?'

Ah. Interesting character, this Matthew. I take a deep breath. Fuck it then, here we go.

'Challenging. Yes, I think that's the best way of describing it. Very . . . challenging.'

2

There was a boy in my class at primary school who was so chronically shy he wouldn't answer to his own name during the morning register.

'He's here, miss,' we'd prepare to shout out on his behalf, as Mrs Kemp rattled through the Hs, the Js and the Ks, through Hugh Letwin, Daisy Lewis and Gill Lomax, at last arriving at The Great Silent One himself.

Occasionally, I wonder what became of Simon Lowenstein. He never seemed to mind that we answered for him, no embarrassment on his freckly face as he stared straight ahead with that benign, even intelligent expression. Now, all these years later, I have begun to think that maybe we got him wrong — that he wasn't painfully shy at all. Rather, it was for some other reason that he didn't want to be Simon Lowenstein. Maybe, in his head, he was Simon Smith or Simon Ali or *Sarah* Lowenstein, who knows? Unwilling to recognise himself as himself, maybe Simon Lowenstein had the powerful idea that somehow he was living the wrong life.

Maybe.

Anyhow, answering for Simon Lowenstein gave me and the boy I shared a desk with a good idea. We started answering for each other. It seemed wickedly exciting to say 'Yes, miss' when Andrew Fineman's name was called out – he was, still is, so different from me – and there was a delightful feeling of . . . well, liberation, I suppose you could call it, hearing Andrew affirming that he indeed was Charles Green.

Most of the rest of the class didn't notice our subversive little game, never mind Mrs Kemp. And it soon came to my notice that it could be to your advantage to allow certain actions to be ascribed in error to another. One morning, as the notably tetchy Miss Wilson chalks up sums on the blackboard, I stretch forward and with the end of my ruler nudge Dawn Covington's tin pencil case off the edge of her desk. It hits the floor with the most wonderfully satisfying cannonade. Miss Wilson is predictably incensed.

'Leave it!' she bellows, and then with impeccable logic adds, as she always does, 'It can't fall any further.'

There must be something in Dawn Covington's expression which Miss Wilson doesn't like.

'Do you think it's funny?' she shouts.

'No, miss,' replies Dawn.

'Stand up, girl.' She stands, a little shakily, and I can still picture her in front of me, black hair against her white shirt, rigid with fear. 'Did you do that deliberately?'

'No, miss.'

'Come out to the front.' Dawn Covington turns to look at me. If she's not *certain* that I am responsible for the downfall of her writing materials, I am easily the most likely candidate. But Dawn Covington is not one of nature's quick thinkers. And she is now frozen in terror of what she and the rest of us knows is about to happen.

'Come out to the front, *now!*'

I'll never forget her lonely walk up the aisle between the desks, the expectant silence that descends on the classroom. The way Miss Wilson takes hold of her, inhumanly somehow, like a sheep to be sheared, how she pulls her dress up a little, and plants three stinging slaps on the back of her leg. I'll never forget the sight of the red fingermarks spreading across her flesh, of her face crumbling into tears, of her long, sad walk back to her desk. Of her terrible discovery of injustice in the world. Most of all, of the look on her face when she turned towards me, her helpless failure to deny responsibility and save herself. And what must have been the expression that she saw on mine: pleasant, a mask. Not so very different from Simon Lowenstein's when his name was called out, I imagine.

Approximately a quarter of a century after this scene took place, I was appointed to my present position, producer of *The Uh-Oh Show*, one of a number of popular television programmes that play sadistic pranks on unsuspecting members of the public.

3

Well, it's a blindie, isn't it? A blind date. These two have clearly had only one phone conversation, so here's what I've gleaned so far. That I— Sorry, that *Matthew* works for some policy think tank attached to Number Ten. That in what little spare time he has, he never meets anyone outside politics. That he broke up with his girlfriend a few months ago (spooky, because so did I). And that he put an advert in Soul Mates in the *Guardian*. Oh yes, and he plays tennis with Gordon Brown. Kate seemed very interested in that particular detail. Gordon,

I confide, has powerful ground strokes but doesn't overly like to run around. It wouldn't be giving much away to reveal that, just as you'd expect, he's fiercely competitive and hates to lose. His weakest shot is probably his serve, which is oddly ineffective (don't know how much longer I can keep this up). Over at the bar, a man who came in about two minutes after Kate is giving her a long, hard stare. He's about my age and height, in a suit. And glasses.

'So, have you had a busy day?' I venture. Haven't discovered what Kate does with herself yet and, indeed, I don't know whether or not 'I've' already asked her on the phone.

'Oh, you know. The usual.'

'Yes, I see.'

Actually, it occurs to me, I don't much mind what she does. Maybe it's the hardball specs, maybe it's the thirties haircut, but this woman has a look about her, a fevered energy that speaks of . . . a sexy intelligence, if that makes sense. I'm afraid I find this particular combination, the idea of a brain the size of a planet in a glamorous package – like Twiglets, cold Champagne and flattery – utterly irresistible. It's not even as if she's said anything particularly clever yet; it's more the idea that she *might*.

I try another approach. 'Are some times of the year busier than others then?' Bit of a long shot, unless she's a travel agent.

'Not really.'

'You must get a lot of stress in your job?' Who doesn't?

'Yeah, a fair amount I suppose.' Is she taking the piss? Has she guessed I'm not Matthew?

'How do you tend to get rid of it?'

'Like this, mostly.' And she picks up her glass, takes a nice, deep swallow. Comes up smiling.

'So how did you get into it? Your line of work? As it were?'

'Straight from college, actually.'

'Really. You didn't mess around with other professions? Make a false start at something else for a while?'

'No. It was my ambition from when I was a child.'

Oh, fuck it then. 'Kate, remind me, *what* is it you do again?'

She laughs. 'I haven't told you yet.'

'Thank Christ for that. Thought I was going mad for a minute there. What is it then? That you do exactly?'

'You can try and guess if you like. Where's the loo in this place?'

And she . . . she *lopes* off. That's really the word for it. A great loping stride that's almost ungainly, but oddly endearing. Her hair is swinging about, her wrists seem to be doing something a little otherworldly. It's the carriage of an Irish wolfhound, or a lurcher quite possibly. In a young woman, the whole performance says *out of control*, which to my mind is a fine quality (see Champagne, Twiglets, flattery above).

The man in the suit and tie at the bar is looking at his watch and scowling. I almost feel a bit sorry for him. But it would never have worked. He's clearly far too serious – a policy wonk, I believe they call such creatures – for a woman with such a twitchy, playful streak.

I whip out the Nokia and dial Andy Fineman, the reason I'm here in the first place. The little boy I used to swap names with is now an estate agent. Every few weeks we like to get together and do things we couldn't do in school, like drink, eat foreign food, and talk about girls in a way our mothers wouldn't entirely approve of.

He's still at the office when I catch him. 'Andy, could we possibly make it tomorrow? I'm coming over all peculiar this evening. It's that pain again.'

'The brain tumour, is this? Or the stroke? Or is it the heart disease?' Andy is my oldest friend.

'The tumour, I think.'

'You dozy twat, you know you're a hypochondriac.'

'Yeah yeah yeah. That's what the doctor said. But he wasn't a specialist. Do you think we *could* make it tomorrow?'

'You could be dead by then.'

'Andy, that's not funny.'

By the time Kate has bounded back from the bog, Matthew has pissed off in disgust. Gone home to gobble a takeaway Chinese and give the latest European policy initiative a good seeing-to, poor fucker.

She drops into her seat and gazes at me brightly, eyebrows set at question mark.

'Not one of the caring professions?' I hazard.

'Correct. Nineteen questions left.'

Oh good, a *games* player. This just gets better and better.

4

As I painted for Kate what I hoped was a reasonably colourful picture of life at the heart of government, I realised I'd been involved in a version of this scene before. It was as the producer of an amusing little item — we call it a 'scam' in the trade — that goes something like this.

It's lunchtime, you're sitting in a café, Pret a Manger, let's say, chowing your chicken tikka ploughman's, reading the *Standard*, minding your own business. Out of a blue sky, an attractive young woman comes rushing up to you all breathless. I'm *so* sorry I'm late, she gasps. Piccadilly Line's murder today. Someone jumped under a train at Arnos Grove, whatever. Anyhow . . . deep sigh . . . bit awkward meeting people through the newspaper like this. I'm glad it's you, though, and not that bald chap over there with the briefcase. I'm Mandy, she says, lights up a big smile and sticks her hand out for you to shake.

At this point, six out of seven blokes say, sorry, Mandy, I think you've made a mistake. You're mixing me up with some-one else. But *one* will go along with it. Maybe he's bored, or lonely. Maybe he fancies the pants off Mandy – and Mandy *is* attractive, though not in an obvious way. Maybe it's been a long time since anyone like Mandy spoke to him of her own free will. Maybe it's love at first sight. Who cares?

One is all you need.

Yeah, hi, Mandy, you say. And then we've got you.

We've got you on the camera in the van parked across the street with the oddly blacked-out windows. We've got you on the camera peeking under the flap of the shoulder bag belonging to the 'tourist' at the next table; we've got you again through the small black lens poking through a hole in the spine of a jumbo Filofax that the nearby 'businessman' is so engrossed in. Even Mandy, sweet, treacherous Mandy, has pointed a camera – and a microphone – straight in front of you when she placed her handbag, rather too carefully you'll realise much later, on the very table you're sitting at.

In a busy urban environment, you'll never spot any of these cameras (most are smaller than a paperback book). And even if *you* do, the next bloke won't. This branch of entertainment has been described as deception comedy.

And now the fun starts. It must be fascinating working in the city, she says. Well, it's not too bad, you reply. Do you find it hard to spend all your money? No, not really. Do you really earn four hundred grand a year? You begin to laugh, nearly blow your cover. I expect that's in a good year, she puts in quickly. (We're going too fast for you. After all, you're not a professional actor, like Mandy.) We've spent hours in the office, she and I, going over the dialogue, working out the best script to gently entangle our punters (we never call them victims) in deeper and deeper shit. What colour is your

Maserati? Red. Did you drive it to work today? Er, not today. Tell me about working with the SAS. Did you ever have to kill anyone? When the punter, let's say a middle-aged cost controller from Finchley, is 'improvising colourfully' (lying through his back teeth), the studio audience find it hysterical.

And then when we've taken the joke as far as it can go – and that can be a long way – the killer moment: the 'reveal', to give it its technical name. Eric (or Hugh, or George, or James or Stuart), says Mandy, can I ask you something?

Sure, what?

Have you ever wanted to be on television?

No, why? (Sudden realisation.) Oh, fuck (bleeped out).

Smile, Eric (Nigel, Henry, Les, Pete), you're on *The Uh-Oh Show*!

5

OK, here's what I know.

She's not an academic. Nothing to do with the media (thank fuck for that). Not politics, or the arts. Neither music nor fashion. She's not something in the City; doesn't work with animals – don't know why I asked that one, just a long shot, a waste of a question, I know; nothing to do with retail.

Of course, why didn't I think of it? Fucking *computers*. Software. Internet. Web design. Has to be.

Nope, though she concedes that she uses a PC in her work. Thanks for nothing there. Who doesn't?

Nothing at all to do with children. Or manufacturing. Or transportation. Not an administrator of any kind. Fuck, *is* she a travel agent?

She isn't.

OK, four questions left, don't blow it.

'Would you be the sort of person who would like another drink? That's not a question, by the way, just a kind offer.'

She would be precisely that sort of person. And she's enjoying this little game, wriggling around in her seat, swinging one checked leg over the other, then thinking better of it, and swinging them back the way she first had them. I find I have been thinking a lot about these legs, possibly to the detriment of my line of interrogation. Her dark eyes are glittering behind the serious specs, the curtain of hair is one moment falling across her cheekbones, the next, tumbling back behind her ears. She can't sit still for a moment, this one, and the phrase, *You got ants in your pants?* pops uninvited into my head, followed immediately by the simpler, con-nected, and highly incendiary thought . . . *in your pants.*

In your pants. One of those thoughts that – like chewing gum on your shoe or that song by Shania Twain – once lodged in your brain, are really rather difficult to shake off.

'Er, I'm struggling here. Any clues you'd care to offer me?' Do you work with insects at all? Ants maybe. Who you've allowed perhaps to colonise your underwear? For reasons of warmth. And in the name of science, of course.

'Oh, no. Much more fun if you can get it on your own.'

A bolt of irritation. Fuck you. If you can get it on your own, indeed. I'm actually rather good at this game in normal circs. But somehow this fidgety woman has put me right off my stroke. *Me* – a government policy adviser. Gordon Brown's tennis partner, for fuck's sake.

'Are you some sort of fucking scientist then?' Whoops. Didn't mean it to come out quite as sharply as it did.

Now she's gone very still. And here's a novelty: she says yes.

Three left. Her eyes have widened. Her breathing seems to have changed. Is that a pink flush rising up her neck? I'm getting close. I have a vivid fantasy – a foreshadowing? – of what it would be like to be in bed with this woman. Careful now. Need to ask something very incisive. A scientist. She's a *scientist*. Went into it straight from college. Fulfilment of a childhood ambition.

Science, though. Christ, it's everything, isn't it, it's so bloody vast. And in an instant I've guessed it. I can see her in a white lab coat, bent over the printer, the data spewing out, hundreds of pages of numbers, the bleeps, ripples and red shifts, all that weird stuff radio telescopes scoop up from the furthest regions of knowable space, the earliest sproutings of measurable time. She probes the origins of the universe. Investigates the most profound mystery of them all: why there is a *here* here. Why there is something rather than nothing. (The hair, the glasses, I *know* I'm right.)

I feel proud and powerfully attracted to her as I say, 'You're a cosmologist. You do black holes and quasars. The big stuff.'

'Nope. Brave guess, though. Two questions left.'

'What? Not even close?'

'Nowhere near. You can have that for nothing.' She's wriggling again. Legs have begun crissing and crossing. A sexy claw seizes the glass for another blast at the Chardonnay.

'You said you weren't an academic.'

'I'm not.'

Well, I'm fucked then, aren't I? She could be bloody anything. I'd need to find a question, two questions, so forensic in their penetrative power that—

And then it seizes me. Something I remember from A level Chemistry. The practical bit of the exam where they give you some unidentified white powder, and then you've got two hours to find out what it is. You carry out a series of tests: you dissolve it in water, see if it will react with this, form crystals with that, is it acid, alkaline, does it burn with a blue flame or orange? By a process of elimination, you can eventually say with certainty that the mystery compound was sodium chloride or zinc permanganate or whatever.

She's gone all still again. A funny disappointed smile has spread across her face.

'Do you by any chance work for the police force?'

She swallows slowly. Nods.

'Are you a police forensic scientist?'

Nods again. Very finally this time.

Oh well. That's my spiffing all-back-to-my-place-for-more-drinks-and-a-couple-of-joints plan knocked on the head, then.

6

Except after a few more drinks she did come back. Remarkable really, that the evening ended in the way it did, given its wholly unlikely beginning. Though the truth, I suppose, is that all beginnings are unlikely, even a little impossible. One's life is chancy enough as it is . . . perhaps it does no harm to improve the odds a little.

Maybe she detected my disappointment that she wasn't a stargazer. I loved the idea of her probing the depths of the cosmos. (My delicious fantasy: we're lying in bed having just had fantastic filthy sex – this is a *fantasy*, right – and— No, wait . . . go back and talk about the sex a bit. OK, it was great, elemental, sinewy stuff. She's wonderfully . . . *supple*. Anyway, she's lying in my arms, we're staring at the car head-lights passing across the ceiling, and she's explaining black holes to me. I mean, I've read the books, I know they're collapsed stars, so dense that they suck everything including light into themselves, and that galaxies spiral around them. I know this stuff, and yet I keep forgetting it, because it is so unknowable, so unimaginable. But she explains it to me, waving her bony hands against the shadows. What black holes are really like. What actually happens inside them. And how they could be the gateway to other universes. And lying here together, listening to her voice against the evening London traffic, for the first time I *get* it. It's a little like falling through space.

We make love again – well, she inspires me, doesn't she? – and, in return, I reveal to her some of the dark secrets of deception comedy . . . No, fuck it, that doesn't play at all. End of fantasy.)

Anyway, after I discovered her secret – 'It seems to put men off, Matthew' – she was no keener to impart any more details about her profession than I was about mine. So we headed into books, films, and restaurants where she was mildly disappointing. Her tastes turned out to be respectable: *Captain Corelli's Mandolin* (the book, not the film)/*The English Patient* (the film, not the book)/Italian food, rather than challenging (*Sabbath's Theatre*/*The Big Lebowski*/Chinese). My heart began to sink when she told me she regularly plays badminton with one of the women from work. And after she revealed she lived in the criminally dull suburb of Ealing, I almost lost all hope.

It was when I began telling her about what *I* did for fun, that matters improved. In particular when I mentioned chess. She loves chess. Her father taught her. She played all through school, but these days can never find anyone to play against. Can't bear the idea of joining a chess club: all those sad women with too much facial hair, those angry men in sandals. (My sentiments *precisely*.)

'We must have a game some time,' I said.

'Matthew, I'd love to,' she replied, the gawky, nervous energy all gone.

And for a moment, *just* for a moment, I almost say, 'Who's Matthew?'

* * *

Actually I find it rather disturbing that I give such a sustained performance as Matthew at Café Rouge. Disturbing when taken together with another couple of signs that all may not be entirely well with me.

First, I think my handwriting is changing. For a start, I'm sure it never used to be as bad as this. Naturally, I do most everything on a keyboard now – scripts, emails and that – but when I came to actually write a short note to someone recently, a message in a birthday card, to Cheryl, my ex, it looked to me like the hand of a child or a sick person. (I read an article about graphology. Apparently they can diagnose serious illness from strange new tics in your lower loops or odd pressure formations on your T-bars.) Also, some of my words were sloping to the left, which is a very bad sign. (If anything, the article said, healthy handwriting should surge forwards positively. A hand that leans backwards expresses a reluctance, a psychic shrinking from something.)

The other worrying thing is that I've started seeing Cheryl everywhere – on the other side of the road; disappearing into shop doorways; sitting on buses. Every passing red Peugeot 205 (her car) gives me a little kick in the guts. I'll probably have to explain about Cheryl at some stage. *Cheryl*, terrible name, don't you think? – hardly better than Beryl. Of course the two of us were always Charles 'n' Cheryl. Or Charlie 'n' Cheryl. Even Chas 'n' Cheryl.

Tall, beautiful, dreamy Cheryl. One of those big blank-canvas faces you could paint almost anything on. I used to say she had a face like a frying pan, a huge flat surface, like Texas. Plenty of room for features to spread out and get comfortable. We had a holiday in the States once, rented a car and drove from New York to California. I found a picture the other day from that trip: Cheryl at Mount Rushmore, the great stone face in the foreground, the carved American presidents, about the same size in the frame, over her shoulder.

Seeing Cheryl everywhere I think is a bad sign. Four months later, I should surely have got over her.

A few weeks ago I went to a party – Rose and Geraldine's from the office. Stepping into their groovy sitting room, I had an instant feeling of physical sickness, like a punch in the stomach. There she was, Cheryl, staring out of the window. Except, of course, it wasn't her, it was another tall woman with broad shoulders and shoulder-length brown hair.

Anyhow, as usual I got excessively pissed and it was at that party where I suppose you could say deception comedy first began to bleed from my professional life into the private. I'm yabbering away to a girlfriend of R. and G. (not nearly as desirable as either of those two *great* girls) and she asks me what I do, and I hear myself saying – not, 'I work with Rose and Geraldine', but, 'I'm a psychiatrist'.

'Really?' she replies. 'What sort of patients do you treat?'

'Oh, all sorts,' I come back without missing a beat. 'Schizophrenics, manics, depressives, phobics, obsessive-compulsives, you name it.'

And for half an hour, more or less, I keep this going, telling her about some of my more interesting cases. Michelle, a repetitive hand-washer, 'scrubbed her wrists raw'; Alex, the brilliant barrister who hears voices but *likes* them, merely wants them to speak one at a time; Kevin, who's excessively normal – 'normotic' is the technical term – who finds it impossible to relate to other people, who I made a senior personnel manager at the BBC.

I couldn't really tell you why I did it, except to say I was bored, and a bit sad, and I desperately didn't want to talk about *The Uh-Oh Show*. Rose and Geraldine were very nice about it on Monday morning.

'We *loved* that silly joke you played on Hilary Bloom,' cackled Rose. They often speak on behalf of each other.

'She totally bought it,' cried G.

(I love these girls. They never fail to make me laugh; they're tremendously fanciable; I'd go out with either at the drop of a hat, except, as they say on *The Antiques Roadshow*, it would be a shame to split up a pair. Rose and Geraldine are flat-mates, the fastest of friends, and I'm sure I'm not the only male at Tuna TV to have quietly entertained the delicious thought of the two of them. You know, *together*.)

'Sorry about that. I couldn't face telling her I worked in horrid old telly for some reason.' Rose and Geraldine haven't quite got to the *horrid old telly* stage yet. They still think it's quite a lark.

Anyhow, back in Café Rouge, I guess it would have been more appropriate to say something like, it's been a lovely evening, would you like to meet again some time? Have that game of chess? But, instead, the words which actually came out of my mouth were, 'You don't fancy a glass of brandy at my flat, do you? It's only five minutes' walk.' And she went very still again and said, 'Yes. That would be very nice.'

And I'm thinking, was it was bold of me to ask, or am I just pissed? And was it bold of her to accept, or – working with the police – does she know how to break a man's neck with a single blow?

7

So we're sat at opposite ends of my long black sofa, getting seri-ously stuck into the Remy Martin, there's a gnarled old Cuban on the hi-fi wailing pitifully about lost love or the price of fish, somehow Kate's managed to point both knees and both feet at me — an exceptionally positive signal, I seem to recall from the *Daily Mail* — when she says, 'Matthew, do you know how to play Pelmanism?' Do wish she'd stop with this Matthew thing.

'Play it? I'm not sure I'd know how to *spell* it,' I reply lightly.

'It's a memory game. I think it was invented by a Professor Pelman.'

'Kate, I think I should tell you that after a few drinks my memory gets quite . . . sketchy.' I smile sweetly at her. 'Er, sorry, what were we talking about?'

'It's best to play it with a few more people, but I think it would still work with two.'

'Is it the one where you're sitting around, one person leaves the room, and all the others have to try and guess who it was?'

Not that one, apparently. Pelmanism turns out to be that very *irritating* game where there are twenty objects on a tray and you have sixty seconds to scrutinise them before a cloth is thrown over and you scribble down as many as you can bring yourself to remember. A low-tech version of the conveyor belt bit in *The Generation Game*. Kate says she's very good at Pelmanism.

So while I'm gadding about the flat collecting small yet *telling* objects — a condom would be too obvious, don't you think? — she's dropped on to her haunches in a tremendously appealing way, flipping through my CDs. *Christ*, hope she doesn't find the Elton John.

'How's this going to work, Kate? I mean I'll know what's on the tray, won't I?' I believe this is a reasonable point.

'Don't worry, you probably won't remember it all. Do you actually *like* Steely Dan then?'

Oh fuck. Steely Dan. Forgot about Steely sodding Dan. 'No, they're my ex's, actually.'

'Can we play Scott Walker? I'm getting a bit sick of this Cuban bloke, to be honest.'

With this one request, she has wiped away all the bad stuff: being a paid hireling of the police state, the badminton after work, living in Ealing, *The English Patient* (the film, not the book).

'Sure. Go ahead.'

Especially *The English Patient*.

It's trickier than you'd think, finding twenty interesting objects to fill a tray, twenty objects that say something about yourself. She didn't actually specify that they should be interesting, but I think they should. After all – I think it was Confucius who said this – you never get a second chance to make a first impression, do you?

Finally, as the great voice swoops and soars through the melodrama of 'Montague Terrace in Blue', I set the tray on the coffee table. She perches on the edge of the sofa in readiness, flicks the hair off her face, takes a deep breath. I whip back what should have been a crisply starched white linen napkin (actually, a nasty tea towel with pub signs on). And here are the twenty objects that meet our gaze:

Bottle of aspirin
One-day Travelcard (Zones One and Two)
Floppy disk (symbolising mastery of technology)
Shell from bathroom (feminine side)
Book of matches from favourite restaurant
    (sensual side)
Novelty spherical dice (fun side)
Champagne stopper (additional fun; abandonment;
    alcoholism)
Chess piece, a white knight (geddit?)
Plastic dog turd (don't ask)

American dollar bill
Credit card
AA battery
Sexy Japanese rollerball
Fridge magnet of Albert Einstein (getting desperate now)
Tin of anchovies
Tube harissa sauce
Pistachio nut
My wristwatch (should be able to remember that one)
Small figure of Buddha (Cheryl gave it to me)
Swiss army knife (there, I *knew* it would come in handy one day).

Maybe I've had a drop too much Remy M, but there is something about this colourful tableau of my life that strikes me as rather artful (annoyed I put the aspirins in now. And the battery). There's something pleasing in the arrangement, the surreal conjunction of floppy disk with dog turd, Einstein with anchovies. I'd like to set it in Perspex, set the whole *moment* in Perspex – the sitting room, the music, the sofa, me, and the girl whose face I can no longer see behind her hair, this girl hunched over the tray, breathing heavily, check trousers straining against bony knees. If I were Damien Hirst I'd do it, and Charles Saatchi would buy it off me for a million quid.

'OK, got it.' Kate is suddenly on her feet, back turned to the tray. 'That must have been a minute, put the tea towel back on.'

I do as I'm told, and now, with the pens and paper provided, we get down to it.

OK, I can remember the watch, the knife, the white knight,

the anchovies, the pistachio, the travel pass. Er . . . the dollar bill, the credit card. The harissa sauce.

Fuck, what else? She's scribbling like a demon, wriggling around like there's ants in her— No, don't start that again. What else? What, what, *what*? The battery. The fucking battery! Yeah, and the aspirins. How many's that? Eleven. Not bad. Keep thinking. What else? She's scribbling, wriggling, staring at the ceiling, wriggling, scribbling . . .

She stops. Turns, smiles at me. I don't believe this.

'You've got them all, haven't you?' She nods. I am rather shocked. There's something a bit . . . indecent about her proficiency at this game. 'Go on then, let's hear it.'

'What about you?' she asks sweetly. 'Do you need more time?'

'I don't think I have a lot more to give, to be honest here.'

She goes through it, barely glancing at her notes. She remembers *everything* on that tray. And she recalls it strategically, grouping the twenty seemingly random objects into fewer, more memorable clusters. She puts Einstein together with the wristwatch and the curved dice; Buddha and the Swiss army knife; the dog poo and the dollar. She produces a whole storyboard of a night out in London (the Travelcard – the *tube* of harissa – the Champagne stopper – pistachio nut – matches from the restaurant – credit card – aspirins). I don't follow all the mnemonic tricks she's employed to create the connections, I just know she's been bloody clever about it. And you want to know what's really scary? She remembers the brands: that it was a Duracell battery, a Maxell floppy disk, a First Direct Visa card, Sainsbury's anchovies, Le Phare du Cap Bon harissa.

'I think the restaurant was called Mr Kong?' she hazards.

'You bloody *know* it was. That's amazing, Kate. I couldn't do that even if I was sober.'

'It can be a curse as well, you know, a good memory.' She's looking at me rather seriously now, her gaze sort of oddly *ticking*, as if she can't decide which of my eyes to look into.

'Yeah, sometimes it's best to forget stuff, I guess. That's definitely my strategy.' I drain off my brandy glass in tribute to her powers. 'How about a game of chess? I'm better at that after a few drinks.'

'I'd love to. Maybe another time, though. Don't you have . . . important government work to do in the morning?'

'What? Oh, *that*. Don't worry about that. This is much more fun than boring old— God, what is it? Transport. That's it. Boring old transport policy.' I shoot her what I hope is a Christ-have-I-had-it-up-to-here-with-bloody-transport-policy sort of an expression.

'Well, it's been a lovely evening, Matthew.'

'Don't go or anything. It's only . . . it's only quarter to two in the morning.' Fuck, how did it get that late?

'Perhaps you should call me a cab.'

'Sure. Before I do, there's just one more thing . . .' And leaning across from the safety of my side of the sofa, I move my mouth up against hers and take a deep breath.

She doesn't respond, and yet neither does she move away. Doesn't seem remotely put out by the gesture. Incredibly, she produces Humphrey Bogart's line when Lauren Bacall boldly plants a kiss on him in *To Have and Have Not*. 'Whadja do that for?' she asks.

'Been wondering whether I'd like it,' I reply as per original screenplay.

(Too much I suppose for her to respond, 'And do you?' To which I retort, 'I don't know yet,' and have another go. Then I add, 'It's even better when you help.')

But I guess she hasn't seen the movie. Because she sort of pecks back at me neutrally like Switzerland, and trips off to the bathroom. I phone the local minicabs and wonder if I have made a mistake, been too pushy on the first date. What would Matthew have done? But no, hang on, women *like* to be desired, don't they? In the proper context — late at night in a boy's flat, for example, after drink has been taken — don't they get confused or offended if you fail to make a pass at them? I mean, what the fuck is she doing here, anyway?

'Something I want to ask you,' I say, her knees on return, I notice, set at a slightly less favourable angle. 'Why did you link the chess piece and the tin of anchovies together like that?' They were the last two objects she remembered. The knight, she said. And finally the anchovies. Sainsbury's anchovies.

'It was silly, really. With that game, you've got to go for any associations you can make. And for some reason I thought of the Knights of St Anchovy. Like in *The Canterbury Tales* or whatever.'

At the door, with escape so near at hand, she releases a longer, more affectionate kiss. Not a full-blown snog by any means, but neither a perfunctory *mwah*. I particularly like the way she grabs hold of my arm with both hands, the better to gain purchase on my face.

'I'll call you,' she says as the lift door grinds open. 'We'll have that game of chess.'

From my window on the fourth floor, I watch the lights of the dented Datsun disappear in the direction of Shepherd's Bush Green. Only afterwards do I realise that she doesn't have my number.

8

Shit.

What if she calls Matthew? To thank him for a wonderful

evening, sort of thing. What if she discovers she's spent the last six hours in the company of an impostor?

Fuck.

What if *he* calls *her* to say, 'Oi, so where were you, then?'

Too agitated for sleep, I pad round the flat. Play 'Montague Terrace in Blue' repetitively. Stare at the trayful of objects, trying to sense some further meaning from them, from the absurdity of this encounter. There's an indentation in the sofa from where she's so recently been sitting. *We'll have that game of chess.*

The phone rings. At this time of night it can only be one person. It's strange, but she – and somehow I'm certain it *is* a she – never rings while I'm asleep. It's as though she knows when I'm still up, as though it's someone across the road who can see my lights burning, though it could just as easily be someone who keeps pretty late hours herself.

I *say* herself. There's no way of knowing for sure.

'Hello?' Silence on the line. In the background, music plays faintly, as if it is coming from another room. 'Ah, that'll be my mystery caller then.' I've found that taking the piss helps dissolve my unease. 'A joy as always to hear from you. What's that I hear? Mahler? Mozart? Robbie Williams? What kind of mood are we in tonight?'

She's never once said a word to me. I don't even hear her breathing. But there's always something, music, a radio or a TV, sometimes just distant traffic noise, that signals a human intelligence, a presence on the line.

I've tried it all. I've tried putting the phone down; she's still there when I pick it up again. I've tried giving her the silent treatment; I always blink first and say something, usually, oh, for fuck's sake, this is ridiculous. Haven't you got anything better to do with your life? Obviously not. Like in movies, I've tried to listen in extra hard for clues – for a dog whining, or the strike of a match, or a shipyard hooter (the dog-owning smoker who lives by the docks). The only time I managed to freak her out was when, after a very long silence on my part, I put my mouth close to the receiver, and in my spookiest, scariest Vincent Price voice intoned the words, 'Why won't you speak to me?' She hung up instantly.

My current strategy, like I say, is the humorous approach; keep up some mildly sarcastic light banter. One, it suggests I'm not rattled. Two, it makes me feel more in control. Three, if I can come up with a corker, it might just make her laugh out loud. And we all know how distinctive a laugh can be. Though if it turns out to be a bloke's laugh, I might just shit myself.

It's got to be someone I know, hasn't it? A former lover. A neighbour. Someone at work. A disturbed friend or acquaintance. Possibly – but unlikely – someone who's been turned over by *The Uh-Oh Show* (they tend to be pathetically thrilled by the attention). Their gratification of course lies in my helplessness. So I'm trying not to sound too helpless.

'So, er . . . what sort of day have you had?'

Nothing.

'Damn, I thought you might just fall for that one. Ah, well. Telly was bloody rubbish tonight, wasn't it?'

I leave a nice long pause. A phone call – even an anonymous one – is actually a very intimate thing. Although she is silent, I have this woman's mouth a few inches from my face. My lips whisper into her ear. I can sense her reality. And the truth is that though I'm half disturbed, I'm also half intrigued.

'Oh, come on, can't you just join in a bit? There's not much incentive in this for me, you know. The conversation *is* getting a tad one-sided.'

Silence.

'I know, let's play twenty questions. You don't have to say anything. You can beep with your phone key. One beep for yes, two for no. Shall we give it a go?'

Silence.

'Shall we try it? Just beep. Yes or no? One or two?'

Silence.

'OK, think of a famous person, alive or dead, and I'll ask you questions. Have you got one yet?'

Silence.

'Right, let's see. Does this person . . . work with animals at all? Is he or she . . . a politician?'

Silence.

'Bit of a long shot this, but is it Natalie Imbruglia?'

I wonder how clever Kate would winkle this weirdo out of her shell. Clever Kate, whose sexy depressions are still keeping me company on the sofa.

I sigh heavily. 'I haven't told many people this, but a few years ago I used to see a shrink. I know it's kind of late, and I don't want to bore you with what's actually quite a long story. But since you asked, in a nutshell, my problem was that I thought I was a dog. It's true. I thought I was a dog. I'm fine now, though. Go on, feel my nose.'

Click.

A small miracle. She's hung up. I stare at the receiver in something close to disbelief.

Two possibilities here. Either that she was about to crack up. Or else, she realised she was on the phone to someone with an even looser set of screws than her own.

9

I imagine that's going to be it from Loopy Loo for the night, so I pour a glass of brandy, fire up the laptop, and hit a book-marked fave on the old www.

I suppose you could describe *Czech-Mates* as a rather . . . specialised site. There's no direct means of knowing whether the individuals depicted within its images are indeed Czech, though there is a definite Eastern European flavour to the whole enterprise (the rather nasty seventies feel to all the backdrops). I used to play with a girl called Danuta. But there was something ultimately rather off-putting about the knowing way she flirted with the camera. Magda is now my current favourite opponent. I'm fond of the serious expression that falls across her magnificent Slavic features as I bang in my latest move, my excitement arising not so much from the fact that during the course of the game she becomes naked – OK, *something* from that, obviously – but more from the way she seems to take it seriously. Sadly, I suppose I must assume that in truth Magda has no input into our contest whatsoever – the chess-board is always very carefully screened by the schematic diagram of our game – that 'Magda' may have posed for these pictures years ago and is now studying International Relations at the Sorbonne. Or is a mother of four. Or is dead. Indeed, it's virtually certain that I am not vying against a human agency at all, merely a chess computer, one which, every now and again, will allow me to win. Nevertheless, the illusion is very powerful.

This particular game has been going about three weeks, a couple of moves per session. We've exchanged quite a few pawns, lost a knight and a bishop apiece, and have now settled comfortably into the mid-game, with no obvious advantage to either player. Time to stir things up a bit.

I type: *K3–K7*.

Magda's image slowly wipes off, is replaced momentarily by a blank rectangle (achingly slow modem) . . . and now she's coming again, this time a particularly fetching shot of her staring hard at the board, face in both hands, elbows akimbo. The classic chess brain-straining position.

How fine to imagine that I've given her something to think about.

Plip.

A tiny pictograph, an envelope, pops up bottom right on my screen. Who's up and awake and sending emails at this time of night? Has to be someone in the States.

Wrong. It's Lindsay. My ex. Actually, my ex-ex. The one before Cheryl. We've been seeing something of one another since C. and I broke up. Recidivism, I think you could call it, when, in times of crisis, you return to an earlier stage of development.

It's a chain email. A list of eighteen 'Instructions For Life' from the Dalai Lama. Apparently if you forward it to four people, your life will improve 'slightly'; to nine people, and your life will improve 'to your liking'; and if you can think of fourteen people you wouldn't be embarrassed to send it to, you will receive 'at least' five surprises in the next three weeks. I take it the Dalai Lama thinks surprises are a good thing. He's obviously never seen *The Uh-Oh Show*. For the most part, it's pretty sensible stuff that it's difficult to argue with: *Learn the Rules so you will know how to break them properly*; *When you lose, don't lose the lesson*; and my personal favourite, *Remember that not getting what you want is sometimes a wonderful stroke of luck*. There is one seriously bad piece of advice — *Approach love and cooking with reckless abandon*. This one, tragically, is Lindsay's personal credo, and in my opinion I think it has done neither her, nor her dinner party guests over the years, any favours whatsoever.

From the long list of people she has sent the Instructions to, Lindsay will obviously be expecting quite a few surprises in the coming weeks.

I flip back to Magda. She's still pondering her next move, so I disconnect, pick up the phone and dial. Surprises, she wants, is it?

'Hello?'

'Lindsay, this is the office of the Dalai Lama.'

'Charlie. What are you doing up so late?'

'Couldn't sleep. What's your excuse?'

'Oh, I was on-line, chatting with some trader on Wall Street . . .'

'*Said* he was a trader on Wall Street . . .'

'Yeah, right. Could be a tractor driver from Spongecake, Ohio.'

Pause. I think I know what's coming.

'Charlie —' a beat, as they say in the movies — 'would you like me to come over this evening?'

'Love you to . . . if you don't think it's too late.'

Fifteen minutes later, Lindsay is brushing her teeth in my bathroom, and I'm lying in bed waiting for her, thinking: this is bloody pointless. It won't help either of us — in the jargon — to 'move on'. In fact, it will only serve to remind me why we split up in the first place. (But it will be good to feel your fine warm body next to mine, Linds.)

I'm drifting off when she slips in alongside me, and for a sickening moment when I put my arms around her and bury my face in her neck I think, Christ, it's Cheryl! I jolt awake with an audible gasp.

'What's the matter?'

'Sorry, nothing. Are you wearing different perfume?'

'I am actually. Do you like it?'

'Mmm.'

It's Cheryl's perfume. What is it? Poison? *Poisson?*

We're not going to do anything. We never do. (Well, we might do in the morning.) We're slipping away, a pair of spoons in a dark drawer. I can hear her breathing becoming deeper. What would it be like falling asleep with Magda? I wonder. Would she wake up in the night with a little cry, having dreamt the perfect response to my knight move?

Or Kate. That hard bony body, all those elbows and knees. Would it really be, as Anthony Burgess once said, like going to bed with a bicycle?

The Knights of St Anchovy indeed. All bollocks. Has to be. Her association was nothing to do with heraldry or the bleeding *Canterbury Tales*. It was this: the white knight in shining armour . . . there was something *fishy* about him.

Face it. It doesn't come a lot fishier than anchovies.

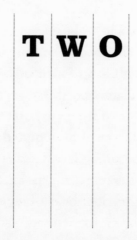

TWO

1

In the post-split era, on occasions like this one when Linds has stayed over, the truth is that the next morning, I prefer to find myself alone. Just me in an empty flat, a few long dark hairs in the sink, and maybe a scribbled Post-it note attached to the fridge: 'Call me XXX L.'

Today when I surface, however, Lindsay is snoring softly, her face, turned towards me on the pillow, once more reminding me — as it did from the first moment we met — of Richard Nixon's. Not literally — that would obviously be a tragedy — it's more the shape of her long head, wider at the jaw than at the temples, which taken together with her biggish nose and its ski-ramp swoop does put one irresistibly in mind of America's thirty-seventh president. (Look, it could have been worse. Could have been Kissinger.) Anyhow, none of this is to say that she's not attractive. She is, very. She has the same exotic appeal that many young women of highly unusual looks seem to have in common: the attraction of Other, tempered with mild concern about what she's going to look like at sixty. Lindsay is a tremendously decent person (to my knowledge, she has never once sought to burgle the offices of an opponent, or carpet-bomb Cambodia) and if I hadn't already done a two-year stretch with her (which of course has served to neutralise her alien glamour), if I wasn't still so raw from Cheryl, and if there weren't so many other . . . *interesting* candidates around, I might even be tempted to suggest another shot. Her only serious failing is a weakness for ethnic fittings and furnishings, those crappy lanterns and tin toys, boxes and candlesticks, all that terrible bric-a-brac from India and the Far East that they flog to us first-time home-owners by the lorryload.

Lindsay is one of the few people I know who does not work in television. She is — on her own admission — a failed actress and musician, who is now making rather a good living designing ring melodies for mobile phones. Naturally, she's involved in a mysterious state-of-the-art Internet venture. Linds says if 'the finance falls into place', and they 'get the start-up right', this little wheeze — 'Imagine it, Charlie!' — could make her a millionaire 'many, many times over'.

I have been imagining it. And on balance I think I would greatly prefer to be a millionaire (m.m.t.o., as stated) than conspiring on a regular basis to fuck over innocent members of the public for the greater glee of the sofa-bound audience. You do what you do, however. I know bugger all about the www beyond the ability to summon up Magda with a few clicks, and mount a sustained challenge on her defences.

One side of Lindsay's great nose — I like big noses, they're characterful – one side is vibrating with each gentle snore, the peculiar face on its cushion looking more than a little like a Picasso this morning.

What's going to become of this slumbering apparition? (What's going to become of any of us, for that matter?)

Will Linds make her millions, buy the big house in Holland Park, hang kilims all over the fucking walls and waft about in some floaty, joss-perfumed, high-tech ever-after? Will she meet and marry the very decent bloke she deserves, have a couple of kids, be one of the mothers at the school gates? Will she take them home in a battered Fiat with a broken aerial? Or a state-of-the-art people carrier? Or a Merc? Or on the bus?

And what about me? Will I ascend to the top of my profession – *don't make me laugh* – OK, through a tremendous effort of will, could I just about manage to creep, crawl, backstab, bully, cheat, manoeuvre . . . generally forge my way to some sort of secure standing in what is simultaneously a deeply insecure and worthless business? And even if I could, would it be worth it?

Or should I go back to my first love?

Unemployment.

At the thought, the first symptom of the day steps into the spotlight and takes a bow, a stabbing pain over my left eye. Not severe, but not so mild you'd miss it either. Right about where the eyebrow is. Signifying what? Brain tumour or stroke, could be either. I lie here, scanning my body for other faint signals from inner space. For this, make no mistake, is how it will start: the dull little ache you wake up with one morning that wasn't there the night before. And six months later, time enough to say your goodbyes and arrange your affairs, as they put it, you're toast.

Or – better or worse, can't decide? – there is always the Other Way. On the tennis court. At the card table. Outside

WH Smith. Out of a blue sky, the massive insult — *WHUMP!* — that fells you like a tree. Just a sharp pain maybe; perhaps for an instant — your last sentient instant — an unbearable pain (if you had to suffer an unbearable pain, this would definitely be the moment to suffer it). And then oblivion. Your world snapped off like a TV set, even before your head cracks the pavement.

Would you know it was the end? In that . . . what, second or two at the most, would you have time to think, oh fuck, here's the mother of all myocardial infarctions, bye bye cruel world, wish I'd slept with more women (specifically Karen Coombs and Laura Spiro). Now I'm going to miss the new Austin Powers movie, the new Moby album. Shit, the car's on a meter . . . ?

The last awful thought: Everything will carry on without me . . . ?

Or would it be more like, Ooh dear, you know I'm really not feeling at all w——?

Sorry, how did I get into this? Oh yeah, looking at Linds. Love always puts me in mind of death.

2

Over breakfast Linds tells me about her love life.

There are a number of runners and riders in the frame. There's the one who's crazy about her (but she's not sure). There's the one *she's* crazy about (but he seems distant). There's the one she *quite* likes (and who seems to quite like her, but never phones). There's the one who only ever calls when he's pissed (he's married, but he's getting a divorce, *yeah, right*); she's moderately keen on him. And there's the one she *can't fucking stand, Charlie*, who she's going out for dinner with tonight.

'If you can't fucking stand him, why are you going out with him?' A reasonable question, I'm sure you will allow.

A small rivulet of egg yolk begins its great adventure down one side of Lindsay's face. Lindsay has always enjoyed a substantial breakfast. (I am a black coffee and banana man myself.) She is currently working her way through juice, coffee, two boiled eggs, a significant pile of toast, plus butter, peanut butter, cheese, jam, marmalade and Marmite. I am anxious about women with too healthy an appetite. I guess the fear is that they'll turn into Hattie Jacques. If Lindsay can be said to eat like any sort of bird, it's a vulture.

'Actually, before you answer that,' I interject, 'what is it that you can't stand about him?'

'Oh, he's ghastly. He's got no sense of humour. Well, he thinks he has, which is worse. He tells just horrible jokes. He drones on incessantly about himself. He's a corporate lawyer. Hardly ever asks about what I'm doing. And the clothes! God, the clothes. He wears really unforgivable clothes . . .'

'What do you mean? Suity lawyer clothes?'

'Much worse. Ironed blue jeans, with a crease? Suede waistcoat? Cowboy boots?'

'Oh dear.'

'And the hair. Straight out of the seventies.'

'Not . . . not a *ponytail*?'

'It isn't long hair. But it's layered or feathered or something. And very expensively cut. It reminds me of the Bay City Rollers.'

'Jesus.'

'He's obviously incredibly vain. In restaurants, you keep catching him taking sneaky little glances at himself in the mirror. Admiring what he sees. And he's a total bore. Never once says anything remotely interesting.'

'How exactly did you meet Mr Personality?'

'It was a blind date. Someone fixed me up with him.'

'Lindsay, why are you going out for dinner with this prick?'

'Well, he's rich. He picks me up in his lovely rich person's car. He's quite handsome, once you get past the hair and the clothes. He knows a lot about stock flotations; with this Internet thing I can ask him all the really basic things that I'm too embarrassed to ask anyone else. And he loves explaining it all, you know, *knowingly*. And, and, and. And a girl likes to be taken out every now and again, Charlie.'

Oh. That old thing.

She digs her spoon deep into the eggshell, gouges out a wobbling, dripping section of yellow and white which she transfers into her surprisingly large mouth. The knife flashes into the peanut butter. She applies it to a fresh piece of toast like cement on a brick. And now there's a big mouth-shaped corner missing.

Lindsay looks a bit extraterrestrial today, sitting up straight, hair combed, all big-eyed in my kitchen, eyes shining with early morning intensity through the rising steam from the coffee mug. I can picture the spaceship that's waiting to collect her, dogs barking at the alien craft as it sits in the communal gardens, engines thrumming, trails of dry ice running off into the flowerbeds.

Is this why we split up? Because my girlfriend ate too heartily? Or for a more serious reason — that she wasn't someone else?

Cheryl, for example.

'You don't . . . ?' I begin. 'You haven't . . . ?'

'What, fucked him?'

My stomach turns at the thought. '*No*. You know . . . snogged him.'

'Oh yeah. He's quite a good snogger, actually.' She makes another corner of toast disappear.

I am Lindsay's ex. We are just friends. I am supposed to take this sort of information in my stride. So why do I want to pick up what's left of her boiled egg and mash it into her strange lantern-jawed face?

3

Sometimes I bus it. When I'm running late I cab it. But most mornings I take the tube. As I drop into my seat, whatever it is that's roosting just above my left eyebrow gives a little kick − *one thousand volts!* − just to let me know that it's still on board.

I've picked up one of those papers they give away in the Underground, but today my fellow passengers seem more compelling than news of Ken Livingstone's latest wheeze. A girl opposite is smiling secretly to herself. Now she's shaking her head − *dear oh dear, I don't know.* I have the strong impression she's thinking fondly about last night. About her boyfriend. A vivid image comes to me, the two of them on their bed in − where? I glance up at the Central Line map − Hanger Lane? No . . . Perivale, much better, all that sexual longing in the outer suburbs. The two of them in an upstairs bedroom in Perivale, duvet thrown aside. His complete, muscular . . . possession of her. Her thrilling abandon; the fabulous, shuddering orgasm. (Sorry. But chaps do have these thoughts on the tube.)

In the next seat, a young man with ill-advised spectacles and major spots is reading a business manual about tax shelters. Every now and again his eyes lift off the page and defocus over the adverts above my head. He's dreaming about great avoidance schemes, legendary offshore company structures. A Chinese girl is pulling a funny face, probing a cave in a tooth with the tip of her tongue. I can imagine the fleshy pink organ squishing around in its hollow.

Two thousand volts. Fuck, maybe this *is* the first stirrings of a stroke. What a pitiful place to be carried off, the crowded carriage of a Central Line train. One minute you're sitting there reading your fucking *Metro*, or your *Captain Corelli's bleeding Mandolin*, and the next – *forty thousand volts!* – you're lolling against the person alongside you, dribbling. When they shrug away to escape your pressing shoulder, you pitch forward into the floor, your face landing on someone's shoe.

Actually, I think my somatic symptoms are getting worse. I can produce pains in my body the way some people get notes out of a musical instrument.

Want to know how?

Just calmly attend to your bodily sensations for a moment. Feel anything? Maybe a little twinge somewhere. Almost nothing, perhaps just a discernible spasm of . . . pain is too strong a word for it, just a spasm of *feeling*. In your wrist, in the back of your neck, in a toe, from your gut, it doesn't matter. But when it arrives – and it will – hold that spasm. Lock on to it. Zoom into it, as it were, and ask yourself, what the fuck is that? No really, what the fuck *is* that? By and large, your body is supposed to keep quiet. So what is that funny feeling? Fuck, there it is again. Is it just a random bodily stirring, the human equivalent of the central heating pipes clanking, or is it the tumour – the one that's been growing inside you painlessly for months . . . years – finally beginning to make its presence felt? The more you worry about this possibility – and I *do* worry about this; a *lot* – the more you focus on this site, the more likely you are to reproduce the feeling – yes, there it is again – and this time, maybe a little stronger than before. So now you're on a roll. Your brain, supersensitised to signals from that particular area, begins to amplify those signals, in a full-blown feedback loop. It's like worrying away at an itch; scratching makes it itchier. But just because I know how this process works doesn't mean that I am free of it, that I can stop worrying. The terrible truth: just because you're a hypochondriac, it doesn't mean you won't get ill.

My change is at Tottenham Court Road on to the Northern Line to Camden Town. As I make my way up Camden High Street towards Chalk Farm Road, I remember another bad sign, along with the galloping hypo, the crumbling handwriting, the seeing Cheryl everywhere and the spontaneous role-playing that I seem to be increasingly prone to.

I've been finding other people's words in my mouth. Saying stuff that just isn't me.

The other day I opened my Visa card bill and was met with a surprisingly high figure. Actually, it was borderline sickening. Anyway, the phrase that fell from my lips was – and here I quote – 'Fucking Horatio!' This isn't the sort of thing I normally go around uttering. But I knew I had heard it somewhere recently, and unconsciously squirrelled it away for future usage (occasions demanding shock/outrage/alarm, etc.). Then it came to me. It was Geraldine at work. She blurted it out one lunchtime after reading something horrifying in a magazine (probably *Marie Claire*; how many times a day men think about sex or whatever). 'Fucking Horatio!' Sounds like the sort of dyspeptic exclamation a retired brigadier would come out with after stumbling across a particularly indigestible piece of news in that morning's *Daily Telegraph*: a statement from Gerry Adams; BP's share price. 'Fucking Horatio!' An old man's expression, yet in the voice of his tall, fair daughter, irresistible.

There are more – others who pop up speaking in my voice. Or is it me speaking in their voice? Whatever, it's not natural.

Here are some of the alien words and phrases that I've found myself parroting in the last few weeks:

Fuck this for a row of ducks (one of Andy Fineman's; never used it until lately).

Oakey-cokey (Cheryl's; she says it all the time; a truly deplorable verbal tic).

Say again (for Sorry? Pardon? Would you repeat that? I hate 'say again' with its techno-military undertone. Every bastard in television says 'say again', including – *especially* – Peter Marcus, my boss).

Take a view (believed to be Peter Marcus's first words. As in, 'We'll definitely need to take a view about that at some stage,' i.e. decide later; cf. 'Let's not worry about that now').

A mad woman's crap (all over the place, chaotic. As in, 'This editing schedule is a mad woman's crap.' Australianism. Heard it on a late-night comedy show).

Thang (as in 'that whole relationship thang'. Caught it off Barry at work. Can't stop saying it).

Oh yeah. And one more bit of evidence that if the wheels haven't technically come off yet, the screws are definitely loosening: that birthday card I was writing the other day – the one to Cheryl – I couldn't decide whether to sign it Charlie (happy, light, and gay in the old sense) or Charles (formal; person of gravity). Neither persona seemed to quite fit the situation. And you want to get these things right, don't you, in a card to the much-mooned-over ex? Then, the exact same thing happened yesterday at work. I was doing an email to lovely Heather in Personnel, about days off in lieu or some such nonsense, and as I came to sign it, I faltered. Another attack of persona-failure. Was I Charles, someone whose days off in lieu are to be taken seriously, or good old, likeable, fun-boy Charlie?

In both cases, I simply wrote 'C'.

4

Tuna Television stands somewhat north of Camden Town yet somewhat south of Chalk Farm. If it were in New York, they'd call this odd zone of quirky shops, brave restaurants and tragic pubs NoCaSoCha. As it is, we just tell people, well, if you're coming from Camden, walk out of the tube and head north up the High Street; if you're coming from Chalk Farm, walk out of the tube and head south. We're on the third floor of a sixties office building, between the theatrical bookshop and the Tibetan café. (If you pass The Roundhouse or Mornington Crescent you've fucked it up.)

Tuna, in common with the rest of the independent TV industry, is open-plan. The main area is a sprawling archipelago of 'desking', which is supposed to make for better communication. You're *meant* to be able to overhear everyone else's conversations, the better to know what they're doing, the better to be able to *contribute*. To my mind, however, the layout only serves to render it impossible to concentrate on very much at all, except possibly how good Emma, the new researcher, looks in those tight trousers, and how much both Barry and Ian, our goateed APs, yearn to get within them.

Thankfully, being a series producer, I am entitled to a 'bubble', one of the minuscule offices off to the side. The first three or four feet of the walls of my bubble are partition board, but the remainder to the ceiling is glass. Thus I can see out (keeping an eye on the troops) and they can see in (what's he doing in there? Watching important videotape rushes? Or the afternoon film? No way of telling, happily).

This morning, it looks like I can make it to the safety of my bubble without having to stop and talk to anyone. Rose and Geraldine have clearly only recently arrived; they're still fiddling with their Starbucks Grande Lattes and firing up their

PCs. The goatee boys, Ian and Barry — two almost identically bearded creatures — are already phone-bashing (technical term for intensive phoning: Can we come and film in your café? How much to hire your tame monkey for the day? Could you please surrender your firstborn? Whatever). To the untrained eye, Ian and Barry are quite difficult to tell apart. Both wear a lot of black. Both are serious, ambitious — what they're doing working on this stupid show is beyond me — and it's depressingly plain that either could be my boss in five years' time. The single biggest difference between them is that Barry keeps his wisp of beard on the end of his chin; Ian's is just below his bottom lip. Ian and Barry, like Rose and Geraldine, are assistant producers.

We've also got four researchers — Emma in the nice tight trousers, for example — a secretary and a production assistant, various runners and nameless work experience characters . . . but, hey, enough introductions for now. Come into my office, and let's see about getting us a cup of coffee.

'Charles?' Oh shit. One of the pesky researchers wants something. It's Robyn. With a Y. So pale and young that she reminds me of a pre-term foetus. Or a plump white larva. She doesn't seem quite fully formed. Her milky face is a little pudgy, as if she's still carrying puppy fat.

I smile as warmly as I can manage. 'Robyn. With a Y.' My little joke.

'Do you still want me to go ahead and book the Princess Diana lookalike for the "Café Royal" scam?' The 'Café Royal' scam — our delightful wheeze where unsuspecting members of the public, blamelessly eating their beans on toast at a greasy spoon, are joined by various members of the 'royal household'. When the 'royals' fall into conversation with the punters — 'please, I beg you, don't make a fuss' — they explain they are in plain clothes as part of a new initiative to 'get more in touch with the ordinary lives of their subjects'. (And yes, *isn't* it amazing how different they look on telly with all the make-up and whatever.) So maybe you can help me, asks 'Her Majesty', or 'Prince Edward', or 'Princess Anne'. Do you hunt? Does your house have a garden? How many acres? Do you find it difficult keeping servants? What sort of art do you collect? Peter Marcus, the show's executive producer, and I are still arguing the toss over whether to include the late Princess of Wales as a final gaff-blowing walk-on.

'Actually,' I tell Robyn, 'we still need to take a view about that one. Hold off for a while, would you?' Television's Rule One: never make a decision until the latest possible moment.

All over the world, TV producer offices are the same. There is always a desk, a telephone, a PC, a TV, a VCR, a comfy chair for guests. There is always a shelf of videotapes of the other crappy shows that you've made. Always picture publicity material from the other crappy shows. Always any awards you can lay claim to (none, in the case of the present writer). Always several interesting unread books (inevitably freebies). And always scores of Post-it notes which have settled everywhere, like butterflies. They bear either a phone number with no name, or a name with no number. They fade in the summer sun; six months later – your contract not having been renewed – another producer will be peeling them off the very spots where they first landed. Finally there is always a novelty prop (also usually a freebie), an object that says, I may sit in this soulless hutch all day long suffering from Sad Building Disease, but actually I'm quite a quirky, fun individual.

My novelty prop is Iris, Goddess of Parking, a three-inch-high wind-up plastic angel that you attach to the dashboard of your car. Her wings flap when you're hunting for a parking space. I bought her in New York.

I set her going when I can't decide which I'm more frightened of, losing this job or keeping it.

5

You remember Newton's Laws of Motion, in particular the one that claims 'For every action there is an equal and opposite reaction'? Well, I think the same may hold true for television.

We are currently limping to the end of series two of *The Uh-Oh Show*. My first thought about this is: Please God, let it be a respectable success — respectable in ratings terms; it'll never be respectable any other way — let us, in the jargon, get away with it, so we'll all have more work next year. And then there's the equal and opposite thought: Please God, let it be a minor flop — not an absolute fucking turkey — no, let there not be too much disgrace, let the Channel just quietly decline to recommission it, and let us all find jobs on other more agreeable programmes. Like many practitioners in television, I live in a delicate equilibrium between fear and boredom.

Richard and Judy are in good cranky form in the rerun this morning. I've become mildly addicted to this show, more for the personal tics and foibles of R. & J. themselves than any of their guests. I like it particularly when Judy looks like she's had a bad night, and you can read the suffering in her face — pouchy, is the word I am looking for — and Richard is acting ratty; getting borderline hysterical when things foul up, wrong captions, cues a little late, that sort of thing. This is why Richard and Judy's programme is so popular. They're real. We share their pain, and in doing so, we forget our own.

Annoyingly, the phone rings.

'Charles . . . Peter.' His laconic drawl. 'Just to warn you that the divine Miss Birkendale is in the building.'

'Oh fuck, thanks for telling me. What does *she* want?'

'To come to the weekly meeting, would you believe? She's got a photographer in tow from *Yes* magazine. They're doing a profile. I suppose she wants to convey the impression that she's one of the gang.'

'That's quite funny, isn't it?'

'There is a certain irony.'

'I shall be charm personified.'

'I'd expect nothing less.'

And fuck, here she is, sweeping towards me through the open-plan, a small, almost elfin figure in unsuitably tight trousers, on unsuitably tall heels, sunglasses perched in her hair (it's been raining all morning, did I mention it?), swinging a D&G tote bag, photographer and make-up artist in her wake.

Erica Birkendale, the 'glamorous' presenter of *The Uh-Oh Show*, is still one of the best known women in Britain, if no longer one of the most in demand. She first came to the public's notice in the early eighties on the kids' show *Get It, Got It, Good!*, where the ripeness of her bottom was as much admired as anything that came out of her mouth. Twice voted Rear of the Year in that turbulent decade, she reached the high-water mark of her fame in 1987 when she landed her own chat show, *Erica!*, notoriously ambushing a member of the Conservative cabinet of the time by asking if he knew the price of a loaf of bread (he didn't). Since then, year after year, in the teeth of ferocious competition – this is, after all, an industry where there is always someone younger, blonder, and cheaper snapping at your ankles – Erica Birkendale has somehow managed to keep her face on the nation's television screens. Erica is thirty-eight. Erica has been thirty-eight for the last three years. Erica will never be thirty-nine, for if she were, one year later, she would have to be forty. And Erica will never be forty, though if she endures, she may be fifty.

Like a vehicle with a regrettably high mileage, Erica has been 'clocked'. Her real age is a mystery. Only she and her absurdly tough agent, Hughie Hughes, know the truth, and neither is telling. Erica is not notably brilliant at any of the recognised TV skills. Neither a gifted interviewer (the bread question was a fluke) nor very good at handling what we call 'real people' ('Can't stand them, darling. They smell of frying'), she isn't even particularly good at reading the Autocue. I guess her single greatest talent is the way she looks at the television camera. It's a subtly *sideways* look, there's a *teasing* quality to it that makes male viewers want to fuck her, and miraculously – we've done research on this – women believe she'd be a good mate.

'Charlie.'

'Erica.'

I rise to greet The Star. She offers me a cheek. The mask looks like it's taken the best part of three hours to put in place, so I'm careful not to make actual contact. As she lowers herself into the comfy chair, I hear a knee joint crackle.

'You don't mind if . . .' She waves at her make-up lady and snapper.

'Of course not,' I reply.

Erica offers up her face for inspection. Make-up does something with a pot of powder and a small paint brush. Now a hair brush. Now the fine point of a comb handle. Now just fingertips. Make-up steps away to survey its fine-tuning. Make-up is satisfied.

'Lighting sympathetic?' says Erica. It's not a question.

'We'll go with available,' says the lensman. 'Very *verité*.'

'So,' she says to me, teasingly. 'This is Erica and producer Charlie Green dreaming up the wicked wheezes for next week's edition of *The Uh-Oh Show*. Do you think you should have a clipboard or something?'

My reply is drowned in the roar of the camera's motor-drive.

6

We hold the weekly production meeting for *The Uh-Oh Show* in Tuna Television's boardroom. Today it's lit up like a film set for the benefit of *Yes* magazine. Four one-kilowatt 'blondes' stand in the corners, bouncing light off the ceiling. A couple of smaller 'redheads' have been strategically placed to favour the star. One is Erica's keylight, the principal source of illumination for her famous features. The other is a backlight, angled to send a warm glow through her beautifully teased hair. Like a flower turning towards the sun, Erica instinctively finds her light. She's been chewing a pen thoughtfully (the photographer *loved* that; his motordrive had multiple orgasms). At one point she wore a groovy pair of glasses to 'read' a 'script'. When I looked carefully, I noticed there were no lenses in them. This was probably her publicist's idea, conveying intelligence and 'growing older with her audience' in one 'candid' image. Erica will have no worries about this. If she hates any of the pics, they'll burn the negatives.

'So, Charlie,' purrs Peter Marcus, 'remind me what scams we're shooting this week.'

Peter Marcus, already a dandy by television standards, has clearly raised his game for the camera this morning (why the fuck did no one tell *me*?). I'd swear he's had a crafty little haircut. A ravishing yellow silk tie spills creamily down the front of a fresh pink shirt. He's wearing his most gorgeous Paul Smith suit. Rose and Geraldine seem a bit shinier than usual. Even Robyn with a Y has had a change of nappy and a spoonful of Calpol, and looks almost human. I am suddenly very aware that every stitch of clothing I'm dressed in today comes from The Gap.

The meeting has been a complete waste of time. It's supposed to be a forum for brainstorming new scams. But this late in the series, everyone is either burnt out or was useless in the first place. The only ideas to come up were retreads. (*Again* someone suggested that one where the fucking phone rings in the call box, you answer it, and guess what. It's someone famous who thinks *you're* someone famous. This time it's Tony Blair – *oh please, my aching sides*, he's got a wrong number – he thinks you're Peter Mandelson. What should he do about fucking Ireland? Or fucking Europe? Or fucking John Prescott? Please, not that one, never *ever* that one again.)

I take a deep breath. 'We're doing "Prize Turkey" tomorrow morning. In Acton, I believe.' I should know this stuff. 'Then "Heartbreak Jack Russell" on Thursday. In Essex, for some reason . . .'

'No filming fee for the shopping mall we're using,' pipes up Barry. 'It's a contra-deal type thang. They get a shot of the exterior. Nothing in writing, obviously.' Peter Marcus's eyebrows lift a fraction of a millimetre. Approval or disdain? Impossible, as always, to tell. 'And it's not a Jack Russell any more,' continues Barry. 'A poodle turned out to be half the price.' He drums his fingernails on the table top for emphasis and I have a powerful urge to rip the stupid beard off his face and ram it down his throat.

'Heartbreak Jack Russell' is the tender tale of a small dog caught between a man and a woman who have reached the end of love. Neither member of the quarrelling couple wants to keep little Bertie. The helpless punter is ensnared as a go-between, shuttling endlessly with the dog between neighbouring benches where the irreconcilable protagonists are camped out, grimly refusing to budge. The key to the scam is that Jack Russells are funny. Poodles are emphatically *not* (they're stupid). And if you don't know that, you shouldn't be in this business. A three-thousand volter catches me under the left eyebrow, just to let me know it's still awake.

'On Monday,' I continue wearily, 'we're doing "Porno Priest" . . .'

'That sounds like a *saucy* one,' says Erica, doing her trademark teasing face, which she holds for a few seconds to allow the snapper to get a decent shot of it.

'"Porno Priest" is local, Kentish Town. And we're in Chingford on Thursday with "Café Royal".'

'I take it we're still taking a view about the Diana lookalike,' says Peter.

'I honestly don't think we'll get away with it,' I reply. 'Issues of taste and all that.'

'It would be a great closer for the item,' says Peter. 'Shoot it anyway, and take a view later?'

'It'll cost a day's fee for the actress. Not as much as the poodle, admittedly.'

'What do you think, Erica?' A classic Peter Marcus diversionary tactic.

Erica does something with the alignment of her head and shoulders. She pauses, turns somehow, pauses again. Bites her lip. Looks down at the table. Takes a piece of hair and tucks it behind an ear. Blinks. The old presenter trick, giving the cameras enough time to swing on to you, frame up and focus. Everyone has gone quiet. Now for some reason she's staring straight at me. Oh fuck, she's going to emote.

'I think . . . I think she was an extraordinary woman. It was such, *such* a terrible waste.'

I nod. Peter nods conclusively. So that's settled then.

Only when I get back to the bubble does it occur to me: have we decided to go with Diana lookalike or drop her?

7

I've developed a cranky-old-man lunchtime regime. Every day, I realise, I do the exact same thing. I go round the corner to the organic bakery, pick up a wholemeal cheese salad sandwich, a cup of vegetable soup, and beetle straight back to the office. There, I gather up as many of the day's tabloids as I can find, retreat to my bubble, switch on *The Jerry Springer Show* and gobble down lunch in a lovely warm bath of trash culture.

I enjoy Jerry Springer's show not for the terrible people who come on to yell at each other, but more for Jerry's reaction to them. The gleeful, kid-in-the-candy-store grin that he makes no attempt to conceal when Clyde and Jolene start effing and blinding at one another. The expression on the face of this coiffured sophisticate that says, isn't this great; being so famous, and making all this money just because of all the stupid folks out there who are prepared to swear and scream and whack each other for our amusement. That, and the irresistible cornball sign-off, 'Take care of yourselves . . .' (*pause for sincerity*) '. . . and each other.'

Is it bad to do this day after day? To be such a creature of habit? Woody Allen, the chronically hypochondriacal filmmaker, is another slave to routine. He has said he hates change because it reminds him of approaching death. I relate to this strongly. Firsts fill me with a nameless dread. The first grey hair. The first tooth to break on a bread roll. The first fall on the pavement. (Not long ago, I saw an elderly man trip and fall in Regent Street. People rushed to his aid, of course. He wasn't hurt, only shaken. But the horrifying detail was the look in his eyes, the fear that he'd crossed some invisible line and entered another category. That he was now amongst *the fallen*, irredeemably marked.)

It's been called life's sad secret. Things change.

Geraldine is standing outside with a baguette and a cappuccino, eyebrows set to question mark. As I wave her in, she raises her elbows and bumps open my door with her hip, a little movie that I just *know* will be going round my head for the rest of the day. Geraldine is a big girl, physically not a million miles from Cheryl, my ex, though blonde not dark; cheerful not brooding; and sensible not hairline-cracked. Geraldine is relaxed and easy within her large frame. As she settles into the comfy chair for guests, I think I can imagine her army officer father; I'd guess it's his long English face with the high forehead that she's inherited. I can picture the big house in Hampshire. The dogs, the pony, the brothers. Their sunlit, happy childhood. In my mind's ear, I can hear Brigadier Brown bemoaning his daughter's turn of career. 'Johnny Wildblood's boy would have married her like a shot. But she insists on living in some slum in London, working on a moronic TV show with a ghastly crowd of pansies and drug-takers.'

We munch our sandwiches silently together as the creatures in Jerry's bear-pit yell and bleep at each other, a small giggle escaping Geraldine every now and again. Outside, the desking has been depopulated. The goatee boys have dragged Emma off to drink expensive bottled beer in some groovy goatee watering hole. Remaining are Robyn with a Y, who is playing with her Fuzzy Felts, and Rose, her face buried in a book. I know, because I looked earlier, that it is *Mansfield Park* by Jane Austen, a work so far off my planet that I know I shall never read it.

Rose is small and dark, a little simian, her mocking eyes beneath sexy, hooded lids. Rose is the dangerous, scheming anarchist of the two girls. The bomb-maker. She radiates sexual abandon; I imagine that she would writhe a lot (forgive me). Geraldine would be more . . . sensuously serene. (Look, I'm sorry. It's just that I *have* thought about these things.) Anyhow, together they have this terrific rapport that I am a little in awe of. The present ten-minute Jerry Springer break may be the longest they spend apart all day.

Geraldine scrunches her sandwich wrapper into a ball, lobs it against the wall opposite, where it drops perfectly into the bin. She burps impressively. With a rattling flourish at the end, like a bloke would (I love her even more for this touch). We both burst out laughing.

'Ah well, back to "Prize Turkey",' she trumpets.

'Prize Turkey': your doorbell rings and, blow me down, here's a man from *Competitor's Digest* congratulating you on winning a prize in their recent draw. Not the jackpot, but still well worth having, a lovely fresh turkey for Christmas. If you wouldn't mind signing for delivery, he'll fetch it from the van. And when he comes back, it's with a magnificent forty-pound *live* bird. This is Tommy, he says. We recommend that you keep Tommy in the back garden until the big day. No, I'm sorry, you've signed for him now, we can't take him back. He won't be any trouble. He'll become part of the family. You can even take him for walks in the park. And here's a leaflet about how to do the necessary when the time comes. And a free packet of stuffing.

'Geraldine, I take it the turkey *is* still a turkey? It hasn't become a budgie or a fucking seal or anything?'

'Still a turkey when I last looked.'

As I watch her stride back to her desk – there really *is* something a bit military about her carriage – for the thousandth time I ponder what it would be like to go out with this happy, handsome girl. One long laugh, I should think. Laughter without the loopiness. She'd bear you a string of healthy blonde children with bone structure going all the way back to the Norman fucking Conquest.

But what would become of Rose? How could you separate

these twin stars? Would the solution be to have them both? Devise some alternating shift system. Rose — curly black hair against the pillow; toes in the air, signalling frantically — Rose on Monday, Wednesday, Friday; Geraldine — big, warm, cool blonde — on Tuesday, Thursday, Saturday; Rose again on Sunday, then Tuesday, Thursday, Saturday, with Geraldine switching to the Monday/Wednesday/Friday cycle . . .

This pleasant logistical reverie is interrupted by the telephone. I mute the telly and pick up.

'Charles. It's Kate. From last night? Forensic scientist?'

'Hi,' I bleat weakly.

But the thought ringing through my head is, *fucking Horatio*!

8

Specifically, how in the name of fucking Horatio did she find me here, at Tuna Television, when at the last count, if memory serves, I was a top Downing Street aide? For some reason, the vision of Kate that comes back to me now is her *knees*. Bony knees straining against the Bohemian check trousers, as she sat hunched over the contents of my idiotic tray. The knees, and the sexual flush that rose up her throat. And the exciting depression she left in my sofa after she left.

'Have I impressed you with my detective work?' she asks not particularly menacingly.

'Er, yes. Congratulations.' Fuck, what is it, twelve hours since we parted? 'Did you, er . . . try Number Ten? At all?'

'Actually, *Charles*, I had a strong feeling you weren't Gordon Brown's tennis partner.'

I don't know whether to feel hurt or relieved. 'Was it the no glasses? And the no suit?'

'No, not those.'

'Was it the stuff in the flat? The books. Too much P. G. Wodehouse, Elmore Leonard. Nothing about politics. Or policy. Or anything remotely governmental. Though I could be the sort who doesn't take their work home with them.' A fair point, indisputably.

'You could, that's true. But I knew you weren't. And it wasn't the books as a matter of fact.'

'Was it the Steely Dan?'

She laughs. 'No, I thought the Steely Dan was actually a very authentic touch.'

Mentally, I lick my finger and dab one up to her. 'What was it, then?'

'It was the credit card. In the Pelmanism.'

Of course. It had my name on it. How fucking stupid can you get?

'Ah. Bit of a slip, that. Still . . . how did you know to find me here?'

'There was a letter from your employer. About terms and conditions. It was tucked under a magazine. I couldn't help . . . noticing it when you were finding objects for the game.'

'Ah, snooping.'

'Do you do this often . . . *Charles?*' Regaining the moral high ground. 'You seemed very practised. At the verbals, anyhow.'

'Yes. I mean, no. I mean . . . are you annoyed?'

'Puzzled.'

'Were you concerned? Even for a moment? I could have been some sort of bad person.'

'Just as unlikely as a Tony Blair aide.'

'Serial killer?' I attempt weakly.

'Serial *liar*, maybe.'

I allow a pause to fall on the conversation. On the telly, some fat women are mouthing obscenities at one another. They seem to be quarrelling about the man with the unnaturally small head who sits between them, smiling ruefully and fiddling with his bootlace tie. In the wide shot you can see the stage crew standing by to drag them apart when the fingernails fly. Jerry is so happy he could shit. I am hoping Kate will take my silence as contrition. Who is going to blink first?

She does.

'I think Charles is a much better name than . . . Matthew.'

'Do you? I've been having trouble with it lately. Listen, Kate. Would you like to meet up again? Properly, I mean. I'll try and explain.'

It's her turn to go for the moody pause. And now I remember the way she kissed me good night, grabbing my arm as she rose up on her heels. Now, I very much want her to say yes, she *would* like to meet up again.

'Do you like exhibitions?'

My heart sinks. I *hate* exhibitions. All that irritating shuffling around. All that standing up. 'Sure, what have you got in mind?'

'There's a photographer called Walker Evans. He's on at a gallery I read about. I think you'll find him interesting.'

'Great.' An hour of clouds and lakes and rock formations, and then off to the nearest bar. How bad can it be?

After she rings off, I realise what it is that I've forgotten. But when I try 1471, the posh woman who answers only says, sorry, the caller withheld their number. Please go and fuck yourself.

9

Oprah can be quite entertaining too, with her cast of authors, therapists and heal-your-life artists. Today she's got some bald bloke on who's a 'life counsellor'. Apparently if you give more, you'll get more. That seems to be the gist of his message to the world. Oh yeah, and any relationship is a negotiation. I'm just puzzling over the fine print of the negotiations which led up to Cheryl and me splitting up – 'Charlie, just fuck off.' 'No, Cheryl, *you* fuck off' – when through the glass, I see Erica and Peter Marcus weaving their way across the floor towards me.

They've obviously been out for a splashy lunch together. I can tell from Peter's high colour. And also, 3.30 in the afternoon is *exactly* the time the guilty slope back to the office after spending a couple of happy hours in the favoured restie *du jour*. Discreetly I flip from Oprah to the VCR and press Play. Up comes the last edition of *The Uh-Oh Show*. Erica doing her long walk on: down the stairs, a little landing (where she pauses, cut to the mid-shot, waves), more stairs, a runway, three further steps to spring up, and finally the high stool that she hops on to (reverse angle, favouring her arse) . . . perkily. Back to the main wide shot now; as the applause dies away, crane in towards her (stay wide enough to catch her crossing her legs) and into a mid-shot for the opening spiel. Not so much an entrance, more an agility course.

Erica and Peter part at my bubble door with a practised exchange – *mwah, mwah* – and she lowers herself into the comfy chair with considerably less brio than the version I have just witnessed.

'Nice lunch?' I hazard.

'To be honest, I'm getting a little tired of The Ivy. You keep bumping into the same old faces.'

I shoot her a sympathetic look, the one that's supposed to say, hey, I know, that's always happening to me down the Curry Mahal. But I think maybe it comes out wrong (these nuances are very subtle). I think it looks more like, oh, don't make me puke, you ego-maniacal stuck-up cunt.

Erica flicks open the clasp of her lizard-skin handbag and produces a sheaf of fax paper.

'Charles. My links for next week's show. Do you think they should be funnier?'

'Funnier, Erica?'

'More . . . *funny*. Do you think there should be more jokes in them?'

'I thought they were OK, actually.'

A pause. A slightly *chilly* pause. 'There aren't many laughs. I don't seem to be getting many laughs.'

'I thought you didn't really *do* laughs, Erica. Warmth, of course. And humour. And your lovely sense of . . . mischief.' That balls-aching teasy-weasy business. 'The odd laugh, naturally. But not . . . *laugh* laughs. Not gags. Not gags as such.'

The temperature seems to have dropped a few degrees.

'Hughie thinks my scripts should be funnier.'

Aha. The hand of Hughie. 'What kind of funny material does Hughie think should be in your scripts?'

'*Funny* funny material, Charles. There are people who write it.'

'I'm not against you doing funny material, Erica. But wouldn't it be a bit of a departure? It's not exactly what you're known for, brilliant as you are. Do you see what I mean?'

The star has gone very quiet. Small icicles are forming on the ceiling. I'm only trying to save this silly vain cow from herself. Christ, let her smirk and flirt; let her wince, pout, insinuate; let her even utter something half-amusing. But the idea of Erica Birkendale trying to be *funny*? Think of Heinrich Himmler cracking jokes and you'll have the general picture.

Now she starts to speak in a quiet, rather disturbing voice. 'I think it is possible to be warm, and humorous, and mischievous *and* funny,' she says. She names half a dozen female TV performers – all, like Erica, instantly identifiable by

Christian name alone. 'Francesca is funny.' Francesca has a sense of humour. 'Layla is very funny.' Layla uses a lot of cocaine. 'Billie is a riot.' Billie is borderline certifiable.

'Erica, you don't *need* to be funny,' I tell her. 'You are unique. You have something none of those women have.' Arthritis. 'You have earned the *affection* of the public. You are practically an institution.'

'A national treasure,' she says coldly.

'Exactly!'

Erica rises suddenly, knee joints popping. 'I'll leave you my thoughts,' she says. Dropping the fax paper on my desk, she releases an arctic smile, and vanishes in a puff of ice crystals.

I unfold the fax paper. Her 'thoughts' consist of scribbled comments in the margins of the script of next week's show. Remarks like 'joke here' and 'gag about turkeys'. In large, spidery, mad person's capital letters through the whole of her introduction, she's scrawled the single word, 'FUNNIER!!!!'

I realise I have just made three big mistakes.

One. Never — *ever* — disagree with the star.

Two. In my list of Erica's qualities (warmth, humour, mischief), I failed to include sexy.

Three. I called her a national treasure. Actually, she used the words 'national treasure' and I agreed with her. But it was Alan Bennett who defined national treasure. You are a national treasure, he said — *fuck, fuck, fuck* — you are a national treasure if you can still eat a boiled egg at seventy.

Still, perhaps she didn't notice, eh?

THREE

1

There's a vigorous close-of-play drink culture at Tuna Television. On Mondays, because you need a little reward, don't you, for getting through the trauma of Monday; Tuesday, I'll come back to Tuesday; Wednesday, because we've heaved our way through the week's balls-aching midpoint, and it's downhill from here on in (so let's celebrate); Thursday, well, Thursday is the new Friday; and Friday because it's Friday, and it's long been custom and practice within the TV industry to get reasonably shit-faced on a Friday.

Today, though, is Tuesday. The day when there's no rationale behind going for a drink after work, except that the alternative is to go home.

'Same again?' says Geraldine. It's not a question. Rose and

I drain our glasses in readiness. Within minutes, all remaining thoughts of Erica Birkendale will have been drowned in another bottle of chilled New Zealand Chardonnay.

The three of us have gone to a groovy new café-bar on Chalk Farm Road called Zyplxqnk. (Zyplxqnk rose from the ruins of the former occupant of this site, a short-lived Polish bar-restaurant concept called Foodski-Drinkski. Before that, it was Myfanwy's Kitchen – Modern Welsh; say no more – and before that, a suicidal attempt at a German gastrodome, Wurst Come, Wurst Served. Before that, it was a vehicle repair shop.)

Actually, it's hard to think of two better people to forget your sorrows with than Rose and Geraldine.

Rose, intense, sexy Rose, feet dangling off the bar stool a long way from the floor, knocking it back, smoking like a train, cackling and chuckling at the wickedness in the world (her own, other people's, she's not fussy). And Geraldine: slower, more deliberate; can match Rose drink for drink, fag for fag, but somehow doesn't seem as . . . driven. Not for the first time do I think Rose is the kite, Geraldine the long, curving string that anchors her to the ground.

As we refill our glasses, I tell them about Kate. For some reason I withhold the precise details of how we met. I tell them we were fixed up by a friend.

'Fuck, Charlie, a *copper*!' This is Rose. 'Did you snog her?'

'Well, there was a . . . tender little scene towards the end.'

The girls howl. 'How could you snog a copper?' Rose.

'Did you fancy her?' Geraldine.

'Or were you pissed?'

'Both, very probably.'

At the other side of the bar, Barry and Ian are perched on bar stools, nudging knees with Emma. Even from here I can see their micro-beards twitching with excitement, their heads dip-dipping towards the object of their frenzy. Emma's trousers are exquisitely tightly packed this evening; in fact I begin to feel a little tense myself, just contemplating the straining fabric. A cluster of researchers and nameless characters on work experience sit by the door, amongst them Robyn with a Y, who has a big happy smile on her larva-features as she gurgles milk through a straw and munches the complimentary rusks.

'So what's she like then?' Geraldine.

'Can you remember?' Rose.

'French-looking. Very slim. Dark hair that kept swinging across her eyes. Rather fidgety. A bit gangly. A curious walk. Loose-limbed . . .'

'Sounds like a chimp.' Rose.

'Did she have any hair *on* her face?' Geraldine.

'Seriously, there was something in the way she moved . . .'

And now Rose sings, shocking, because it's rather beautiful, '"Attracts me like no other lover . . ."'

Geraldine takes it up, more like singing in church. '"Something in the way she WOOO-OOS me . . ."' Her eyes bulge on the 'woo-oos'.

We laugh. I tell them about the Pelmanism, Kate's phenomenal memory.

'So what does she do all day?' asks Rose. 'Stare through a microscope at spit and sperm?' I know I shall want to rerun the way that she just phrased 'spit and sperm'; the wonderful sibilance; the warm glow at the end of 'sperm'. I put it in the folder where I left Geraldine opening my door with her hip.

'To be honest, I have no idea. We didn't talk about work very much.'

'Maybe she's not allowed to. Could be dead hush-hush.' Geraldine.

'So you didn't bring out the waccy baccy, what with this bird being in the filth and that?'

'Technically, I imagine she works for the Home Office.'

The girls look at one another. *Ooh, get him.*

'Home Office!'

'Fancy!'

'Speaking of which, I don't think I can drink much more of this battery acid. You don't feel like coming back for a herbal nightcap, do you?'

Half an hour later, the three of us are seated on my long black sofa. The TV plays silently, an ancient Cuban mourns on the hi-fi, and Rose is running a lighter flame over the corner of a significant cube of hashish.

2

'Plastic shit.' Rose.

'Floppy dick.' Geraldine.

'Penknife. Swiss navy penknife.' Rose.

We're playing a special stoned version of Pelmanism with the collection of objects that was still on the coffee table from last night. Under these relaxed rules, players get as long as they want to do the memorising part of the exercise. Despite this advantage, Rose and Geraldine have so far between them only managed to recall twelve things that were on the tray, and one – 'hairgrip?' Geraldine – that wasn't.

'Shit.' Rose.

'You've just had that.' Me.

'No, shit, I can't believe that policewoman remembered all twenty. It's jolly hard, isn't it?'

'Not for a trained professional whose brain hasn't been turned to slurry by soft drugs and New Zealand Chardonnay,'

I quip lightly. 'Do you want to skin one up, then?' I pass the joint-making impedimenta to Geraldine. She begins to roll with a facility that I am confident would horrify Brigadier Daddy.

In my book, this homely scene counts as pretty close to heaven: two fantastically attractive girls relax on my sofa; there are drinks; there are mild narcotics. Music tinkles lightly in the background. Should a powerful hunger suddenly strike, major stocks of chocolate, ice cream and frozen pizza brood impressively within the darkness of the fridge.

These fantastically attractive girls on my sofa – sorry, am I repeating myself? – each is somehow the antidote to the other. I can gaze at small, sexy, spiky Rose – now purring, now trouble-making – and when my brain is full of her heavy-lidded, almost Levantine life-force, I snap my vision over to Geraldine . . . and Rose is dissolved; in blondeness, in something very English – in something to do with the shape of her forehead – it's to do with cricket pitches, Labradors and the smell of horses (Christ, this stuff is *strong*).

I've kicked my shoes off and put my feet up on the table in front of us. So has Geraldine. Even Rose has managed to park her heels on the very edge. My black socks flanked by Geraldine's yellow socks and Rose's red socks. And our feet have started harmonising with the music. The Cuban is absolutely fucking *gutted* now; someone must have pinched his woman. Or said something horrid to him at the post office. We are feeling his pain and interpreting it through the medium of our toes.

For some reason, we find this irresistibly amusing.

But there's a sad undertow to my heaven because, much as I like to flirt with the idea, Rose and Geraldine are, of course, fundamentally unavailable. They're mates more than they're potential prey (you know what I mean). We're colleagues. And in the end, how could one ever separate them?

They have, it's true, both made fleeting references to extinct boyfriends; Geraldine used to go out with someone called Hugh; and Rose has some kind of tangled previous with a Swiss musician called Guy – pronounced like the clarified butter they use in curries. I suppose one day they'll have men, children, separate lives. But not just yet. For the moment, Rose and Geraldine seem perfectly happy with each other.

I roll another one. And then one more (just to be on the safe side). We play that game where you flip between TV channels trying to make funny speech conjunctions. The best one is:

Jeremy Paxman: 'So as Northern Ireland faces yet another critical weekend, the question being asked tonight is—'

Captain Peacock: 'Are you free, Mr Humphries?'

Mr Humphries: 'I'm free, Captain Peacock.'

We become mildly gripped by an insect sex docco: preying mantises mating, and the female eating the male for dessert. The last thing I remember is Rose saying blearily, 'Do you think he'd be terribly offended if she said afterwards, "Actually, I'll just have a black coffee"?'

When I wake up, I realise the three of us have been asleep on the sofa like the Babes in the Wood. Up at one end, Rose has made a nest for herself with some cushions. Geraldine has zizzed off where she sat, long yellow feet sticking out in front of her. I get up quietly, and watch the girls breathing for a few moments.

It's half-past midnight. I scan the CD pile to find something suitable to bring them back to life. I have a wicked urge to crank up the volume, and let them have it with the intro to 'That's the Way (I Like It)' by KC and the Sunshine Band. Rose would, if it was her.

But now — shockingly — the phone is ringing. The girls stir slowly into life as I pick up.

'Hello?'

Silence. Oh fuck, Ann Onymous again. Well, at least it rules R. and G. off the list of suspects.

'Look, I'm just in the middle of things here,' I explain. 'Do you think you could possibly call back in about twenty minutes? Then we can have a nice long chat.'

The oddest thing: two beeps come down the phone followed by the dialling tone. Two beeps. *Two for no.*

'Who was that?' asks Rose, rubbing her eyes.

'Fucked if I know,' I reply truthfully. I call the local minicabs and agree to meet the sleepy girls at eight thirty tomorrow morning for 'Prize fucking Turkey'.

Oddly, now I don't feel tired. So I power up the Hewlett-Packard, click on 'Favourites', and in a few seconds, I am face to face with my sexy Slavic adversary.

Magda — down to her last two items of clothing — is curled in the brown leather armchair studying the board with a fierce concentration. Her magnificent cheekbones seem to fill the screen. The little symbol starts to flash, signifying she's about to reply to my previous and, if I may say so, provocative *K3–K7*.

Shit. She's mounted an audacious counterattack deep into my king's side of the board. Her bishop simultaneously threatens two of my major pieces, and I'm bound to lose another pawn here, whatever else happens. As the next image downloads, I see she has removed her top, and now sports a look of defiance. She's not staring at the chessboard for a change, but straight out of the screen at me. Go on, then, Boris Spassky, what are you going to do about that?

It suddenly occurs to me, I bet Kate will turn out to be

bloody brilliant at chess. Bound to be, with that Pentium Five brain of hers. Will I mind losing? No, not really. But the better question is, will I be a worthy opponent? Will she lose whatever respect she has for me if I play like a complete cunt? With Magda, happily, the issue doesn't arise. She has no respect for me in the first place.

I log out of *Czech-Mates* and hit the email. No late-night note from Linds wondering if I'd care for some company. Of course. She's out with Prickface tonight.

I power down.

At four in the morning, heart pounding, I drag myself out of a nightmare. I am rescued by the little corner of my mind that finally remembers, oh, yes, this is a dream. That crazy bloke with the blood dripping off his axe won't be able to follow if you . . . Just. Wake. Up. Except my pursuer wasn't a bloke; it was a woman. In a suit of armour. As she approached, I had an overwhelming feeling of nameless dread. And when she lifted her visor, I found myself staring into the cold, dead eyes of Erica Birkendale.

So what's all that about, then?

3

'Good morning, sir. Would I be talking to the head of the household?'

'You would.'

'Excellent. You'd be Mr . . .'

Howard, who trained at RADA and once played Malvolio to some acclaim at Stratford, is today Man from *Competitor's Digest*. On the TV monitor, in the back of the undistinguished Ford van with blacked-out windows, I watch a shot of him fiddling with his paperwork. Rose and Geraldine sit behind me, suppressing their giggles (they still think this is fun).

'Phelps. Norman Phelps.' The head of the household looks like an early retiree. Cavalry-twill trousers, checked shirt, that type. (What the fuck *is* cavalry twill? Can you have *infantry* twill?)

'Of course. Mr Phelps.' Howard makes a reassuring mark on the documentation. 'Well, congratulations, Mr Phelps. I have some good news for you.'

The searching look in the punters' faces at this stage of the scam never ceases to fill me with wonder. It's something between innocence, curiosity and fear. I'm watching a nice steady close-up of this Phelps, and I feel it: the nauseating mixture of excitement and self-loathing that characterises the deception comedy genre. On the one hand: yes, yes, he's biting! And on the other: oh fuck, I really don't think I can bear to watch this.

'I represent *Competitor's Digest* – this is my colleague Miss Cole – and it's our happy task to inform you that you have won a prize in our monthly draw.'

'Really? How, er . . .' How nice? How much? How *what*, shitface? 'How remarkable.'

'Yes. Unfortunately, *not* the ten million on this occasion.' Love that *not*.

'No . . .' Absorbing all this spurious material. Already accepting the disappointment.

'But a nice prize none the less. Let me just check what you qualify for.'

More business with the paperwork. Miguel, the cameraman, shooting through the blacked-out side windows of the van, tightens up on our punter. Phelps actually runs his tongue over his top lip in anticipation. He's joined in the doorway by a woman.

'Muriel, this chap is from the . . . *Competitor's Digest*. Apparently we've won a prize.'

We haven't planned it with the precision of a military operation – after all, no one's life is at stake. We've just turned up in what seems to be a likely residential street in Acton (not too busy, not too quiet; a street where you wouldn't notice an extra couple of unmarked vans; a street where you can *park*). And we *are* getting usable pictures – there's Miguel's tasty long-lens shot (some out-of-focus foreground privet; rather moody, in fact); there's a shot of Phelps from Howard's buttonhole (fish-eye but deliciously 'covert'); and a third shot from Miss Cole's handbag. Phelps sounds clear as a bell, thanks to the rifle-mike pointing at him through the spine of Howard's ring-file.

'Mr Phelps . . . *Mrs* Phelps, is it? I'm delighted to tell you that you have won a lovely fresh turkey. If you'd just sign here, I'll go and fetch it from my van.'

The Phelps creatures exchange looks. They seem neither disappointed nor pleased. Fresh turkeys seem to be a topic that they have no particular views on. Muriel smiles at Miss Cole (*Hair*, *The Mousetrap*, episodes of *EastEnders* and *The Bill*). Miss Cole no doubt smiles back. The function of Miss Cole – aside from her splendid low-angle handbag shot – is to keep the punters standing in the doorway.

Now – priceless – Muriel turns to Norman; says, 'We can have it for lunch on Sunday when the boys are over.'

They have bought the whole scenario. They have assumed – as we wished them to – that the *Competitor's Digest* Prize Draw was another one of those lurid communications which say on the envelope, 'Act today. You may have already won the gross national product of Guatemala.' Only now, maybe, they're wishing they'd paid it a little more attention – opened it, read it, dealt with the nightmarish collection of YES stickers, NO stickers, MAYBE, CAN'T DECIDE and OH FUCK, DO WHAT YOU LIKE stickers. Perhaps they regret having so little respect for the details of the *Competitor's Digest* Prize Draw that they transferred them directly from the doormat to the dustbin.

And now their expressions are changing. Mrs Phelps' hand flutters to her mouth. Mr P. looks paralysed with confusion. Miguel stays tight on their faces – in the trade, this is the 'money shot'. Howard, I know, is returning up their garden path with a horribly huge, and unmistakably live turkey on the end of a lead. He will have taken the trouble to felt-tip 'Phelps' on a luggage label and put it round the beast's neck.

'Here we are. This is Tommy. He's a beauty, isn't he?'

Now Howard will take his foot off the pedal. He'll allow the miserable Phelpses to make the running with the comedy here. And they're doing quite nicely already, both staring in something like shock at the rudely sentient and undeniably substantial entity that is Tommy.

Tommy, I know, will be the only character in this drama to maintain his dignity. He is, of course, a seasoned old pro. We booked him through an animals agency – he's appeared in a couple of commercials, and was up for a part once in a Ridley Scott movie. Tommy is certainly the only artist out here today with his own trailer (a mini-van plus handler). He's costing us about the same as Miss Cole and Howard put together.

'Is this some sort of joke?' asks Mr Phelps.

'No, sir. Not at all. He's all yours,' replies Howard. Important to rebuff the joke notion firmly and instantly.

'But the thing's alive,' argues Mrs P., accurately.

'Very healthy bird, madam. Quite a gleam in his eye.' Howard pauses. Let them twist on the hook.

'Well, I'm afraid you'll have to take it away. We can't have this . . . *here*,' says Mr Phelps. Howard falls silent. If in doubt, say nothing. The punter will usually come in with something helpful. 'I mean, what on earth are we supposed to do with it, for goodness' sake?'

'Oh, Tommy will be fine in the garden. He's much too big for any cats to bother with. And his . . . his muck will be very good for your roses. They're very good with children. And when the time comes, well, they do have a lot of meat on them.'

The Phelpses eyes have gone very wide, picturing these ghastly scenarios.

'I'm sorry, there's no question. I can't have this bloody great . . .' Mr P. is losing the power of speech.

'Turkey, sir.' A comic touch from Howard.

'I can't have this bloody great thing in my back garden. You'll have to take him away.'

'I'm afraid I can't do that, sir. There's no provision.'

No provision – one of those powerfully meaningless phrases that work so effectively on people of a certain cast of mind. Phelps is silenced for a moment, staring in dismay at the horny-clawed brute. Intercut with close-ups of Tommy, this will have the studio audience peeing into their knickers.

'You can't just take him back?' A pleading note has entered Phelps' tone. This is turning cruel. Good.

'No, sir,' Howard states regretfully. 'There's no provision. Tommy's been properly assigned to you.'

'What do you think, Muriel?'

Muriel doesn't know what to think. The spectacle of the massive alien bird on her doorstep has numbed her senses. These things just don't happen in Acton.

I sense we're getting close to the endgame. I press a button and whisper into Howard's tiny wireless ear-piece, 'Very nice. Do the killing thing now.'

'I assure you he'll be no trouble,' says Howard warmly. 'I'll leave you these instructions on killing, plucking and gutting. And on the next page, there are some recipes. I can especially recommend the honey-glaze, madam. Tommy's a big lad, so I expect he'll need quite a long time in the oven.'

Mrs Phelps' mouth has dropped open. But a steely expression has come over Mr P. And now with a curt, 'Muriel,' he pulls his wife inside the hall and slams the door in the bemused faces of Howard, Miss Cole and Tommy, and the three camera lenses trained on him.

'Fuck. OK, stop the tapes. Thank you, Howard, thank you, Tommy. Let's reset everything to go again in twenty minutes, please. Rose and Geraldine, can you do the biz?'

I step from the van into the daylight. Rose and Geraldine tumble out and head for the Phelpses' front door. It's their job to charm these old fools into signing a piece of paper that grants permission to Tuna Television to exploit, in any way it sees fit, the material we've just shot ('in perpetuity, throughout the Universe'). Although we didn't get a 'reveal', the sickening (uh-oh) realisation that it was all a prank for TV, the Phelpses might still make the final edit.

But when R. and G. return, it is with a very blank release form. The Phelpses were not only unwilling to sign, they wouldn't even open the door.

Fuckers. Where's their sense of humour, eh?

4

We carry on for the rest of the day, cruising around Acton, parking up, launching our turkey prank on unsuspecting householders. And though we capture some funny moments – an Italian au pair screaming and squealing at the sight of the monster; a furious yapping Airedale, straining at the leash; a retired butcher who insists Tommy would be inedible – something's not quite right about any of it. There isn't the single great take that we can make the centrepiece of the item, its victim all smiles in the studio audience afterwards, for Erica to talk at, patronise and generally poke with a stick.

'What we needed,' I say to R. and G. when we return to base and repair for postoperative stress medication to Genghis Lounge (Mongolian tapas bar concept), 'was a bloody good bust-up. Some effing and blinding. Get that bleeping thing out of my bleeping garden, you bleeping bleep.'

'Yeah, like that guy in "Pretend to Be my Sibling",' recalls Rose.

'Maybe not quite like that guy,' I reply.

'Pretend to Be my Sibling' – a minor classic in cruelty television. There you are, minding your own business (the way all these horrible jokes begin) when an attractive young woman comes up to you in the street, all flustered and pleading. I wonder if I could ask you an enormous favour, she says. I work in an office over the road there, and my boss is really angry with me. I think I might be about to get the sack. You see . . . (deep sigh) . . . I overslept *again*. He rang me on the mobile this morning. Where the hell are you? Why aren't you here for this meeting? (He used some quite bad language, actually.) Well . . . (another sigh) . . . all I could think of telling him was that I was at the airport, meeting my sister-stroke-brother who'd just flown in from overseas. Really, says my boss. How nice. I'd like to meet her-stroke-him. Bring her-stroke-him in. Third and final sigh. Do you think – I quite understand if you won't – but *would* you please just pretend to be my sister-stroke-brother? Just for two minutes. Just so I can introduce you to Mr Fairbrass. He's such a suspicious man. It's literally across the road. I'll be *ever* so grateful.

Well, do you?

Derrick Royce did. I had a bad feeling about him from the start. In fact I nearly buzzed through to the actress and said, Sally, not that guy in jeans and the nylon bomber jacket with the orange lining. But it was too late. She'd buttonholed him, and he was buying the schtick – 'yeah, sure, I'll be your bruvver' – and they go over the road, into the cluttered little office above the travel agents. And Mr Fairbrass (*Macbeth*; *Last of the Summer Wine*; *Brookside*) says come in, sit down – that chair *there*, the one that's perfect for the close-up; the room is bristling with tiny cameras – and he gently starts giving this guy the third degree. Where have you flown in from, what airline, how long were you away, what were you doing over there? And this Derrick Royce is lying like a good 'un. He's been working in Florida, on computers, he rents an apartment in Orlando – near the park? asks Mr Fairbrass; not too far, says Derrick without missing a beat – and soon the conversation takes quite a nasty edge. Fairbrass is quizzing him intensively about his life – how long have you been in computers; where did you train; what system do you use? – and Derrick is improvising brilliantly, but in the room next door where we're watching, we can feel the needle. And then Fairbrass goes in for the kill: I don't believe you're brother and sister at all. *Course we are.* You don't look alike. *So what?* You don't even know your sister's name, do you? (He doesn't; she's been careful not to give a name.) What's her name, then? And now he's fucked. In a great sweaty close-up, the realisation dawns. He's been done up like a kipper, and he doesn't even know the worst part (that it's all on tape). Fairbrass will let him sweat for a minute or two, and then ask quietly if he's ever appeared on television (that old sickener). But now the terrible thing happens. In one muscular leap, Derrick flies across the desk, pulls Fairbrass on to the floor, and starts punching the shit out of him. By the time we get to them, he's squatting on the actor, banging his head against a filing cabinet, yelling, 'Have some of that, you arsehole.' When we drag him off and finally convince him that the whole thing was a scam for TV, he takes it in fairly good part. He sees the funny side. He congratulates Fairbrass on his performance – 'you had me well fooled, mate' – and even offers to drive him to hospital.

Like I say, we could have done with a bust-up on 'Prize Turkey'. But not quite like that one.

5

Rose and Geraldine and I split another bottle of the Ulan Bator Pinot Noir. I can't really recommend it, to be honest. The top note of yak is a bit too prominent.

'Listen,' I ask them, 'I need some girl advice. Where could I take Kate tomorrow evening after we've seen this Walker Evans exhibition?'

'Ooh, I dunno,' says Rose. 'Where does a policewoman feel comfortable? The Met Bar? The Pig and Whistle? Anywhere called Bobby's?'

Oh please. I wish I'd never started this.

'The main thing,' says Geraldine, 'is to make sure that by the end of the evening you've taken down her particulars.'

I can tell this could go on for some time. I head off for dinner with Linds.

'Bring her a single red rose,' shouts Rose as I'm going through the doors. 'Or a truncheon wrapped in Cellophane.'

I, along with the rest of the civilised world, have largely grown out of them, but Lindsay is a curry hound. She still loves to get inside one of those traditional Bangladeshi flock-wallpaper-puffy-menu-pappadums-and-chutney-to-start places and order the hottest thing she can find. So tonight we're in Curry Carnival, with its annoying chilli-pepper icons all over the menu denoting the spice-factor of the various dishes. (Where are the little Alka-Seltzer icons for how grim you'll feel in the morning?)

Linds is eager to tell me about last night, her dinner with Prickface, the corporate lawyer (*his lovely rich person's car —* why can't I forget that phrase of hers?). It appears he took her to some very smart Lebanese restaurant near Hyde Park Corner where the manager seemed to know him. They had a banquette. Nicer to sit side by side than facing each other, didn't she think? More sophisticated. And with the drinks came some appetisers, a lot of funny things skewered on a dagger.

'Did you have testicles?' I ask wearily.

'Mmm. They were *heaven*.'

I don't know why, but I find the idea of women enjoying sheep's testicles rather irritating. Aren't they supposed to pull a face and go 'Yuck'? Mind you, this is Linds. The only parts of a sheep she wouldn't eat are its eyebrows.

Onion bhajis arrive. Tandoori chicken, the colour of a pillar-box. Two pints of Heineken (none of your girly halves for Linds). She applies the sauce, a shade to do your bathroom in.

Anyway, Giles — that's his name, Giles — he wasn't nearly half as up his own arse as he usually is (I paraphrase). He was quite attentive last night, managed to ask several questions about her life, complimented the outfit — black Nicole Farhi jobby — and didn't once get caught flirting with himself in any passing mirrors.

'Golly. Anyone would think he was making a big play for you,' I say breezily.

'I ended up telling him quite a bit about you, actually, Charlie.'

'Did you? What?'

'How we met. How we . . . how we split.'

How we met. A media birthday party in Belsize Park, the usual great throng of people talking too loud, too much. (What are you doing at the moment? Oh, still Crimewatching. You? Gen Game, for my sins.) I force my way through to the kitchen, and there you are, in the tight green silk dress, hair up, feeding on Marks and Spencer miniature spring rolls, eyes blazing with an alien light. And I think, fuck me, it's Richard Nixon in a frock. But a powerfully sexy version of the old criminal. I'm struck by the drama of the way the green silk travels over your hips, I'm fascinated by the way your face moves when you chew. I do my standard all-purpose party conversation line.

'Where do you fit into this jigsaw then?'

'I'm just a neighbour, actually. It was either invite me, or have me complain about the noise.'

You pop another couple of spring rolls; they vanish as though they were peanuts. I think, she probably hasn't eaten all day. That thing women do.

I talk to a bunch of other people. I'd only just started working on *Uh-Oh* then, so I was still quite excited. *No, it's really fascinating to see how people act under pressure. And the little cameras are amazing.* Like it was a respectable experiment, not a nasty vehicle for generating laughter at the expense of un-suspecting members of the community.

Anyhow, all evening we keep returning to one another, Linds and I, each time a little deeper in drunkenness. You think I'm funny and sweet. I think you're funny and gorgeous (despite, or is it because of your unusual looks). I persuade you to give me a tour of your flat, one floor down.

You tell me you're an actress and a singer, so I ask you to sing something for me. You do a bit of Kurt Weill, later, a speech from *Blithe Spirit*. I borrow your guitar and, putting it over my knee as if I know how to play, I assume the mournful twang of an American country singer, and speak the lines

> *Sittin' in a chair*
> *Drinkin' beer*
> *In ma underwear.*
> *Life gets tedious —*
> *Don't it!!*

I twang one string, for a melancholy finish.

You think this is uproariously funny. And moments later — after one of those heart-thumping-sitting-on-the-sofa-staring-at-each-other pauses, our mouths find each other.

At some point later, I once again become aware of the music and the crowd over our heads. But we do not complain.

6

How we split: an altogether darker tale. Maybe I'll save it for later.

'So, last night,' I ask Linds over the king prawn vindaloo, 'you and Giles — did you . . . ?' I crunch into a pappadum for dramatic effect.

'What, shag him? I was quite tempted. He's rather good-looking in an obvious sort of way. I suppose I will eventually.' She says it in a tone of gloomy inevitability. Like getting round to filling in a tax return.

'You wouldn't say you were *over*excited at the prospect?'

'I think it would be fine at the time. In itself. But afterwards would be a problem. The thought, oh God, I actually slept with *him*.'

'The Bay City Rollers issue.'

'The hair is a serious negative.'

'And the sense-of-humour failure.'

'He'd be perfectly all right to go to bed with, but afterwards he'll still be there, with all that vanity and self-obsession and humourlessness. We have nothing in common. It would be like you going to bed with a brainless page three model.'

'Ghastly.'

'No, seriously.'

'But you think you will eventually.'

'He's taking me to the opera at the weekend, which is kind of hard to resist. And he's invited me to his house in France. He'll just wear me down, that's what'll happen.'

'One night, one glass of wine too many . . .'

'And that'll be it.'

Linds forks an indecently large load of curry into her mouth. There was a time when I found her appetite, its voracity, a turn-on. The thought of sexual fires being stoked. Now it just looks cranky.

'I thought women found it hard to go to bed with men they don't actually like — that old proverb: men fall in love through their eyes, women fall in love through their ears.'

'I suppose he's not *all* bad. He's from a completely different world to mine, which is *kind* of interesting. He's quite old-fashioned, which is sweet in a way. And he is *fucking* loaded.' On the f-word, a few grains of pilau rice spatter on to the tablecloth.

'Actually there's someone *I've* started seeing.' Enough of poxy Giles and his fabulous wealth.

'What, *seeing* seeing, or just seeing?'

'What's the difference?'

'Have you kissed her?'

'I suppose I have, yes.'

'Well, then, *seeing* seeing.'

I tell her about Kate. Once again, I omit the exact details of how we met. I tell her about the twenty questions, the Pelmanism, the fact that she's a chess player. (Linds used to call the pawns 'prawns'. How annoying is that?)

But what are we really doing here? Are we taunting each other with our new loves in the making? Or coming to terms with our revised status: the friendly exes, sorted enough to be able to talk about each other's potential partners without raising a shit-storm of sexual jealousy.

'Bloody hell, a cop. With twenty-twenty recall. Better make sure you get your stories straight with *her*.' She feeds a table-spoonful of k. p. vindaloo into the furnace. (Why isn't she the size of a house?)

Twenty-twenty recall: a reference to a number of conflicting accounts of my whereabouts that I gave to Linds around the time I started seeing Cheryl ('The important thing about telling lies, Charlie, is you have to remember which ones you told' – extract from our final conversation as a fully functioning couple). But she's mentioned it tonight without rancour. Even with a little affection. So that's what we're doing here. We're getting all grown up. She can bang on about the man she's going to allow to fuck her, and I about a woman who I hope to, and neither of us is sobbing or shouting or slamming doors. Our skins have thickened. Our grazes have healed.

And yet . . .

And yet, why does the thought of this Giles fill me with a nameless dread? Could it be that even though I don't really want Linds, neither do I entirely want to let her go?

We part with a friendly kiss in the street outside – no suggestions of back to my place this evening. She sets off towards her flat, I towards mine. After a few yards, I glance round to discover . . . that she's glanced round too. We wave, and walk on in the directions of our separate lives.

When I get home, there's an email waiting. It's from Linds. 'Good luck with Kate XXXL.'

I press Reply to Author and type 'Good luck yourself with Prickface.' Then I delete 'Prickface', and type 'The Haircut'. Then I delete that and type 'Giles'. I press Send.

Oh yes. Very fucking all grown up.

7

Bad thing number one. Bad thing that feels all the more bad for happening first thing in the morning. Haven't even prised the lid off the fucking coffee . . . *that* first thing.

Peter Marcus shimmers in, drapes himself elegantly on the comfy chair for guests.

'Charles. A tactical question. Or more strategic than tactical possibly.' What the fuck is he talking about? 'If we get another series of *Uh-Oh*, and I say *if*, because the channel will almost certainly want to take a view about how long they want to keep it going. *If* we get another series, how . . . how *dedicated* are you to continuing to work on it?'

A lone siren wails through my brain cells. The creature nesting above my left eyebrow stirs in his sleep. Turns over on to his other side. Stretches about a bit. Goes back to its dream. This is a scary question. The wrong answer to this sort of enquiry can take your career down a three-year cul-de-sac with only a very narrow turning circle at the end. Or end it overnight. This question is like that move in chess where a piece simultaneously threatens several other pieces. The calculation is: which is it better to lose?

How dedicated am I to working on another series of *The Uh-Oh Show*? There's the truth (I'd rather eat my own liver), and then there's what it's politic to say. But this in turn depends on where the question is coming from. Has Erica complained to her agent, Hughie Hughes, about yesterday's conversation (in which, if memory serves, I implied she was a humourless old bitch), and now has Hughie complained to Peter? Do they want to ease me off the show mid-run? Or (sorry, actually *and*/or) has there been a steer from the channel that they will indeed be looking for what they like to call 'fresh ideas' at the end of the current series? And if so, would it be a good idea to get on board one of these fresh ideas at an early stage? And if it *would* be a good idea, *which* fresh idea? Or is what lies behind Peter's question a desire to keep me on *The Uh-Oh Show*, and have me go down with the ship? Put it this way, with Peter it is *never* a casual enquiry.

Unfortunately, the four other projects that Tuna TV has 'in development' at the moment are every bit as unappetising as *Uh-Oh*.

The first is known in the building as *Helicopter Life Swaps*, a hideously embarrassing idea where people with diametrically opposed lifestyles (West End playboy and Orkney Island lighthouse-keeper) are dramatically air-lifted into each other's lives for a week . . . 'with hilarious and fascinating consequences', as it says in the proposal document. Once a day, they're allowed to phone each other for advice.

Then there's *Go for Broke*, a very nasty quiz format in which members of the public may win a lot of money, but they also stand to lose. If they get questions wrong, they can forfeit their savings, their possessions, even their homes. A particularly unpleasant touch is the live link to the team of repo-men who storm into the house and take away items to the value of the question you fucked up on. 'I'm sorry, Winnie-the-Pooh's middle name is 'the'; Elvis is incorrect. Bernie the Bailiff, let's have his stereo, his golf clubs and the video, please.'

There's an idea knocking about based on Stanley Milgram's classic experiments on conformity: where punters— sorry, *subjects*, were told to deliver electric shocks to other subjects who answered questions incorrectly. For every wrong answer, the 'voltage' was increased. Of course it was all a sham. The shocks were fake. The quiz 'contestants' were deliberately getting it wrong. But despite the realistic electrical sound effects and the harrowing screams for mercy, most subjects obeyed instructions to give increasingly severe shocks, right up to and including 'lethal'. When some protested, they were told things like, 'I'm sorry. These are the instructions. Please deliver the shock.' And mostly they did. This research has been cited as evidence for the way 'ordinary' Germans followed orders to take part in atrocities between 1939 and 1945. Peter Marcus thinks it would make a cracking TV show.

And then there's *Fuck or Die*. A version of that game where you have to say whether you would rather fuck someone or die. Trickier than you'd think. Cameron Diaz, no problem, right? But Ann Widdecombe? The teacher you hated most at school? Bernard Manning? Peter thinks Channel Five might take a punt on it.

So how dedicated am I to *The Uh-Oh Show*?

'Well, Peter,' I reply, 'I think there really will come a time when I would want to take a view.'

He smiles gnomically. 'I thought that would be your attitude. Thanks. That's helpful.'

I don't *think* he is taking the piss.

8

Bad thing number two.

The phone rings.

'Charles Green?' A male voice. Thin and edgy. A suggestion of a lisp. *Charlth*.

'Speaking.'

'Are you the cunt in charge of *The Uh-Oh Show?*' Oh fuck, a loony. You get them now and again.

'I'm the producer, yes.'

'You're the producer, are you?' *Produther*. 'Well, I think I'll just call you cunt. Listen to me carefully, cunt.' *Lithen*. 'My grand-dad is seriously ill in hospital because of you and your show.'

'I'm sorry, who am I speaking to?'

'Never you fucking mind, cunt. Do you know what you did? When you knocked on his door yesterday and pulled that fucking stupid stunt? Do you know what you did?' The nervy, chilling voice. What is that lisping accent? Not quite English. 'To a fucking war hero? Who went up the beach in Normandy? Who saw his mates get their bollocks shot off?' *Mateth*. And *Bollockth*. This isn't the class bully at school. This is the smaller, weirder, madder one (Neil Skinner who liked to soak labora-tory mice in lighter fluid. 'How do you make a mouse go woof?' His grotesque joke).

A horrible pause falls on the line. Is he choking up? There's a long, fruity sniff. 'My grandfather has suffered a stroke.' *Thtroke*. 'That's what the doctor said. "Your grandfather has suffered a stroke." And you're gonna suffer too, cunt.' *Thuffer*.

'Do you think you could explain exactly what you say has happened?'

'He collapthed after he told you lot to pith off. He told you to pith off, shut the door, and collapthed. I'm at the hospital now. He's thuffered a thtroke.'

'Look, I'm terribly sorry to hear about your grandfather, of course, but I don't think it can have been quite that simple. We're always most careful to ensure a non-confrontational—'

'I think it was *exactly* that simple, cunt.' *Thimple.* The quiet menace of his voice. 'You stressed him. You put him in hospital with your fucking bad joke. And now — are you listening very carefully? — if he dies, so do you. Do you understand?' *If he dieth, tho do you.*

'Look, I'm very sorry but I really—'

'Do. You. Under. Thtand?'

'Well, no, not really.'

He rings off.

9

I sit here for a few minutes, waiting for the phone to ring again. Ha-ha, did you fall for it? What a hoot, winding up the man who makes a living winding up other people. But something tells me this is not a joke.

The VHS copy of the tape we shot yesterday is sitting on top of my TV set. I stick it in the VCR and start viewing on fast forward. None of the people seem old enough to be the alleged stroke victim. Phelps looks mid-to-late fifties. He would have been a toddler on D-Day. We're looking for a man of . . . well, if he was, say, twenty in 1944, that puts him, fuck, somewhere in his mid-to-late seventies. If he was more like thirty, then we're looking at an *eighty*-year-old. We didn't try 'Prize Turkey' on anyone nearly as ancient. The oldest punter was probably that Holderness bloke, and he didn't tell us to piss off exactly.

I fast forward to Holderness. Press Play.

'Good morning. Am I talking to the head of the household?'

'You are.' The camera focusing up on the weather-beaten face. The thick white hair. The great barrel of a chest behind the old man's V-neck pullie. But he can't be anywhere near seventy-five or eighty.

'Excellent. You'd be Mr . . .'

'You tell me, mate.'

'Er, I'll have it here somewhere,' says Howard, playing for time.

Bad thing number three. In this little lull, Miguel has quickly zoomed right into the punter's eyeballs, to fine-tune his focus. (Eyes are the most telling part of any face – they're the bit you want most in focus – so that's what cameramen do; they use your crow's-feet for range-finding.) Miguel quickly pulls out again to a head and shoulders. But it's horribly clear. From the tightly packed contour lines, Holderness is one of those fit old geezers who could be any age. His gaze flicks between Howard and Miss Cole. He glances up the garden path towards our unmarked van. Seems to stare straight down the camera lens, eyes glittering. I feel a chill run through my shoulder blades. *If he dieth, tho do you.*

'According to my records,' continues Howard, 'the house-holder here at number ninety-three has won a prize in our monthly draw. Allow me to explain. I'm from *Competitor's Digest*, and this is my assistant, Miss Cole.'

'Look, mate, I don't know what you're selling, but I've already got one. OK?'

'I'm not selling anything, sir.' Howard, slightly shocked at the accusation. 'I'm here to award you your prize. Rather a good one, as it happens.'

'Go on then. Let's hear it.'

'I do need a name, however.' Howard is scrabbling through his notes.

'Holderness. It's not a secret. We're in the phone book.'

'Mr Holderness. Of course. It's right here. I'm delighted to say you have won a lovely fresh turkey. Sign here, and I'll fetch it directly from my vehicle.'

Exit Howard. Holderness turns towards Miss Cole.

'Where'd he say you were from, love? *Reader's Digest?*'

'*Competitor's Digest*, sir.'

He nods; does something with his mouth. Perhaps he doesn't believe a word. Doesn't matter. He's game. Seen it all. And now he's smiling because he's caught sight of Howard coming up the path with Tommy. He's giggling. He's actually saying, 'Oh dear, oh dear.'

'Here we are, this is Tommy. He's a beauty, isn't he, sir?'

'Sure is,' says Holderness.

'He'll be perfectly happy in your back garden, sir, much too big for the cats to bother. And apparently his . . . his muck will be very good for the roses. Is there a Mrs Holderness, sir? Would she like to have a look at Tommy?'

'She's upstairs having a little sleep.'

'Well, what would you like to do with him, sir?' Howard floundering slightly at the warm reception, the lack of horror. 'There is a leaflet with advice about plucking and feathering. And some recipes . . .'

'Stick him in the garden, mate. He'll give the missus a nice surprise when she wakes up.'

'In the garden,' says Howard, defeated.

'Yep. Straight through. If you're quick about it, he won't get a chance to cack on the carpet.'

End of joke. No conflict, no story. Stop the tapes, I can remember saying. Howard, tell him it's a gag. Reset everyone, ready to roll again in fifteen minutes. No need to send Rose and Geraldine out to get the consent form signed because we can't use it.

And that's exactly the point where the Holderness sequence

ends — with a rainstorm of shash on the tape, and now . . . the following take. Another house, the screaming au pair this time.

Fuck. What happened next?

10

Bad thing number four.

I go on to the Internet. Type 'Holderness' into a search engine. It finds 9,665 possible sites. Seed merchants. Catapult manufacturers. A village in Hampshire. Inventor of a solution to a very complicated equation. You name it, there's a Holderness with something to do with it.

There's even a Holderness on a site dedicated to organised crime. Holderness, I discover, is the name of a reasonably well-known West London gangster family who specialise in extortion, racketeering, drugs, and money-laundering. In the past, they have also been involved in the control of prostitutes, the fixing of horse races and counterfeiting currency. Oh yes, and killing people. Their name was linked — though the connection was never proved — to the celebrated slaughter of a club owner whose body was found on waste ground with thirty-five knives in it. Not knife *wounds*. Actual *knives*. One for every thousand pounds of the disputed sum in question.

The head of the clan, now retired, is a Harry Holderness, who I see won a medal for courage during the D-Day landings.

11

Next bad thing.

Around four in the afternoon, I manage to reach Howard

on the telephone. He's been filming some children's drama. I ask him if anything in particular happened yesterday 'in the aftermath of Holderness, that big old bloke who wanted to put Tommy in the back garden. I wasn't watching.'

'Why? Is there a problem, Charles?'

'No, just curious.'

'Well, actually, he got quite shirty when I said it was all a joke for the telly. He said he wasn't bothered, he'd take the bird anyway. I said, sorry, Tommy's a working professional and all that – tried to make light of it – but he said he didn't care, he'd won his prize fair and square. He made a grab for Tommy's lead, so I just said, sorry you've been bothered, sir, and legged it up the drive. Is he kicking up now, or what?'

'Er, no. It's nothing really. Thanks, Howard. See you next week, eh? "Heartbreak Jack Russell".'

'Yeah, sure.'

Bad thing number six. I was going to put *final* bad thing, but who knows now?

I call the hospital, the one they would have taken him to. Ask for a condition check on a patient, a Mr Harry Holderness. I give the address. (I've looked in the phone book. There *is* an H. Holderness living there.)

'Are you a member of the family, sir?' the nurse asks when she finally comes back to the phone.

'Not exactly. I'm his lawyer actually.'

'Ah, I see. Well, I'm sorry, sir. Mr Holderness passed away about an hour ago. He never regained consciousness.'

FOUR

1

I do not feel like a man under a death sentence. In fact I am remarkably calm, I tell myself, as the cab bowls through West London towards the gallery where I am meeting Kate. Remarkably calm. The words ring through my head like a mantra: It's amazing, he is really quite remarkably calm.

After all, it's a joke, isn't it? It will never happen. The lisping phone-caller isn't going to turn up on my doorstep with a sawn-off shotgun. For one thing, he doesn't know what I look like or where I live (though I suppose he could find out). For another, it's by no means clear that Grandpa Holderness died as a result of a stressful encounter with our giant turkey; indeed, the evidence suggests he found the whole thing a bit of a laugh. In addition — face it — if he was eighty-odd, he could have keeled over at any moment from almost any cause. For a further thing, the criminal classes do not tend to risk their liberty assassinating innocent members of the public who by chance become mixed up in their affairs. They only hurt their own. That's what they say, isn't it? And for a final thing . . . it'll never happen. TV producers don't get bumped off because someone takes offence at the way a particular piece of filming turned out. It's all a joke, isn't it?

Well, *isn't* it?

Calm. Remarkably calm. Really quite remarkably calm.

There are three important sources for my really quite remarkable sense of calm. The first is the undeniably powerful logic in the arguments marshalled above. The second is my God-gifted ability to simply ignore, or defer, problems. My motto is: ignore it, and it may just go away. If it doesn't, *then* worry about it. And the third is represented by the four large whiskies I downed in happy hour at the Genghis Lounge shortly before hailing this taxi. These whiskies are doing their best to drown the one fly in the ointment: the nagging doubt brought on by that cynical old saying, if you are not panicking, you have completely failed to understand the seriousness of the situation.

Kate is sitting on the steps in front of the gallery, wrists on her knees, reading a paperback. She springs to her feet, brushing the dust from the seat of her checked trousers. I refrain from asking if I can help at all, and file the vision alongside Geraldine/door/hip, and Rose/spit and sperm.

'Hi,' she beams. Do we kiss? Don't we? What's the protocol here?

'Hi,' I return. 'Good to see you.' And I go for one, on the east side. A perfumed curtain of hair swings pleasantly into my face. But she's doing something kissy in return. And now – blow me – she's actually going for a second. We retract,

I come in again from the west, gently scraping my cheek against hers, giving her a bit of man-beard. The power of *Other*.

We stand and blink at one another in the sunshine. Her eyes are doing that funny ticking thing where she can't decide which of mine to look in. But I've felt the heat and the scent rising off her neck. I have registered the pink gums in her smile; the springy, agile way she got to her feet, dropped the book in her bag, threw the strap over her shoulder. I do not want to trudge round a poxy gallery with this woman. I want to take her to a bar, maybe a couple of bars and then a restaurant. And then to bed. If not tonight, then soon. Christ, if we really must look at pictures – photos, not even proper paintings – let's get on with it.

But Walker Evans is a revelation.

The exhibition is a series of images he took of New Yorkers in the twenties. In the street, on the subway, at the luncheonette. The men in their suits and coats, their young work faces toughened by the city. There's something infinitely sad about these Manhattan office workers in the last century's bright, confident youth. There's one in particular, a three-quarter profile of a rather lovely young woman in a fur coat and cloche hat standing by a shop window in Fulton Street in 1929. A banner across the road reads 'Fulton Billiard Parlour'. She looks about the same age as Kate: high forehead, dark eyes, a prominent nose and wide full lips. An upward flick of black hair has escaped from her hat and is parked on one cheek, threatening her left eye. Her face wears the blank urban mask adopted for the city. Yet beneath it, as she stares off to her left through the passing crowds, there's a faintly perturbed expression. Is she waiting for someone? A lunch companion? Maybe her partner in a dying love affair, for certainly there is no delicious expectation in her gaze. Or perhaps she has merely come up for the day from Bumfuck NJ to marvel at the shops and buildings.

'What do you think she's thinking?' I ask.

Kate sidles up alongside me and peers into the photograph. Her eyes flash across the silvery print.

'Her boyfriend is the manager of the Fulton Billiard Parlour, and she's spotted him across the street, chatting to a woman. She's thinking, is it an innocent conversation? Or is there something going on here that I should know about?'

Now I look again, her eyes do seem focused on something in the distance. And it's true, there are the faintest beginnings of confusion upon her dark, dramatic features.

My head and Kate's are very close together. I can smell her, a sexy animal blend of perfume and leather jacket. Her breath is making tiny condensation marks on the glass. They vanish almost instantly.

'He bought her the fur coat, didn't he?' I speculate quietly.

'He did. She's very pretty. I wonder how they met.'

'In the billiard parlour. She came in one evening to meet someone else.'

The image is perfectly enigmatic. Only two things are clear. The first is that she does not know she is being photographed. And the second is that everyone contained in this fleeting moment in a New York street is now dead. Felled as surely by the passage of more than seventy years as by a hail of machine-gun fire.

Sorry, I sometimes get like this in the face of art. Especially old art. Like that exhibition of Ingres portraits that Linds dragged me to. I suppose the pictures were extraordinarily good. But as we trailed round, all I could think of was: the artist, his subjects, all these people, these generals, industrialists, rich men's wives, their children, their lapdogs . . . every one of them, dust.

I look over at Kate, this live woman staring hard at the image of the dead one. Kate in her black hair and glasses, her leather jacket and checked trousers. I'm thinking, can't we stop all this looking at pictures of dead people and just go home together? I suppose this is why I hate bloody galleries, and trailing round old churches. It's the living haunting the dead, isn't it? The butterfly wheeling through the graveyard (sorry, will snap out of this any minute).

'Have you seen this?' she asks. Mounted on the wall is a description of Walker Evans' working methods. And as I read, I begin to realise there's a more prosaic explanation for the mild puzzlement of the girl in the cloche hat.

It turns out Walker Evans was in my business. He was an early pioneer of the hidden camera. To get nice and close to the punters – sorry, his *subjects* – without them realising they were being photographed, he used a special piece of apparatus. The lens on the front of his camera was a fake. It seemed to point forwards, but it actually took pictures sideways, through a system of mirrors. To get his shot, Walker Evans could stand right next to the beautiful girl in Fulton Street. She would have been aware of him photographing *something*, but she'd never have guessed it was her.

And that, I think, explains what's troubling her. She's looking off to the left, the direction that Evans' camera would appear to be pointing in, and she's thinking, why is he taking pictures of a fire hydrant? Or a mail truck? Or the fat guy in the coat? What the fuck is so fascinating over there?

I guess if you look at anything long enough, its meaning is eventually revealed to you.

By the exit, in big letters, there's a quote from the old sneaky snapper himself. 'Stare. It is the best way to educate your eye and more. Stare, pry, listen, eavesdrop. Die knowing something. You are not here long.'

You are not here long.

I can feel the four whiskies fading in my bloodstream.

'Kate? Are you, er . . . thirsty at all?'

2

Why do people *repair* to a bar? Is it because of what goes on there – human repair, after a morale breakdown or nerve failure, or a punctured spirit? Let's see . . . I should think a couple of glasses of Argentine Merlot will have you on your feet. Try that, and if there's still a problem, pop back and we'll sort you out with some double brandies.

We've squashed ourselves into a booth in the first pub we came to, a foul local in urgent need of a good doing-over in armchairs, blonde wood and yuppies. Some red-faced men in baggy jumpers are murmuring at each other by the bar. An obvious married couple sit side by side, drinking, smoking and gazing into space. A fat boy in a T-shirt with a pint is playing the trivia machine. The silly fucker doesn't know what currency they use in Denmark. It's kroner, you moron.

'Charles, is anything the matter?'

'What do you mean?'

'You look a bit . . . a bit agitated.'

Fuck, do I? 'How do you mean, agitated?'

'You seem distracted. You keep sort of glancing about.'

'Sorry. Difficult day.' I drain the whisky in one go. 'Kate, that girl in the cloche hat in 1929. She wasn't staring at her boyfriend.'

'No?' She looks at me with something close to pity.

I explain my theory.

'You'll have to tell me about your work with hidden cameras,' she says, returning from the bar with more repair fluid. I realise she is talking to me like a nurse.

'It's all rather ghastly at the moment, to be honest. Listen, Kate, can I ask you something? Do you ever think about death at all?'

'Death? How exactly?' She cocks her head to one side, appealingly.

'You know. Dying. Extinction. The final taxi. Did I mention that I am a bit of a hypochondriac?'

The topic of mortality should not be underestimated as a powerful weapon in the armoury of seduction. A well-timed canter round the theme of human life being but a brief candle flame between two endless slabs of nothingness can do wonders to kick-start a slow-moving evening. I've discovered that a quick look into the abyss – its cold, horrible finality – can ratchet up the sexual chemistry very nicely.

It first happened with a girl at university, Barbara Lesquinny. She was my age, a student of Theoretical Physics, rather grave in demeanour, but so utterly fanciable, it made your eyes water. (If there was also a suggestion that she may have been a twenty-four-carat, five-star basket case, I was prepared to overlook it.) One evening in February – a good month for this sort of conversation – in my room at our hall of residence, we swapped theories about the big D. My position, I believe, was that the fact of death renders our lives absurd or meaningless, whichever is the more terrible. Hers was an even more hardline view, which, if I recall it correctly, appeared to cast doubt on the actual fact of existence itself (I think she was from Canada). Anyhow, after about an hour and a half of all this stuff – fuelled by several powerful joints – we concluded that the cosmos was a pretty sorry place for human beings to be meaningful within. And then, following one of those embarrassing little pauses, we fell at one another with a passion and frenzy that only such a terrifying glimpse beyond the curtain can properly deliver.

Our affair lasted a month. It ended when she started going out with a Maths lecturer who could *prove* that space and time were imaginary. Someone told me that eventually she'd thrown herself off a high building. But that can't be true, because every now and again I see her name mentioned in the business pages in connection with the John Lewis Partnership.

'Actually I have been thinking about death quite a bit lately,' says Kate. 'Someone died on the next badminton court to mine. Dropped dead from a heart attack. Wasn't even forty.'

Great! I mean, an obvious tragedy for the family and all, but very good as a chilly reminder of the frailty of the thread which we hang by. If we can be so easily snuffed out tomorrow, shouldn't we be having fun . . . tonight?

'God, how awful. Was there a history of heart disease? Parents died young? High blood pressure or anything?'

She shakes her head.

'Oh, don't tell me. He was as fit as a butcher's dog. Ate well, barely drank, never smoked. Never took a day off sick in his life. A perfectly normal, happy healthy bloke and then . . . *pow*. Curtains. Finito Benito. Good night Vienna. Over and out.' I've started gibbering.

'Actually, I think she used to run marathons.'

'*She*? A *woman*?'

'The blood just drained from her face, Charles. It was awful.'

Excellent. The second Bells is busily going about its repair job, plugging the holes that the lisping creep punched into my bodywork. And despite my dread of falling-down-dead stories, I feel I can ride this one quite thrillingly close to the precipice.

'Horrible thought, that you can be . . .' pause for dramatic effect, 'snuffed out like a light.' Kate's gone rather serious. 'And then that's it. That's your lot. No second helpings. For all eternity.'

For all eternity. The phrase tolls like a bell across the conversation.

'You believe this is all there is?' says Kate.

You can't use morbid dread to ignite passion in anyone who believes in an afterlife, of course. So right now I'm hoping she doesn't turn out to be a fucking reincarnationist.

'I'm afraid I'm utterly convinced.' Looked into it thoroughly, of course. Regrettably, the only sensible conclusion to reach. Bit of a pity, but there you are.

'Me too. Depressing, isn't it?'

I resist the urge to cheer. Instead I pull a face. One that says, yup, it looks like we're alone and adrift in a scary Godless universe, Kate. We'd better cling to whatever happiness we can find.

Then she says, 'Charles, shall we have that game of chess?'

Now I very nearly *do* cheer. And I don't again think of dead Harry Holderness, or his lisping grandson, or Erica Birkendale, or Peter Marcus or Cheryl, or Loopy Loo or any of my other tormentors for a whole twelve hours.

3

Actually, Cheryl was my most famous victory with the death conversation turning sexual.

I found myself sitting next to her at a dinner party a couple of summers ago. The tall dreamy girl with the huge face who was wearing some shivering clingy number that practically ordered your eyes to roam over its fascinating surfaces. It was the usual crowd: a gobshite band of telly people and associated lowlife, all making clever remarks, laughing too loud, and knocking it back something chronic. Cheryl was someone's friend and it was clear she was different. She didn't seem to

vibrate at the same frequency as the rest of us. She had a stillness, a quietude that is rather rare in the jittery milieu I and
my chirrupy chums inhabit. From a distance, I'd have guessed
that she was a painter, or possibly an artist's muse; at a pinch,
something to do with antiques. She reminded me of one of
those slow, beautiful girls you find working in auction houses,
or certain posh shops in Kensington or Belgravia. So when I
got talking to her, it was a surprise – and something of a disappointment – to discover she was just a media beast like the
rest of us, a producer of children's television, actually infants'
television, a show for babies, more or less, called *The
Bibblybums*.

Our hostess had sat us together. Linds passed the evening
up the other end of the table, laughing like a drain at Nick
and Oliver, their wickedly camp ancedotes fresh from the set
of *Newsroom South East*. Today, am I grateful to Andrea for that
subversive piece of seat-planning? I can't honestly say I know
the answer to that question. I'm not even sure Andrea did it
consciously, that she knew Linds and I were bumping along
the bottom somehow, and – to mix up the metaphors a bit –
threw a big sexy pebble into the pond.

If there had been no Cheryl, would Linds and I still be
together? I doubt it. But if there had been no Cheryl, would
Linds and I have split up a month after this dinner party? Ditto,
I doubt it. We'd have limped on in our desultory fashion until
some other crisis – some other woman, or some other bloke
– blew in to finish us off.

Anyhow, back at the table, once I'd stopped drooling over
her wonderfully statuesque frame, and started to actually listen
to what she was saying, I discovered Cheryl had a way of
making the most commonplace statements sound almost profound. It was partly the words she chose, partly the order she
put them in and partly a quality in her pattern of speech. She

said things *oddly*. As if English were not her first language. I remember at one point burbling at her, 'This spaghetti is rather marvellous, don't you think?' And she actually thinking about it for a few moments and replying, 'Rather hard work, the *winding* one has to do.' And then a little later, I splutter, 'Tell me about *The Bibblybums*. Is it a pain or an absolute joy?' Again she seems to think the question needs a proper answer, not a smart-arse one-liner. 'Well,' she says after a bit, 'I suppose at the moment it's a joyful pain.' The clincher comes when I ask her what she actually watches on television. Slowly, she turns her huge face on to me like a sunflower, operates the eyelashes once, twice, and says, 'My set exploded last year. A vase of roses fell off a shelf and poured water down the back. The next day I went out and bought a new vase.'

I'm afraid I fell for her in that instant.

The following morning I phone Andrea, thanking her for a delightful evening. We launch into a debriefing about the food (the sauce was *putanesca*, which means prostitute in Italian), the guests (how nice to see Greg and Nikki not at each other's throats for a change), the booze (Michael surely didn't need to drink *quite* so much), the gossip (Holly will never get that job in a million years . . . will she?), finally bringing the subject round to the woman in the neighbouring seat.

'What did you make of Cheryl?' asks Andrea. How did I know this would be the last topic on the agenda?

'I thought she was very . . . very striking.'

'Cheryl's a dear. I love her to bits, but she's completely away with the fairies.'

'Really?'

'She's on her own planet. Planet Cheryl. And you know she hasn't been out with anyone for a year. Such a terrible waste, don't you think?'

My agony of conscience is short-lived. Five minutes later I call *The Bibblybums* office – 'You don't fancy a drink one evening this week, do you?' / 'That sounds nice, one can become thirsty in these evenings' – and so it is that a few days later, I find myself in a groovy drinkerie in Soho, orbiting Planet Cheryl with a view to mounting a manned landing.

She's even lovelier the second time out, in white jeans and a shiny green blouse. Her face, as I gaze at it from the viewing platform of my bar stool, seems extraordinarily wide, almost lunar. And when she speaks, it's with an odd deliberation quite unlike any of the frenzied babble spewing from the mouths of our fellow creatures of the night. Eventually it comes to me. She is Russian, or Serbian, sent here to penetrate children's television and sabotage the minds of a generation. Or she's an android, who perhaps hasn't been fitted with the absolute very latest language chip. She orders cider.

'Cider,' I recall saying. 'I don't know many women who drink cider.' Outside of a students' union or a bench of derelicts.

She ponders my statement. 'No, nor do I, really,' she says finally. 'Why do you think that is?'

'I suppose it's considered a bit rustic. You know, backward. The association with mad alcoholic tramps.'

Her eyes, huge liquid craters, hold me in their gaze and I wonder what she sees. Human male, early to mid-thirties, not bad-looking, hair going a bit at the temples, linen suit, made a bit of an effort, right thumbnail rather badly chewed. Simple views about the cultural aspects of cider drinking.

'My parents have a house in France,' she says. 'I used to drink French cider in the holidays. It was cloudy and you could taste the apples.'

I have a vision of her around seventeen or eighteen, in jeans and a gingham blouse, for some reason, at a quiet little bar in the deep emptiness of the French countryside. She's towering over the boys of the village, the close-eyed pasty youths who've watched her return year after year, biding their time, wondering if their chance will ever come. And there is one, isn't there? The handsome one, with the smoky good looks and the moped, from whom, one summer evening, she'll accept a ride up to the old church at the head of the valley, and there allow him to kiss her.

Strictly speaking, she's not being difficult. It would be unfair to call her uphill. But there's definitely something that feels like wading through treacle in my attempts to set this woman's blue touchpaper alight. Maybe it's the aura of otherworldliness that's hard for a chap to get beyond. Anyhow, I do my best. I give her all my best lines. I tell her a joke. (I know you should never tell women jokes; they prefer conversations, apparently.) She even laughs — a wondrous sight, like seeing the moon laugh. But there's still a reserve and a distance that I don't quite know what to do about.

It's the same on the next few occasions we meet, perfectly civil encounters in state-of-the-art venues where she sips cider, looks incandescent and mouths strange circumlocutions, while I, dazzled by the sheer spectacle of her, put up a huge barrage of . . . of jolly chat, hoping — in the manner of mud and walls — that some of it will stick.

So I feel like I'm not really getting anywhere, and I'm beginning to think, oh fuck it, what's the point, and what am I doing with you anyway? I've got a girlfriend who doesn't talk in riddles, well, not riddles exactly — do I mean Delphic utterances? — anyhow, there is a riddle at the heart of you, and maybe life's too short to bother to solve it. I'm beginning to think all of the above when one night something happens.

We've arranged to meet in All Bar One. I can't be bothered to think of any more splashy ultra-fashionable happening metropolitan places, and she's beginning to *irritate* me now with her serene unreachability. And this night, because I'm annoyed, and close to giving up, I guess – and guilty, because I've told Linds yet another lie about who I'm seeing – I say the first thing off the top of my head, which is about a plane crash on the news this morning. In particular, the academic on the *Today* programme who said that compared to cars, *mile-for-mile*, yes, modern aeroplanes are incredibly reliable, and you've got more chance of winning the sodding lottery than being exterminated in an airline accident. But if you do the maths *journey-for-journey*, your chances are definitely better in a Datsun Cherry than a 747.

'The thing about car accidents is that they're so sudden,' I say cheerfully. 'But in a plane crash, the passengers are often hideously aware for quite a long time that they're in the deepest possible – terminal – shit. On the other hand, in a car wreck, you might suffer horrible agony and die on the way to hospital. But when your jumbo jet crashes into the side of the mountain, I would think it's all over pretty quickly. Anyway . . .' I smile and clink my glass against hers, 'how are you this evening?'

But she opens up like a flower.

She says: 'That would be the worst possible thing, Charles. *Knowing*. In advance. That it was all going to end.'

And I say: 'But we do, don't we? All of us. That's it's going to end. All right, granted, not in half an hour's time in a fireball in a forest, hanging upside down in your seat next to some bloke from Kent who had the meatballs and the Rioja. And hopefully, not until after a nice long, satisfying innings. But we know it's going to end, all right.'

And that's it. The rest of the evening is swallowed up in the most glorious – I think the word is *thanatological* – think-tank. She blooms. Her morbid dread is easily as morbid and as dreadful as my own though, technically, she is agnostic on the subject of an afterlife. Her father is a believer, her mother a sceptic; her heart says, wouldn't it be lovely if there was a further spiritual realm? her head says, don't make me laugh. Cheryl's eyes become vast at the bigness of the thoughts we are thinking. At a dramatic high point in the argument – parallel universes, and would things be any better there? – I suggest we continue this discussion back at my place, where I have a fine bottle of single malt whisky and access to takeaway foods. And blow me down, she agrees. Less than an hour later I have her on my sofa, glugging Glenfiddich, talking about her childhood, her pet guinea pigs, Pyramus and Thisbe, and the moving burial ceremony that took place after they succumbed to the Grim Reaper (in the form of next-door's wolfhounds).

'They went together. It's what they would have wanted.' I don't know whether she's being serious or ironic, but I hardly care. Between a third and a half of the way down the bottle, during a little lull in the conversation, I lean across experimentally, and position a gentle kiss on her mouth.

'Sorry,' I say. 'It's all this talk of death.'

She says: 'I know.'

And the next moment, her eyelids close for business, her face slowly comes towards mine, and miraculously, we chew over the vexing problem of mortality without a word escaping our lips.

4

The same sofa. About eighteen months later. Around the same time of night. Quite possibly the same broken-hearted Cuban on the hi-fi, mourning the loss of a damn fine parking space.

The death thing hasn't moved much further forward with Kate – perhaps because we agree about it essentially – but I have had a brainwave.

Over the years, in the literature of chess, I have come across a number of obscure and bizarre forms of the game. *The Oxford Companion to Chess* makes reference to Hexagonal Chess, for three players with six-sided 'squares'. There's Double-Move Chess, where each player takes two moves at a time. Progressive Chess, where white makes the first move; then black takes two moves; then white three; black, four and so on. There's Losing Chess, where the aim is to force your opponent to capture all your pieces. Alice Chess, where you have one set of pieces, two boards and a mirror. Pieces begin their move on one board, and travel (as it were through the mirror) to the other board. And there's Living Chess, where humans play the part of the pieces on a giant board.

The Companion, however, is silent upon a particular variant that I suppose may be called Alco-Chess. And it is a spectacularly fine edition of this somewhat adult game that a few years ago several of my friends clubbed together to buy me for my thirtieth birthday. It contains a big glass board, and instead of ordinary pieces, there are drinking glasses. Tiny shot glasses for the pawns; larger, appropriately shaped vessels for the knights, rooks and bishops. The tallest glasses on the board are the two kings. Not quite as tall are the queens. And here is the deep genius of Alco-Chess: it isn't played black versus white, but vodka versus whisky. Or lemon vodka versus pepper vodka, brandy versus tequila. Baileys versus Cointreau. Crème de menthe versus triple sec. Whatever you have in the house frankly (though obviously Diet Coke versus Fanta is a pointless abomination). The only rule that separates it from conventional chess is that when you capture a piece, you drink it.

Kate, to my enormous excitement, is fascinated by the idea. This evening she is playing Spanish brandy – I can drink any amount of Fundador – and she carefully fills her sixteen pieces with the best part of a bottle. I charge my little glass troops with vodka, her drink of choice from the bar tonight. As vodka is the lighter spirit, and closest, as it were, to white, I begin.

Her front rank of tawny brown pawns look incredibly inviting. I have an immediate urge to mow them down, one after the other. I open with a conventional pawn to king's bishop move, designed to prompt a pawn exchange as quickly as possible. She makes the reply that convention dictates, and soon we are clinking shot glasses and downing the first spoils of combat.

We are both lying on the carpet, the safest way for this game to be played, in my opinion. Kate is up on one elbow, studying the board with an intensity that I find I admire tremendously. I also admire the lovely, *contained* way she's spread her length along the floor, one long, thin leg resting on top of the other. The drama of her hip seems infinitely more absorbing than anything I shall be likely to stage on the board tonight. We quickly do another couple of pawns apiece and then a knight exchange. I really have to take my hat off to her: she's embraced the spirit of this little-known variant, gamely offering and accepting these opening exchanges in a way a more boring opponent might eschew. The rules are not explicit on whether the contents of each captured piece must be strictly consumed before play resumes. She is a little behind – those knights are, what, a triple measure maybe? – but I am empty. So I prompt another pawn exchange, and then, emboldened, set my guns on the magnificent prize that is her queen (with a view to sacrificing my own into the bargain, of course, and if that doesn't get everyone nicely pissed, then nothing will). I find my gaze keeps flitting to her legs. As she concentrates on the current position, my eye travels down the long limbs in their checked trousers in the direction of her ankles. Once there, we immediately set off on the return journey.

But fuck, what's this? She's just made a move that, on the face of it, invites me to capture her queen at the cost of a mere knight. She's looking across the board at me, smiling oddly through those serious glasses, the curtain of hair swaying slightly to the warbling Cuban. It's a terrible trap, of course. Got to be. I can sense something awful to do with one of her lurking bishops, but I'm a little too fuzzy, and a little too happy to bother to work it out.

'OK, I'll buy it,' I say, and claim my huge royal Fundador.

The smile falls from her face, and the next ten minutes are a nightmare. One by one, my pieces are driven off the board. It's a bravura display of merciless attack chess. Her moves have real depth and power. I'm utterly outclassed. Every time it's my turn, there seems to be only one move I can make. A line of un-drunk vodka glasses forms behind her side of the board. The end can't be long in coming.

I pick up my king, and take a glug of Smirnoff to signify resignation.

'Stop it, you're hurting me,' I bleat.

Kate smiles. 'I enjoyed that, Charles.'

'I walked right into it, didn't I?'

'Oh, I wouldn't say that. It was reasonably well disguised.' She is magnanimous in her total victory.

While I polish off a couple of her un-drunk pawns, she tells me what she loves about chess — the fact that it's open, that everything is out there on the board, that if there's a problem, the answer will inevitably be staring you in the face, that the trick is simply to think hard enough. Not like life, where facts can be concealed, where there can be information you are not given, where lies may be told. There's nowhere to lie on the chessboard, is there?

And while she's banging on about the application of pure reason and logic – and that's exactly what I felt in that scary period after I 'captured' her queen: the inescapable crushing force of inevitability – I am wondering what it would be like to be a small car on a motoring tour through the hills and curves of her body. It's the sweep of her hip that's done it. The gentle gradient of the climb up from her ankles (maybe stop for a bite at Knee?) and then on to the summit (pause to admire the panoramic views) before the exhilarating plunge down the other slope (warnings to check your brakes).

'I can't believe you're really a forensic scientist,' I say foolishly, apropos of nothing (the hour is growing late and my bloodstream is full of chess pieces).

'Oh?' Her face, its black glasses and shiny curtains of hair, floats over the squares of the glass chessboard.

'You don't *seem* like one exactly.'

'Really? What are they like then?'

'Big girls. You know, big serious girls with horrid specs.'

'I've got specs.'

'I know, but yours are nice.'

I haul myself to my feet to change the music. What we need here is some moody romantic endgame stuff. I flick through the piles of CDs. Not Pink Floyd, *The Division Bell*. Not fucking Carlos Santana. Hardly The Smiths. How about music 'from the motion picture' *Gladiator*? I don't think so. (Christ, who buys this stuff?) Here's quite an amusing collection of TV themes, but ironic rather than seductive, I fancy. Elton John, *Goodbye Yellow Brick Road* (must bin this before anyone sees it). Maria Callas? Hmm, not really. Ella Fitzgerald sings Cole Porter? Love it, but on balance, probably not. Elvis love songs?

Ditto. Bob Dylan? Too distracting. All that funny phrasing and whining empha-*seeeees*.

Got it. Miles Davis. *Kind of Blue*. Very cool. Very sophisticated, late night. And hypnotic in its spell, I think you'll find.

By the time I get back, she's relocated to the sofa. Lovely jazz notes fall softly around us like musical snow. Her eyes are doing that ticking thing, but she's wearing a very promising expression.

'I'm a bit embarrassed about that last game,' I tell her. 'One little slip, and you did me up like the proverbial smoked herring.'

'Sorry, I couldn't resist it.'

'Don't apologise. It's hard to stop yourself sometimes.'

And now we kiss. Technically, I started it, I suppose. But she responds — somewhat experimentally at first, the way the detective in movies dabs a pinkie into the white powder discovered at the crime scene, takes a tiny, tentative lick and declares, 'Chinese heroin, a hundred per cent pure.' She gets a little warmer, but still with a definite reserve; I can feel it in her lips. I slide an arm round her back to draw her towards me — I feel the bumps of her spine — but she arches like a cat, breaks away from me smiling oddly, not ready, or willing.

'Let's have another game,' I suggest. 'I'll make a really big effort this time. I let myself down before. And my parents,' I add satirically.

'Shall we play for something?' she asks. 'An incentive, to make it more exciting.' To my surprise, she reaches for one of the vodka bishops and downs it like a Cossack.

'I'm quite excited as it is, to be honest, Kate. What have you got in mind?'

'Can I tell you a story?' she asks.

She tells me a story. A rather thrilling one, about a boy she used to play chess with at university. Robert Zamovic is a student of Mathematics, but he doesn't look like your typical maths geek; you know . . . disturbed. This Zamovic is a broodingly handsome, dark-eyed fucker. And arrogant with it. He really fancies himself. Mr Z. is undeniably good at chess, but not as good as he thinks he is. In his own opinion, he's brilliant, and he has all the annoying flamboyant gestures to go with it, including banging the pieces down when he makes a move. Zamovic doesn't have a particularly impressive record against Kate — they've won and lost about the same number of games, and drawn many. None the less — and here's the twist — the contempt in which he holds her game — 'women shouldn't play chess' — is only matched by his undisguised admiration for her loose-limbed, pale-skinned body (I paraphrase). One evening at the chess society — how very different, all this, to my own dissolute university career — Zamovic offers Kate a private challenge: a unique series of games, seven in all, one point for a win, half a point each for a draw, the winner (the games to continue until there is a clear winner) to do what they will to the loser. His meaning is clear.

'What would I possibly want to do with you?' Kate had asked.

'Use your imagination,' Mr Z. had replied.

Kate is shocked, even disgusted at first. But an idea begins to take hold in her mind. A week or so later, the terms of the bet are laid: Kate to sleep with the appalling (though good-looking) mathematician if she loses; Zamovic, should he falter, to walk naked down Oxford Road, Manchester from Cavendish Street to St Peter's Square during the hours of daylight.

'You know, Charles,' says Kate, 'they were the most exciting seven games of chess I have ever played in my life. The sense of . . . of jeopardy was totally adrenalising. I played out of my skin. I think he did too.'

111

'What happened?' I croak weakly.

'I'd have let him off, but he insisted. A bet is a bet, he said.'

'What do you mean?'

'The police wouldn't believe he was wandering round the city centre with no clothes on because of a chess game. So he was taken to a psychiatric unit for assessment. Unfortunately it was a Friday afternoon and the duty shrink was off sick. So he had to stay until the Monday.' She downs another vodka pawn. 'Apparently he played quite a bit of chess over that weekend with some of the other inmates. And I guess he must have lost quite badly, because he was never quite the same afterwards. He stopped banging the pieces down the way he used to.' She gazes at me with a peculiar expression on her face. 'I discovered that chess is so much more interesting when there's something to lose. Or something to win.'

I have a horrible feeling about what's coming next. Or is it a wonderful feeling? 'Is this what you're about to suggest? That we play seven games . . . ?'

'How about one?'

'I won't need to get my kit off and stroll round Shepherd's Bush Green if I lose?'

'No.'

'Though if I win, you'll. Or rather, if I win, I'll. We will, as it were. What you're saying is, that if you lose, you'll . . .'

'Yes, Charles.'

Well, fucking Horatio. How about that for a turn up for the books? 'I don't stand a chance, do I?'

She does something funny with her eyebrows. Draws the curtain of hair behind an ear. 'What makes you so sure that I'll want to win?'

5

Have you ever drunk yourself sober? The strange window of clarity that opens up late at night, after several hours of drinking like a fish. The odd feeling that despite the extravagantly large number of alcohol units put away – greatly in excess of the Government's present guidelines – you suddenly discover that you are stone-cold sensible. As though you're at the still centre of the cyclone. All around is a maelstrom of drunken confusion, but *here in your head*, you're thinking clearly, seeing things as they are. The woman you were lusting after half an hour ago is revealed as a drooling hag. Human life, a meaningless farce. You feel capable of anything, except possibly the operation of heavy machinery and fine needlework.

I am suddenly very sober.

Not because I have reached this Zen-like aperture, but because of that thing she said. *What makes me so sure that she'll want to win?*

We resume our positions on the carpet, reset the board and refill the pieces. The little shot glass pawns are particularly hard to top up with vodka when one's hands are shaking. I play the king's bishop pawn opening again to get an exchange going pretty quickly and she readily complies. I can barely look her in the eye as we clink glasses and continue. More pawns follow, and the same knight exchange as the opening to the last game. We get into some attritional mid-game stuff. My eyes flit to the delicious checked countryside beyond the board. No, pay attention, you fool. Just fucking concentrate.

And now her bishop does something a bit tasty, swooping halfway up the board out of fucking nowhere. Shit shit shit, what's this? *Think.*

I reply by bringing out my second knight.

'That's a bishop, actually,' says Kate.

'Is it? So it is. The sherry glass. Easily mixed up with these other blighters. Sorry.' Whoops. Embarrassing. *Think.*

No, I'm sorry, it *is* distracting to have those legs lying there in front of me, ending — or is it beginning? — in the way they do. And then there's the face. Not classically beautiful, but very . . . what's the word? . . . very watchable in its serious, delicate-featured way. And sexy, perhaps because of its very lack of classical beauty. I gaze at her for a while, as she surveys the board, dark eyes crunching the data, computing the possibilities. I know I shall never be as good as Kate at this game. In fact, the sad truth — has she realised it yet? — I'm not very good at chess at all. I don't have the application, the depth of intellect, the fucking random access memory. You need to think too hard. I do try to make those chessy calculations: if I do this, then she'll do that, and then I can do this, and all that balls-aching carry-on. But I find happier thoughts are always drifting into my head. For example, did I mention that Kate's trousers are fastened by a single green button. Oh, and now that I look again, I can see that a zip up the side also plays a part in the proceedings. Could it *really* be like going to bed with a bicycle?

Tragic, don't you think? To love a game, and be so crap at it.

She catches me staring at her. 'Your move, isn't it?'

'Fuck, is it? I thought I moved.'

'You moved the bishop back to where it came from. Now you have to make a legal move.'

Oh Christ. This is hopeless. I'm not trying hard enough. What must she think of me?

Con. Cen. Trate.

And then I see it: a sweet little sequence of one-two-three moves which will knock out her queen, threaten check and, who knows, maybe checkmate. But *wait*. Could be a trap. Go carefully here. Yes, it's almost certainly a trap. She's breathing differently. She can sense I've spotted it and she's waiting for me to blunder right in. But hang on, what makes me so sure that she wants to win? What the fuck was that all about? Maybe she's left the door open deliberately. I stare at the position on the board until my eyeballs throb. Is she surrendering herself? Or am I already in the mincer and she's just waiting to turn the handle?

I never find out.

Because when I wake up on this same spot on the carpet, it's a quarter to three in the morning and she is gone. A Post-it note is stuck to the board. 'Match suspended.'

FIVE

1

Six hours later I'm lying in bed, but getting close to the scientific tipping point where boredom and anxiety finally equal inertia and hangover ($b + a = i + h$) and the next moment, you find yourself on your feet, heading for the bathroom, the electric kettle, another day in the working world. This morning, however, I seem to have lost the will to turn off the *Today* programme. It's not that the news is especially compelling: the markets are expecting another turbulent ride; seven have been shot in Philadelphia; French air traffic controllers are threatening action; at Lords, there's been an England batting collapse; and one of Hollywood's greatest leading men has died at the age of ninety-one. In fact, I'm just beginning to wonder if there's been a military coup and they're playing a generic edition, when the phone rings.

Kate. My stomach lurches. I snap off the radio, clear my throat, try to psych myself into the right blend of apology and charm. *Terribly sorry to drop off on you like that. Can we play with Ribena next time?*

But it's only Loopy Loo.

'Oh, it's you. How are you this morning?' In the background I can hear Chris Tarrant on Capital Radio. So that's narrowed it down nicely to ten million people. 'You off to work in a minute?'

Beep.

How about that? She beeped. One beep for yes. Two for no.

'Hey, great to hear you. Even if it's only a beep. Er, do you feel like actually speaking at all?'

Beep beep.

'No. A bit too much to hope for, I expect. Look, let me ask you something. Do I know you?'

Beep.

'I do. Fantastic. Are you a man or a woman?'

Silence.

'Come on, you can at least give me that one. Are you male or female?'

Silence.

'Oh yeah, sorry. Got to put the question in the right format, haven't I? Are. You. A. Woman?'

Beep.

'I thought so. Only a woman could get so . . . obsessive. No offence, obviously. So who the fuck are you? Are you someone I work with?'

Beep beep.

'Someone I used to work with?'

Beep beep.

'Have we been . . . sorry for asking but, have we been . . . intimate?'

Beep beep.

'Not even close?'

Beep beep.

'Would you like to be?'

Silence.

'Come on. Is that what this is all about? Would you like to be? Be honest.'

Beep beep beep beep beep beep beep beep.

'OK, you've made your point. I'll take that as a no.'

Beep.

'Hmm. Well, I'm none the wiser, really. Care to offer me any clues?'

Beep beep.

'But I do definitely know you?'

Beep.

'And you do always beep the truth?'

Beep beep.

'You don't?'

Beep beep.

'You mean you could be telling lies?'

Beep.

A bolt of rage. 'Oh, fuck you. How much time do you think I have to waste on this stupid game? It's like talking to fucking Sooty and Sweep.' And I slam the phone down in a way I feel sure will shorten its life.

When I pick up a minute later, she, he or whatever is on the other end is gone. I dial 1471. Once again the posh woman informs me, Sorry. The caller withheld their number. So, you're well buggered on that one.

2

Robyn with a Y bobs up outside my bubble and waves her feelers, or whatever larvae do when they want to attract attention. While I wait for the latest dose of ibuprofen to kick in, I've been hiding behind an absurdly thick audience research document, sincerely trusting that the world will leave me alone.

Apparently 78 per cent of the viewing public believe Erica Birkendale would be kind to animals, 85 per cent think she would be sensible with money, and a staggering 90 per cent of male C2DEs would be prepared to give her one (not exactly how the question was phrased, but you get the idea). ABC1 males were only slightly less taken with the old bitch, 69 per cent finding her either 'moderately' or 'extremely' sexually attractive. I am gratified to read that her scores are weakest with young people. In a focus group of sixteen- to eighteen-year-olds for example, remarks were made like 'she looks like that woman next door who works on the perfume counter at Debenhams' and 'you can't imagine her doing an e, can you?' Nevertheless, a full 65 per cent of the adult population agreed with the statement, 'If I were in hospital, I would rather be visited by Erica Birkendale than by a member of my own family.' Three-quarters believed she is 'more trustworthy than the Prime Minister, the Chancellor, the Leader of the Opposition and the Leader of the Liberal Democrats'. Only Trevor McDonald scored higher. And perhaps the most astonishing statistic of all, 80 per cent of those questioned concurred with the view that 'Erica Birkendale is a much-loved part of the tapestry of the nation.'

Mind you, they never ask the really *telling* ones, do they? Like if you had a gun, two bullets, and you are locked in a room with Erica Birkendale, Vanessa Feltz and Chris Evans, who do you shoot? (Erica, of course. Twice, just to make sure.)

'Someone phoned for you,' says Robyn with a Y when I wave her in. A smile spreads itself across the pale, formless terrain that one day will become a human face.

'Oh yes?'

'About ten minutes ago. Just before you got in.'

'Anyone in particular?' As she opens her mouth, I swear I see a bubble come out of it and float up towards the surface. Today I think she reminds me of a sea creature, one of those sad, blobby things with tiny fins, and curious arrangements of eyes and lips.

'He didn't leave a name. But he said to be sure to let you know he called.'

'Ah.'

'And that you'd be hearing from him again quite soon.'

'I see. Any . . . any *clues* at all, as to who it might have been?' One of those surreal fish that are all face. Blamelessly hoovering the coral until some passing sea monster mistakes it for an hors-d'oeuvre.

'He said you'd know. He said he had a funeral to organise, and then he would be getting right back to you.'

3

Calm. Remarkably calm. Really quite remarkably calm.

People in television react in different ways when things go wrong. There are those whose knuckles become very white, and before long you find they're shouting at everybody in sight with the specific exception of anyone in a position to shout back. Then there are the panic merchants, who flap helplessly when the shit hits the fan and issue all sorts of meaningless – and usually contradictory – instructions, people whose personal hysteria soon infects the rest of the team. There are the blame-meisters whose first concern is to pin the fault on someone else. In a similar vein are the arse-coverers (as long as it's not their fault, it doesn't matter). I suppose somewhere in the TV business there must be a few brilliantly decisive individuals who know exactly what's to be done in any crisis and assign crisp, concise directions accordingly but I have never met any. And then there's my own technique: the bigger the pile of cack that I find myself in, the calmer I become. I don't do rage, panic, witch-hunts, cover-ups or surgical decision-making. I just become calm. As if calm itself will lead to the solution. I guess the rationale is that you're more likely to come up with the answer in a calm atmosphere than a frenzy. Sometimes it works, of course; sometimes the crisis just goes away by itself, so at least while it lasted you haven't been consumed in a shitstorm of horror. If you wanted to be kind, you could call my attitude a form of serenity in the face of adversity. If you didn't, you might describe it as the calm of the rabbit, eyeball-to-eyeball with the python.

Anyhow, calm. *Very* calm. Really quite *remarkably* calm.

Peter Marcus shimmers in, closes the door behind him, takes the comfy chair for guests, laces his fingers behind his head, parks his legs out in front of him, one polished brown brogue resting on top of the other. He looks relaxed and contemplative, almost whimsical. Naturally all my early warning systems are at the highest state of readiness.

'What did you make of the Erica research?' he asks. It was he who left the slab-like document on my desk.

'Fascinating. It seems there's an enormous amount of affection out there.' For the horrendous old trout.

'The stuff about money and animals was interesting, I thought.' Was it?

'She hates animals, doesn't she? The fuss she made when we wanted that Labrador in the studio.' *Charles, if that creature sticks its nose in my fanny, I'm telling you, I walk.*

'She is perceived in terms of words like "kind" and "caring".' 'Selfish' and 'cow', I'd have thought. 'Whereas the show itself attracts adjectives like "cruel" and "mischievous". There's a contradiction, isn't there?' *What the fuck is he getting at?*

'There's that . . . that funny face she pulls.' *The one that makes me want to gag every time she does it.*

'The audience allow her to tease them,' Peter purrs, 'but from a standpoint of kindness and caringness, it seems.' *I'm lost.*

'Kids aren't particularly over-enamoured apparently.'

'No. There are clearly some generational issues. I'm glad you've got such a good feel for the data.' *Uh?*

'Amazing really. What people think they know about a figure they've never met.'

'Exactly. That's why I think it's important that we take a view now about the next phase. The post-*Uh-Oh* phase, if you like.'

Oh fuck, here it is. Caught in the radar sweep. Large, unidentified – presumed hostile – object heading fast in this direction. Scramble all available defences.

'Tuna needs to develop a raft of new shows for Erica. To cement our connection with her, and Erica's connection with the channel. Maybe something to do with animals. Or money. Or both. Ideas that play to her particular qualities. But that could also help build her appeal to a younger audience.'

'Who have you got in mind, Peter?'

'Charles, I think you're someone who would be able to take an appropriately sophisticated view of the nature of the landscape. Of course you could keep your office. We might even be able to find you a bit more money.' *Defences weakening.*

Stand by for immediate impact. 'Corporately, I'd say that Project Erica is of the greatest importance. I'd like it if you could begin immediately. Barry can act up and produce the rest of the series. What do you say?'

KA-BOOOOM.

'Peter, it sounds a . . . fascinating challenge.'

4

It's always 'a raft' of TV shows, isn't it?

Like, a show's a show. Two shows are just a couple of shows. But three shows, and all of a sudden you've got a raft. What's a raft? A bundle of planks, lashed together. Hmm. My first idea. We go to a tropical location, get a bundle of planks, lash them together, put Erica on board, tow them out to sea, and wait to discover how long it takes for her to be eaten by sharks. (Actually they wouldn't dare. Too much professional respect.)

Ideas to play to her 'particular qualities'. What *are* her qualities? I get a fresh sheet of paper and draw a line down the middle. On one side I write 'Good Qualities'. On the other, 'Bad Qualities'. In the good column I write:

Turns up on time
Speaks English
Does a passable imitation of a TV star
People believe they like her/trust her
Full driving licence.

Under bad qualities, I put:

Irascible old bag
Self-obsessed

Egomaniac (if different from above)
Haunted by celebrity
Contempt for public
Hates animals
Hates children
Hates *people* really
Obsessive dieter
Mutton dressed as lamb
Admires Margaret Thatcher
Treacherous scheming bitch.

Of course it's obvious she's had me bumped off the show. For calling her a national treasure. And forgetting she was sexy. Or more accurately, 'sexy'. And Peter's line about the money will turn out to be just that, a line. But overall, the central mystery remains. Is what's happened a Good Thing, a Bad Thing or a Disaster?

On the face of it, it certainly *feels* good that I don't have to work on *The Uh-Oh Show* any more. In fact it feels fucking wonderful (though being a television producer with nothing to produce could be construed as a bad thing). What *definitely* feels like a bad thing is that Peter wants to give me a new title, Head of Special Projects. In my experience, this is just the sort of bogus nom de pointless job they stick on you shortly before the trap door opens and you find yourself tumbling through empty space.

The key thing is how you land. If you come up smelling of roses, you can bounce right back. But if it's the other thing, suddenly you'll find even the Seafood Channel isn't returning your calls.

It does, however, have a certain cachet to it, Head of Special Projects. 'Head' sounds good. So does 'Special'. 'Projects' is a bit iffy, smacking as it does of large-scale engineering works.

But all put together, Head of Special Projects sounds kind of important, even a little clandestine. In the Genghis Lounge, I shall have to tap the side of my nose and use phrases like 'commercially sensitive, I'm afraid'. (This is probably the same silly thought entertained by anyone who's ever been made Head of Special Projects, in the few giddy months before they become totally unemployable.)

In the meanwhile, Barry looks like he's won the fucking lottery. His spine seems straighter. He's lost some of that slacker generation slouch. He came in here a few minutes ago, trying hard to keep the swagger under control, goatee all a-waggle. 'Charles, Peter has filled me in. We need to do a handover thang.'

'Sure, Barry. Let's do the thang whenever you like.'

Except, what's to hand over? I'm sure he knows more about what's going on with this silly show than I do.

5

I feel curiously light-headed. The sort of sensation you might have, I imagine, when the worst has already happened but you simply haven't realised it yet. The feeling of the lobster in the tank, immediately after pondering: Why is that bloke pointing at me like that?

At lunchtime, I deviate from routine and take a minicab to Acton. Getting the driver to drop me a little way away, I stroll through the pleasantly sun-dappled streets towards the particular boulevard I have an urge to revisit.

Madrigal Road, which only forty-eight hours ago had seemed to bristle ridiculously with intrigue — with unfamiliar personnel, oddly parked vans, tiny cameras, trained actors and giant poultry — today slumbers in its afternoon torpor. We had chosen it for its low garden walls (easy to shoot over), convenience of parking and a general air of suburban respectability. The houses are mainly semis; there's the odd detached, but none of that multiple doorbell thing denoting flatland. And this is one *long* street, nearly two miles of it on the map. The theory was that we'd pick a house at one end, play our turkey joke, and move the whole caravanserai along, two hundred yards at a time, ringing on doorbells, until we got a corker of a take. The very randomness of the scam was part of its appeal. Mere flukery that we should happen to call on the *eminence grise* of a West London crime family especially noted for its flamboyant displays of sickening violence. Pure chance that he should drop dead as a result. And completely illogical that the producer should be held responsible by a grieving grandson with a lisp and most probably a handy way about him with a machete. Common sense tells you there was no malicious intent. By the sound of things, he could have got into a state and turned up his toes over anything. A steep gas bill. An unfavourable racing result. The way that woman on the telly waves her hand around and says, 'Just look at those tightly packed isobars.'

I'm just beginning to think, This is nuts. What the fuck am I doing here? when I notice a woman standing at the gate of number 93. She's looking at me, a large, weathered blonde, round fifty, I should guess. As I get closer, I see the skin across her breastbone is all speckled and burnished. Something about the Marbella suntan and the gold jewellery reminds me of Erica Birkendale. I intend to walk straight past but suddenly she is speaking to me.

'*Acton Herald*, right?'

'Sorry?'

'You're Andrew from the *Acton Herald*.'

'What made you say that?'

'You look like a journo. Harry could smell them a mile off. He used to say there was something about their shoulders. Come in, love.'

'Thanks. But if you've got people . . .' If your house is crawling with knife-wielding thugs . . .

'No, it's fine.'

I follow what is undoubtedly the figure of the most recent Mrs Harry Holderness up the garden path and in through the front door.

A shiny marble floor, very nasty indeed. Some marble cherubs, if anything even nastier. In the sitting room, a pale green leather sofa suite floats in a sea of pale green carpet, its pile of a depth to significantly impede locomotion. There's an onyx coffee table, a life-sized porcelain leopard. In the corner squats a TV set the size of a wardrobe. French windows give on to a back garden dominated by a white marble fountain of almost breathtaking hugeness.

'That's quite a . . . a water feature,' I venture.

'Harry loved fountains. It's an exact copy of the one in the square in Estepona. We bought it for his seventy-fifth birthday. Coffee, love?'

While the widow busies herself in the kitchen, I wander politely round the room, checking out the family photographs: the younger Harry with various sets of children; older Harry in the company of a number of larcenous-looking young men; Harry seen together with 'showbiz personalities'; Harry beaming alongside a white-haired old mum-type figure. Harry in one of those all-the-family-together shots, the old rogue and his new missus, at a wedding by the look of it, surrounded by several dozen men, women, children, babies. His sons would be the guys around fifty or sixty, I guess, the grandsons around my own age. I peer into the photo, trying to pick out the one with the lisp. And then I spot him. The short, weird-looking fucker with a ponytail. Got to be.

'You'll want a few pictures, won't you? For the tribute?' Mrs Holderness comes wading through the carpeting and hands me a coffee mug. Amusingly it is emblazoned with the crest of Her Majesty's Prison Service. 'Sit yourself down, love.' As I sink, and continue to sink, into the armchair – this is one of those you have to fight your way out of – I notice her toenails are painted gold. 'You got no notebook then?' she points out reasonably.

'I thought we could keep it informal.'

'Good idea. I've got you a list of his achievements.' She passes me a hand-written sheet. It's the Harry Holderness c.v., the clean version. The schools in Shepherd's Bush. The army. The war heroism. The business career in the wholesale fruit and veg trade. The good works for charity. Connections in the world of greyhounds and horse racing. Prowess on the golf course late in life. Enjoyment of grandchildren and great-grandchildren. Underplaying the interest in torture, murder, extortion and control of prostitutes.

'Mrs Holderness, how do you see this piece?'

'What Harry wanted was a story putting down all the good things in his life, surrounded by adverts with black borders from the friends and family – In Deepest Sympathy, In Loving Memory. He reckoned you'd sell a whole page of those, so he said the write-up should be nice and friendly with it.'

'It's what he would have wanted.'

'It's what he *did* want – a warm tribute in his local paper with none of them phrases like "colourful past" and, what was the other one? Oh yeah, "persistent rumours of links with organised crime".'

Then I twig. The piece of paper. The methodical, old-fashioned handwriting. It's Harry's.

'Was your husband expecting to . . . to pass on, Mrs Holderness? When he did.'

'He always believed he'd go before his mum. His mum's still alive. Still lives in Acton.' She shoots me a meaningful look. 'Still takes the local rag, old as she is.'

She must be knocking on the ton, but that's what this is all about, isn't it? Suburban shame. Harry doesn't want his mum to read anything horrid about her boy in the local paper. Doesn't want the neighbours to have anything to gossip about. Like that woman from over the road who was done for nicking a tin of pilchards from Sainsbury's in 1958 and no one's ever forgotten it. Or him who was never quite right in the head who exposed himself to a schoolgirl and forty years later is still known as Frankie the flasher.

'How exactly did he die, Mrs Holderness?'

'Peacefully in his sleep.' She stares at me, unblinking.

'Really? His death wasn't . . . provoked by anything.'

'How do you mean?'

'Nothing brought it on, as it were.'

'I'm not with you.'

'Well . . . the rumour. That it was something to do with a television show. And a turkey. A live turkey, they say.'

'That is a lie.' The gangster's widow gives me a flash of the old man's steel. 'Andrew, listen very carefully. If that's what *they* say, whoever *they* are, *they* have got their facts one hundred per cent wrong. And if what *they* say ever appears in your newspaper or anywhere else, there are some people who will get very upset with you. Harry died peacefully in his sleep. Is that very clear, love?'

'Er, yes. Very clear. No worries on that score, rest assured.' Love that 'love'. 'Tell me, Mrs Holderness. How are the rest of the family taking it?'

'My husband wasn't a young man, but it still comes as a bit

of a shock. One of the grandsons is very cut up. He was very close to Harry.'

'Really.'

'Harry was more of a dad to Luke than his own father, what with Luke's dad being . . . being away such a lot.'

'I see.'

'Yeah, Luke is one hurting little boy at the moment.'

6

I tell Mrs H. that 'the picture editor' will call round later in the day to carefully select the best snaps to decorate the *Herald*'s fulsome tribute.

'Thanks, Andrew,' she said on the doorstep. 'I hope you don't think I'm a heartless bitch, just because I'm not weeping and wailing and that. I did love him in my way. I'm just relieved that it was over quickly. That he didn't linger or suffer. It was his greatest fear, you know, becoming a vegetable.'

Understandable really. What with Harry's legitimate business being in the wholesale greengrocery trade, coming into contact with courgettes and aubergines and the like on a daily basis. You'd never want to become one of *them*, would you?

By the time I get back to the office, I think I get it. The business over how he died. It's a pride thing. In the eyes of the world, the Grand Old Man of a West London crime family should die a Grand Old Death. A death befitting his status. On the golf course would do, after a perfectly judged chip on to the eighteenth. Or in the arms of the young wife. Better still, the mistress. Even, at a pinch, peacefully in his sleep. In the eyes of the world – in the eyes of rival crime families – the great man can't afford to have a *silly* death. And this one is just too ridiculous: death due to a stroke following a mild altercation over the ownership of a turkey. It's a joke, isn't it? Have you heard about old Harry Holderness, stuffed by a turkey? That's got to be the explanation, hasn't it? In death, the family are protecting their brand name from becoming a laughing stock.

But Luke is one hurting little boy at the moment.

By four o'clock, as part of my new responsibilities in the arena of Special Projects, I've identified a few more of Erica Birkendale's particular qualities.

Rampant insincerity
Naked careerism
Inability to appreciate subtlety (tendency to see everything in black and white).

But a problem: when it comes to performing successfully on television, which category should I put these under? Good or bad?

So what about a new show for her? Something to do with animals. Or money. Or both. Maybe a quiz where sheep compete with goats for big cash prizes? No, better idea. Erica goes to live on a farm for six months. A fascinating insight into the tough economic realities in the life of today's small farmer. And she's in it for *real*, not just staying at the nearby five-star hotel and limo-ing in for the links. Erica gets up at 5 a.m. for the milking, she mucks out the pigs — would the pigs agree to work with her? — she takes the bullocks to market, or whatever you do with bullocks. She feeds the chickens, collects the eggs, generally gets covered in shit, breaks every fingernail and utterly knackers herself. And of course she cries. At some point, she definitely loses it. Sobs, but pulls herself together, takes a deep breath and delivers those baby baa lambs.

Wrings the neck of the clapped-out rooster. Whatever unpleasant task cruel nature bowls at her.

A worry, though: *Erica on the Farm* could turn out to be a surprise hit. The 'glam' TV presenter getting all down and dirty could totally reinvent her and the old monster could become more famous and insufferable than ever. Hmm. Maybe quietly forget this one.

I become aware of a small commotion outside my bubble. Some of the girls are shrieking; with laughter or surprise, it's difficult to say. They're all staring and pointing and chattering about something on Barry's desk. Rose has her hand clamped over her mouth and her eyes have gone very wide. Geraldine is giggling and cracking jokes. Barry's goatee is spasming unpleasantly. Robyn with a Y looks like someone's bashed her head against a rock. I push my way through the gaggle.

In front of Barry lies a large, opened Jiffy bag, addressed to 'The Producer, *The Uh-Oh Show*'. From the lack of a stamp, it's obviously been dropped off by hand at the front desk. Inside, wrapped in newspaper, Barry has discovered a pair of Sainsbury's rainbow trout, still in their packet. The use-by date has been circled in the same fat red felt-tip pen employed to address the envelope. The date is tomorrow's. And now that I look again, I see the newspaper is the *Acton Herald*.

'It's in *The Godfather*,' says Barry rather quietly. 'The traditional Mafia signal of death.'

'Sainsbury's trout?' says Geraldine.

'It means you should shortly expect to be sleeping with the fishes,' replies Barry.

Robyn with a Y gives a little gasp.

'Great movie,' says Rose.

7

On my desk now, the evidence rest nose to tail in their plastic wrapping. Dead as they are, they're rather beautiful, these two – surreal marvels of nature, all silvery and freckled, absurdly at odds with the tacky particle board and neon light fittings of their surroundings. I begin to wonder about them. Was theirs a carefree infancy in a Highlands river? Or a miserable overcrowded childhood in a fish farm, the trout version of *Angela's Ashes*. Were they ever lovers? Do trout fancy other trout? Could a boy trout think of a girl trout, oh she of fair face and fin. Did they once dart and dance around one another joyfully, and then do whatever fish do to each other? W. C. Fields famously said, 'I never drink water, fish fuck in it.' But actually they don't, do they? After all the mating rituals, doesn't the girl squeeze several thousand eggs on to a weed, and the chap, if he can manage it, comes all over them? (Do fish have orgasms? When I was a child, one of my goldfish used to lie at the surface, panting, but I think that was fin-rot.)

All things considered, might it not be better to *be* a trout, a lovely muscular being in harmony with its medium and with little in the way of anxiety, except perhaps a vague unease about that fat worm with the hook through it?

Calm. Remarkably calm. Really quite remarkably calm.

I've told Barry and the scandalised onlookers that the parcel was obviously intended for me. That I have a pretty shrewd idea which jolly prankster friend of mine had sent it. And now that it's safely in my bubble, I've been scouring it for clues.

To be honest, I know very little about the Italian Mafia beyond what I've gleaned from the cinema. I do feel certain, however, that a proper mobster wishing to send the classic 'fishes' notification of an impending change in one's sleeping arrangements would be sure to first remove them from the packet. The symbol loses much of its power without the fishy stench and a smear of blood. In addition, the presence of the Sainsbury's logo, plus the refrigeration and cooking instructions, only serve to further erode the chilly portent of its ability to make the recipient cack his *pantaloni*. Besides, the *Acton Herald*, fine organ though it may be, carries none of the *forza* of a *La Stampa* or an *Il Giornale*, or one of the more colourful Italian football papers. So on the whole, in my professional opinion, I'd have to say this was a badly produced piece of scary business.

On the other hand, the circling of the use-by date is an interesting modern flourish, suggesting as it does a possible time frame for the proposed outrage. Though should the hit or whack fail to materialise by the date in question, I suppose it would still be unwise to consider the fishes commitment as dissolved.

Of the handwriting on the Jiffy bag, one can say little. The author of the words 'The Producer, *The Uh-Oh Show*' has spelt them correctly and the punctuation is impeccable. I scan the pages of the *Acton Herald*, searching for additional wisdom, but none emerges.

Later in the afternoon I call Daisy on reception.

'You don't happen to remember who dropped off a package for *The Uh-Oh Show* this afternoon, addressed to the producer?'

'Dispatch rider. He left it on the counter.'

'You don't recall what he looked like, by any chance?'

'He had his helmet on.'

'I see. Thanks, Daisy.'

'I remember he was unusually short.'

'Really?'

'Little guy. About five five. And one other thing.'

'Yes?'

'He had a ponytail.'

8

OK, fuck *calm, calm, remarkably calm* and all that shit.

Now I'm scared.

The guy's been in the building, for Christ's sake. Lispy fucking Luke has been on my territory. I can smell his scent. I can feel his hot breath . . . well, not on my neck exactly, on my elbow maybe. In any case, threatening telephone calls are one thing, but taking the trouble to mount a threatening fish delivery is of another order of intimidation entirely.

Where is my police forensic scientist when I need her?

I call Linds.

'You don't fancy coming away for the weekend, do you?' I ask.

'This is a bit out of the blue, Charlie. What did you have in mind?'

'Don't know, really. I just fancied getting out of town for a bit. Seeing some fields and cows and stuff.'

'You hate fields. You once said to me, I hate fucking fields. You quoted somebody.'

'Yeah, Bruce Robinson. He said the countryside was all birds shouting and shit everywhere.'

She laughs. 'That was it.'

'How about the coast then? I fancy some fresh air.'

'I'd love to. But Giles is taking me to the opera this weekend. He's got tickets for Glyndebourne.'

'Oh fuck, I think you said. So are you and he sort of . . . creeping closer to one another?'

'Actually, he's rather wonderful, Charlie.' Hang on a moment. Only a few days ago, he was the one she couldn't stand.

'An intimate moment has transpired. I can hear it in your voice.'

She sighs and I feel a bit sick. 'I think I'm rather smitten.'

'You've . . .' Allowed him to pollute your body with his filthy rich person's prick. 'Is there something you want to tell me?'

'We did it, Charlie. Last night. We had a lovely evening and he drove me back to my place. I asked him in for coffee.'

'Great.' Not all that great actually.

'He was surprisingly . . . considerate.' So he didn't just tip you over the back of the sofa and pull your frock up then?

'Really?'

'Mmm. It was rather dreamy actually.' Let me guess. The sort of dream you have after six pints of lager and a king prawn vindaloo.

'Fantastic. That's brilliant news.'

'What does one wear to Glyndebourne? Do you know?'

'Oh, something posh and floaty, I should imagine. Isn't there a lot of lolling about swigging champagne on lawns?'

'Is there? Sounds heaven.'

'Yeah.'

'You'll have to meet Giles. I think the two of you would really get on.'

'I'd like to.' I'd rather eat my own liver.

'Sorry about this weekend.'

'No, that's OK. You two young lovers just go off and have plenty of fun, you hear?'

'We'll try.'

When we hang up, I cut the line gently with my finger. Then I slam the phone down so hard in its cradle that everyone turns to look.

9

Somehow I feel much safer walking down Chalk Farm Road between Rose and Geraldine. How could anything horrid happen to me sandwiched between the cool blonde Englishwoman and the wicked little sprite?

Also, it occurs to me, Lisping Luke doesn't know what I look like. Nor can I think of an easy way he could find out. Could it be that the phone call and all that business with the trout and the use by date was solely designed to fill me with dread? *If he dieth, tho do you.* It's got to be bollocks, hasn't it? If I die, then it would all come out about Harry and the turkey, and the Holderness brand will be irreparably tarnished. On the other hand, if I'm just found one morning with my throat slit, who's to know it was the work of the grieving grandson? On the *other* other hand, if I come clean about Harry's death and go to the police for protection, my already compromised career will be holed below the waterline: a fatality to an inno-cent member of the public is one of the worst things that can happen in the course of a TV show, and anyone who can be blamed for it may as well contemplate a new life in another hemisphere. On the *other* other other hand, my TV career seems to have a serious question mark hanging over it already.

No. Here's the way to look at it: if it comes out about Harry, I'm fucked twice over. First by the industry that I love (ha-ha), but secondly, and more importantly, by certain nameless 'people'. *There are some people who would get very upset with you. Is that very clear, love?* If it doesn't come out about Harry, I'm fucked merely once over, by Lisping Luke . . . maybe. My best hope is that shorty is just trying to frighten me.

Calm. Remarkably calm. Really quite— Oh, don't start all that again.

Zyplxqnk, I notice when we get there, has been restyled as Myxpqlncx. The woman behind the bar with rather a lot of studs in her face explains that customers were finding the old name a bit difficult to say. In addition to the alteration in nomenclature, the menu has been streamlined. From now on they will simply be offering a daily soup, a main dish and a dessert. Tonight it's a peanut broth with crusty cob; baked herring in yoghurt with home fries and beetroot salsa; and a Thai-spiced milk pudding. The drinks menu has also been made more attractive to consumers. They're introducing a wine of the day (today's is English Sauvignon Blanc), a guest beer (Mindfucker from Dorset) and a featured cocktail (the Marine Martini, evidently the same as an ordinary Martini, but instead of an olive or a twist of lemon, they use a pickled cockle).

We all agree the makeover has been a tremendous success, order three Marine Martinis and privately agree to come back next week for the closing down party.

'A masterstroke,' says Geraldine, taking a sip of her M.M.

'A lovely fusion of the sea and dangerously strong drink,' says Rose.

'Actually, I think it might have gone better with a whelk,' I add in all seriousness. (Honestly, I think it would. It's the *body*. Oh, never mind.)

At the other side of the bar, Barry is buying drinks for Emma. There's an insouciance about him this evening that definitely wasn't there this morning — the misplaced arrogance one assumes when first placed at the helm of a network television show, no matter how tacky. The beardlet is tracing curious arcs through the air. I think I once saw a docco about courtship patterns in male gibbons, and they do much the same thing, though fewer of them work in TV.

'So what happened?' asks Rose about halfway down the featured cocktail. 'Why have you suddenly deserted us?'

Geraldine joins in. 'Did you jump or . . . ?'

She leaves it hanging there. And I have the urge to tell them everything. How threats have been made against my life; how my ex-ex has fallen for a Porsche-owning throwback to the 1970s; how I passed out in front of my current romantic lead, and now she's vanished off the radar; how I've entered a Kafkaesque dialogue with an anonymous phone-caller; how a woman who seventy-eight per cent of the population associate with the words 'caring' and 'compassionate' has stiffed me with the panache of a Neapolitan assassin; how my boss has finessed me into accepting a job that is the television equivalent of moving to Eastbourne (God's waiting room); how I still miss Cheryl.

'Bit of a complex tale to be honest,' I reply.

And then the terrible thing happens.

Into Myxpqlncx walks the unmistakably small and pony-tailed figure of Lisping Luke Holderness.

10

He's even stranger in real life than in the photos. A short, hard-looking creature with an oversized rocky head. Dark, thinning hair is swept into what I now see is a *plait*. Fuck, how weird is that? And he's wearing a raincoat, a long pale trench coat of the sort favoured by detectives in cop shows and American secret service guys, the kind of garment that could easily conceal a machete. Or a baseball bat. Or a shotgun. Or a fucking sam missile. A foot taller and he would be terri-fying. As it is, his visual signature reads *short mad bastard*.

'Who are you staring so hard at?' asks Geraldine.

For a moment I contemplate replying, that bloke at the bar actually, who has expressed an interest in killing me. But when I think of trying to explain what I mean by that statement, I am overcome by a great weariness.

'Sorry, bit distracted. What were you saying?'

Luke the Lisp, I notice, has bought a half of Mindfucker and is engaging the girl with the face full of studs in light con-versation. She's bantering with him as she serves customers, takes the money and generally hangs around waiting for the big moment when someone is pissed enough to order the baked herring in yoghurt. Every now and again he scans the room, the boulder of a head turning slowly as it eyeballs the chattering yuppies. He seems to linger particularly on Barry, who I guess may conform to your average crim's stereotype of your average TV producer (goatee, glasses, turtleneck, chatting up bird in incredibly tight trousers).

I can't leave, not just yet. It would be too obvious. But I can't stay either. My heart is racing, my palms have gone tropical. I can't concentrate on a word either of these girls is saying to me.

'. . . which, Charlie? You just said, "Yes, please".' Rose is looking at me like I'm stupid or something.

'Sorry, could you repeat that? I'm feeling a bit peculiar.'

'I asked if you wanted the same again or something else.'

'No.'

'What do you mean no? Are you all right?'

'Don't go to the bar.'

'What?'

'Stay with me.

'What's the matter?'

'Oh fuck, don't look. He's coming this way.'

I recall from O level Biology that a sudden jolt of adrenalin is supposed to prepare the body for fight or flight. It catalyses the survival mechanism that evolved for the moment when Ancient Ancestor glanced upwards and clocked the sabre-toothed tiger in the tree tying on the serviette and smacking the lips. Your pupils dilate, your airways widen, blood diverts from your internal organs to your muscles and you either run the beast through with a sharpened stick or leg it back to the safety of the cave.

But aside from fight and flight, there is a third way.

Fright.

The sort of fear that leaves your airways nice and spacious and your muscles flooded with nutrients, but your bum parked firmly on the bar stool and your brain jammed in neutral. And this is no mere jolt of adrenalin. This feels like a fucking Zambezi of the stuff.

'Thorry to bother you. I wath wondering if you've theen Charlie Green thith evening. Charlie Green from Tuna TV.'

The face up close is disturbed rather than overtly violent. He's more like the schoolboy who used to torch rodents than the one who crushed your crisps and gave Chinese burns. A vein throbs in his temple. His eyes are arctic blue. They look pained. Something about the way his tongue moves inside his mouth makes it look as if the words themselves taste rotten, as though they've gone off. Round his thick neck on a chain hangs what looks awfully like a human tooth.

'Hath he been in at all, do you know?' He's staring right at me. I am mesmerised by the tooth. A fat molar, yellowed, with a long root. Is it one of *his*, I want to know. And if it isn't, how exactly did he come by it? I'm dealing him what I hope is the blankest expression in my pack, but I realise I am incapable of speech. I look at Rose.

Rose looks at Geraldine.

And Geraldine says, 'Actually, I think you'll find Charlie in the Genghis Lounge tonight. Are you supposed to be meeting him?'

'Yeth. Thomething like that. Cheerth.'

11

It's the military background, I decide in the minicab back to mine. It's the way her father would have behaved. For good or ill, that sort act decisively, rather than stewing endlessly in a morass of equivocation. Attacking the insurgents, or selecting a marmalade at breakfast, I can imagine the brigadier going about both with a ruthless efficiency. When I finally stop shaking, I congratulate her.

'You saved my bacon there. I owe you one.'

'Odd-looking feller,' says Geraldine. 'You didn't wish to make his acquaintance, I gather?'

I take a deep breath. 'That bloke is such a bore, I can't tell you. He's been calling me for weeks about his stupid idea for a scam for the show. Honestly, what's it coming to when a humble TV practitioner can't have a quiet drink at the end of a hard day's toil without being pestered by the bloody *viewers*.'

'I thought he must have been your dealer,' says Rose. 'Or dentist.'

In the flat, I pour large drinks and Rose rolls a suitably challenging spliff. Twenty minutes later, I am feeling a *lot* more relaxed about life.

We chatter. About my new role, dreaming up rafts. About Barry, and whether he'll ever manage to get off with Emma. About Peter Marcus and the possible sources of his enigmatic mystique. About ghosts and whether we believe in them. Morphic resonance, that thing where if enough people think about an idea, then *you* start thinking about it too. How, if you cross your fingers and touch them to your nose, it feels like you've got two noses.

We flip channels, playing that game.

Tennis commentator: 'So after three hours and twelve minutes here on Number One Court, Mark Philippoussis has . . .'

Newsreader: '. . . destroyed hundreds of buildings and left thousands homeless without power or fresh water.'

We watch a debate on *Newsnight* on dumbing down in the

media. But we soon grow bored — particularly of the bald twat academic on the link from the Midlands — so we catch the end of that programme where contestants have to pick their partner's arse out of a line-up.

Around midnight, the dented Datsun comes to ferry them home.

I fire up *Czech-Mates*. Magda is still sitting there topless amidst the heavy brown furniture, the look on her face insolently goading me to come up with something, if I think I'm smart enough. Her bishop, threatening all sorts of havoc on my king's side, is no less menacing than it was the last time I looked. What would the brigadier do in this position? Whatever it was, it would be swift, surgical and decisive. Action this day.

I type *R4–R8*, a powerfully diversionary strike into Magda's soft underbelly (as it were). Press Enter.

And now the picture is changing, and it's a close-up: Magda's face cupped in two sets of red fingernails, pondering her response. The symbol starts to flash. Here comes her move.

Q3–Q8 Checkmate.

Fuck. Oh well, maybe surgical isn't for everyone. As I disconnect, the phone starts to trill. Whoever it is must have put me on Ringback.

'Hello.'

Silence.

'Oh you. What do you want?'

Silence.

'Oh, OK. I'll ask you questions. Are you still a girl this evening?'

Beep.

'Thank God for that. Are you quite sure that we've met?'

Beep.

'But you could be telling lies?'

Beep.

'Why do you tell lies? I mean, it's not in the spirit of the thing, is it? Are you telling lies because you're worried I'll work out who you are?'

Beep.

'Have you told many lies?'

Beep beep.

'How many? What, more than five, let's say?'

Beep beep.

'More than two?'

Beep beep.

'Just one?'

Beep.

'You've told me one lie.'

Beep.

'Although that could be a lie in itself.'

Beep.

'Are you enjoying this?'

Silence.

'Come on, you can answer that. Are you enjoying this?'

Beep.

'Are you masturbating at this moment?' (Sorry, had to ask.)

Beep beep beep beep beep beep beep beep beep . . .

'OK, OK. Look, you ask me something. I'm running out of ideas.'

Silence.

'Will you *ever* speak to me, do you think?'

Silence.

'Can I take that as a maybe?'

Beep.

'I can?'

Beep.

'Well, that's great news. I look forward to it, honestly. When do you think it might be? Weeks rather than months, I hope.'

Silence.

'Tell you what, let's have a new code. You can do three beeps for I don't know.'

Beep beep beep.

'You don't know when you'll speak to me?'

Beep beep.

'But you will one day?'

Beep.

'Fine. Shall we go to bed now?'

Beep.

'Well, good night then.'

Beeeeeep. A longish sort of beep. And she hangs up.

Some sort of victory, I guess.

12

Five minutes later, while I'm brushing my teeth, the phone rings again. If it's bloody Loopy Loo, wanting another bedtime chat . . .

But it isn't.

'Charlth?' My blood freezes.

'Yes?'

'Have you got a minute?'

'Who is this?'

'You know perfectly well who thith ith, you mitherable cunt. Come to the window.'

'What do you mean?'

'Come to your front window.'

'I'm sorry, it's a bit late.' What sort of a ridiculous thing to say is that, to a bloke who wants to kill you? I'm sorry, it's a bit late. How's he supposed to react? Ooh, is it? Sorry, I'll come back another time then.

'I can thee your lightth on. Come to the window, I want to show you thomething.'

He's outside. In the street outside my flat. Oh shit. Correction, make that shit de la shit. What if he's got a fucking sniper's rifle, ready to take the roof of my skull off the minute my soft pale face appears at the windowpane. I drop to my knees and, clinging to the digital cordless, I slither into my darkened bedroom. *This* is what the brigadier would do. He'd use a bit of fucking natural cunning, a bit of *nous*.

'Look, will you please stop harassing me?'

'Don't be a cunt all your life. Come to the window.'

Gingerly, I get to my feet at one side of the bedroom window. Slowly, I push the curtain aside until I can see down into the street below. Across the road, perfectly framed in a pool of orange sodium light, trench coat flapping, mobile telephone to his ear, stands the appalling spectacle of Luke Holderness. This counts as one of the worst things I have ever laid eyes upon.

'What do you want to show me?' I ask, only a touch more relaxed now I see he doesn't actually have a bazooka trained in my direction.

'That I know where you live.'

'Congratulations. How did you find out?' Stockholm syndrome: establish a dialogue with the enemy; humanise yourself, so that when the time comes, he fatally hesitates before doing you in, allowing the Special Forces the vital few extra seconds to burst in and blow the fucker away.

'A helpful young lady in a bar told me. Name of Robyn. You got children working for you, Charlth.'

'Tell me about it. She should never have given you my home address.'

'I was very persuasive.' *Perthuathive.* 'I told her she'd be doing you a big favour.'

'Jesus. Good thing you didn't speak to anyone who's actually got it in for me.'

'Hey, cunty. That was almotht funny.'

'Look, I'd love to stay up chatting all evening but—'

'Don't fucking push it. By the way, I can thee you peeking.' He waves conspicuously. I let the curtain fall back into place.

'Listen, I realise you must be terribly upset about your grandfather. But he was an elderly man, from what I understand. And if, as it turns out, he was in such . . . such precarious health, anything could have carried him off.' Not a bad little speech, I should have thought, in the circs.

'Very comforting, Charlth. Maybe you'd like to invite me in and we could sit down and talk about it.'

For a moment, I consider the idea. An appeal to his reason. Perhaps even a bit of a manly heart-to-heart where the granite-headed gangster ends up sobbing on my shoulder – 'He meant the world to me, did my old granddad.' We become pally. We frequent dog tracks together; hardnut drinking dens where he introduces me to the fascinating ways of the criminal demi monde. In return, I take him to . . . to, er. Where exactly? A theme bar in Camden? Some pretentious dump in Covent Garden full of silly people in serious glasses? A studio recording of *Ready Steady Cook*?

'Actually I don't think that would be awfully convenient right now.'

'Wouldn't it? Wouldn't it be *awfully convenient*? Oh well, never mind. You're a dead man anyway. Thleep well, cunt-faith.'

S I X

1

'Good morning, ladies and gentlemen. Second Officer Simon Beamish here. May I take this opportunity of welcoming you all on board our service down to Toulouse this morning. Journey time today should be just under two hours and as no significant air traffic delays have been reported, we plan to have you down on the ground pretty much on schedule, safely in time for lunch. Our cabin crew will shortly be serving you with a light snack, and it'll be our pleasure to offer you a selection of drinks from the bar with our compliments. Once again may I thank you for choosing to travel with us today, and can I recommend that you do try to get as pissed as possible in the short time available.'

The gin and tonic is doing a grand job, naturally, but it's

mainly an intoxicating feeling of relief that is currently coursing through my system. Relief that started to build as I watched Luke Holderness climb on to his motorcycle and roar off in the direction of Shepherd's Bush. That grew stronger when I scanned the impressive list of departures that just-buggeroffsomewherehot.com had availability on the next morning. That climaxed a few moments ago, when I felt the plane's undercarriage retract and I saw the light sparkling on the reservoir a thousand feet below in West Drayton, or whatever it is down there.

Somewhere, my murderous tormentor broods in his fetid hutch. But I have literally and metaphorically risen above him. I am in the air, weightless, bound for the soft light and herby scents of Southern France. There's a drink in my hand, a book on my knee. The traveller in the next seat is neither overweight, malodorous, nor in pressing need of conversation. Matters at this little locus in space-time are just about perfect. In fact, about the only thing that could puncture my sense of . . . of happiness actually, would be the sight of Luke Holderness's head suddenly rising up from behind the seat in front of me. That, or a catastrophic loss of cabin pressure.

And, of course, I'll be seeing Cheryl.

I called her last night. I had my spiel planned out. Look, I know we've broken up and all, and I accept that, and I'm not going to plead with you again to give it another try. I know, it's over. You and I aren't the answer to each other. But Cheryl, I'm in the most awful fix − I can't explain − you'll have to trust me. I need to hide away somewhere for a few weeks. And I was wondering, if your parents' house in France was free, whether they'd mind if I just sort of camped out until all this blows away. I have such . . . such happy memories of the place. No, scrub that last bit, too hopelessly maudlin. Make it fond memories. Obviously I can still recall how it all works.

Where the switch for the electricity is, how to put on the water, remembering to be nice to Monsieur Wotnot, what's he called, the sulky old twat in the Renault who comes to collect the fallen apples? Sorry, correction. Delete sulky old twat, insert charming old character. Also, I'd be more than happy to pay for Madame Thingy and her dim-bulb son to come over every day and clean. And basically they might prefer to have me staying there than the place lying empty.

But it was her flatmate, Jilly, who answered the phone. Who said hello, how are you? Who said, actually Cheryl was in France at the moment.

'What, at her parents' place?'

'That's the one.'

'On her own?'

'So I believe.'

I always rather liked Jilly. A dull, sensible girl, she nevertheless felt like an ally in the problem with Cheryl. When I'd stayed over, and Cheryl had come out with something particularly Cherylesque at breakfast – 'I wonder if plants can hear, if that's why they call them ears of corn' – Jilly would shoot me a knowing look across the marmalade that spoke of devotion mingled with wry amusement. Gorgeous barmy Cheryl, it seemed to be saying. You lucky dog to be sharing her bed.

'Jilly? She hasn't gone there . . . with a chap?'

'Not unless he's very small and I didn't spot her packing him.'

So I called the house. Woke her up actually, explained my predicament as outlined above ('what's he called, that funny old chap who comes for the fallen apples?' 'Monsieur Beauregard.' 'That's him.' Never was a sour-faced old bastard less aptly named). I promised I'd be no trouble. And she'd said, As it happens Charlie – Charlie, not Charles – it might be good to have you on the scene for a while. I didn't press for details, I said I'd turn up on the terrace tomorrow with a case of something dry and sparkling by way of a present for the house, as it were.

My call to Peter Marcus the following morning felt slightly more sensitive. But as it turned out, he was worryingly accommodating.

'I think it's an inspired idea, Charles. Taking time out to think. More of us should do it.'

'I will be working, of course. Dreaming up ideas for Erica's raft. But away from the familiar old terrain, allowing the brain to float more freely, untrammelled by notions of what's considered possible.'

'Very exciting,' he purred.

'And you're quite comfortable that I take a week or two out of the office on this?'

'Perfectly.' Great to know I'm so fucking indispensable.

'I'll obviously be phoning in regularly.'

'No need. Just go, stare at some clouds, and come back with a couple of dozen ideas for Erica. If just one gets commissioned, we'll consider it a success.'

'I'll leave a contact phone number with Daisy.'

'Charles, relax. Enjoy. Be creative. Be fertile.'

Hmm. Since when does your boss urge you to relax, to enjoy? And how about that 'be fertile'? Was it a subtle way of telling me to fuck off?

I press the little button in the side of my armrest. A short time later, replacement gin, tonic and ice cubes are reprising their familiar melody in my plastic tumbler. Far below, the airliner's shadow follows the course of a French river that I should know the name of. It suddenly occurs to me that since I have been in genuine mortal danger, the creature living behind my left eyebrow hasn't twitched even once.

2

I remember the first time I did this drive from the airport, the forty-odd miles through leafy old France, the roads getting narrower at each turnoff, the villages getting remoter and sleepier, until we arrived – Cheryl and I, when we were Cheryl and I – at their village, an almost creepily somnolent cluster of shops and houses huddled at the intersection of two exceedingly minor roads. After a blind left turn at the *boulangerie* – 'listen out for tractors, but basically you've got to hope to Christ there's nothing coming the other way,' her father had advised down the phone that first time – there's another mile and a half of pitted track, the blackberries flogging the flanks of the hire car, the ground steadily rising, until suddenly you find yourself emerging at the top of a small valley. Below lies the narcoleptic settlement of Yech, the aerial plan laying bare the full scale of its attractions and amenities. Apart from the *boulangerie* referred to above, there is one restaurant – 'There's no menu,' Cheryl had told me cheerfully. 'She just cooks whatever she has in' – a petrol pump (it would be overstating the case to call it a garage), a medieval village hall, a shop that sells things like old buttons and stuffed birds that doubles as a post office (open for approximately two hours a week), and a fucking huge ugly grey church.

'However did they . . . discover it? Your parents?' I'd asked her.

'The village? It took them ages.' Before landing on exactly the right mix of tedium and despair.

'You pronounce it . . . ?'

'Yech.' Like a small dog being sick.

'What do they get up to here?' Apart from the roller-disco, and the rest of the giddy social whirl, obviously.

'Daddy reads. Mummy paints. They go for walks. Go to bed early.'

Hmm. Well, there is always that, I remember thinking.

But the house itself was completely charming. Long and low-beamed, it sat comfortably on its hillside, the terrace overlooking the chimneypots of Yech, the perfect spot for hour after hour of serious loafing. We'd lounge there side by side, my eyes lifting off the improving novel every now and again to catch a dramatic piece of action in the village below. Monsieur Beauregard's Renault grinding off in the direction of the *supermarché*. Monsieur Beauregard's Renault returning. Madame Thingy and her low-wattage *fils* encountering the woman who operates the old button and stuffed bird franchise. The two ladies conversing for twenty minutes – what the fuck about? – Einstein scuffing his shoes against the bus stop. Then twirling round it like he was Fred Astaire. Then sitting down on the kerb and staring at his boots. And all this in just one morning. Oh no, never a dull moment in Yech, that's for sure.

Back then, Cheryl and I sink deliciously into the tomblike peace of rural France. She cooks and picks wild flowers and gets all dreamy. I feel the overwound spring start to uncoil. At night we sit on the terrace with our drinks, listening to the dogs barking as the light fails. Bats loop the loop in celebration of the dusk. Sometimes we take torches and stumble down the pitted track to the empty restaurant, where *la patronne* rouses herself from her pastis-induced stupor, mutters something – 'Did you catch what she said, Charlie?' 'It could have been "entrecote", but she may have just been clearing her throat' – and she lurches off to the kitchen where pans are rattled and breaking glass is heard sporadically.

I gaze at Cheryl pathetically across the candle flame. And when we wander home, we sleep the long, drugged sleep of the countryside. Ten, eleven hours sometimes. In London I'm lucky to do six. In the morning . . . Cheryl's huge eyes are looking at me across the pillow, there's a particular expression in them, and we don't surface until much before lunchtime.

The car journey is achingly familiar, the very scenery somehow imbued with the essence of her. I pull into the short driveway and park in front of the house. I walk round the side on to the terrace, where I picture her at this time of day, sprawled on a lounger perhaps, snoozing beneath a French fashion magazine, or listening to her Discman. At a pinch, attempting yet another impressionist study of Yech with her mother's watercolours. Except this afternoon she is doing none of these things. She is seated at the white plastic dining table, smoking a cigarette – Cheryl doesn't smoke – and laughing at something that has just been said by the bullish young man who lolls insolently in the chair opposite.

3

'Charles,' she squeals, leaping to her feet. 'How wonderful.'

She's advancing on me, closing in for the kiss, the frying-pan face getting wider and wider in my field of vision, the features beginning to spread out. I'm going for what protocol suggests, a safe cheek-to-cheek jobby appropriate for ex-lovers, but she does a swerve and plants one on my lips. Even manages a little half-hug. I'm slightly taken aback by the warmth of the welcome.

'Come and meet Jamie.'

She tugs me across the terrace as Jamie hauls himself to his feet, a tall, fleshy character – rugger bugger is my first thought

— who squeezes my hand with just a tad too much grip I'd say for a first meeting.

'Jamie Munslow,' he says.

'Charles Green,' I respond. The exchange feels like two playing cards falling, one on top of the other. After the flight and the drive, I'm suddenly aware of the deep background silence into which our words have been spoken. The theatricality of the setting, this hillside terrace, the two Englishmen, the one English woman.

'Jamie works for . . . who is it again, Jamie?'

Jamie mentions a firm with a long name. 'We're international tax consultants. Lots of clients in this part of the world.'

He's in leisurewear this afternoon: deck shoes, no socks; white jeans that end at the knee; a sharply tailored short-sleeved shirt with a man on a polo pony motif. Some variety of fiercely expensive timepiece gleams in a forest of arm hair.

'Jamie's been down to Nice and Cannes and Monte Carlo,' says Cheryl. Jamie gives a little shrug that makes me want to hit him.

'That must have been fun,' I say brightly.

'Cannes is a zoo,' says Jamie, 'and Monte's a bugger to park in.'

I nod sympathetically. Yes, it can often be tricky finding a space in Shepherd's Bush in the week too.

'Have you just sort of popped up for the day?' I enquire lightly. When are you leaving?

'Jamie's taking a week driving up through France,' gushes Cheryl.

'Thought I'd break up the journey by dropping in on a few pals en route.'

'Nice idea,' I add with as much enthusiasm as I can muster. 'How do you guys know each other?'

'We met at a wedding last year,' says Cheryl. 'That friend

of Jilly's. Jamie's promised to give me some tax advice, haven't you? What was that thing you said . . . ?'

'You can legitimately avoid, but you can't lawfully evade.'

Cheryl pulls a face, like she's trying to memorise the mantra. 'Legitimately avoid, can't lawfully evade,' she repeats. Like she gives a shit.

But what friend? What wedding? Last year Cheryl and I were still romantically linked. Unless it was around the time we started getting scratchy with one another. And now I come to think of it, perhaps there was a weekend. But hadn't she described it as a 'hen event'?

'What line are you in?' asks Jamie, and I can feel myself beginning to shrivel. His nose looks like it may have been broken once. Or maybe it's naturally thick, like the rest of his features. There's a lazy, rough-hewn, blubbery quality to them. If you squinted, you could imagine he was wearing a stocking over his head. He looks to me like the sort of bloke who wouldn't give a fuck what I, or anyone else, thought about anything.

'Television, I'm afraid.'

'Aha. Another one. Well, maybe you will know the answer to this. Cheryl was a touch vague on the subject.' She smiles in the most sick-making fashion, and Jamie starts up about the latest big, boring takeover farrago in the satellite television industry, with its huge implications for the regulatory bodies, its massive conflicts of powerful interests, its fascinating international taxation ramifications. 'It seems to me the individual governments are bound to have to get involved,' he drones, 'but what's your take on it all?'

I want to answer, oh fuck off, you pompous twat. Ask me a proper question. And anyway, what are you doing here? But because I don't want to spoil the mood, I resign myself to reply, actually that's not quite my line. I produce deception comedy, maybe you've heard of it.

And then I'm saved. His mobile is ringing. He flips open the *Star Trek* communicator-style flipper. 'Hello? Oh hi, Bob.'

It's the office. He gets up and prowls the terrace, I guess spieling to London about the clients he's seen. How Serge in Antibes might still need a little sweetening; how Marco and his brother bought the whole package, even the messy bits; how they had to be looking at triage now with the K-Pax partners; how the Cap Ferrat syndicate would be holding fire before they filed. Cheryl is gazing at him with something like wonderment on the great plain of her face.

When he comes off the mobe, she says: 'How do you chaps fancy a spot of lunch?'

4

Blubber-chops isn't clearing off. Not for several days by the sound of things. Over a rather fine spread of the local hams, pâtés, cheeses, bread and tomatoes – washed down with some of the fizzy that I procured in Toulouse – it becomes depressingly clear that the taxing Mr Munslow plans to hang around until at least the weekend, and possibly beyond.

So now we're all lined up in a row on the terrace on sun-loungers, reading, digesting, and in my case brooding. Cheryl lies in the middle, her long, slim legs aimed in the direction of Yech, in whose hot, dusty streets at this time no visible life form stirs. She is still a little tipsy from lunch I'd say, because she seems to be finding every remark of Jamie's irresistible.

'Does anyone actually live down there?' he asks.

Cheryl giggles. Oh stop, my aching sides.

'Big church for such a tiny village,' he adds. 'Practically a cathedral.'

'Yes!' she cries, like the idea has never occurred to her before.

'What's it like in the rush hour?'

'Oh, you know,' says Cheryl, on the verge of hysteria, 'just crazy.' And to emphasise her point, she reaches over and lays a hand on his arm.

'They say people live longer in this region,' I murmur from behind my book. 'Though perhaps it just seems longer.'

She looks round at me like I'm not well or something.

'Do you remember that God-awful speech the best man made at the wedding?' asks Jamie, apropos of nothing.

Cheryl creases with silent amusement. 'Charles, you should have heard it. It was so embarrassing.'

'Really?'

Did that 'really' of mine come out a bit . . . jaded and cynical? I only ask because she's giving me another funny look.

Jamie says, 'I thought the remark about the groom and the Italian whore was in particularly poor taste, considering how many old people were present.'

'Have you ever been a best man, Jamie?' she asks.

'Yeah. Actually I have.'

'What was your best gag?' I hear myself saying.

'Didn't really do gags, as such,' he replies. 'More sort of colourful stories. Though actually, there was one. I said . . . I don't know how many people here today know this, but Hugh – Hugh was the groom, always a bit of a scruff at school, all his life really – only last month, I said, Hugh was voted Best-Dressed Man of the Year. And then I said . . . the year was 1977.'

Cheryl does a gaspy little laugh. The laugh I have come to know as the one she does when she wants to find something funny. Like the time she laughed at a joke of mine before I had reached the actual punchline.

'Got quite a big reaction on the day too,' says Jamie.

'Who fancies a stroll into downtown Yech?' I ask. Only, if I have to listen to much more of this, I think I may be sick.

5

It wasn't supposed to be an actual full-on walk. It just sort of evolved. At the point where we could have turned down the pitted track into the village, Cheryl said, if we carry on along here, we'll reach the head of the valley eventually, so we kept on going.

Actually, it's rather perfect. Hot, but not too hot. Nice clear paths. A pleasing amount of interesting bird and insect life to keep an eye on. When we pass cottages and farmhouses, all the slavering white-eyed dogs have either been chained up or howl harmlessly behind gates. None, at any rate, are in a position to come pelting out with a view to sinking their fangs into my balls.

We fall into a comfortable stride, sometimes three-abreast, at other times two in front, one behind – or one in front, two behind – the permutations continually altering in the way of country walks. For ten minutes I find myself alongside Cheryl, with Jamie a steady ten yards ahead. But then he allows us to draw level, by pointing out something fascinating like a dead creature in a hedge or a distant view of a steeple. And for the next ten minutes it becomes Cheryl and Jamie side by side, with me trailing along behind. Then Cheryl will contrive a reason to stop – to marvel at a cloud of butterflies, or admire the composition of a view – and suddenly I'll find myself in step with Blubber-lips, as Cheryl once again leads the advance, both of us forced to admire her tall, slender body as it makes its progress into the future.

'Fine girl,' says Jamie. 'You two were an item for quite a while, I gather.' Something about that 'were' falls heavily on my heart.

'Yes, you could say that.'

'Neither of you seeing anyone at the moment, I don't suppose?'

I get a sudden picture of Kate behind the glass chessboard, stretched out along my carpet like a range of hills. 'Actually, there is someone.'

'Glad to hear it. It doesn't do to mope.'

'What makes you think I'd be moping?' You cheeky cunt.

'Well, Cheryl's a great girl. Not too many where that one came from. Still, it's good that you two can remain friends. Never could with any of my exes.'

'Really, why's that, then?' Did they perhaps eventually realise that you were a pompous, arrogant twat?

'I guess once we split up, I found I had nothing left to say to them. And vice versa, I'm sure.'

We walk on in silence for a bit after that. A bumble bee the size of a man's thumb crosses our path. High overhead, a pair of eagles circle.

'What does she do, this someone you're seeing?' asks Jamie after a while.

'Actually, she's a police forensic scientist.'

'Christ. How did you meet her?'

'Long story. I say "seeing", but she's a touch on the tricky side.'

'Tricky, how exactly?'

'Elusive. Hard to pin down, as it were. But clever. Smart as a whip.' Why am I telling him all this?

'You want some free advice?'

Not really. 'Go on then.'

'All women in my experience – smart ones, dim ones,

babes, dogs – they all respond to wit. Tickle a woman's sense of humour and you'll discover her erogenous zone.'

'You've found that, have you?'

'Get a woman laughing, and you're halfway to getting her into bed.'

'Thanks. I'll try and remember that.'

'Charles, you didn't tell me you were seeing anyone.' This is Cheryl, a little later, after she's had twenty minutes *à deux* with the King of Comedy. Now it's the two of us, slogging up a hill, Bob Hope trailing back in the rear there, practising his snappy one-liners.

'You didn't ask.'

'And she's a police scientist?'

'That she is.'

'Golly. Is she very . . . serious?'

'Not overly. Cheryl, tell me something. I feel like a bit of a gooseberry here. Are you and . . .' I jerk a thumb over my shoulder, 'are you and he sort of . . . ?'

'You're not a gooseberry, Charles.'

'But are you and he sort of . . . brewing up to anything?'

'I shouldn't think so,' she replies, like she doesn't know for sure. 'How about you and your scientist?'

'Probably a bit early to say. But do you like him?'

'Jamie? He's sweet.'

How very Cheryl. Whatever else you might say of Jamie – good-looking (in an ugly sort of way), fit, rich (probably), confident, well-connected, good tan . . . er, actually I'm running out now – the one thing you wouldn't call him is sweet.

'But look, I don't want to get in your way . . .' If you two young people want to start rutting like deer.

'Charles, you are not a gooseberry.'

'Sure?'

'Sure.'

'No kind of soft fruit at all?'

'Don't be silly.'

But they do look awfully bloody . . . pally, the next time it's their turn to form the dyad, leaving me gooseberrying along in their wake. Jamie up ahead, giving her all his best lines — Christ, I hate to think — and she hee-hawing like the front row at the Comedy Store.

Fuck it, I remember Cheryl when she was mysterious, an enigma to be solved, like a Nazi code. And what can she be laughing at? Jamie Munslow is as funny as a leaky heart valve.

'So tell me some of your best lines,' I ask him the next time it falls to us to walk together, Cheryl in front, scouting for the turning to Yech (this walk has gone on plenty long enough). 'Stuff that you've found particularly effective with the opposite species.'

Jamie gives me a stocking-mask stare. He can't tell if I'm taking the piss.

'Doesn't really work like that,' he replies, his gaze now returned to the happy sight of Cheryl's arse, doing its regular uppy-downy, arsy thing.

'Just one memorable sound bite.'

We walk on in silence for a bit, as he dredges his brain for a sparkling example of the old rapier-like wordplay.

'Because with me,' I continue, 'I find that death can actually be quite helpful in getting an evening going with a swing. Bringing up the subject of mortality.'

Another armed robber glare. 'Sounds more like a passion-killer.'

'Not at all. A quick excursion round the theme of extinction — in the right circumstances — in the right hands — if you set up the right train of thought — you'd be amazed how fast it can have them struggling out of their skimpy white knick-knocks.'

Good grief. He's laughing. Not a pretty sight. He looks almost ashamed to be caught at it. His is a face better suited to saying things like, Clive's position in derivatives may get a bit bumpy further down the line.

'Well, that's a good one,' he chortles. 'Death in the abstract? Or stuff about illnesses and hospices?'

But up ahead, something's happened. Cheryl has frozen to the path. Her elbows are up. Her hands are at her face. She's staring at the ground in horror. She's breathing oddly, fighting to get a purchase on her lungs. By the time she manages to actually scream, I'm at her side, one manly arm round her shoulder, the other free to deal with . . . whatever it is. Blubber-boy, gratifyingly — immensely gratifyingly — is rooted to the spot in confusion.

'Hey, hey. It's OK. What is it?'

She points off into the field, trembling and beginning to cry.

'Snake,' she sobs. 'Big brown snake.' A shuddery convulsion. 'I almost stepped on it.'

And now she is heaving with tears and fright and I put both arms round her and make reassuring noises. 'It's OK, it's fine. It's gone away. It was much more frightened of you. It was probably asleep on the path. They almost never bite. It's fine now. Really. He's gone. Everything's OK. You're fine. You're safe.' Her breast is squashed against my chest. I can smell her hair, her perfume. God, I've missed the way our bodies . . . fit. God bless you, Mr Snake.

She looks up at me, the huge flat face shattered by trauma. 'Charlie, it was horrible.' She shivers a couple of times. 'Mon-strous, ugly . . .' Her words trail off. She roars a revolted yuucchh! A sound not dissimilar to the name of our own sleepy village. Slowly, she regains her composure. I release her, and she starts fishing about for tissues. 'Sorry,' she mumbles. 'Sorry to be such a girl about it.'

Jamie breaks the magic spell. 'You OK, Cheryl?' he enquires.

'Yes. Sorry. Fine now. God, I hate snakes.'

When we march back, it's three abreast all the way, clapping and talking in loud voices to announce our presence to any further serpents who may be lying asleep across our route.

6

Cheryl is out of sorts for the rest of the day. Every now and again she drifts off into a private silence – reliving this latest, or some past horror – returning to the present with an actual physical shudder that I must say I find strangely exciting.

But Jamie has blown it. By his complete failure to be the knight in shining armour at the moment of maximum peril, we all know that he's brought subtle disgrace upon himself. The mood around him has changed. Metaphorically, I enjoy thinking to myself, he's cacked his pants.

Dinner is a long, unfocused affair that takes Cheryl an age to prepare. I know this mood of hers. It's the one that says, please just ignore me. Leave me be, to cook or sketch or clean or poke around in the garden or whatever. (Assume Swedish accent at this point) I vont to be alone. So for long periods, Jamie and I are left with each other on the terrace, interrupted only by his repeated visitations to the kitchen with offers of help, all declined.

Life becomes marginally more comfortable when I discover a bottle of Cheryl's dad's Famous Grouse and dispense us a couple of gentlemen's measures. Jamie then becomes discursive, embarking on a long soliloquy about European financial harmonisation. But I find I prefer listening to the howling of a dog from a distant farmyard, and the way another dog across the valley appears to be answering. Bats wheel. Jamie burbles on. The dogs duet. The funny burping noise starts up from the direction of the river, which Cheryl once alleged was frogs. I am oddly happy.

When the food finally appears, it's gone dark and we are weak with hunger. I can positively identify chicken, potato and onions, but after that it's largely guesswork. We both make approving noises, though perhaps we are a little underspecific in our praise. Jamie kicks off with, 'This is very good. Very, very good.' I manage, 'It's a sort of French country stew, is it?' to which Cheryl replies a touch sharply, 'Sort of.' Almost certainly, I will later discover we have been wolfing a regional classic, involving the painstaking reduction of several highly complex sauces and stocks. But for now, it's mostly just the sound of people chewing. And the dogs.

'Bloody good,' says Jamie after a particularly long-extended piece of canine recitative.

'Mmm,' I add enthusiastically. 'I love chicken.'

Encouraged by these good notices, Cheryl produces a dessert, a tragic, leaden affair involving apricots, custard, pie crust and a liqueur, possibly schnapps. No one can finish it.

'I can't,' says Jamie. 'That first course finished me off.'

'I don't seem to have any more room,' I add, only a tad more diplomatically.

'Pastry is my weakness,' she confesses enigmatically.

A huge moth flies into Cheryl's face, mistaking it for a small airstrip or some such. It hangs, flapping on a strand of hair across her forehead and for a split second, she looks as though she might panic. But then she brushes it away without a murmur.

We sit under the stars for a while, but the conversation has been crushed under the weight of everything that's not being said. That and the pudding.

Eventually Jamie rises, declaring, 'Leave the washing-up. I'll do it first thing in the morning. I'm up early to see a man about a golf course in Toulouse.' He offers Cheryl a chaste good night kiss, nods at me, and vanishes into the blackness of the house.

We sit for a long time, candles flickering in the warm French night. For some reason, I'm scared to speak, as if whatever I say will come out all trite and pointless. Cheryl has put her feet up on Jamie's vacated chair and is gazing at the orange moon. An odd mood is coming off her, a kind of calm disquiet, a serene unease.

'Charlie,' she says in a soft voice, 'would you say that Jamie was the competitive type?'

'Don't know, really. Why do you ask?' What the fuck is it now?

'Well, boys always know about other boys, don't they? They can read them better than girls can.'

'Can they?' The hardball handshake. The strutting around the terrace on the mobile. The cacked-trousers body language after he fatally missed his moment. 'Yes, maybe he is a touch on the competitive side. Why?'

'Just wondering.' She rises silently and floats towards me in the gloom, like an owl on final approach to a fieldmouse. 'Night night. Thanks for rescuing me from that filthy snake.' And with a warm, nonlingering kiss on the lips, she is gone.

I pour myself a nightcap from the Famous Grouse bottle and settle back to watch the stars. It's a spectacularly clear night. They're all out there: Pegasus, the Plough, Cassiopeia. If I turn my head sideways, through my peripheral vision I can make out a ghostly white path across the sky, that elusive view of our own celestial doughnut of stars, the Milky Way galaxy.

For a few moments, I try thinking about the strange and violent creature who has driven me to this spot. But now that he is so many miles away, Lispy Luke seems ridiculous to me, barely more than a cartoon character. And how about Kate? Twitchy, sexy Kate. Somehow she doesn't feel like a living, breathing human either. My brain is filled, overwhelmed, perhaps even a little stupefied, by Cheryl. By her physical reality. I can still feel the impression the side of her nose made against mine when we pecked just now.

Filthy snake, she said. Just which filthy snake could she be talking about?

7

The following morning is an idyll.

Jamie has been as good as his word, and has fucked off to Toulouse after leaving the kitchen spotless. I didn't hear him leave, so deep was my sleep. I couldn't even tell you why I woke up. After ten hours' solid shut-eye, maybe the brain just protests: hey, come on, man, throw some stuff at me.

When I step on to the blazing terrace, I see Cheryl has already got the paint set out, and is embarking on another attempt to solve the age-old conundrum of how to do justice to the rooftops of Yech.

'I'm not a very good watercolourist,' she once said to me, on this same spot, with this same subject in her gunsights. 'But I am dogged.'

I settle on to a nearby sun-lounger with my laptop to contemplate a more recent problem. I write:

Ideas for Erica

1.

Hmm. What was it Peter Marcus said? Stare at some clouds and be fertile. Right then.

Cheryl looks wonderful this morning in her painterly trousers and baggy white shirt. She's got her feet up on the low wall overlooking Yech, with the pad across her knees. As I gaze at her over the lid of my laptop I'm seeing her in profile, the angle at which you can never quite imagine what a large, flat area the front of her face will turn out to contain. Sorry, let's think . . .

1. Erica Up Close and Personal With . . . A series of face-to-face confrontations with some of the most fascinating figures of our era. From Boy George to George (some other George). They let her into their lovely homes and show her their stuff. This hasn't the remotest chance of getting commissioned, but the silly cow will like seeing it on the raft. Or is it *in* the raft? Never mind.

2.

Cheryl has particularly fine feet, I always thought. Most people's feet are a pretty scary spectacle, truth be told. Either they're all mashed up and dead-looking: car-wreck feet. Or else, they're the scabby and mutant type, with alarming livid patches. And hairs. Cheryl's, which are currently parked so elegantly up on the terrace wall, are simply an inspiration. I used to tell her, darling, your feet are a joy to behold. And to think, they've been together for years. Sorry . . .

2. Erica Birkendale's Stars In Their Shoes ... Erica hosts the quiz where celebrities let their feet do the talking. All we see of the mystery guest is his/her feet as they go about their daily business. A celebrity panel (usual suspects) attempt to guess their owner's identity from the clues on the ground ... carpets, other shoes, small dogs, etc. (Footwear manufacturer to sponsor?) Fuck it, worse ideas have got on the telly.

3. What's the Worst Idea You've Ever Had? ... Erica Birkendale presents the series where members of the public – and big-name stars – recount and redeem their personal disasters. From DIY to romance, from the workplace to ... some other place.

'Charles?'

'Yes.' It's Charles again this morning I see, not Charlie.

'What would you call the colour of the roof next to the roof of the *boulangerie*?'

'Hmm.'

'A blacky-brown? Or a browny-black? I find it helps to put it into words sometimes.'

'I'd say . . .' I haven't a fucking clue. 'I'd say . . . actually, isn't there a note of purple in there too?'

She looks at me for a moment – as if I may or may not be an imbecile; she's thinking about it – and then again at the roof in question. Then she dips her brush in the jar of water, waggles it in a pigment and resumes without a word.

4. Erica's True Colours ... Erica hosts the awkward dilemmas show where members of the public have to predict how well-known celebrities (as opposed to unknown celebrities) would react in a crisis. Then we see whether they're right, as we play the film of the specially staged crisis we put them through.

Come on now, respect. Four top ideas for the raft already, and it's not even lunchtime.

8

We were having such a lovely time, Cheryl and I, loafing around the terrace; she painting, I having one brilliant – OK, crap – idea after another; she occasionally asking what colour some feature of the landscape was, I now and again enquiring if she could think of another phrase for 'big-name celebrities'. It was quite like old times, the two of us rubbing along side by side, doing our separate things, but together.

It was The Way We Were.

In the past at times like these, I used to play a game with Cheryl. Actually, it would be more correct to say that I used to play a game involving Cheryl, because she was always dreamily unaware of taking part. The object was to plant a tune in her head by whistling it around her (despite the widely held notion that women don't really whistle). Two or three minutes might go by, sometimes five or ten. And then the wonderful moment, as she put her lips together and – concentrating hard on some difficult detail of her watercolour, the sign on the *boulangerie* or the petrol pump – out would come 'Some Enchanted Evening' or the overture to *The Marriage of Figaro* or that one by Moby.

So this afternoon, because I can't resist it, idly I whistle scraps of 'The Way We Were' ('mishty warder-coloured maaaaaaaam-riche').

In the past too, at times like these, OK, well . . . once;

once when we were out here, she painting, I with my nose in a book, we both looked up at the same moment, with the same thought. It must have been the same thought because when I put my book down, walked over to her chair and offered her my hand, she gently put her brush in its jar, her pad on the warm yellow tiles, and accepted it.

I can't say for certain that the next hour was the happiest in my life, but it must have been right up there with the contenders.

'The Way We Were' thing didn't quite work out today. Because when she did start whistling a tune, it was from *South Pacific*. The one that goes, 'I'm Gonna Wash That Man Right Outa My Hair'.

Anyhow, the idyll begins to crack when I hear the sound of Jamie's car coming up the pitted track. And it shatters completely when the ugly great oaf comes bounding on to the terrace, waving a bunch of flowers. He's dressed in a beautifully cut lightweight suit, its shade of pale blue dangerously close to Ice Cream Salesman. However – sickeningly – even I have to admit that it's gorgeous.

'How lovely,' squeals Cheryl. (What is it about women and flowers?) 'I'll put them in water and try to paint them.'

'Good meeting?' I ask, trying to sound friendly.

'Bloody good. Building a golf course has some really interesting tax issues around it. The guy I saw this morning is doing twenty over the next three years. If you've got any spare moolah hanging about, my advice is, stick it into golf. Golf's exploding.'

'It'll do better than in the Cheltenham and Gloucester?'

He doesn't even deign to dignify my query with a reply. Instead he squares up to Cheryl and says, 'So what have you two bunnies been up to while I've been hard at work?'

Unforgivably, she giggles.

'Aha,' he cries. 'More great works of art. Let's see.' She holds up her latest study of the timeless Yech skyline. He plants his feet apart and takes a good serious peer at it. 'That is very good,' he declares, glancing over the terrace to check the details of the original. 'You've got a real flair for this, haven't you?'

A red flood tide is creeping up Cheryl's neck. And I'm thinking, twelve hours ago this guy was the hesitant loser in the smelly trousers. Now he's Mr Fucking Charm, spraying flowers, flattery and financial wisdom all over the place. Where has all this irrepressible confidence suddenly come from?

'I'll just slip out of these office togs,' he says, heading indoors. 'Let me take us all out tonight. My treat. You can be important tax clients.'

A lizard has scrambled up the low wall of the terrace and is blinking at me, as if any second he might speak. Cheryl is doing something funny with her hair, twirling a piece round in her fingers with a peculiar expression on her face. Oh Christ.

Don't tell me she fancies him.

9

He's driving us in his rich person's car – Cheryl up front, me stewing in the back – to a chic little village about forty-five minutes away, a restaurant he's heard of whose speciality is seafood, even though we're many miles from the coast. Cheryl disappeared for a couple of hours before we set off, emerging . . . well, dazzling is the only word for it, in a little black dress (earrings and a row of pearls) and enough warm, bare flesh on show, as the Rolling Stones so memorably put it, to make a dead man come.

All the way there, my eyes keep returning to her naked shoulders, which seem to sparkle in the moonlight (I think she may have dusted them with that sparkly stuff). Her perfume is mingling with the car's smell of expensive leather. Jamie is driving with such cool manly brio — really mastering that gear knob — that more than once, I find myself hoping that he'll steer us into a ditch.

In comparison to Yech, Bléaux is Las Vegas. Its main street boasts half a dozen restaurants, in addition to several bars and cafés. Jamie leads us into the one called *Le Crapaud d'argent*.

'It means The Silver Toad,' he tells us as if we didn't know, though annoyingly, I didn't.

'I knew it was the silver something,' I say shirtily.

Proper French waiters, poker-faced old guys in white jackets, busy around us. The menus that Cheryl and I are handed do not feature prices. The place has the deep hush of serious food, and serious money.

'Bill Gates brought his wife here on their honeymoon,' Jamie tells Cheryl. What total bollocks.

'He's especially fond of the table near the windows,' I quip. She doesn't get it.

A grey-haired corpulent fellow, about sixty, looks like a European banker, comes to discuss our order. Jamie talks to him in fluent French, which makes me want to hit him.

'He recommends the lobster this evening,' says Jamie, like we couldn't follow the conversation (the truth: I thought he was tipping the sea bass).

Next up is a fish-faced character who turns out to be the international financier in charge of the wine this evening. A long conversation follows, during which I concentrate on the man's wobbling double chins. I can't bring myself to look at Cheryl, who will no doubt be hoovering up Jamie's every bon mot.

Eventually Jamie announces, 'The sommelier has an '89 Château de Fatseaux.' Something like that, anyway. 'For my money, it's between that and the '92 Hoshe de Poshe de la Gauche. Or if you prefer something jollier, there's a very good white Burgundy on the list.' He's looking at me like I give a shit. 'The '94 Bonne de la Ronne au Coupon.'

'You decide,' Cheryl tells him. Jamie squeezes off another couple of hundred French words and the matter is settled.

I feel like I've gone from a set in front overnight, to two sets to one down, and 5–3 in the fourth, Munslow serving for the match.

'Jamie, this is very sweet of you,' Cheryl gurgles.

'My pleasure,' he says graciously.

'Yeah, thanks.'

Three members of the distinguished banking clan who wait tables here approach with silver salvers. They pause beside each of us and, at an invisible signal, simultaneously lift away the covers in a flourish. Cheryl's hand flies to her mouth. Even Fuck-face can't choke a 'Blimey!'

Claws taped shut, but very much alive, one of the largest lobsters I have ever seen waves its spiny feelers at me from the platter. It's a monster. And so are its two colleagues, currently being displayed to my awe-struck dining companions. White barnacles are encrusted to the creature's massive foreclaws. I wonder how old he is, where he grew up, what adventures he may have had frolicking about the Mediterranean, before so incautiously crossing the threshold of the treacherous pot. I realise I'm gazing at an alien life form. If he can make out any-thing sensible through those peppercorn eyes, it could be that he's gazing right back at me: not his assassin, not even his assassin's paymaster (that's F-face), but certainly a major con-spirator in the present murder plot. I toy with the idea of say-ing, no don't jab him in the back of the head with a screwdriver, or drop him alive in the pan of boiling water, or whatever ghastly method you plan to stiff him with. No, here's what I want you to do: put him in a bucket, and tomorrow I shall drive to the coast, delicately untape his claws and release him into the sea.

'Looks like a beauty,' says Jamie. He nods to his lobster-wrangler. Back goes the lid. He's a gonner.

Cheryl looks vaguely uneasy. But nods anyway. Manages a thin smile. Her lobster vanishes under its silvery dome. It's a massacre out here.

Paul McCartney once said he wouldn't eat anything with a face. I don't go that far, though to my mind it's still in bad taste to eat anything you've been formally introduced to.

In flawless English, I tell my lobster-bearer, 'Do you know, actually I think I'll have the lamb.' Just don't bring the fucking creature through here on a lead beforehand.

10

The lobster was delicious – I tried a bit of Cheryl's – and the lamb was as perfect as any I've ever had. The conversation was *slightly* strained, what with Jamie directing all his remarks at Cheryl, and Cheryl going all girly, and playing with her hair and working her eyelashes, and me getting a bit pissed and ratty on the Château Whateverthefuckitwas. To his credit, though, without a whimper, Blubber-features dropped a platinum credit card on what must have been a whopper of a bill and drove us back for late night brandies on the terrace.

Cheryl and Jamie have pushed their chairs close together. With their feet up on the low wall, they're gazing out contemplatively at the glittering spectacle that is Yech by night, murmuring in low voices. I sit on the wall itself, feeling distinctly spare-partish.

Cheryl's head is sort of drooping towards Jamie's shoulder. It won't make it, not unless she extends her neck by about nine inches, or he relocates his upper body leftwards by about the same distance, but you get the idea. There's a hideous magnetism at work here.

I should just go off to bed and leave them to it, except I can't quite bring myself to. The alternative is to haunt the terrace like a bad smell and I can't bear that idea either. I guess I could just roll gently off the edge, like a scuba-diver from the side of a boat, crashing a couple of hundred feet down the hillside into the outskirts of Yech. That should help put a dampener on the evening.

'Gosh, this is lovely,' says Cheryl dreamily.

'Almost perfect,' replies B-features with a rather pointed glance in my direction.

'Do you know anything about astronomy?' she asks softly, the head now at an almost impossible angle.

'I know a star when I see one,' he says throatily. 'And I see one now.'

She breathes out heavily through her nose. I drain my brandy balloon. But even in the face of this sick-making love-talk, still I cannot rise and take my leave. I'm paralysed.

And now he throws a baboon-like arm round her shoulder. She rests her head on the back of it.

For Christ's sake, get up and go to bed! Don't put yourself through another second of this torture. Where's your self-respect, man?

'Are you superstitious?' he asks her.

'Why?'

'I just saw a shooting star. So I made a wish.'

'What was it?'

'If I tell you, it won't come true. And I very much want it to come true, Cheryl.'

'Do you?'

'Very much.'

'I've made a wish too, Jamie.'

'Really?'

'Want to hear it?'

'Not if it won't come true.'

'It's OK, I'll whisper.'

And she puts her mouth very close to his ear, and now they're both laughing softly. Jamie shoots me another glance. And somehow I know Cheryl has said, I wish Charles would bugger off to bed.

When I stand up, my legs feel a bit wobbly. 'Well, good night, you two,' I manage. You two snakes in the grass.

'Night, Charles,' they echo, without taking their eyes off the sky.

I stomp into the house and find myself in the kitchen. The brandy bottle stands half-full on the long wooden table. I unscrew the top and take a few deep slugs. Then a few more. Then a couple more just to be sure. By the time I put it down, things don't seem nearly as terrible. And when my head hits the pillow – their whispers and sniggers still carrying on the warm night air in through my open bedroom window – I feel almost nothing at all.

My first conscious thought is: someone's trying to break into the house. It's a rhythmical thumping, like a burglar attempting to force a door. I press the Indiglo button on my watch. Four fifteen a.m. I lift myself on to one elbow and my head swoons. It feels like I've been beaten up. I train my attention away from the urgent complaints of my own body – pain, thirst, non-specific generalised dread – and back on to the creaking, thumping. Creak-thump. Creak-thump. And now, creak-thump-*moan*. Suddenly it's all too obvious what I'm hearing. My heart sinks. A fist of anger punches its way out through my chest. I realise that my mouth has assumed an odd shape. I shut my eyes and a single shivering sob passes through me.

In counterpoint to the percussion of thumping and the woodwind of creaking, a string section has joined the concerto: Cheryl's sawing little cries, quiet at first, but growing steadily louder, and then deeper, until horrifyingly, they become full-throated roars of almost blood-curdling intensity.

And then all is silent.

11

'Good morning, ladies and gentlemen. First Officer Simon Beamish here. I'd like to take this opportunity to welcome you on board our service to London's Heathrow Airport this morning. No delays have been advised to us by French air traffic control, so we should be arriving on schedule, at one p.m. London time. The cabin crew will shortly be serving you with a light snack, and it's our pleasure to be able to offer you a selection of drinks from the bar with our compliments. Once again may I thank you for choosing to travel with us today, and may I strongly suggest that if you have recently suffered some humiliation or heartbreak, you get stuck into the miniatures as fast as decently possible.'

Tonic fizzes, ice cubes crackle. Yech recedes over my shoulder at the rate of five hundred miles per hour. I open my free copy of *The Independent* and there under the headline, 'Gangland Says Goodbye to a Legend', is a striking photograph taken at a funeral in West London. A grim-faced collection of mourners are gathered outside a church. Men who, for the most part, look unaccustomed to the wearing of suits. One, I notice, is handcuffed between a pair of prison officers.

At the centre of the shot, supported by several relatives, is a dangerously elderly woman.

There are two people in the picture who I recognise. The first is the legend's widow, 'being comforted' by members of her family. The second stands slightly outside the main group, staring directly at the camera, a shortish, large-headed young man whose hair has been pulled back into a ponytail. Pinned to the lapel of his dark jacket is some sort of badge or brooch. It is in the shape of a fish.

For the hundredth time, my mind's ear treats me to a replay of last night's awful sexual recital. Cheryl's final climactic help-less . . . bellow before it all went quiet.

No, sorry. Give me a lisping homicidal psychopath any day. Anything rather than that.

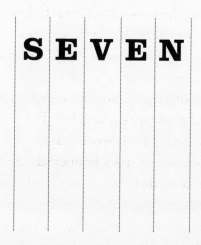

SEVEN

1

You see, on top of everything else, Cheryl was never a screamer.

Well, not with me she wasn't. So all that throaty yelling, all the scarier for being so *deep*, so animal, was like hearing a close friend suddenly speaking a strange new language. Or organ music coming from a kazoo. Or getting into your Renault Twingo and finding that you've actually *taken off* from the North Circular. Or, to be more strictly accurate, watching as a loathed rival gets behind the wheel of your Twingo and makes the fucker *fly*, when the best you could ever manage was 75 before the doors started rattling. Or . . .

Actually, no metaphor is more powerful than the horrible reality. And once again the scandalous trio strike up their unforgettable tune in my head (the truly terrible detail being the way each one of her moans was subtly different to the last).

Creak-thump-cry. Creak-thump-cry-ee. Creak-thump-CRY. Creak-thump-LOUDER CRY. Creak-thump-FULL ON YELL. Creak-thump-THIS IS FUCKING WONDERFUL BUT NOW I'M A BIT FRIGHTENED KIND OF YELL. Creak-thump-NOT FRIGHTENED ANY MORE, EQUAL TO IT, BUT AWE-STRUCK BY OWN SENSES SORT OF YELL. Creak-thump-SIMILAR YELL TO LAST TIME BUT NOW EXTRA DRAMA BECAUSE CRISIS POINT IN VIEW.

Look, I won't go on.

The captain points the plane's nose in the direction of Merry Old LHR and snaps the seat belt signs on. As we descend through the clouds, my mood reduces altitude accordingly. I've left Cheryl joyously shagging the blubberous oaf in Southern France, and I'm returning . . . to what exactly? A mirage of a job (that jolly scene across the sand dunes will turn out to be my leaving-do). A phantasm of a relationship. (What does she mean 'match suspended'? Like, *cancelled*? Or just postponed for a while?) They're the big ones, aren't they, Love and Work, the twin pillars of one's existence?

In addition, I can also anticipate further persecution at the hands of a violent criminal with a penchant for dental jewellery and fish symbolism. Plus more pointless dialogue with an anonymous phone-caller who, from the spectacular richness of the English language, is prepared to employ just three words.

Gloom cloaks me like a fog. As I wait for my bag to make its appearance on the carousel, I call Linds on the mobile.

'How was Glyndebourne?' I enquire.

'Heaven, Charlie.'

'What did you see?' As if I g.a.f.

'*Cosi Fan Tutte*.'

'All Women Are The Same.'

'Who's rattled your cage then?' Whoops. That last bit must have come out a bit . . . bitter.

'Sorry. Been away for the weekend. Still a touch ratty from the flight. Anyway, how's . . .' Oh fuck, what's his name? 'How's himself?'

'Giles is great.'

'And the two of you?'

'I guess you could say we were an item now.'

'You could? Really? What, officially?'

'I guess so.'

A long way away, I spot my bag rising out of the shoot and tumbling helplessly on to the conveyor belt. For some reason, I find this sight peculiarly annoying.

'What qualifies it as an item, then? I mean, what are the various hurdles it has to clear, the criteria it has to satisfy, before one can make that claim? That one is an item. Part of an item.'

She sighs. 'Charlie, do you want to give me another call when you're in a better mood?'

'No, honestly. I'm very interested in this. I mean, you weren't an item when we last spoke, were you? But now you are. You're not an item after one . . . one *shag*, so is one an item after two shags? Or three? Or is it something else? Am I missing something here?'

She hangs up. The woman waiting alongside shoots me a funny look. And now my mobile bleeps. The posh lady who lives in my phone tells me I have three new messages. She outlines my main menu options. I elect to listen.

It's a long silence. In the background, a radio plays. ' . . . so, Clement, it was an incorrect challenge. You gain another point and you have thirty-four seconds on Things I Like to do in Bed, starting now . . .' Loopy Loo checking in.

Second message is from Geraldine. Inviting me round for dinner last night. 'Rose is cooking, and we thought we wouldn't bother with conversation, we'd just have party games – charades and In the Manner of the Word, and stuff.' *Fuck*, how exquisitely infuriating. How much better to have spent the evening with R. and G. eating, laughing, *playing*, than trailing round with Cheryl and that tosser in a funk of sexual jealousy and general mortification of the soul.

'Third new message. Message received today, at 9.05 a.m.,' says the posh lady. 'Charlth,' begins the familiar voice. 'Where have you been? You're not hiding from me, are you, cunty? Becauth you know what they thay, don't you? You can run, Charlth, but you can't hide. Oh, and by the way, I've put a little prethent through your letter bokth. Hope you like it. Be theeing you, cunty.'

'To hear the message again, press one,' says the posh lady. 'To save the message, press two. To delete the message, press three. To come round to my place, where we can send out for a takeaway, watch a video, and have vigorous sex, press four.'

2

What little present has he put through my letter bokth? Has he sent something in the post? Or has the crazy fucker been into the building, up in the lift, has he peered through the flap into my hallway? Seen my umbrellas and tennis rackets, my books . . . the stuff of my life. I can imagine his ice-blue eyes framed in the slot, as he takes in the empty flat. A chill runs through me. What if I'd been at home? Would I have had the nerve to pretend not to have noticed him squatting there? To have sauntered into the bathroom for a minute, wandered back through the hall, to have suddenly produced the bottle of bleach from behind my back and aimed it directly through the letterbox into those inhuman eyeballs. To have drawn satisfaction from the terrible howls of anguish on the other side of my safely locked door. Would I?

Don't make me laugh.

I eddy with the crowd into the arrivals hall, that febrile locus of travel anxiety. Expectant rows of faces line the railings, craning for a glimpse of loved ones coming through From The Other Side. A girl with flowers and helium balloons awaits a lover. A woman and child, a daddy. Here is a pair of white-haired old fuckers with his 'n' hers expressions of infinite suffering (look, there she is, the daughter back from Canada with the bearded fiancé: 'Mum, this is Earl'). And everywhere, drivers holding up their signs: hungover minicab drivers with their hopeful Biro-scrawled scraps of cardboard; liveried chauffeurs, their pick-ups advertised in white plastic lettering against black, like the greetings board in the lobby of some regional hotel ('The Ramada Inn welcomes . . . The Monday Club').

Just for a second, just for a sickening, heart-stopping moment, as I wheel my bag down the arcade of faces, faces to left and right, for one horrible, bowel-loosening instant, I clock *his* face. Luke Holderness. Here in the throng of those who wait. A flash of sheen off the big, bony head, hair pulled back from the rock-like skull.

How the fuck did he find out that I'd be on this flight? Who *knew*?

He's ducked behind the crowds lining the railings. I catch a glimpse of trench coat moving parallel with me towards the place where the railings run out. Where, if no one's come to meet you, if no friend or relative or protector has come to cover you in smiles, hugs, kisses; to scoop you up, take you away from all this, to deliver you . . .

Where, if there's no one here for you, cunty, you're on your own.

Where it'll just be him and me.

And whatever's under that trench coat.

There have been other moments in my life like this, moments of Maximum Shit, when it's possible to state with absolute certainty that very shortly, something truly horrible will happen. Like when I was best man at Andy Fineman's wedding, and the father of the bride got up and delivered an effortlessly brilliant speech. It was funny and touching, and perfectly pitched, and people in the audience were wiping away tears of laughter. And I'm sitting there, dying inside, because for one, I hate speaking in public; two, in my pocket I have my own speech which I just know is going to be crap by comparison; and three, I'm on next. So the bride's father – confident and assured, the old bastard – he's riding warm waves of big laughter, my heart is hammering in its cage, and then I hear him use the words '. . . so in conclusion . . .' For the first time in my life, I know why people talk about wishing that the ground would swallow them up. The terrible, gut-wrenching, irresistible feeling of *not wanting to be here* meeting the immovable fact of *you fucking are here, matey.* The seconds tick, the moment draws nearer, until finally – there's no escape – I must stand up, my legs feel weak, I take a deep breath, oh fuck it then, here we go . . . (and actually, on this occasion, it isn't so bad. I make an important discovery: at public events, when people have taken a drink, they *want* to laugh. If you've got a half-decent script, they'll generally chuckle).

Here and now in the arrivals hall, Holderness only yards away (it's obvious where he must have hidden himself, behind a particularly large welcoming party; oh Christ, that ghastly tooth round his neck, those arctic eyes), I'm feeling that same nauseating fear. The one that says, OK, now you really cannot take a view. Or worry about it later. Or indulge in a bit of masterly inactivity on the grounds that the problem might just . . . fucking evaporate. Now you must do something . . . because if you don't, what will follow will definitely be awful.

The moment of Maximum Shit is at hand.

I've slowed down. I can feel a trolley bumping into the backs of my ankles. To my left and right, as I am funnelled towards my fate, drivers hold up their signs. DEXTER. TOWERHOUSE PLC. MRS VAN GELDER. PORTEOUS. DR MONTAGUE. TEXAS INSTRUMENTS. CRETIKOS. THOROGOOD. DAVE WARREN. SHELL OIL.

Oh, to be the man from Shell Oil right now. Or respectable, unruffled Dr Montague. Fuck it, at this point I'd pay to swap places with Mrs Van Gelder.

I veer right, to the opposite railing. Walk up to a tall, wide man in a dark suit, about sixty, grey hair, grey moustache. Holding up a piece of paper with 'GOUGH' printed on it.

'Car for Gough?' I ask, trying hard to keep the pleasant expression plastered on my face.

His features light up. 'Blimey, you're early. I only just got here.'

I slide the bag under the rail and follow it. 'Can we just . . . leave straight away, do you think?'

'Follow me.' And we're off across the concourse. Despite a limp, he's setting an urgent, things-to-do pace. 'Your flight must have got in ahead of schedule. Or your bag came off quick.'

'Yeah.' I daren't look back.

'Good one, was it?'

'Oh, you know.'

'Get a chance to watch any of the movies?'

'Er, not really.'

'Sleeping, was you?'

'Reading.'

'Ah.' That seems to shut him up for a bit.

As the lift doors finally close behind us, I make myself turn and stare out. A long way away, in the peculiar neon-lit darkness of the arrivals hall, a small figure in a pale trench coat stands by a pillar.

I wouldn't absolutely swear it was Lisping Luke Holderness. But neither would I swear that it wasn't.

3

It's an old brown Bentley, with one of those numberplates that starts with three letters — that old. But lovingly cared for by the look of the high shine on the bodywork. The boot swallows up my luggage — 'You travel very light' — and we're away. Down the ramps, through the roundabouts, into the Heathrow tunnel, and on to the spur road that leads to the M4 and Central London. The walnut veneer gleams, the interior smells of soft, warm leather. Our progress is sedate, but somehow incredibly reassuring.

'Beautiful car,' I comment in an effort to woo my rescuer.

'Lovely, isn't she? They don't make them like this any more.'

'I bet they don't.'

'Nearly thirty years old, she is now.'

'Is it really?' Can't bring myself to say 'she'. 'I know thirty-year-old *people* who are in worse nick than this.' He laughs, gratified by my silver-tongued flattery. 'Bet it sucks up the petrol.'

'Something ferocious.'

'And parts must be expensive.' The sum total of my automotive knowledge.

'The garage charges like a wounded bull. I do most of the running repairs and maintenance myself.'

'Really?' How fascinating.

'Course, there are bits you have to leave to the professionals.'

'Of course.'

'Cylinders and that.'

'Drive shaft.' Just a long shot.

He says hmm, and goes quiet for a bit. We listen to the engine's silky thrum. I realise I love being driven in this car.

'You drive yourself?' he asks eventually.

'I *can* drive.'

'How did you find the driving over there, then?' Alarm bell.

'The driving.' Remind me, *who* am I supposed to be in this scene again?

'What are they like, behind the wheel? Because you hear so many different stories.'

'Well, that's just it, really. You can't generalise. Some are a bit potty. And some are very sensible.' Life is richly complex, don't you find?

He gives a driverly shrug. The one that says, yep, we see 'em all out here on the road, us drivers. All sorts. Truly we do.

And I'm wondering: who will this Gough I'm playing the part of turn out to be? Despite the luxurious eccentricity of the vehicle (it's a wedding car, isn't it, the pride of the minicab fleet) Gough will be in Sales or Marketing, oven chips, or office supplies. Or IT support – that's another big one. We'll be making for some ghastly building off the North Circular Road. Swing doors giving on to a nasty lobby with blue carpeting and spongy sofas. The girl on the switchboard will offer Gough a cup of coffee while he's waiting. Reg is still in his meeting, he shouldn't be too long, though. Milk and sugar?

'Like to hear some music?' asks the big man.

'Sure.'

I'm expecting Classic FM, or perhaps Radio Two. But instead he fires up a CD: love songs by Elvis Presley. And then – to the accompaniment of 'Are You Lonesome Tonight', which sounds through these lovely clear speakers, as I sink into the back seat, the sun starting to stream through the grey clouds, just fucking immaculate – he does a very surprising thing. At the junction with the M4, instead of heading where everyone's heading, right towards Central London, we bear left.

M4 West.

When we got into town, when the mistake became obvious, I was going to say: did you say Gough? Oh Christ, I think there's been the most awful mix-up. I'm *Bough*. With a B. They look alike, don't they? Well, they can do when you've come off a flight and you haven't got the right specs on. Look, I'm terribly sorry. Can I write you a cheque?

But now, as we head away from the capital – 'Bristol 91 Miles' – a curious sense of happy paralysis comes over me. Is it the fact that our present course setting is taking me away from my tormentors? Or is it the pleasure of riding in this deliciously big car – I feel like a fucking Royal – this safe, solid, wide man at the controls. Or is it the Elvis?

'I adore Elvis,' I say pathetically after 'Love Me Tender'.

'Did you ever see him live? No, you can't have. You're too young.'

'Did you?'

'I did. In Las Vegas, on our honeymoon, not long before he died. He was very overweight, he wore those high collars to hide all the chins . . .'

'I heard they used to have to pad his knee. So when he dropped on to it for the big finish, it wouldn't shatter. What was he like? When you saw him?'

The M4 corridor glides past. In the rear-view mirror, as I observe my saviour choosing his words, I have the distinct impression that his eyes are moistening. 'He was wonderful, Alistair. Bloody wonderful.'

Hmm.

Alistair Gough. I guess there are worse names to be saddled with.

4

I'm guessing Bristol. Or somewhere in Wiltshire. But then we hit the M5 and begin heading seriously south-west. I suppose I could still just about manage to contrive some lousy excuse: I knew there must have been a mistake when we went past that last junction. What an extraordinary coincidence. That there should have been an Alistair Gough and an Alistair Bough, both returning to the same part of the country on the same day.

But perhaps we have passed a point of no return. Perhaps for a while, I shall just have to go with it. Whatever *it* turns out to be.

His mobile rings. It looks ridiculously small in his great, fat paw. I have a funny feeling that I know who this will be.

'Sorry?' he says. 'Sorry? Alistair Gough, did you say?' He passes the phone over his shoulder. 'For you. Shocking line.'

Through the crackle I can make out the sound effects of a busy airport terminal. 'Hello?'

A grown-up no-nonsense voice cuts through the mush. 'This is Alistair Gough speaking. Are you the driver who's supposed to be picking me up at Heathrow today?'

'Hi!' Like he's a long-lost friend. 'How are you?'

'Actually, I'm wondering where you've got to. I've been waiting here for over an hour. I've been paging you. Are you actually *in* the airport?'

'I'm sorry, I'm not. *Circumstances*,' I add enigmatically.

'You've been held up.'

'I regret to say so.'

'But you're on your way.' A statement of fact.

'Oh yes. Definitely.'

'So when can I expect you?' Push-ee.

'Not for a while, I'm afraid.'

'What's your recommendation? Should I make my own way there?'

'I couldn't honestly recommend that.'

'How much longer will you be?' I'm beginning to dislike this bloke.

'Another one. One and a half at the most? Maybe two at the most?'

I hear him take a deep breath. There's a long pause, and then a heavy sigh. It's fatigue combined with fury, plus a side order of utter helplessness. 'Shall we make it five thirty, then, at the meeting point in the arrivals hall?'

'Six? Just to be on the safe side?'

'Six then.' Sulky. Defeated.

'One thing: let me give you a different mobile number to call from now on, if you need to.' My own number. 'Thanks for phoning,' I chirp merrily when he's copied it down.

He hangs up without a word.

I hand the phone back to my driver. 'Sorry about that,' I tell him. I make a noise that sounds like *tsk*. 'Seems they can find you just about anywhere these days.' Bloody old *they*, with their pesky questions. He watches in the rear-view as I shake my head in wonderment at what a small and irksome world it is now. 'What do you get to the gallon then?' I throw my arm expansively along the top of the back seat. 'What's the best you can get out of . . . out of *her*?'

'Varies. In town, it's a joke, frankly. On a long run like this, ooh, let's think . . .'

We pass a sign that reads 'WELCOME TO DEVON'. I feel ridiculously . . . well, I'm sorry, the word is *content*.

5

His mobile rings again. This time he does a lot of listening, throwing in the occasional 'yup' and 'righto'.

When he hangs up, he says, 'That was HQ. Bad news, I'm afraid. Toby's been delayed — he didn't say why — says he won't be able to get down until tomorrow now. But he's left a number where you can reach him. And that you're to make yourself at home.'

'I see. Thank you.'

'You haven't met Toby's father, Mr Gulliver?'

'I can't say I have.' True. I can't say I have.

'A fine man. A very fine man, I think you'll find, Alistair. I had the pleasure of serving under him in Her Majesty's Armed Forces.'

'Really?'

'Never had a better commanding officer than Digby Gulliver. It wasn't just me, all his men loved him.'

'Really?'

'In some ways, he was almost too introverted to be a CO. Brooding, you'd call him. And it was no secret that he liked a few whiskies of an evening. Could have a dreadful temper on him the next day too. But it was the essential decency of the man. It shone through. Oddly, you know, I think people wanted to protect him.'

I can't say 'really' again, can I? I go with, 'I see.'

The big man nods, drifts into some sort of private reverie. Out of the window, Devon rolls by to an Elvis soundtrack. The same CD again, *Elvis from The Heart*. His greatest love songs, digitally remastered.

'Very good of you to have picked me up like this,' I say after a couple more tracks. 'I could have taken the train.'

'No trouble. I had nothing else on today. And besides, Digby insisted.'

'He did?'

'He said to me, Victor, Alistair is an old college friend of my son's. He's been out of the country for five years and we can't have him fighting the bloody railways on his first day back.'

'Well, I certainly appreciate it. Five years . . . *is* quite a long time.'

'Did you miss home at all? Or was you able to shoot back for the odd break? Christmas and that. You can't beat a British Christmas, can you?'

'I've never been fond of Christmas, to be honest. All that false cheer. And Noel Edmonds all over the telly.'

'Oh, they've got rid of him.'

'Really? That's wonderful.'

'Yeah. It's all that bird with the big gob now. What's her name?'

'Angela Rippon?'

'Carol Something. It'll come to me.'

My driver goes quiet for a few miles; turns on to a road signed for Buckfastleigh and Plymouth. 'Elvis again?' he suggests.

'Fine by me.'

We listen all the way through 'The Wonder of You', 'I Just Can't Help Believing' and 'Always on My Mind' before I can bring myself to ask.

'Victor . . . ?'

'Vic, please.'

'Vic? How's old Toby keeping these days?' I ask. 'Not having seen him for a while,' I add unnecessarily.

'We've hardly seen much of him ourselves, to be honest. That practice of his keeps him pretty busy.'

'I see.'

Vic seems unwilling to offer me any more. On a whim, I ask, 'And Toby's mother . . . ?'

'What about her?' Whoops. Careful now.

'How . . . how is she?'

Vic takes a deep breath. And with a horrifying certainty, I know, I just know, he is going to say, dead. Dead these last twenty years. And if you didn't know that, you're no friend of Toby Gulliver's, so just who the hell are you, matey?

But he doesn't. Instead, in a quiet voice, he says, 'Maybe Toby never mentioned it. Celia finally left Digby.'

'Oh. I'm sorry to hear it.'

Vic shakes his head sadly in the rear-view. 'It's broken his spirit, truth be told.' And then he adds with unexpected venom, 'Heartless fucking bitch.'

'Sorry. I had no idea.'

'Pardon my French.'

'Not at all. Very . . . very distressing for everyone, I imagine.'

Vic snorts. His huge knuckles are very white against the Bentley's broad steering wheel.

6

It's Totnes.

And, oddly, like Charles Ryder in *Brideshead Revisited*, I have been here before. Though this was hardly the pre-war idyll with teddy bears, strawberries and a friend's willowy sister to fall in love with. This was fifteen years ago. I'd come down in the long summer vacation to stay with a university chum. His parents were away on a field trip in China — botanists, if memory serves — so we spent an agreeable month in their house, smoking draw and getting pissed in the local pubs. Even then, the quaint Devonian town huddling beneath the walls of its ruined Saxon fort was a magnet for all kinds of free spirits. Hippies, healers, students, psychics, mystics, yogics, proto-type crusties, drunks and dope fanciers were drawn by the pleasant summer climate, the Neolithic resonances from nearby Dartmoor, and plentiful supplies of class-B drugs. I remember one evening in a grungy bar with sticky carpets, trying exceptionally hard to seduce a beautiful girl with henna-coloured hair and tattooed ear lobes. After many pints, she sweetly allowed me to kiss her; she said I had a powerful aura — the lager, I think — but ultimately she couldn't be enticed back to Keith's parents' house, pleading she had to be up early for an astral projection workshop. Keith laughed a lot when I told him that. No one in Totnes, he'd scoffed, is *ever* up early for *anything*.

Digby's place turns out to be about three miles out of town, the houses once again giving way to fields and woods. We take a turning between trees, follow a winding road between high hedges, and suddenly, like Brideshead, we are upon it. A lovely old crumbling brown brick villa, covered in wisteria or what-ever you call that stuff when buildings decide to grow a beard. Bouncing towards it through the agreeably overgrown park-land, it's clear that nature has been given a generously free hand here. Between trees, a tractor rusts in a bed of nettles. The corrugated iron roof of one of the outbuildings is falling in. As we pull up, two dogs come streaking towards us through the long grass. Smaller than greyhounds, but built on the same general lines, they seem extravagantly fond of Vic, who greets them like children except, in my experience, you rarely allow children to lick your face in public.

'Alistair, meet Smear and Stain.' The animals crane their pointy faces up at me, and wave their tails enthusiastically.

'Delighted, I'm sure.' I pat. I tousle. I rub throats. All the things dogs are said to take as indicators of well-meaning. 'Unusual names.'

'Daughters of the late Smudge. They're lurchers. Ooh, they like *you*. Come on, let's go and meet the boss.'

The dogs' claws click on the cold flagstones of the hallway. From the chill in the air, from the musty smell, and because I once used to go out with a girl who belonged to this social tribe, I recognise it immediately: down-at-heel-landed-gentry chic. The house will be filled with classy old bits of furniture, scratched and faded to fuckery, every sofa and armchair impregnated with ancient animal hairs. Too big to heat or light effectively, the whole place will be freezing, gloomy and damp. I can picture the winter evenings, the cruel draught spilling through the ill-fitting windows, the spores of mould marching up the curtains. The dinners, at which you need to wear three layers of clothes. Eating off chipped monogrammed china. And the food you never get anywhere else: mulligatawny soup, beef cobbler, a slab of Walls vanilla ice cream with tinned peaches. Afterwards, while you're making small talk in the drawing room, you'll actually see your breath. To make bearable the thought of turning in for the night (think freshly dug grave), you'll need to skull an indecently large amount of brandy. The next morning, you'll wear a scarf and most probably a hat down to breakfast, and later in the day you'll discover that what you thought was a hangover is actually a filthy head cold that will take weeks to clear up.

I follow Vic into a long, dark sitting room, curtains half

drawn against the sunlight. At the far end, almost lost in the gloom, an elderly figure jammed into an armchair is watching the cricket on TV and eating a sandwich. On a side table, there's a glass of whisky. The perfume of cheese and onion mingles unpleasantly with the dust and damp.

'Digby, this is Alistair, Toby's friend.'

He's older than Vic, maybe seventy. Rather portly when he gets to his feet. In scruffy brown corduroy trousers, and one of those pale checked Viyella shirts favoured by male retirees. On top is a V-neck pullover, the colour of chimpanzee sick. A streak of egg yolk decorates the front. Or maybe it's a bird strike. His face is one of the most tragic I've ever seen.

'Digby Gulliver,' he says, pained dark eyes never leaving mine. The hair, what there is of it, is white and lank. Loose sandpapery skin hangs down his face, pooling beneath the spot where a chin might once have held sway. His long, gloomy features remind me of one of those melancholy chessmen they discovered on the Isle of Lewis. Or a melting candle. The long ears, the pendulous lower lip, even the eyes seem to be on the slide, their outer corners joining the general drift south.

'You've obviously met Vic.' A deep voice. Complex, with many notes in it.

Vic grins. 'We had a nice old Elvis session on the way down, didn't we, Alistair?'

'We did, Vic.'

'Vic enjoys his Elvis,' says Digby, like he's announcing a death in the family.

'Uh-huh-*huh*,' sings Vic, straight out of 'Good Luck Charm'. Digby manages a sad smile; he's heard it many times before. I smile too, but I'm thinking, what am I doing here? Who the fuck *are* these people?

Digby flicks his gaze to the TV set. 'Follow the cricket at all?'

'Not really, to be honest.'

'Australia giving us a roasting, as usual. Trescothick's out.' He gazes at me like I'm supposed to know what the fuck he's talking about. 'Big where you've just come from, I imagine?'

'Sorry?'

'Cricket. They're keen on their cricket there?'

'Oh yes. They are quite. That's true, actually.'

A longer look. He blinks a couple of times, and I can feel myself starting to wither.

'You know, you're not at all how I pictured one of Toby's friends,' he says eventually.

'Really? Is that good or bad?' I ask as winningly as I can.

'I was expecting someone more like that boy he brought back from boarding school one summer.'

'Ah.'

'Morose little fellow. From the city, never seen proper countryside before. Can affect some people. The emptiness. Turns them strange. Will you have a drink?'

'That's very kind . . .'

'Get yourself settled in, then report back for cocktails. How's that sound?'

Digby lowers himself back into his armchair. His watery eyes fixate on the big colour telly he's sitting much too close to. He takes a slow, old-man bite of sandwich. I become aware of his huge, hornlike thumbnail; the smell rising off him, part whisky, part onion, part old man's guts – that worrying stew of innards and pipes and God knows what else.

'Come on,' says Vic, grabbing my bag. 'I'll show you to your billet.'

7

The estate is bigger than I thought. I follow the limping figure of Vic through the grounds. We pass a neglected orchard, derelict henhouses, a poisonous-looking lake. My 'billet' turns out to be the left half of a pair of tiny redbrick terraced cottages, set in the middle of a large and rather well-tended vegetable garden, about five minutes' walk from the big house. Inside, there's a sitting room and kitchen on the ground floor, with a bedroom and bathroom up a flight of those cramped, twisty wooden stairs that inevitably spell concussion to anyone over five foot five at some point in the proceedings (late nights and early mornings, favourite). The whole place is simply appointed, to a somewhat more modern design – seventies rather than twenties – than the main house. I note with particular approval a TV set, and a telephone, one of those where you have to put your finger in a hole and actually *dial*. Small collections of paperback books and magazines have been thoughtfully placed in the two main rooms. On romantic weekends away, Linds and I have stayed in nastier places than this where you don't see much change out of a hundred quid a night (incl. cooked breakfast).

I throw my bag on to the bed and walk over to the window (a journey of three steps). I look out across the vegetable garden to fields dotted with sheep. And then to trees. Then hills, featuring further sheep. No haywain, but it's your full-on picture postcard countryside. I look at my watch. It's ten past six on a Monday evening. Suddenly I have a vision of NoCaSoCha at this hour. Fume-choked Haverstock Hill. Me, Rose and Geraldine in Zyplxqnk – sorry, Myxpqlncx – giggling over the Marine Martinis. Emma in her tight trousers. A powerful wave of nostalgia catches me under the port bow. What the fuck *am* I doing here? In the middle of bloody Devon, staring at a hillside of bloody sheep, when I could be in London's fashionable NW1 postal district, drinking, chattering, you know . . . generally *carousing*.

I pick up the bedside phone and call Peter Marcus.

'Charles, have you been thinking brilliant thoughts?'

'Possibly. It's not always easy to tell. I was just checking in, really.'

'Well, you needn't worry, all's well here. Barry's doing a fine job taking over the reins. Have all the time off you need. I wouldn't mind seeing what you've got on paper some time. Could you bear to fax me something I can give to Erica? To show her that we care. By the end of the week, shall we say?'

'Sure, Peter.'

'Thanks, Charles.'

I shouldn't worry, should I? Barry is doing a fine job, is he? I can take all the 'time off' I need, can I?

I look at the mobile again: 6.15. Come on, Gough, you silly fucker, *phone me*.

A knock at the door. Vic, I guess. Come to collect me for more orientation in the ways of curious Digby and his ramshackle old house. I feed myself carefully into the staircase and make it to the front door without serious abrasion.

But it's not Vic. It's Magda.

Or rather a tall, strikingly beautiful young woman who looks so much like her that I gasp audibly.

'Sorry, did I startle you?' she asks.

'No, sorry. You look astonishingly similar to someone I know.'

'Digby asked me to get you on parade for evening drinks.' She hoists a huge smile on to her broad, Slavic features. 'So what sort of high jinks did you and Toby get up to at uni then?'

Uni. She actually said 'uni'. I take a deep breath. Fuck it, here we go again. 'Oh, you know. The usual crazy old uni stuff.'

8

Magda is my new neighbour. She lives in the next-door cottage. Unfortunately, her real name is Trish. She's Digby's housekeeper, although by training, she's keen to tell me, she's really a nutritionist. It's her organic vegetable garden that's currently throbbing so magnificently with tomatoes, cabbages and peas, and all that other stuff one normally only comes across in packets. Trish is an infinitely better advertisement for the benefits of eating well than her employer. Trish, who I just *know* I shall not be able to think of as anything but Magda.

Evening sunlight spills through the trees on to the overgrown path ahead. As we skirt the lake and head up towards the house, a duck calls after us absurdly. I can't help laughing.

'It's ridiculously lovely,' I tell her. You are too.

'We're very lucky here, really.'

'Does Toby get a chance to get back home much?' I've been out of the country for five years. I feel I can ask.

'Mostly just at Christmas. With Frances and the children.'

'What have they told you about me then?' I ask with a mischievous twinkle.

This turns out to be a brilliant question.

Apparently Toby's friend Alistair is a gifted young doctor who, pissed off with the NHS and horrified by the cynical greed he discovered in private practice, upped sticks to the Far East to work with remote tribespeople, delivering babies, setting broken bones, doing other worthy medical shit (I paraphrase). However, as a result of the worsening civil war in the region, and the growing danger to foreign aid workers, several of whom have been beheaded in recent months, Dr Gough has reluctantly returned to the old country to take stock, consider his position, and spend a few days down in Devon with his old mucker from uni, Toby Gulliver.

'You didn't pick up much of a tan,' Trish points out.

'Terribly bad for the skin, too much sun,' I reply authoritatively. 'Very real danger of carcinoma.' See, I knew those hours hunched over the *Home Health Companion* would pay off one day. 'Had to work hard to maintain the pale and interesting look.'

She doesn't honk up at the cheesiness of my line. I realise that I am trying to flirt with her.

We pass the ruins of some sort of overgrown barn, or garage. It's impossible to tell. 'Remarkable place, this,' I comment. 'Delightfully . . . unspoilt.'

She laughs. 'You could put it that way.'

'How long has it been in this state?'

Her face goes rather serious and I instantly know what the answer will be: since Celia fucked off. Leaving big, sad Digby with a hole in his life that no amount of Scotch, cricket, and cheese and onion sandwiches will ever fill.

'It's always been a bit chaotic, to be honest. But things have definitely got worse . . .'

'. . . after Toby's mother . . .' I allow my words to trail away.

She casts her big eyes on me and nods. I feel slightly dizzy.

As we step through the doorway of the big house, I turn off the mobe in my trouser pocket. The voicemail will just have to deal with the real Alistair Gough and his grotesquely ballsed-up travel arrangements.

'England all out for seventy-one. Fucking dismal performance. What'll you have?'

Digby is stooped over the drinks cart in the sitting room, rattling bottles. The curtains are drawn, lamps glow weakly behind their shades. Evening has officially been declared. Trish goes off to prepare his supper.

'Whisky, please.'

'How do you take it?'

'Just by itself, please.'

'No ice or anything?'

'No, thanks.'

'Good man. Can't stand ice myself. Only gets in the way.'

Digby pours the largest glass of Famous Grouse I have ever seen and hands it to me.

'That's . . . that's quite a drink,' I say weakly.

'Only gentlemen's measures served here.' His voice is rich, rising from deep within his chest, an organ chord full of over- and undertones. He picks up his own glass – if anything, even fuller – and carefully clinks it against mine. 'Been a long time since we saw any chums of Toby down here. Cheers.'

I watch fascinated, as the weathered, old-man hand brings the glass to his moist lips. He tips about a third away, like he's putting something powerful down a blocked sink. The sand-papery wattles shake. The subsiding eyeballs take on a slightly crazy lustre.

'Before I forget . . .' He fumbles into the pocket of his deplorable old trousers and produces a scrap of paper. 'Toby's number, where he's gone. He called again. Wants you to give him a bell. Says he doesn't think he can get down here before the weekend now.'

Excellent. 'Oh, shame.'

'You can amuse yourself, though, can you?'

'Oh sure. No problem.'

'There's some good walking. Do you walk?'

'I've been known to walk.' When there isn't a taxi.

'Used to be a great walker in my time. Now I find I've been everywhere. Toby tells me you're a reader.'

'I . . . I do read, yes.'

'Got an interesting library here. Just across the hall. Might like to take a look in there. Bit of a jumble, I'm afraid. Not catalogued or anything, but you'll probably find something.'

He does something vaguely obscene with his mouth and pours another third of the Scotch into it, wincing slightly as it gurgles through the pipe work. He plods across to a sofa – he's slightly bow-legged, I notice – and indicates an armchair for me.

'Toby hardly ever brought anyone home,' he says. 'Never a very gregarious boy. Like his father in that way, really.'

Digby gazes at me mournfully. I feel I have to say something.

'College feels like a long time ago.' Can't quarrel with that.

'Withdrawn sort of a teenager. His mother and I used to worry about him. I wondered at one time if he wasn't going to end up batting for the other side.'

'Ah.'

A look of mild horror appears on his face. 'Although nowadays, of course, none of that matters any more. Live and let live.' He thinks he may have offended me.

'Of course.'

'People's personal business, their own . . . business.'

'Yes.'

'No shame. No longer any stigma.'

'Things have moved on a lot. My girlfriend and I were only talking about it the other evening.'

He looks visibly relieved. His mouth does the thing again, and he administers the final third of the Scotch to the system.

'Toby said you were in the armed forces.'

Digby's up again, treading back to the drinks cart. Is it my imagination, or do I see a path worn in the carpet between the sofa and the booze?

'I was a professional soldier, though never much of a warrior. Missed all the best stuff.'

He dispenses himself another magnificently generous

measure of Famous G.; returns with a photo in a silver frame which he hands to me: Digby as a young man in the uniform of an army officer, leaning against a mantelpiece with a cigarette in his hand. Thinner, taller somehow, but with the same melancholy look about him, the same hot dark eyes in the long pale face.

'Handsome devil, eh?'

And then Magda's head — sorry, *Trish's* — pops round the door.

'Digby, sorry to interrupt. There's a call for you. From an Alistair Gough?'

9

Oh fuck it, then. Call the cops. Lead me off in chains. Do whatever one does to people who impersonate other people at airports. Cast me out from these gently ruined surroundings, this soft world of hills and trees, sheep and dogs (not to mention beautiful housekeeper/nutritionists with amazing Slavic faces). Return me to the jittery, snarling metropolis. To the paranoid horrors of television. To the lisping lunatic who, one way or another, is going to ruin my life.

But Digby says, 'No, *this* is Alistair Gough. Must be for you, Alistair. Take it in the morning room, if you like.'

So I follow Trish across the hall into a long, wood-panelled room overlooking the drive. Back numbers of *Country Life* are heaped on every spare surface. Through the windows, I can see Vic the Wheel playing joyously with Smear and Stain, something touching about the big man frolicking with the pencil-thin dogs.

'Press the button that says Talk.' She smiles. Not a split second of her sashaying exit fails to imprint heavily on both my retinas.

I take a deep breath, and stare hard at the button in question. Then quietly, almost under my breath, I speak a line I think I remember from *Kind Hearts and Coronets*, the lovely old movie in which Alec Guinness plays seven members of the D'Ascoyne family.

'The west wing is Chaucerian, but with none of the concomitant vulgarity.' It's Guinness's marvellously restrained upper-class twang I'm trying to locate; not its depth – I'd never get that – just the general style. I repeat the line to make sure. Then I try one from *The Bridge on the River Kwai*: Guinness as Colonel Nicholson when he sees the detonator cable trailing above the riverbank. 'Oh my God. They're going to blow up the bridge.'

Then I press Talk as advised.

I say, 'Is that Dr Gough?' Fuck, it's come out more like the old twat in *Star Wars*.

'Yes, it is,' he replies. Sounding extremely peaky, and not without cause.

'This is Digby Gulliver. Toby's father.'

'Ah, hello.'

'How was your flight?'

'Fine, thanks. But I don't seem to have made contact with anyone at the airport. It's been hours.'

'I do apologise. I'm afraid we've got something of a spanner in the ointment at the moment.'

'Oh.'

'I'm sorry to say that my son isn't going to be able to get down here for a few days. He's, er . . . been called away urgently.'

'Oh.'

'He won't be here before the weekend, he thinks.'

'Oh.'

'Terribly irksome for you, no doubt. But Toby will explain all. He says he hopes you will understand, and he's very much looking forward to seeing you again. And I'm to make sure, what was it? Oh yes . . . that you have somewhere to stay in the meanwhile.'

'Er. Yes, of course. Not to worry. I'm sure my . . . my sister can put me up.'

'Toby will be most relieved. If you call again on Friday, we may have a better idea of his ETA.'

'Thanks. I will. There's nowhere I can call him in the meanwhile?'

'I'm sorry, there isn't. He's going to be totally . . . what was the word he used? Incommunicado. I'm afraid we shall have to rely on him phoning in to base.'

'I see.' Heavy sigh. 'You know it's odd, you sound very similar to that driver I spoke to earlier.'

'How funny, everyone says that. Well, if there's nothing else I can help you with . . .'

'I don't think there is . . .'

'Well, goodbye then.'

'Bye.'

Crikey. I'm obviously losing it. For a moment back there, I even began to feel a bit sorry for him.

10

By the time I return to the sitting room, Digby has taken the opportunity to become completely pie-eyed. He's lolling in the TV chair with a big napkin jammed into his shirt collar. Trish has put a plate of scrambled eggs on his lap. On the screen, the titles come up to *Tooth and Claw*, the wildlife show where each week, in horrific close-up and slo-mo replay, members of one species stalk, attack, kill and snack off members of another species.

'Oh good,' slurs Digby. 'It's cheetah. Vicious buggers, cheetah. Buggers'll tear your throat out.' He waggles a fork in the air. 'Why don't you two young people go off and have some fun somewhere?'

So it is that half an hour later, Trish and I are snuggled into a cosy lounge bar in downtown Totnes, two pints of a cloudy Devonian bitter between us, she going on about nutrition, specifically the nutritional aspects of beer – 'beer is the liquid equivalent of bread, more or less, but without the dairy fats, obviously' – me marvelling at how such a dull statement could emerge from such a splendid face.

'Hovis doesn't get you pissed either,' I add in an effort to brighten up the conversation.

'That's right.'

'No one's ever had a hangover after too many jam sandwiches.'

And I am rewarded with a laugh. A little tentative as laughs go, but a laugh to be sure. The eyes widen. The remarkable cheekbones gain sharper definition. The magnificent lips part to reveal a favourable proportion of dazzling white teeth mounted in sexy pink gum. Something fascinating happens with the tendons in her neck that I know I shall want to provoke again.

'That's true,' she confirms.

OK. The horrible truth – apparent after only half an hour in her company – Trish is a tragic bore. I know with a crushing certainty that nothing stimulating or amusing will ever escape this woman's lips. Here are some selected highlights:

Why she trained as a nutritionist: 'Well, it's important to eat properly, isn't it?'

What she likes best about her job: 'Working with *people*.'

On Digby Gulliver: 'Far too fond of whisky. In common with a lot of men of his generation, not that interested in vegetables.'

But what he's *really* like? You know, *deep down*?: 'Oh, a sweetie.'

On Vic: 'A poppet.'

On London: 'Dirty. Unhealthy. Too many people.'

On the West Country: 'People have got more time for you down here.'

On alcohol: 'Everything's fine in moderation.'

Sorry . . . are you still awake? See what I mean? Trish is one of those big, beautiful women who can have no idea how lovely they are. Because if she did, then she would surely find something better to say, or maybe just go down the silent route. Anyhow, the grotesque disparity between what she looks like (smoky Balkan temptress) and what she *sounds* like (particularly banal character in *The Archers*) is making me dizzy.

I'll give her this though: she can hold her drink. Because we're both a couple of pints down the line, and they're having no discernible effect on her, neither in style nor content. Whereas I can definitely begin to feel my guy ropes slipping their pegs, my tongue loosening, a steadily growing desire to say something stupid.

'You obviously don't consider beer a pollutant then,' I say, returning with a pair of fresh pints.

'I detox every month.' She takes a healthy pull at her drink, leaving behind a creamy moustache. 'For ten days no alcohol, caffeine, proteins or dairy.'

'Christ, you must feel terrible.'

'Actually, you feel really good. Really, you know . . . alive.'

'Why bother to tox up in the first place? Why not keep clear of toxins altogether and feel great all the time?' I have a powerful urge to lean across the table and suck the foam off her upper lip.

'A little bit of what you fancy is good for you. We were taught you should have everything—'

'Let me guess, in moderation.'

Fuck, how depressing. This is almost the exact opposite of my own position, which is that if a thing is worth doing, it's worth doing to excess. She's not even a hardline food crank, who could at least fill you with horror at some sinister diet involving fish oil and yarrow stalks. Clearly, sadly, Trish is totally sensible. No chink, no flaw through which to prise her open. But standards are lower in the country, aren't they? Because of the sheer paucity of population, you end up being pally with people you'd utterly blank in the city. Out in the sticks, you'll talk to anything with a pulse.

'Do you think that makes me awfully dull, Alistair?'

'No. Of course not. Why do you ask?'

'I did a personality quiz in a magazine yesterday. And when I checked my answers, I thought I came out very dull.'

'I'm sure you didn't really.' Forgive me, Lord.

'Would you like to try it?'

'Sure.' Yes. Please. Anything.

She tells me to write the numbers one to eleven down the side of a piece of paper.

1.

2.

3.

4.

5.

6.

7.

8.

9.

10.

11.

Against numbers one and two, she asks me to write any two whole numbers (no fractions).

1. 67
2. 25

In slots three and seven, she tells me, I should put the names of two members of the opposite sex, alive or dead. Two women.
'What, *any* two women?'
'Any two.'
'Alive or dead?' Important to get these things right.
'Alive or dead.'

3. Erica Birkendale
4.
5.
6.
7. Trish (don't know your surname)

Now in spaces four to six, I should write three names of friends and family.

4. Linds
5. Andy Fineman
6. Geraldine

And finally, in eight to eleven, she tells me to put four song titles.
'What, any four song titles?'
'That's right.'
'It's a recognised scientific test, this?'
'It's supposed to tap the unconscious.'
'Can they all be Elvis songs?'

'Whatever comes to mind.'

8. 'Suspicion'
9. 'The Wonder of You'
10. 'Are You Lonesome Tonight'
11. 'All Shook Up'

'Now,' she says knowingly, 'shall I tell you what it all means?'

'I'm on tenterhooks.' Whatever the fuck they are.

'Well, number one and two don't mean anything. Ignore them.'

'You mean I've wasted my time thinking up two perfectly good whole numbers?'

'I think the idea is to engage your logical brain, freeing the illogical, creative side.'

'I see.' It *is* a load of old bollocks then.

'Number three is someone you love.'

Now I laugh. Indecently loud, I'd say for a weekday evening in this part of the country. 'Well, that's a good one,' I tell her. 'I've put Erica Birkendale.'

Trish looks at me blankly. To her enormous credit, I realise that she's never heard of the foul old bitch.

'Number eight, the first song title, describes your attitude to Erica Thingy.'

'Well, that's a bit more like it. I've got "Suspicion".'

'Four is who you most care about.'

'Linds. Lindsay, my ex. Actually, my ex-ex.'

'Five is the person who knows you best.'

'Andy Fineman. An old schoolfriend. He does know me rather well, it's true.'

'Six is your guardian angel.'

'Geraldine. A . . . er, another friend. She did recently help me out of a jam.'

'And seven is someone you fancy.'

'Ha. I've. I've put. Ha. Actually. Well.' Heavy sigh. Fuck it. 'I've put you, Trish.'

11

The song title at number ten is allegedly a summation of oneself ('Are You Lonesome Tonight'). Eleven characterises one's life at this point ('All Shook Up'). Number nine ('The Wonder of You') purports to describe one's attitude to the person one fancies named in number seven (Trish). If it wasn't all so horribly accurate – with the obvious exception of loving Erica Birkendale – I'd have had no hesitation in pissing copiously over this ridiculous piece of psychobabble. In a good-natured way, naturally.

Trish wasn't in the least fazed by the declaration from my unconscious. She smiled rather sweetly and quickly changed the subject to how she'd answered the test. If memory serves, she loved her father, cared most about her mother and fancied George Clooney. Her guardian angel was her sister. The song that summed her up was 'Happy Birthday' and her life at this point was 'Smooth' (a hit for Carlos Santana).

'That does make me *quite* dull, don't you think?' she asked.

'Catastrophically', I should have thought, was the *mot juste* here. 'Not at all,' I replied. 'I'd say you come out admirably sane.'

We went on to have a somewhat stressful dinner together at a Thai restaurant. Her face I could have looked at for hours. Days, maybe. But there's only so much one wants to hear about the nutritional aspects of peanuts. At one point, I tried to draw her out about Toby. She was saying little beyond the fact that she found it hard to imagine me as one of his friends.

'Really? Why's that, then?' I asked.

'You're all sort of chatty and cheerful. Toby's more . . .'

'. . . gloomy and morose?' Just a guess.

She smiled thinly. Actually, I don't think she can like him very much.

Eventually we minicabbed it back to the house. As we walked in silence through the moonlit grounds towards our twin cottages, an owl hooted to its mates, or whoever it is that owls hoot to.

'Well, good night, Alistair,' said Trish as we stood outside our respective doorways fumbling with keys. 'It's been a nice evening.'

'Night, Trish. I've had a good time.' Bit of stretch, but you know what I mean.

'I liked the name of that song you picked for me,' she said.

'"The Wonder of You". It's Elvis. From his schlocky Las Vegas period.'

'I never really liked Elvis,' she replied, 'but it was a sweet thought.'

Then she vanished, leaving me with the thought: is it possible to desire someone whose words cause large areas of one's upper brain to close down with boredom? Someone who doesn't like Elvis?

So now I'm back in my billet, feet up, *Newsnight* on low, eyelids drooping. And I'm just thinking . . . actually, I could probably bear three or four more days of this country lark, fuck off out of here before the return of the prodigal, when the mobile rings.

'Hello?'

Silence.

'Oh, it's you. How did you get this number? Off my answerphone, right?'

Silence.

'Come on. You can do it. One for yes. Two for no. Three for not sure.'

Silence.

'Oh, for Christ's sake, we had all this worked out. Why are we suddenly going backwards?'

Silence.

'Look, what's the matter? Have I done something to upset you? Is there something you want to tell me?'

'Yeth, cunty. Ath a matter of fact there ith.'

12

Somehow, in all the excitement, the subterfuge, the deception, I'd forgotten *him*: the very reason I'm in Devon tonight and not West London.

'Who did you think I wath just then?' asks my boulder-headed persecutor.

'It's a long story.'

'I'm not in a hurry.'

'Mr Holderness. Luke. How can I put this? What happened to your grandfather was an accident. He was a very . . .' Never say 'old'. 'He was a very *elderly* man. Anything might have . . .' Never say 'killed'. 'Anything might have taken him away. The fact that it was . . . an animated discussion, let's call it, over a turkey is just a turn of fate. He might as easily have had a row with the newsagent over a paper bill. And, Luke, please trust me. No one need ever know the . . . the exact circumstances of your grandfather's . . .' never say 'death', 'your grandfather's passing.'

Silence.

'Are you still there?'

'I'm lithening.'

'Look, I saw the report of his funeral. I realise how upset you must be. But blaming me is not going to help you come to terms with your loss. Grief is a complex process.' Yes, I watched a docco about it. How does it go? 'There are several distinct stages. First there's the shock and disbelief. Then comes anger and resentment . . .' Shit, what comes after that? 'This angry phase is entirely natural. But it will pass. And then there will be . . .' Fuck, what? 'There will be acceptance. Yes, that's it. Acceptance. That's what we've got to work towards.'

'Acctheptanth.'

'That's the one.'

'Do you know what I think would help my acctheptanth?'

'What, Luke?' That's three times I've Luke-ed him. Maybe the horrible cunt's going soft.

'The thight of your thkull cracking open under my baith-ball bat.'

'Ah.'

'Yeth, I think I'd find that very therapeutic.' And he laughs. A ghastly sort of Mutley *heh-heh-heh*.

'Oh, big joke. Big fucking joke. You think it's funny running round threatening innocent television producers? Well, it isn't. I'm scared, OK, Luke? Not just for my own sake, but for *you*. That's right, I'm frightened for *you*, Luke. For what may happen to *you*.' Jesus, where am I getting this stuff? I sound like a particularly crappy episode of *Columbo*.

A long, meaningful pause. 'Let someone help you, Luke.' Go for it, why not? 'Let *me* help you.'

Now he leaves a long, meaningful pause. 'You want to help me?'

'Yes.'

'Why would you do that?'

Good question. Why *would* I do that? Why wouldn't I just

go to the police and report the crazy bastard? Oh yeah. Because then everyone would find out that someone died on my show, and that would be the end of my TV career. Also, the police might not take it seriously (as far as I know, it's not yet illegal to send someone a pair of Sainsbury's trout). Oh yeah, and he might get me anyway. Best hope: keep talking to the sick fuck.

'Why would I help you? So something good can come out of something bad.' Oh please. Don't make me ill.

'Tho thomething good can come out of thomething bad. That'th very moving, Charlth.'

'I know you're hurting.' Stop, I'm going to gag. 'Let's just stay calm, and talk.'

'What should we talk about?'

'Whatever comes to mind. The first thing that comes off the top of your head.'

And now he's doing the horrible wheezing *heh-heh-heh* laugh again.

'What's so amusing?'

'The firtht thing off the top of my head.'

'Yeah?'

'It'th the top of *your* head, Charlth. All thmashed in.' More *heh-heh-heh*.

On the television set with the sound down, Jeremy Paxman is conducting a civilised debate. A silver-haired man in a nice tie is being eminently reasonable about something or other. A woman in a beige jacket is smiling patiently a lot. A clergyman of some hue expresses mild concern. On a monitor, against a background of spires, a bald man in glasses is getting increasingly narked (no warm wine and Twiglets for *him* in the green room after the show). But this is the way we proceed with disagreements in this country. By recourse to discussion. To reasoned argument. To the cut and thrust of logic, not the bish and bosh of the cudgel. A sudden shaft of clarity spears through the fug of Thai food and beer fumes in my head.

'Holderness. Do me a favour, will you? Take that baseball bat of yours and just shove it up your arse, OK?'

Then I press End, depower the mobe, and drift off to sleep on an unfamiliar feeling of triumph.

E I G H T

1

To: Peter Marcus, Tuna Television
From: Charles Green
Subject: Ideas for Erica

Dear Peter,

Here's today's instalment of ideas for Erica's raft. Again I have left them very much at an outline stage. Getting out of the office has been very liberating for the creative juices, I must say. I trust you will let me know when – if ever! – you'd like me to return. In the meanwhile, I shall continue to stare at clouds and be fertile.

All best,

Charles

1. TV Star Island: Erica Birkendale plus nine other major television performers are holed up in a luxury hotel on a desert island. Each week, viewers vote to remove the one they can stand the least. The one who remains at the end of the series gets their own chat show, if they do not already have one.

2. Endure with Erica: members of the public are trapped on a desert island with Erica Birkendale. Each week they compete amongst themselves to decide who should be allowed off.

3. Hell is Other People: half a dozen of the nation's biggest gobshites (they know who they are) are brought together in a studio late at night. The doors are locked, and they are then instructed to argue among themselves on a series of prearranged topics. When audience monitoring equipment reveals no one is any longer watching, they are allowed to go to bed.

4. Erica's up for it: action girl (*girl!*) Erica Birkendale has a go at tough challenges set by the viewers. Whether it's baking a pavlova, playing a set of tennis against Venus Williams or running the British economy for half an hour, this is the show where Erica is always – up for it!

5. The Sick Pet Bank (combining Erica's research positives relating to animals and money): the show where viewers win money to pay for operations for their sick pets. The cat with cataracts. The dog dogged by some fucking dog thing. The goldfish hooked on amphetamines.

6. Erica Birkendale, Forever Young: now that 50 is the new 40, 40 the new 30, and 30 the new 20, in this era of kidults, adulteenies, and no one acting their age any more, Erica Birkendale presents the show that makes youth culture safe for people old enough to know better.

7. Erica and Friends: Erica Birkendale's one-woman show.

As you can tell, the last forty-eight hours under Digby's roof have proved to be highly productive. Each morning I've woken up with a head full of fresh ideas, which I've duly whacked off to Peter Marcus on the old email before breakfast. (*Erica and Friends* was a joke by the way, but like I say, you'll see more terrible sights on ITV almost daily.)

Meanwhile, I have been free to come and go as I please. This morning, for example, I have been following Trish around her organic vegetable garden, admiring the dramatic way her legs soar from the top of her green wellingtons and speculating about the small sweaty patch which soaks through her blouse in the region of her lower back when she's bent over doing something intimate to the runner beans or whatever the fuck those spindly green things are.

My other principal activities in the Digby Gulliver universe have been, in no particular order:

1. **Going for a lovely long country walk with Vic, Spit and Smut.**
2. **Listening to Vic's views on**
   (a) **Motor vehicles.**
   (b) **Dogs in general, lurchers in particular.**
   (c) **Money ('money comes to money, Alistair').**

(d) The villages, towns and cities of the UK ('Birmingham, ever been there? What a fucking dismal place that is').

(e) 'The daughter.' Ali. Living with a footballer.

(f) 'The wife.' Not named as yet. Lives Hitchin.

(g) 'My ladyfriend.' Carole. Lives Torquay.

(h) Digby ('you should have known him in his prime').

(i) Toby ('I know he's your pal and all, but he could take more interest in his old dad').

3. Keeping away from that darkened sitting room where Digby is to be found at all hours watching television and sipping whisky.

What else?

4. Reading Hugh Trevor-Roper's *The Last Days of Hitler*. Paperback edition kindly placed in small pile on bedside table.

5. Watching *Newsnight*.

6. Going to bed earlier, and considerably less pissed than would be the case in London.

7. Trying to keep in mind that for the moment I am Alistair Gough, actual medical doctor, and not Charles Green, producer of television deception comedy, especially when Vic solicits my opinion on any matter. Or after some vapid remark of Trish's, when I feel a cloudburst of undoctorly cynicism about to come over me.

8. Regularly remembering that I am *not* actually Dr Alistair Gough, as described above, but Charles Green, producer of television

deception comedy, native of London, co-owner with the Halifax Bank of Flat 16, Romney Mansions, friend of Rose, Geraldine, Andy Fineman and Linds, ex-lover of Cheryl, and general all-round metropolitan creature.

And that I can't stay here for ever.

2

Because it really is awfully agreeable. Indeed, the phrase that keeps crossing my mind, like a message on a banner trailed in the sky behind a light plane, is THIS IS VERY NEARLY FUCKING IDYLLIC.

The sun shines. Everything is terribly *green*. I breathe fresh Devon air, not the stale exhaust of Chalk Farm Road. Instead of toxic cocktails in absurd theme bars, I drink good, healthy English beer in charming country pubs (OK, a *bit* of an exaggeration, make that an unpretentious Totnes boozer). I have formed a positive ongoing relationship with two creatures from the world of nature (Smeg and Slut). I have only *one* lovely young woman to admire, flirt with and harbour thoughts about instead of a confusing roll call of colleagues, ex-lovers and vanishing police forensic scientists picked up under false pretences. And despite my role as 'friend of Toby' – I have the sense that Toby is not necessarily Mr Popular round here – despite that, under this roof I have found a genuine sense of welcome, as opposed to the fear and loathing that's the custom and practice within the television industry.

It's true that my new cast of chums aren't necessarily the sharpest bunch of individuals one has ever been cooped up with. None could lean plausibly against the bar at Myxpqlncx,

Marine Martini in hand, and toss off the perfect world-weary *aperçu* with which to sum up another hard day in the wicked old metropolis. But I find I have become rather fond of them, mainly, I suppose, because of their unquestioning acceptance of a newcomer in the social structure, more accustomed, as I am, to an environment where one's first thought is, What's this bastard doing here? Is she/he going to steal my job? No, I'd say 'this is very nearly fucking idyllic' sums up my mood fairly precisely at this moment, seated, as I am, in a deckchair, laptop on my knees, a fine view of the organic vegetable garden in my gunsights, and prominent within that view, no more than ten feet away, the magnificent figure of Magda (sorry, today she truly does resemble the cerebral Czech beauty), boots planted wide apart, pivoting dramatically at the waist to give the tomato beds a sound poking.

I am fertile. I type:

1. Erica Grows It Alone: TV's Erica Birkendale spends a year in the North Wales hills living – surviving – on what she is able to produce for herself on a five-acre small-holding. Turnips, radishes, mangetout, whatever can be induced to grow in her lonely outpost. In addition, at the start of the series she is given a piglet, which she must fatten and eventually slaughter, not wasting any part of it (using its intestines for sausages, eyelids for soup, grinding its hoofs for glue and all that puke-making stuff).

2. Erica Sits Among the Cabbages and Peas

'What are you writing?' Magda is squinting at me in the sun-light, her hands on her knees like a cricket umpire. Sweat has plastered strands of her raven hair to her forehead. Mentally I right-click on this image and transfer it to the same folder that contains the little reel of Geraldine operating my office door with her hip.

'Letter to my sister. I'm telling her all about you.'

'What does she do, your sister?' Magda has straightened up. She's scraping her hair behind her ears and the vision of this nutritionally correct young woman, lovely bare arms raised to the sky, is almost blinding.

'She works in television. On a hidden camera show.'

'Golly. That sounds glamorous.'

'Not really. She says she spends all day having to be nice to horrid people and horrid to nice people.'

'Oh.' I've lost her. She hasn't a clue what I'm on about.

'Shall I tell you what I've written to her about you?'

'Go on then.' She starts doing something delicate with a seedling that means she doesn't have to look me in the eye.

I 'read' from my screen: 'Trish is Toby's father's house-keeper. But really she's a nutritionist. She reminds me of Magda, that friend of yours who went to live in Prague with the chess-player. Trish is the most sensible person I have ever met. She believes in moderation in all things. My plan is to take her to the pub, get her tiddly somehow, and then, her tongue loosened by alcohol, I shall discover The Truth behind the enigma. I hope she doesn't have a more attractive offer for tonight, because I'm aiming to ask her out.'

She's still fiddling with her seedling, carefully flicking earth off its roots. But she's coiled one ankle round another – quite a good trick in gumboots – and I do believe the flush on her fine cheekbones didn't arrive there through fresh air and exertion alone.

'What's your sister's name?' she asks.

'Rose,' I respond without missing a beat.

'Well, I don't. Have a more attractive offer. For tonight, that is.'

'Fantastic.'

Trish drops on to one knee. Fashioning the index and fore-fingers of her left hand into a gardening tool, she eases them slowly and deliberately into the soft soil of the vegetable bed. She wiggles them around a bit, withdraws, positions the seedling carefully in the resultant hole, then does some further squishing, patting and tamping. For some reason I find it very hard to tear my gaze away from this spectacle.

I type:

Erica's Highland Fling: Erica Birkendale is marooned in a remote Scottish community where there are ten single men for every eligible woman. Week by week, we watch as she receives the attentions of the blacksmith, the cobbler, the lighthouse-keeper, the bee-keeper, the village idiot, the weird one who still lives with his mother, the lot of them. In the final *live* episode, viewers phone-vote to decide which one gets to go on a 'dream date' with one of television's best-loved celebrities.

Come on, be fair. You've sat through worse.

3

I dream up a couple more preposterous ideas and fire them off to Peter M. Then I drag the deck chair into a favourable position to read a few more pages of *The Last Days of Hitler*, and to watch Trish as she plays a hose over her preciously tended vegetables, something irresistible in the solemn way she's aiming her stream (women *don't* generally, do they? You know what I mean).

At one point I find myself praising her tomatoes.

'Fine-looking tomatoes,' I offer.

'Thanks. Like to try one?'

'Sure would.'

She makes a bit of a show about selecting a nice one, finally twisting it off and handing it to me, a rich, red jobby, all heavy and warm. 'One hundred per cent organic,' she says. 'Never been near any nasty chemicals.'

In my experience, you've got to be a bit cautious about a tomato that you can't get into your mouth whole. Particularly if your plan is to take a bite out of it in the presence of a woman you're trying to impress — or at the very least, not look like a complete pilchard in front of. You know what I'm talking about: no matter how carefully you plan the attack, the surprising tendency of even the most innocuous-looking specimen to suddenly projectile-void a stream of crimson pips straight down your best white shirt.

I did it in France once, on holiday with Cheryl, with one of those socking great French tomatoes that grow to the size of apples, which is maybe what gives you the idea that you can bite into them like that. Big mistake. Fucking thing as good as yacked all over me. We were picking dried pips out of the hire car for days. Still, it amused Cheryl. In fact, as I remember, she laughed louder and longer at that than any witty remark I ever came up with.

Clearly one technique is to get a tooth, maybe a couple of teeth, into the flesh of the beast, and then work slowly, using suction to hoover away the treacherous pulpy or pip-like material, though this can have the disadvantage of making you look like a rabbit or a pervert. And you can still get it wrong, with a split and consequent blowout remaining a distinct possibility if there is a weakness elsewhere in the fruit.

A nightmare, in short, polishing off any variety of tomato other than cherry in front of an attractive member of the opposite species without the aid of a bib. So my strategy is to get this bastard in three. A first mediumish-sized bite (maximum danger) but with plenty of suction on hand, should there be the threat of a blowout. A good manly second bite, but taking care to feel how the pips lie, to avoid any secondary unpleasantness. Pop the third bit away whole.

When I manage to pull it off, she looks impressed. I feel like I've passed some sort of test.

'Delicious,' I declare (in truth, it wasn't nearly as nice as one of those small sweet jimmies that cost an arm and a leg at Marks and Spencer), 'though I do kind of miss that tang of pesticide.'

She laughs and mock-slaps me on the arm.

Half an hour later, I fancy I can still feel a glow where her fingers landed.

4

Mid-afternoon, still in the deck chair, my nose in *Hitler* (Führer doped up to the eyeballs; things in the bunker getting really shitty now) when I spy Vic with his walking boots on, Snot and Spunk in a high state of excitement. I ask if I can tag along.

For a heavy-set man with a limp, Vic sets off at a pretty uncompromising lick. Soon, all traces of habitation are left behind, and the vista becomes one of unrelenting countryside. All right, there are a few farms dotted about the landscape, and we pass a couple of . . . what are they, woodcutters' cottages, I suppose? But in the main, it's your classic rural Devon scene: hills, trees, fields, grass. Wherever you look, it's shades of green. Light green, dark green, mid-green. All the greens. Except for blobs of white (sheep) and the occasional splodge of brown (horse). Sorry, never been much good at descriptions.

We're tramping along the top of some valley, the dogs streaking away every few minutes to investigate urgent matters in the undergrowth.

'What do you think to the new Renault?' asks Vic. 'Good-looking motor. But, you know. Those French.' I notice he's wearing a quilted grey anorak with orange stickers, popular among people who work in car dealerships.

'I'm honestly not terribly good on cars. My first ever car was a second-hand Austin Allegro. It had a square steering wheel.'

Vic laughs. 'Dear me. I remember those. What a bloody joke, eh?' He laughs again, and shakes his head in wonderment at the comedy of British automotive design.

The day is magnificent. Way overhead, a tiny fighter plane leaves a white jet trail against the blue. So high, the pilot must be able to see the curvature of the earth. Where did I read that space is nearer than one thinks? Only an hour away by car . . . but straight up. I recently came across another astonishing fact. The sun, which is currently doing such a fine job lighting up the general environs, contains 99.86 per cent of the mass in our solar system. Two-thirds of the tiny remainder is locked in the giant planet Jupiter. So everything else (including the earth) makes up less than one-twentieth of one per cent of the mass of the whole solar system. I paused when I read that. Truly we are a grain of sand orbiting a grapefruit. Or should that be a pumpkin? And another thing. On the radio today: scientists think they've discovered the location of the black hole that our doughnut of a galaxy revolves around. If you set off from Totnes, travelling at the speed of light, it would take you 26,000 years to get there. I like to think big thoughts in the countryside. I find it helps put one's troubles into perspective.

'Vic, does Toby's dad *always* drink like that?' (Last night

Digby was paralytic again, after what he rather grandly calls 'cocktails'. Secret recipe passed down the generations: find a glass. Fill it with Famous Grouse. Repeat as necessary.)

Vic laughs. 'Why? Would you say he had a problem?'

Yeah. He's only got one mouth. 'I imagine he does exceed the current Department of Health guidelines. Does he drink *all* day?'

'He *tipples* through the day, to be honest – a steady trickle to keep the system ticking over, as he says. Then he gives it the gun in the evening. He probably does a bottle every day or two.'

'He knows it'll probably kill him?' Apparently.

Vic shakes his head. 'Hasn't done yet. He's a tough old boy. Women or worry are more likely to finish him off.'

'What's he worried about?'

'The summer fair for one.'

'The summer fair?'

'Every year, the owners of the big house put on a do for the locals. It became a tradition. Nothing fancy; you know, stalls, tombola, sale of handicraft, displays of rural whatnot.'

'Sounds fun.'

'Digby and Celia always used to do it. But when she . . . when she left, it knocked the stuffing out of him. He didn't have the heart for it any longer. But this year we've nagged him into giving it another go. Stop moping, start living, sort of thing.'

'Good idea.'

'Yeah, except now muggins here has got to organise it all. Matter of fact, we're still short of a celebrity to declare the whole shooting match officially open.'

'What sort of celebrity?'

'We had Larry Grayson one year, when he lived at Torquay.'

'Funny man.'

'That bird off the local telly would do. Except she's said she can't.'

'Is that what he's worried about?'

'He's worried it may bring back too many memories.'

We walk on in silence for a bit. The dogs have fallen alongside us now, temporarily all chased out. A small breeze blows the fur back off their fine, noble faces. I have an urge to ask Vic where he came by his limp.

'What was Toby's mum like?'

'Celia? Beautiful woman. Very classy. But, pardon my French, if she were a bloke, you'd call her a complete arsehole.'

I laugh. 'It's true. You can't call a woman an arsehole, can you? It doesn't work. I guess the nearest thing would be "a pain in the arse".'

'That doesn't even begin to cover it.'

'Would you say Toby was close to her?'

Vic pulls a face. 'Couldn't rightly tell you *who* Toby's close to, Alistair.'

5

Trish has attempted to make herself look more glamorous this evening. Standing, waiting to get served at the bar of the grim Totnes pub we've taken ourselves off to, I can see she's wearing some kind of brown linen frock; earrings are in evidence; a flash of mascara may even have been applied to the eyelashes. The overall effect, however, is to render her far less attractive than when she rose so magnificently from behind the runner beans, sweat sticking the hair to her face, soil all over her fingers. There was even a moment back there this morning, me tap-tapping away into the laptop, she tying back tendrils, nipping at things with the secateurs, when a vision came to me of a purer, more peaceful, more *purposeful* way of life. A life where one's days were in tune with the natural order, where a beautiful, *uncomplicated* woman stood by one's side (not a twitching metropolitan neurotic), where one did proper work (not conspiring to take the piss out of hard-working members of the general public). It was a fleeting glimpse of a future together. But the next moment she'd cried, 'Oh, *gross*.' And I'd said, 'What is it?' and on the end of her trowel, she brought me the putrefying remains of a small bird. Larvae were causing its tiny body to writhe. She was staring at it with a mixture of horror and fascination.

'Dry-roasted, OK? They didn't have ordinary.'

Trish sets down the pair of pints, and places herself in the seat opposite. My heart sinks. What could I have been thinking of? That horse manure about the letter to my sister, how my aim was to ask her out, if she didn't have a more attractive offer. Get her tiddly and discover the truth behind the enigma, *oh please*. Strikingly lovely as she is — even with a foam moustache — it's only a quarter past eight, and we're already struggling to find things to talk about. There are *at least* two more hours in this foul tavern, and then the very real possibility of a grisly Chinese meal to follow. Christ, I could have been watching *Inspector Morse*. I could have finished *The Last Days of Hitler*. Instead, I'm labouring to discover a topic that will make this woman sparkle.

'I've been reading a book that was left in my cottage.' Worth a punt, don't you think?

'Really?'

'It's about the end of the last war.'

'The Falklands?'

'World War Two.' Maybe you've heard of it.

'Oh yes. We did that at school. Or was it World War One? Hitler was in both, wasn't he?'

'You're right. Once as a corporal. Once as Führer of Germany.'

'Did you know that Digby has a painting by Hitler?'

I choke on my beer. 'You're joking.'

'It's in the library.'

'He's not a . . . He doesn't have any sort of . . . unhealthy interest in the Nazis? At all, as such?'

'I don't think so. He says he wants to get rid of it.'

'Bloody hell. What's it like?'

'It's not very good or anything. Just buildings. And a church. I probably shouldn't have mentioned it. Shall I tell you what I've been reading?'

'Go on then.'

'That one about men are from Mars . . .'

'. . . women are from Muswell Hill.'

She does laugh. But I sense an opening here.

'Why are you interested in that?' I enquire, as if I didn't know.

She does the deep sigh. The one freighted with loss, regret, disappointment, ennui, missed opportunities, chances blown; general hopelessness in the face of an uncaring universe. She says, 'Oh, you know.'

'Chap trouble, eh?'

She nods her head.

'Care to talk about it?'

Christ, just try to stop her. All the way through the next pint, it's Roger this and Roger that. How Roger was great, and a laugh, how you could have a fine old time with Roger, how Roger made her feel good. How Roger made her feel (pause, lowers voice) like a *woman* (not like a hamster, then). But how Roger had his dark side as well. How Roger Had Moods. How Roger found it difficult getting close to anyone because Roger's mother had starved Roger of affection as a child. How Roger said it was *his* fault, not hers. How he needed 'some space'. How finally, she'd given Roger all the 'space' he could possibly want. And how eventually she discovered that while Roger was off somewhere supposedly 'having space', Roger had in fact started 'seeing' an eighteen-year-old who worked in Somerfield. Roger being the evil little shit who'd wormed his way into Trish's affections and then fucked off a bit more sharply than is generally considered polite. The same Roger who evidently now regrets his mistake and has been turning up sporadically begging for a second chance, though she's having none of it.

'What does this loathsome creep do for a living?' I ask, just to check whether my mouth still works.

'Oh, don't say it like that. He couldn't help it. He's quite sweet really.'

How like a woman. To remain pathetically loyal to the author of her misery. Whereas with me and Cheryl . . . well, I was about to say, I've cut her out like a cancer. Except at the thought of her, I feel something soft and rather tearful round about where the second button of my jacket is. And when I speak, I find my words have an odd thickness to them.

'One's got to look forward, Trish. You know, like in the song, pick yourself up, dust yourself down, start all over again.'

'You're right.'

'If at first you don't succeed, you should try, try and try again . . . and *then* give up. There's no point being a damn fool about it.'

'It's true.'

'Life,' I confide sagely, 'is one damn thing after another.' I drain my pint. 'No one said it would be easy. Or fair. Or interesting. There, I've given you every bit of wisdom I know.'

She smiles. And I feel my guy ropes slipping their pegs

again, an odd floating feeling as I gaze into her marvellous Slavic features.

'So what about you?' she asks. 'What happened with you and . . . *your* last special friend?'

'Cheryl.'

'That's a nice name.'

'Do you think? I never really liked it, to be honest. Almost as bad as Beryl.'

'What happened with you and Cheryl?'

'I think I'll need another pint for that story.'

6

'Charlie, just fuck off.'

'No, Cheryl, *you* fuck off.'

That was the matchless piece of dialogue that officially slammed the door on our relationship. Pinteresque, you could call it. Ortonesque in its black finality. Certainly a long way from my first perception of Cheryl as unlike others; as someone who danced to the rhythm of a different tune. The lone, special inhabitant of Planet Cheryl who even spoke the language in a weird and fascinating way.

By the end of the affair, in the way of these things, the qualities that I first found enchanting about Cheryl had switched polarity to become irredeemable character flaws. What had once been her delicious girly dreaminess, I came to see as pathological distance, her fundamental unreachability. The mysterious way she used to speak, always slightly off the point, like some tragic heroine in a Chekhov play, I discovered was a subtle form of evasion. Her marvellous stillness, her thrilling quietude became her *disturbing* stillness, her *infuriating* quietude. And the fact that she produced *The Bibblybums*, which I used to think of as noble and specialised work – maybe even a higher calling (you know, engaging the developing brains of a generation) – well, I now realised she was simply churning out the dumbest of dumb kids' shows.

The sex was still pretty top drawer, though. No complaints in that department.

What did she see in me? Perhaps, in the end, only someone who was crazy about *her*. Yes, I could make her laugh, and engage her, and all that other stuff people are supposed to do for each other. I was nice to her friends (not that she had many), I got on with her parents (put it this way, their mouths didn't drop open with horror when we met for the first time), we even managed to have some fun. Some of the time. But it was never a riot. Never a relationship that was *on fire*. On our motoring trip across the States, me at the wheel, she behind sunglasses, feet up on the dash with the map across her knees, I often felt that although Cheryl was technically beside me, *she wasn't actually there*. A hundred miles or so of scenery could roll by, the country music radio station begin to fade, I'd say something . . . and you could feel her struggling to the surface to voice a reply. I guess I was proud of my tall, beautiful girl-friend, but a little alienated as well.

It ended, as it began, at a dinner party, not quite a year after that first evening at Andrea's. We hadn't been getting on. From seeing one another nearly every night, we'd recently begun spending more time apart. When we did come together, the silences between us were growing deeper, more ominous. I would ask her what was on her mind, was something worry-ing her, why did she seem so . . . distant? She would tell me to lighten up. There was a permanent sense of anxiety about us. I think everyone noticed it. Once I even phoned Jilly, her sensible flatmate. Just for a chat, apparently, but really for some inside dope.

I'd said, 'So how are you two getting on? Is she all right, do you think? Not a bit down at the moment?'

And she'd replied, 'Oh no. I'd say she was very *up*, actually.'

Linds had invited us round for dinner. She was being very grown up about me and Cheryl, and it certainly helped that there was a new young man in her life that week. The long kitchen table buzzed and babbled with the jolly chatter of Chardonnay-fuelled media folk. But Cheryl neither buzzed nor babbled. Her chatter, what there was of it, was far from jolly. Indeed, her pain and boredom at the entire evening were plain for all to see. All right, Linds' friends Lucy and Jake can be a bit wearing, and Bernadette didn't need to talk about herself quite so much, and the new boyfriend *was* ever so slightly uphill. But Cheryl's great flat face was like a poster hoarding that read 'Get Me Out Of Here'. In the taxi home, we were silent. Back in my flat, I broached the topic.

'Well, you were the life and soul of the party,' I quipped.

'What was in that fish pie she served us?'

'Fish, I imagine. Is something bothering you?'

'What type of fish?'

'*All* types of fish, I should think. Look, this isn't about fish, is it?'

'Do you think Bernadette is a happy person?'

'This great sulk. It's not about fish. Or Bernadette. What's the matter, Cheryl?'

'I think Lucy and Jake are happy.'

'You hated them.'

'I don't hate anyone, Charlie.'

'Bollocks. It was written all over your face. You thought they were awful. And, well they are, slightly. But there was no need to advertise it quite so clearly.'

'Can we go to bed? I'm tired.'

'What the fuck is the matter with you? You've had a face

like thunder all evening. For *weeks*, actually. Look, I ask you a straight question, just give me a straight answer. What's wrong?'

'Did she open the wine we brought? Did we drink it?'

'We drank everything in the house, Cheryl. Is it *us*? Is it *me*?'

'Is what you?'

'Are you tired of *us*?'

'Of *us*, or of *you*?'

'What's the fucking difference?'

'Well, *you* is singular, *us* is plural.'

'Don't fucking speak to me like that. Like. Like. Like this is some fucking game, some philosophical, fucking linguistic hair-splitting seminar. Answer my fucking question.'

'Charlie, just fuck off.'

'No, Cheryl, *you* fuck off.'

And that was it. The moment the relationship was cancelled. Cheryl sat there thinking about it for a moment. Then she picked herself up off the sofa, put on her coat, grabbed her handbag, and walked out of the door. I remember thinking, she'll be back. She'll have to come back at some stage. She's got stuff here. Except that over the next few days I discovered there wasn't a single item of her property in the flat. Not a paperback book. Not a jar of moisturiser. Not one crumpled pair of knickers.

She agreed to meet me a week later in Café Rouge. Her shoulders were set at an unfriendly new angle and, to my shock, I realised she was talking about us in the past tense, like we were history.

I guess I thought we were only having a row.

7

Trish is looking at me with a rather serious expression. I suppose I must have been going on a bit.

She says, 'Cheryl doesn't sound like a very nice person to me.'

'I don't think *nice* came into it really.'

'I think you should always make the effort. A smile doesn't cost anything . . .'

'I wasn't drawn to her for her *niceness*. It was more her *weirdness*.'

'People should be straight with each other. They shouldn't play games.'

'Really? Wouldn't it be terribly . . . terribly *dull* if there were no games? Anyway, it's impossible for people to be absolutely straight with each other. Even if we wanted to, we don't always know what we think. Don't always know our own minds. I often don't know what I think until I say it. Sometimes it comes out as a complete surprise.'

Trish looks at me oddly, as if this is the first time she's entertained such an idea.

'I always know what I think,' she asserts.

'Bet you don't.' Bet you don't absolutely know for certain whether you'd like to go to bed with me. Clearly, one way or the other. Bet you're ambiguous on that one. (OK, perhaps it's a bad example.)

'Gosh, you are funny, Alistair.' Who?

Oh yeah, Alistair. Fuck, pay attention, for Christ's sake. 'Funny ha-ha, I hope.'

She takes a long pull on her pint, providing me with an excellent view of her noble cheekbones. She sets down her glass and smiles. Funny peculiar, then.

'Trish, have you ever played that game where I say a word,

and then you say the first thing that comes into your head?'

'No. How does it go?'

'Well . . . I say a word, and then you say the first thing that comes into your head.' Pause for appreciation of irony. None follows. 'OK, this is just for practice. Tree.'

'Leaf.'

'Bird.'

'Bath.'

'Up.'

'Down.'

'Big.' Let me guess.

'Small.'

'Black.' Wait for it.

'White.'

'North.' The tension is unbearable.

'South.'

'Roger.'

Her mouth drops open to answer, but nothing comes out.

'Roger,' I repeat. She's staring at me, faintly dumbstruck. 'Go on. What was the first thing you thought of?'

Now her fingers are at her lips, and a pink flood-tide is surging up her throat.

'Actually . . . actually, I don't think I want to say.'

'But it was something surprising.'

'Yes, it was a bit.'

I cheer inwardly at my clever-cleverness (saw it in a movie, didn't I). 'Something you didn't think you'd think.'

'Yes.'

'Go on. What was it?'

She does a deep sigh. 'My brother as it happens.' She takes another hearty draw on her pint, so her eyes needn't meet mine. And just then, my pocket starts ringing.

'Hello?'

Silence.

'Oh . . .' I was going to say 'Christ', but it's not very brilliant-young-doctor-like. 'It's you.' Loopy Loo, I'm hoping.

Silence.

'How have you been, OK?'

Beep. Phew.

'Good to hear. Anything to report at all?'

Beep.

'Really? Well, that makes a positive change. Are you going to tell me?'

Beep beep.

'I'm going to have to wheedle it out of you, right?'

Beep.

'What have you got on in the background, there? Not *Inspector Morse*?'

Beep.

'Really? Which one?'

Silence.

'Look, I'm just in the middle of things right now. Do you think you could possibly call back? Tomorrow maybe?'

Beep.

'Well, bye then.'

Silence.

And then she hangs up.

I do that non-specific *tsk* noise again, the one, combined with a roll of the eyeballs, that speaks of the peskiness of unwished-for telephone calls. From acquaintances too colourless to talk about. On matters of profound unimportance.

But I'm glad we've had this conversation. About Roger and Cheryl. It's not that it's made her any less banal ('a smile doesn't cost anything'), it's more that the sharing of grief does seem to have forged a closer bond between us. Moved us *past* something. I guess the death of love conversation is a branch

line of the death conversation. And, remembering the fascinated way she'd gawped at the dead bird this morning, alive
with maggots, it occurs to me that perhaps the full-on, 'isn't
death just too horrible?' dialogue might just open some unexpected floodgates. Anyhow, for now I'm grateful that
someone has listened to *me*, to *my* woes for a change.

When Trish goes to buy a final round — oh fuck, might as
well — I thumb my way through the mobile's menu to Call
Register, and then to Calls Received. And here's the funny
thing.

Alongside the time of Loopy Loo's call, in the space where
I expect it to display the words 'number withheld', in their
place is a London telephone number.

8

In the Chinese restaurant, I have an inspired idea.

'Look,' I say, gesticulating with a naked spare rib bone, 'you
and I have both been wounded in love. But think of it, there's
treacherous Roger gadding about Totnes with a fat smile on
his face,' shagging the sexy Devonian checkout girl. 'There's
Cheryl . . . doing whatever Cheryl's doing,' pointing her toes
at the ceiling with that great blubbery oaf on top of her. 'I
mean, in all fairness, these people shouldn't be allowed to get
away with it. They should be punished, Trish.'

'Punished? How exactly?' Trish feeds herself a sizzling king
prawn without taking her eyes off my own.

'Something . . . *unfortunate* should happen to them. Does
Roger keep tropical fish? Maybe all his fish could be found
floating on the surface. Is he inordinately proud of his car?
Perhaps it would benefit from an interesting new paint finish.
Do you see what I'm getting at? I find a way of . . . enabling

Roger to suffer a setback on your behalf. In return, you ensure some exquisitely unpleasant event befalls Cheryl. And no one suspects it was us, because we are complete strangers. There was a film about it.'

She gazes at me for a few seconds. 'It's not very sensible, is it, Alistair?'

Oh, bollocks to sensible. Fuck all this moderation in all things. 'No, not sensible, but it would be great mischief, don't you agree?'

'It's not very mature either.'

You've got the rest of your life to be mature in, you silly bint. 'No, not desperately mature.'

'Would you like the last of the fried rice?'

'That's OK. You can have it.' I'll finish off the Chinese Beaujolais.

In the minicab back to the house, my hand inching closer to hers on the back seat of the smelly Austin Montego, I say, 'I'm glad you told me about Roger, Trish. And that I told you about Cheryl. I feel it's . . . it's brought us closer together.' Us victims of love. 'You know, Trish, I really think you're a great girl and . . .'

'FIRST LEFT AFTER THESE TREES,' she yells.

We crunch down the pitted drive in silence. I pay the driver the piddling rural fare — was it sixpence? I forget — and I rush round to open Trish's door. She rises out of the tragic vehicle like a goddess. I'm standing close enough to catch her perfume, intermingled intoxicatingly as it is with garlic and ginger. We stand for a moment in the warm night, watching the car's single working taillight weave its way back to the main road.

'Do you fancy a glass of brandy in my billet?' I ask. 'It's very decent stuff.' On top of the beer and the red wine, we would get disgustingly drunk, and one thing could lead almost inevitably to another.

'It's late, Alistair.'

We set off walking through the moonlight towards our silly little cottages.

'Just a quick one? A nightcap?' Please?

She's thinking about it. And her eyes in the gloom have gone very wide. 'Maybe next time.'

Outside our doors, I mutter a sulky, 'Well, good night then.' And she moves towards me; I feel her lips on mine in a gentle parting-of-the-ways kiss. I catch hold of her arm, try to pull her towards me, seeking to extend the embrace, to transform it through the strength of my desire for her. But she steps away.

'I'm still a bit . . . raw, Alistair,' she says. 'But perhaps next time? When I'm a bit more, you know . . .'

'More . . . whatever.'

'Yeah, whatever. Would you like to do that?'

'Sure. Whatever.'

'No, I mean it.'

And her face, in the fleeting seconds before she melts away into the blackness, looks to me like it holds a promise.

9

Lying in my bed, tuning into the profound silence of the countryside at night and yet again asking myself, what the fuck am I doing here? (Answer: don't know yet. Watch this space), I have a sudden thought. It occurs to me that just a few feet away — most probably just on the other side of that wall — Trish will be lying in *her* bed. Instantly I picture her all freshly bathed, pink-skinned, raven hair against the pillow, eyelids gently closing over the latest issue of *Organic Vegetables Monthly*, a touch sad, still a bit *raw* from the whole Roger experience.

Am I still a bit raw from the Cheryl experience? I wonder. Also, I muse, is it really feasible to have a relationship with someone who replies 'bath' to 'bird'? Who says things like 'a smile doesn't cost anything'? Or come to that, 'would you like the rest of the fried rice?'

The mobile rings again. Golly, I *am* popular out here in the sticks.

'Hello.'

'Good evening, Charlth.'

'Oh. You. How are you?' You lisping homicidal flake.

'Have you mithed me?'

'Desperately.' Go on, start threatening me. It's late. I'm going to sleep in a moment.

'Thorry to hear that.'

'Ah, well.'

'There it ith.'

'Mr Holderness, Luke, is there any actual point to this call?'

'Not really, Charlth. Just pathing the time of night. You're not thinking of returning to London then?'

'No. I'm quite happy here for the time being.'

'I don't thuppose you want to tell me where "here" ith?'

'Not just now. But thanks for asking.'

'Even if I athk nithely?'

'Sorry.'

'Becauth I am prepared to meet and discuth thith.'

'Without the use of a baseball bat?'

'Hmm. Have to think about that one.' The Mutley laugh.

'Good night, Luke.'

'Good night, Charlth. Pleathant talking to you.'

'Sorry to be unhelpful.'

'Not at all. You've been motht obliging.'

*　　*　　*

I'm lying in bed, drifting off, hoping that Trish will visit my dreams, when I remember. I snap on the light, grab the mobe, thumb through to Call Register, then Calls Received, and store Loopy Loo's telephone number. Silly cow obviously forgot to 141. I'll call her tomorrow.

No, fuck it. I'll call her now. See how she likes it.

I dial the 0207 London number – don't recognise the three-digit code – it rings.

'Hello?' comes the reply. *'Hello?'*

And now it's my turn to remain silent. My lips hang open but no words escape as a voice at the other end whispers into the night, 'Hello? Hello? Can't hear you. Hello? Look, I'm not hearing anything. Hang up and try again.'

A man's voice.

10

Birds chirrup and spider webs gleam in the early morning sunlight as I make my way up to the big house. The ducks on the poison lake mark my passage with a fusillade of quacking, but I am in no mood to return their greeting. I'm still feeling rattled from a series of disturbing dreams.

In the last one, I find myself hurtling through the enclosed tubes of some sort of white porcelain helter-skelter. Except, I realise, this is no helter-skelter. This is a toilet. I can't see what lies at the end. I have only the strong feeling that whatever it is, it will be very bad. I'm going faster and faster, there's no way to stop, when suddenly the tube vents into the top of a huge empty chamber, like the inside of a cave. And I'm falling. Or floating. Falling, floating down through space towards, oh God . . . a sea of shit. I can make out the stiff brown peaks. As I'm falling, floating towards my terrible fate,

I notice a balcony, a stylish, Philip Starck sort of balcony, built into the side of the cavern, upon which, at a small table, Luke Holderness and Erica Birkendale are having an intimate candle-lit dinner together. They look up and smile sadly as I drift down past them.

I wake, fighting for breath, heart hammering.

I'm the last to arrive for breakfast. Trish, Vic and Digby are seated round the long kitchen table in a silence dominated by Digby's hangover. It radiates off him like an aura, so powerful you can practically see its awful bruised glow. The only sounds are the clink of spoon against cereal bowl, the rasp of knife against toast. This is only my third breakfast in the Gulliver residence, but already I'm a veteran. I know not to do any of that jolly good morning, lovely day stuff.

Digby's flesh is dropping down his face a little more cata-strophically this morning. The skin itself appears to have com-pletely parted company with the muscle tissue behind it. It hangs like a grey, sandpapery curtain. The eyes are in partic-ularly tragic condition, sinking in despair into their own pouches, while the pouches themselves subside helplessly in the direction of the chin/neck/throat conurbation. I've seen jollier-looking corpses.

Digby is having the full English breakfast, traditional kill or cure treatment for the full English hangover. He groans. He sighs. He forks a sliver of egg into a merger with a piece of sausage and lifts the pair trembling to his lips. But the trem-bling suddenly worsens, becomes reclassified as actual shaking (you could injure yourself trying to take a bite on that), and the fork quickly returns to the plate, still loaded. He tries again, but the amplitude of vibration only widens as the fork nears its target. Frustrated, it returns to base again. Digby stares at his breakfast for a moment and goes in for a third attempt. The knuckles of his right hand whiten with the tighter grip he's put on. This time it's happening for him. It's getting there. Triumphantly, he steers the sausage and egg to his lips, opens his mouth . . . and then he catches me staring at him.

His fork spasms. The slice of sausage falls to the table, rolls to the edge and drops on to the floor. A lurcher lumbers to its feet, clicks across the tiles and snaffles it away.

'*Ffff . . . UCKK!*' A howl of anguish. Digby's tragic eyes boil with frustration and I have the feeling that he's about to cry. He's staring straight through me, shaking his head at the unfair-ness of life. And then an unearthly smile appears on his face, and his shoulders start to heave. 'Fucking breakfast's still alive.' He's gripping his knife and fork as though electric charges were being passed down them. 'How am I supposed to eat my bloody break— my bloody b— my sodding breakfast . . .' Tears roll down his cheeks. 'How am I supposed to eat if . . . if the bugger . . . if the bugger won't . . . if the bugger won't keep still?' And now he's weeping with laughter, rolling around in the chair in a way hardly anyone seems to laugh any more. Vic and Trish are laughing too. And in the gathering hysteria, I start to crack. There's something wonderfully grotesque about the melting candle face in the grip of the comic fire-storm. 'How do you . . .' Digby splutters, creased up, 'how do you . . . I mean how . . . how do you fucking *explain* it?' And now he's literally holding his sides, arms crossed over each other like the arms of a strait-jacket. Vic is rocking up and down in his seat, Trish has one hand at her neck, the other flapping, flapping, she's about to speak, and then the won-drous thing: between gasps for air, she replies, 'I don't know, Digby . . . it was . . . it was . . .' Explosive pause. 'It was quite dead when I cooked it.'

We fall about. The room's gone blurred and teary. The thought crosses my mind that we've all been drugged.

It takes several minutes for things to return to normal, with lots of sighs and 'dear, oh dears' and 'my words'. And from the expressions on people's faces, surprise and pleasure, I have the powerful feeling that Digby hasn't laughed like that in a very long time.

'Sorry about that, Alistair,' he says, still wiping away a tear. 'I don't know what you must think. We don't usually behave like this over breakfast.'

'Not at all. Makes a . . . makes a . . .' Oh fuck, now I'm starting to corpse. 'I mean to say, it makes a refreshing change from the *Today* programme.'

Generous laughter, rather than full-scale on-your-knees hysteria, but the whole episode leaves me feeling that we have been in the presence of something otherworldly. For a brief, hilarious moment, the curtain parted, and we hooted joyously at the cruel indifference of the universe; a vision of sunshine through rain clouds, glimpsed from the speeding train carriage.

Outside the window, a car suddenly pulls to a halt. It must have come from around the front of the house, which is why we didn't hear it approach. A tall, bald man emerges and makes his way towards the kitchen door.

'Well, well,' says Digby, wiping away a last tear, 'here's a turn-up. I didn't think Toby was arriving until Saturday.'

N I N E

1

Ah.

Oh shit.

Now this should be interesting.

People can change a lot over five years; however not so much usually that they completely fail to look like themselves. Sure, they grow fat or thin, old, or bald, but their face stays constant. And their voice, though that too can deepen, or take on a new accent – it remains their voice, doesn't it? True, you might forget what someone looks like after a long time apart, but you're always going to recognise them, aren't you, when you're reintroduced?

So the long and the short of it is that I'm fucked here, basically. If this was a deception comedy scam, and I was the producer in the white van, this is where I'd be saying, 'And . . . *cut*. Very nice. Thank you everyone.'

Like it says on the pinball machine, Game Over.

It's too late to run. Too late to race out of the room saying, 'I want to surprise him,' beetle back to the cottage, fill a bag and leg it across the fields. Too late, because there are only seconds before he's going to walk in through that door. And also, somehow too late in the day. The lie has gone on long enough. I should have ended it. I *would* have ended it, but for the charm of the location, its sense of peace, my morbid fascination with Digby. And Trish, of course. Gorgeous, deathly dull Trish, who just two minutes ago said something funny. Maybe the endorphins still squirting round my synapses from that laughter jag have dulled my sense of jeopardy, because I am weighted to my seat as though I were a sandbag. I have lost the will to struggle. I feel like the felon in the fifties crime caper who offers up his wrists to the policeman saying, 'It's a fair cop, guv.'

Like I say, this should be interesting.

The handle turns, the door swings open, and into the old country kitchen steps a tall, stooped, dark-eyed, bald figure, about my own age, I figure. Looks like some sort of gangling chemist.

Digby, struggling to shrug off the remains of his hangover, rises to greet his son. 'Toby!'

'Dad.'

They shake hands formally.

'We weren't expecting you until yesterday. I mean tomorrow. I mean the day after tomorrow.'

'Yeah. Sorry 'bout that.' Unsmiling. Sulky even.

Digby blithers. 'No. Not at all. Good to see you. And look who's here.'

The palms of my hands have turned into soup. As I stand,

I realise my legs have become weak. The knees don't seem to want to lock in place. My features feel as though they've arranged themselves into a mask of resignation, the expression one makes when the doctor picks his spot and says, 'You'll feel a slight prick.'

Toby's big dark eyes come to rest on mine. A tiny spasm passes across his face. And he says, 'Hey, Alistair, great to see you, mate. Where's your tan?'

2

Ah.

Make that a big fat *hmmm* if you like. Actually, make it a full-on *fuck me, now I'm genuinely confused*. In deception comedy, this is the moment where the cameraman would have zoomed in for the tight shot of my face, every tic and flicker of incomprehension up there on the big screen for the audience to howl at. But this isn't hidden camera. This, unless I have been extremely elaborately hoodwinked, is real life.

Isn't it?

Toby steps towards me and we shake hands. His grip is limp. There are deep scratches down the inside of his wrist. He sort of slaps me on the shoulder, a bit unconvincingly. Says 'hey' again. What did he just ask me? Oh yes. Where's the tan?

'Tried to keep pale and interesting, didn't I? How are *you*?' How I get these two sentences out, I don't know. I realise I am in a muck sweat.

'Bit frazzled, to be honest. Bloody awful drive down. There's been some sort of pile up outside Newton Abbot. All kinds of chaos. And the police no help, of course.'

I do a *tsk*. One of those tell-me-about-it *tsks*.

'I hope my father and his . . . his friends have been keeping you entertained,' he says, a rather unpleasant edge to his voice.

'Oh, definitely. In fact, we were only just . . .' But how to begin to explain what only just took place? That moments ago we were helpless with laughter because Digby had dropped a piece of sausage on to the floor and a passing lurcher had snacked upon it. 'No, absolutely. I've been absolutely fine.'

'Well, you're looking well,' says Toby.

'I, er, I am well. Yes, very well.'

I can't in all truth reciprocate the compliment. Toby looks a long way from what you'd call well. Actually, he looks dreadful. Purple rings circle his eyes. The lank straggles of dark hair clinging to the sides of his domed head are streaked with grey. Tightly packed isobars of a deep frown maintain a grip across his brow. I become aware of Digby, Trish and Vic looking at the two of us oddly. There follows a horrible pause, which Toby appears unwilling to fill.

'*So.*' I clap my hands together, in an effort to pop the air of expectation.

Toby seems to pull himself out of some private reverie. 'Sorry,' he says. 'Has my father shown you round the house yet?'

'Not really, no.' Immediately I have the feeling that I have just landed Digby in it. The old boy squirms slightly.

'You haven't seen the library?' Toby continues.

'No. Your father did tell me about it, though.'

'Dad, you might have shown Alistair the library.'

Digby begins to bluster. 'Such a mess. Everything in such a jumble. Never really been sorted since your mother . . .'

From personal experience, I know that hangovers come and go in waves. And from the look on Digby's face, I'd say that a mountainous one has just caught him squarely amidships. He does a deep swallow, almost existential in its depth, eyelids closing with the effort. When he comes back to the surface, he looks as though he's seen something very terrible down there.

'What held you up, Toby?' I ask as pleasantly as I can.

Toby sends me a level stare. 'Frances, I'm afraid. A last-minute callout. You know she's a psychiatric social worker now. Does emergency cover . . .'

I nod. I knew that.

'. . . some inconsiderate single mother, high as a kite, I've no doubt, picked Monday night to go doolally. So basically I was stuck with Oliver and Josh. And then Josh got another of his asthma attacks. So I had to take him to the hospital. And, and, oh look, sorry if it's all been a *TOTAL BLOODY MUDDLE*.'

Whoops. Baldy nearly lost it there for a moment. His fists are clenched, and a vein in his temple has started to throb in a worrying way. Something about his look of despair just now reminds me of his father – the same sense of helplessness in the face of events.

'Please. Not at all. Not a bit,' I coo. 'I've been enjoying myself hugely.'

I flash a knowing look across the table towards the magnificently sculpted face of Digby's housekeeper, her long fingers curled round a steaming mug of English Breakfast tea.

Toby sighs. 'Sorry. Sorry, Alistair mate. It's really good to see you.'

'Yeah. You too.' Oh, *please*.

Another uncomfortable pause. Digby fills it this time with, 'You two must have a lot to catch up on. Why don't you . . .' He trails off. His train of thought doesn't run that far.

'Fancy a stroll round the grounds?' pleads Toby.

'Sure.'

As we leave, is it my imagination, or is Trish blushing?

3

Say nothing. That's the trick. Let the punter do all the talking, give you all the clues. Except, who's the punter in this scene? Who's fooling who, exactly?

It's hard, but I'm determined not to be the one to blink first. About a minute passes before he speaks, when we're well clear of the house, heading down the path that leads to the lake.

'Sorry about that.'

'Not at all.' What's to be sorry for?

'Bringing up the suntan thing. Bloody silly of me. I forgot, what we agreed.'

'Doesn't matter, honestly.' Uh?

He smiles weirdly. 'I was looking forward to hearing you explain how you didn't tan. Couldn't tan. Because of the rare defect in your pigmentation.'

Uhhhh??????

'Ah well.'

'You still could, of course. Explain. That pale and interesting thing could have just been a cover.'

'Yeah.'

'You could be embarrassed about telling people.' He's looking at me intently. There's a light in his eyes that wasn't there in the kitchen. There, he seemed more like the sulky son returning home. Now he's all keen and down-to-business.

Then he says, 'You seem different in real life, Julian.'

'Really?' Real life? Julian?

'Yes. It's funny how you imagine people when you've only spoken to them on the phone.'

'Yes, it is odd, that.' It's true. It is.

'I'd pictured you as older. And I suppose I was stupidly expecting you to look like the *actual* Alistair Gough. The one I *was* at university with.'

'Ah.' I manage a sort of snigger. 'Can't help you there, I'm afraid.'

'But I think it helps, having you be someone that I *may* have mentioned to my folks over the years. A name they could have a half-memory of.'

'Oh, yes.' Er, definitely.

'Rather than a completely made-up name.'

'No.'

'Or your real name!' He thinks this is an amusing idea.

'No indeed.'

'So how do you want to play this?'

'You tell me. Your patch and everything.'

Toby – and I suppose we must assume he really is Toby, and not Miles or Gervase or Cuthbert or fucking Myfanwy – Toby wants to play it like this: in a while, we'll go back to the house and he'll show me the library. Dad thinks I'm a big reader, so checking out the Gulliver family library will be perfectly natural. Then later, tonight or tomorrow, in any case whenever Digby is dribbling drunk, and Vic is safely asleep or minding his own business, we'll pay it another, longer visit. On this occasion I'll have the time to examine the books more carefully, identifying the ones that will excite the serious collectors, the editions that will fetch 'thousands rather than hundreds'. I'll note their titles, and their exact position on the shelves, so that when it comes to it, Toby can lay his hands on them readily. Toby is sure – he's sorry to repeat himself, but he's absolutely certain – there's 'big money' on those shelves. He's talking Swift, Defoe, Keats, Byron, Shelley, what have you. There are Bibles, ancient atlases, star charts, weapons manuals. He remembers opening a leather-bound volume and finding its date was *fourteen*-bloody-something-or-other. All kinds of expensive-looking shit just sitting up there doing nothing, waiting to get attacked by moths, or damp, or specialist mites whose idea of a good time is throwing a lunch party in a really valuable first edition. I'm the expert, apparently. After I supply him with a list of the top fifteen or twenty most precious titles, when the moment is right, he'll make them disappear – either a few at a time or maybe all at once. Either way, Digby will never notice, he guarantees it. I sell them privately or through my firm, it doesn't matter. We share the profit in the manner agreed.

Toby's quite excited about the whole thing, I can tell.

'You know, Julian, I should have done this years ago. It's the sheer waste that's so sickening. He does nothing with the house. Just look at the place, for God's sake. It's going to shit. And there's no cash, of course; that's all tied up in the property. About time somebody got a grip.'

'How did you get those scratches on your hand, Toby?' I ask by way of a non sequitur, a powerful technique, I have discovered, when you haven't a fucking clue how else to respond.

'Red setter. Just as I was about to slip him the needle. Took my eye off the ball for half a second.' He shakes his head. Smiles ruefully. 'Would you believe I've been a vet for fifteen bloody years, Julian, and it's the first one that's ever got me.'

4

It's a library all right. You don't need to be an antiquarian book dealer to recognise one of those when you see one, even if it is snuggling under half a ton of dust, cobwebs and bat shit.

Books – there are hundreds of the bastards here. Make that thousands, actually. I do a sort of scholarly 'Mmm' as we stand in the doorway and survey the scene.

Books climb all four walls from floor to ceiling. To reach

the topmost volumes, there's even one of those mini-staircase-on-wheels jobs with a handrail. There are piles of books on each of its steps. All around there are more books. There are fucking books everywhere. Tottering heaps, tower-like formations, chest high, that you have to suck your stomach in to squeeze between. Piles that have collapsed and caused other piles to collapse and then further piles. Great drifts of literature subsiding across the carpet like fractured geological strata. Ancient volumes with leather bindings and metal clasps lying cheek by jowl with lurid fifties thrillers. Across everything hangs the musty smell of damp woodpulp. Motes of dust dance in the sunlight slanting in through tall windows.

'First impression?' Toby whispers.

My eyes flick across the chaos. 'Difficult to say.'

'How long do you think you'll need?'

I shoot him my sincere deadpan stare (learnt it off Peter Marcus), the one that says, Stand by, I'm about to say something significant. 'It's really hard to know, Toby. I don't want to guess and then be wildly out.'

'Roughly.'

I take a deep breath. Set my jaw. Narrow my gaze. Fold my arms and do a slow three-sixty turn, my eyes flicking over the shelves professionally – you know, up and down, side to side and stuff. I scratch my head. Sigh.

'I think I shall need to take a view about that.' You prick.

'But it's doable?' His eyes are anxious. The plough-lines on his forehead have deepened.

I smile reassuringly. 'Leave it with me, Toby.' You treacherous cocksucker.

He looks relieved and plants himself in a ratty wing-backed armchair where he picks up a volume at random, turning the pages, not seeing them. With my hands clasped bookishly behind my back, I begin to prowl the room, pulling ancient-looking editions off the shelves, blowing away a little dust here, tap-tapping an impressive binding there, humming, whistling, making odd clicking noises with my tongue to denote absorption, uttering the occasional thoughtful, 'Mmm', a 'Well, well' or two, even the odd '*Hah!*'

But all the time I'm thinking, You toad. You absolute wretched fucking worm. You . . . What's worse than a worm? Maybe, like a maggot or something. Anyhow, you get the drift. I replay the conversation we had a few minutes ago, when we finished the short tour of Digby's ruined estate. As we were making our way back up towards the house.

'Have you met my father's housekeeper?' he asks.

'Trish. Yes, I have.'

'What do you think?'

'What do you mean?'

'What do you think of *her*?'

'She seems . . . very nice.'

'Highly shaggable, don't you think?'

'She's very . . . striking, yes. Very.'

'But shaggable, wouldn't you say?' His eyes are shining horribly.

'Not the word I would have picked.'

'Shaggable in both senses. In the sense that she's a real babe, a *real* babe, and also in the sense that you probably *could* shag her. If you made an effort, she'd probably let you.'

'You think so?'

'She looks open to it. Some women just do. Doesn't even matter whether they're married or not. You just know, if you tried hard enough, you could shag them. She's one of those. Sure of it.'

'How did you come by this . . . fascinating idea?'

I feel slightly sick as the gangling vet expounds his theory, gesturing with his spidery arms for emphasis, pausing occasionally to rake bitten fingernails across the region where hair might once have waved in the breeze.

'It's like a sixth sense. You look at a woman, and right away you can tell from the way she looks back at you whether she's open to the idea. Sometimes you can tell even before she can tell. If she's all closed down, and there's nothing there, you may as well just forget it. You're wasting your time. But if she's open to it . . . when she looks at you, you know, you just *know* that if you were prepared to put in the spadework, you could definitely get into her knickers. Could take hours or days or even weeks, but you'd definitely get there.'

'Spadework?'

'All the chitchat, dinner, flowers, endless flattery.'

'That's how you do it?'

He gives me a funny look. 'I'm a married man, so it doesn't come into it. But just because you're on a diet, doesn't mean you can't look at the menu, does it?'

'I've heard that before somewhere.'

'All I'm saying is that Trish is highly shaggable. And if I were single, I'd be doing my spadework. Are you single, Julian?'

'Sort of.' Then I add without thinking, 'Well, actually there *is* someone.'

With a small shock, I realise I'm not sure who it is I'm referring to.

Is it Kate the copper?

Or Cheryl? (Surely not.)

Linds, perhaps? (Don't be ridiculous.)

Or is it — in fact — Trish?

It occurs to me that this is the second time within only a few days that I've been lectured on the art of seduction. Blubber-chops in Yech had a theory, didn't he? Humour them into bed, that was it. Make them laugh and you're . . . you're laughing. The larcenous vet meanwhile emphasises a supposed pre-existing sexual readiness on the part of the female, over and above any particular technique employed by the male.

Hmm. Which would be more annoying? I wonder. If he's right, or if he's wrong?

5

I drop into the wing-back armchair opposite Toby's, sending up a small cloud of dust.

'Was your father a collector?' I ask quite reasonably. Fuck of a lot of books here.

'His father was the collector. My father just presides over waste and decay.'

A chessboard stands on a small table between us, a game in progress. From the thick layer of dust across the board and pieces, it's clear no one has made a move in a very long time.

'Your father has no interest in these books? He wouldn't know which had any value?'

'Nowadays my father takes no interest in anything less than forty per cent proof. You've seen what he's like, pissed old husk.'

'I gather he's been persuaded to reinstate the summer fair.'

Toby snorts. 'What's your view, then? How long do you need for a proper inspection? A night? A couple of nights?'

'I guess a night should do it.'

'Fine. Dad still likes to mark the weekend by getting extra-specially paralytic.'

'Tell me about your dad. I'm intrigued.'

Toby gives me a funny look.

And then he tells me a story. Not even attempting to keep the scorn out of his voice. About how, as a young man, his father followed the pattern of many young men of his class and generation and joined his own father's old regiment. And although he was a competent officer, and gained promotions at a respectable rate, something conspired to keep him, and each group of men under his command, away from the action. Whenever there was serious soldiering to be done, they were always either posted too soon or too late. Or there was a badly timed tour of duty at battalion headquarters. Or they'd get sent somewhere exotic where nothing was happening.

'My father was too young for World War Two. He missed Suez. Missed Malaya. Missed Aden. Missed Kenya. Missed Cyprus. Missed the Falklands.

'Whenever he was posted to Northern Ireland, it was inevitably during one of the quiet, dull spells. And the years he spent in Germany with the British Army on the Rhine were a joke frankly, doing exercises in the countryside, practising for the Russian invasion. He used to tell us that half our armoured personnel carriers wouldn't start. Then one day some clown would decide to drive his tank through a hausfrau's back garden, and he'd be on the phone for weeks trying to pacify Kraut lawyers demanding compensation . . .

'The horrible truth of it,' says Toby, 'is my father has missed every serious scrap the British Army has been in since the war. He's never fired a shot in anger. He used to be ashamed about it. Now I don't think he gives a shit about anything.'

Toby gets to his feet. The Gulliver melancholy clings to the son's stooped, stringy frame like mist in a hollow.

'I'm glad you could help me do this, Julian,' he says. 'Do I need to get you anything?'

'What sort of thing?'

'Equipment – special gloves, torches, what have you?'

'I have everything I need.' The complete professional.

'Good man. I've got a few calls to make.'

And he slopes off, shuffling between the stacks of books, out of the door.

It takes me a good ten minutes to find it. Hidden behind a pile of bound nineteenth-century volumes of *Punch*, one of a handful of framed pictures stacked against a wall. You wouldn't look at it twice unless you knew. Initialled 'A.H.' in the bottom left-hand corner, it's a watercolour of a European city scene. There are a couple of apartment blocks, another civic building, and a big, gloomy-looking church. Quite technically proficient, I suppose, but all rather ponderously executed, the heavy architecture more convincing than the few tiny figures peopling the cobbled streets. It has to be Vienna, about 1910. Where Hitler was a penniless artist churning out such anodyne views for the makers of frames and pedlars of hand-painted postcards. Carefully, I take the picture over to the armchair and gaze fascinated into the brushstrokes. I guess I'm looking for clues. To madness, to evil, to history. Each of the five civilians in the picture stands alone. There's no sense of animation about any of them. Dwarfed by the walls and roofs towering above, it's as if someone's shouted 'freeze'. A dark foreboding hangs over the whole scene.

And then suddenly it hits me: the surreal nature of this moment, squinting at a watercolour allegedly painted by Adolf Hitler, in a tumbledown mansion in Devon where an elderly broken drunk believes me to be a doctor, an old friend of his son; while this same son believes I am an antiquarian books specialist who has agreed to enter into a criminal conspiracy to help him steal his father's property.

I suddenly have an enormous pang of nostalgia for my old life – my job, my flat, my sexy black sofa with an attractive young woman down one end of it.

What the fuck am I doing here?

6

Guess what? One of my ridiculous ideas for Erica has been 'picked up', as we say in the trade. It's *Erica Birkendale, Forever Young*, the one where she mixes it with a load of twenty-year-olds (music, clubs, lifestyle blah blah blah), allowing the thirty-, forty- and fifty-somethings a look-in at youth culture, while in the process the rancid old tart becomes some kind of iconic, post-modern personage, like Nicholas Parsons, or another of those old beezers who young people seem to take to their hearts for ironic purposes. Actually, it hasn't *quite* been picked up, but the channel are said to be 'biting hard', which is the next best thing. Inevitably they will want to 'tweak it', making subtle changes to the show's emphasis and direction. The first thing they wish to tweak is the title. It may become *Erica's Groove* or *Erica's in the Groove*. Possibly *Erica's Groove Thing*. Apparently, the channel see it as a great 'crossover' idea, the presence of Erica making the horrible music and terrible clothes accessible to that section of the audience who 'aspire downwards on the age ladder' – while simultaneously appealing to upwardly aspiring teenagers as yet lacking the necessary spending power to drink alcohol and do e's. Oh yeah. And it'll be cheap as chips. They're going to shoot the fucker on those digital cameras you can buy in larger branches of Dixons, all in hand-held horror-vision. Erica is thrilled, of course, as it means exposing herself to a whole new generation of viewers. In fact, the very people who watched her the first time round when she was a kid's presenter can now sit down with their own teenage children and marvel at what they can do these days with make-up and embalming fluid. Oh, and you'll never guess who's going to produce it.

Larva-features. Robyn with a Y. Seeing as how she's in touch with young people. You know, what with being one herself.

I get all this from Rose and Geraldine when, a little home-sick and weirded out just now, I walk back to my cottage and call them at work.

'Where the hell *are* you, Charlie?' Geraldine asks

'Devon. It's quite nice here, actually.'

'Come back. We miss you.'

'I miss you too. But it's good to have a change of scene. I'd never have come up with *Erica's Groove* in NoCaSoCha.'

'Oh, was that yours? I thought it was Robyn's.'

'Why would you think that?'

'She's been working on it with Peter Marcus.'

Oh she has, has she?

When Rose comes on the line, I have another serious attack of nostalgia. I can just picture her at her desk at Tuna Television, the phone trapped between ear and chin, uncapping her Grande Latte, eyes half shut, that wicked smile.

'Have you fallen in love with a creamy-faced Devon girl, then?' How did she know?

'Er, love would be too strong a word for it.'

'What's her name?'

'Trish, as a matter of fact.'

'Good name . . .'

'Do you think so?'

'. . . for a bathroom cleaner. What does she do?'

'Actually she's a nutritionist.'

'Ask her if it's true about hard-boiled eggs.'

'What about them?'

'They take more energy to digest than they actually contain. So if you ate nothing but hard boiled eggs, you'd starve to death.'

'I'll come back to you on that one.'

When I hang up, I realise how much I've been missing these

girls, their *side*, their *edge*. But the thought of the actual office makes me slightly queasy. I could hear it there in the background, the hum of the computers' cooling fans, the jangling phones, Barry saying things like, 'I thought the cut-away on the poodle was a knat's too long.'

I email Peter.

To: Peter Marcus
From: Charles Green
Subject: Erica's Groove Thing

Dear Peter,
   Delighted to hear that one plank of Erica's raft is in place. Do you want me to continue thinking up further planks? Or are there other special projects you'd like me to get my teeth into?
   Devon is beautiful. Weather lovely.
   All best,
   Charles

An hour later he replies.

To: Charles Green
From: Peter Marcus
Subject: RE: Erica's Groove Thing Whatever

Charles
   Very good news about Groove Thing. Yes please keep thinking. More ideas welcome.
   Peter

What a cunt, eh? He didn't say, 'Very good news about *Groove Thing* and, by the way, Charles, bloody well done for your brilliant "crossover" idea, which will help keep Tuna TV in business, me, Peter Marcus, in a job, and the company nicely in bed with Erica.' No, none of that. Not, 'More wonderful ideas urgently needed, only you can do it.' Just '*ideas welcome*' (like 'Pets Welcome'). He didn't put 'Dear Charles'. Just 'Charles'.

Or am I reading too much in? It has been known.

7

'How do you take it?' Digby is stationed over the drinks cart, feet planted wide apart to minimise the falling-flat-on-your-arse factor.

'Just straight please,' I remind my host gently.

'No ice or water or anything?'

'Nothing thanks. Just whisky and whisky.'

'Good man. Can't abide cubes. Only get in the way.'

Famous Grouse gouts into my tumbler.

It's a sorry collection of individuals who've gathered for 'cocktails' this evening in the Gulliver sitting room. There's my host (his whisky-pouring arm, I note with alarm, appears to be paralysed). There's Toby, who I see has made a bit of an effort for dinner (shaved and tucked his shirt into his trousers). There's Vic . . .

'What's it to be, Vic?' asks Digby.

'Usual, please,' he replies.

'Can you help yourself?' says Digby. 'Tonic's such a fiddle faddle.'

. . . and there's Trish. Trish, who's slipped away from the kitchen and is sportingly sipping a ginger ale to make up the numbers.

I'm delighted to see that Toby (can of Heineken) is still in a strop with me after a conversation we had earlier today in this same sitting room. I'd found him alone mid-afternoon, irritably paging through the *Daily Telegraph*. I explained that I wouldn't be staying for dinner tonight, owing to an appointment with an important client of mine, a keen buyer of seventeenth-century Flemish manuscripts who lives just outside Paignton (found it on a map, didn't I).

'Since we didn't think you'd be arriving until Saturday, I thought I'd take the opportunity to visit him,' I said. 'I told your father I was seeing an old friend of my family's.'

I think Toby imagined that we'd be sneaking off and doing some scheming together this evening, because he whined like a spoilt child. 'You didn't say you had a client down here.'

'You didn't say you would be delayed. And it's too good a chance to miss. You know, this chap is quite an influential character in the antiquarian book world. It's perfectly possible . . .' I believe I pressed my fingertips together at this point to signify subtlety and discretion, '. . . that he might be able to do *us* some good.'

Toby sniffs. I realise I have become more 'booky' in my dealings with the irritable vet. Metaphorically, I've donned a velvet jacket, somehow lightening my tread, making my movements more delicate – picking away imaginary pieces of fluff from my sleeve and suchlike – generally coming on like the cravat-wearing aesthete with a serious romantic poetry habit.

This evening, as we stand in the grim little circle, me, Toby, Vic and Trish – Digby subsided on to the sofa below us, beaker of booze in a tight grip – Toby enquires sulkily, 'So who's this . . . this *friend* of your family in Paignton then?'

'Peter Marcus. Went to university with my father.' Come on, cunt-face, ask me another.

'You'll be missing a treat,' says Vic. 'Something in that kitchen is smelling lovely.'

'Organic hotpot,' chimes Trish. 'And I've put out an organic fruit tart for you to follow.'

'You won't be joining us?' says Toby, a little horror-struck.

'My Thursday night yoga class,' replies Trish with a small blush.

A metallic crack as Toby's beer can crumples into his fist. I have a hard time keeping a straight face at his all-too-visible dismay at the prospect of a cosy evening in with the two ex-servicemen.

'Watched a fascinating documentary about yogics,' mumbles Digby at our feet. 'Little Indian fellow can suck a whole glass of water up through his cock. Remarkable control.'

Vic pipes up again: 'Who was that fellow at Catterick who used to do the trick with spaghetti?'

Digby chuckles. 'Inhaled it through his nose.'

'That's him.'

'But not if there was any chilli in the sauce.'

Thanks to my mega-Scotch, by the time I'm ready to be on my way, I'm three parts pissed. I leave the men in the sitting room, Digby and Vic on the sofa, rumbling at each other quietly, Toby in an armchair, seething with despair. I put my head round the kitchen door. Trish is rising off her haunches, carrying something hot out of the oven. I have a powerful urge to walk up behind her and put my arms round her waist.

'Have a good session,' I say.

She turns. 'Thanks.'

'Give that fat old sun a salutation from me.' Yoga-talk, innit.

She smiles. 'I will.'

I lower my voice. 'And see you . . . what, about nine?'

She blushes slightly. 'Yes, about then.'

Somewhat unforgivably, I wink. Can't think why, really. Must be all this cloak-and-dagger.

8

I'm sitting in the Totnes Tavern. And because I'm waiting for Trish, and because our last date ended on such a note of promise, I've taken the precaution of downing a couple more large whiskies before she shows up, just to loosen things up even further. I've made a bit of an effort myself this evening (wearing my newest shirt, rather grey and fashionable, I fancy) and right now I'm running through the possible ways the night could turn. I particularly like the one that gets off to a flying start within minutes, lots of staring into each other's eyes, knowing looks, sexual tension dripping all over the place; we set off towards the Chinese or wherever, but before we get ten yards down the road, we subside into a romantic alleyway – the town is cross-hatched with scores of quaint romantic thoroughfares – and her face is in mine, my hands are in her hair and and and . . .

There are a number of variations on this theme (all end with the face/face thing) and then there's the *other* version. The one where we have a balls-aching two hours in the pub, I can't warm the dialogue into any sort of bubbling flirtatiousness, she only wants to talk about sodding vegetables or the like; there follows a deadly knife and forker; when we get back to the house, she sashays off to bed leaving me with a belly full of booze, chow mein and unrequited lust.

If I think about her too much, this hopeful, expectant mood of mine could collapse like a soufflé. I'm perfectly capable of putting a curse on the whole evening by entertaining a treacherous thought like, This is a total waste of time, Charles Green. The woman, strikingly lovely as she is – her beauty even carries with it a *nobility*, yes it does, an assumption of added virtue, that one projects on her as if she were a thoroughbred racehorse or a pedigree cat – sorry, where was I, oh yes, strikingly lovely as she is, Trish is . . . let's be kind . . . she just isn't on your wavelength. You have nothing in common. Oh bollocks, she's a world-class dullard. A crasher of Olympic proportions. I mean, it is possible to say 'a smile doesn't cost anything' ironically, but she didn't. Face it, in a civilised society, how can one go to bed with a woman who believes in moderation. In all things. Even in *that*, presumably.

No, it's really rather hopeless being attracted to someone you have no interest in beyond the fact of attraction itself. The thing feels weightless, fragile, like a great gorgeous soap bubble. If she's attracted to you in return, the affair may float, buoyed up by the power of self-fulfilling prophesy. If she isn't . . . well, all you've got is a stain on the pavement.

Mind you, there were distinctly hopeful signs earlier this afternoon. I was sitting in the doorway of my cottage, banging out more silly ideas for Erica. I had one eye on Trish in her vegetable garden where she was snipping at shoots, trailing fronds, pegging whatnots and generally looking fucking ravishing.

'Interesting to see old Toby again. How well do you know him?' I enquire.

'Not very,' she replies. 'Not as well as you, obviously.'

'Funny how much people can change in five years,' I suggest.

She stops snipping. Straightens. Jams one arm of the secateurs down the back pocket of her jeans (the image immediately joining my small private collection of arresting vignettes).

'How has he changed, would you say?' she asks.

'He seems more careworn than I remember. Perhaps he's worried about his dad.'

She snorts at the idea. Then looks a little embarrassed.

'To be honest, Trish, he's not the same Toby I went to university with. That Toby was . . .' Er . . . yeah? 'That was an altogether different Toby. Are you doing anything this evening, Trish? At all?'

She tells me about yoga. And *after* yoga? I enquire. Nothing particularly, she says, eyes widening. Could we have a drink together? I ask. There's something rather important I want to share with you.

'What sort of thing?' she asks.

'I'd rather tell you tonight. If you don't mind.'

'I hope it's something good.'

'Oh, it's good, all right.'

'You want to give me a clue?'

'It's . . . it's about something rather close to home, as a matter of fact.'

'Care to say any more?'

'It's something you should know.'

'I see.'

'Yes.'

'But you can't talk about it.'

'I will tonight.'

'Around nine then?'

'Great.'

When my fingers return to the laptop, I realise they are trembling.

I'd say we were definitely flirting just then.

9

She's late. I've read the *Totnes Times* from end to end (goodness me, that council recycling initiative sounds exciting). So since I've got a moment, I drag something that was lurking in the back of my mind into the light, and give it a kick to see what kind of state it's in. *'I'm not hearing anything. Hang up and try again.'* Loopy Loo. The man's voice. As sickening a piece of late-night dialogue as I've ever heard (and that includes 'Did you remember to set the alarm?', 'There's someone moving about downstairs' and 'Shit, I think it's burst').

Of course the conversation doesn't prove that Loopy Loo *is* a man. Plenty of other people could have access to that phone. But it was late when I rang. And Loopy Loo does tend to call late herself.

Himself.

Whatever.

Loopy Loo, a *bloke*. How fucking weird is that?

Because of the extra-large load of Famous Grouse now happily careening round the old arterial ringroads, I do something I'd never do if I was stone cold s.: I fish out the mobile, locate the stored number and press Call. Twenty past nine on a weekday evening. Who's going to be at home?

'Hello?' Oh fuck, it's him. The same guy. The same nice, polite middle-class voice.

Silence. (Mine this time.)

'Hello? Sorry, can't hear you. Anyone there?'

Beep. (I beeped).

'Oh.' Fucking right, oh.

Beep beep.

'Ah. Oh dear.'

Beep beep beep.

A long pause and then, 'Hello? Is that, er, you, Charles?'

'It is.'

'Ah . . .' A bloody long pause. A heavy sigh. 'I'm sorry, I don't really know what to say.'

I know this voice, and yet I don't. I feel a mixture of fascination and disgust. 'How about starting by telling me who you are, and why you've been telephoning me.' I say '*telephoning*', like in a fifties film.

Another sigh. 'Sorry. It's a bit difficult. This is rather uncomfortable. Do you think we might talk a little later? When I've had a chance to collect my thoughts.' Something oddly familiar . . .

'Sure.' What the hell? 'What's good for you?'

'Later tonight? Do you mind? Sorry.'

'No, it's fine. Shall we leave it that you'll call me? When you're ready.'

'That would be most thoughtful.' Where have I heard . . . ?

'And you will call?'

'Certainly.'

'Because I do feel you owe me some sort of—'

'Explanation. I realise. I assure you I'll call you back.' Something in his tone makes me believe him.

'Talk later then.'

'Yes. Later. Thanks. Sorry.' No. I can't place it.

He hangs up.

I turn off the mobile and gaze up at the light fittings. Then I say, 'Fuck a duck.' I must have said fuck a duck in quite a loud voice, because I become aware of the table full of young people opposite, staring across their pints and their roll-ups at me. They break out giggling amongst themselves.

I want to explain, Actually, I'm not one of those people who shout expletives in public places. In fact, there's a very good reason for my behaviour just then. You see, it's like this . . .

But it seems easier to bag another Famous Grouse.

10

An hour of yoga has put Trish in a serene place where, if anything, she looks even lovelier. Her skin has a bloom, a sheen to it, which goes all the way around the amazing jawbone and extends down on to her long, fabulous neck. This is a neck you want to consider seriously, to stare at for extended periods of time, put your nose and mouth against, inhale gusts of female stuff from. (Rude to stare at a woman's neck for too long; eventually you're forced to return to the negotiating table of her face.) There's a pinkish glow to her fine, intelligent forehead (nature can be a terrible piss-taker), her eyes shine with a high lustre. I realise I'm not trying all that hard to put out of my mind the exciting shapes her body must have been contorted into, just a few minutes ago in the smelly old church hall.

'How do you feel?' I ask. 'You look . . . wonderful.'

She ignores the compliment. 'You feel all tingly. And a bit spaced out.'

'Is it hard?'

'Some of the positions are. There's one where you're like a backwards crab. You're on your back, with your hands behind your head, and then you push your body off the ground with your hands and feet.'

She sticks her elbows out sideways and flips back her wrists to demonstrate the interesting angles involved. I picture what she must look like in this attitude, suppressing the desire to ask what she wears while this is going on – I'm guessing tight-fitting leotard – and whether one can buy tickets to watch.

'Doesn't the alcohol blur the effect of the yoga?' I ask, nodding towards the nice creamy pint that sits in front of her.

'I don't know really. I don't usually go for a drink afterwards. We'll have to see.'

She takes a sip. Then, holding my gaze, she slowly, deliberately, licks away her foam moustache, as stirring a sight as I've seen in a long time. Was it a sexual signal of unmistakable clarity (what they do in this part of the world to semaphore their interest)? Or just a natural act in a yoga-induced moment of stillness? Either way, I find I am suddenly lost for words. I dive back into my whisky glass.

'So, what did you have to tell me this evening?' she asks, a small smile playing around her mouth. Fuck, she *is* flirting with me.

'It's about Toby.'

'Oh.' A faint look of disappointment, as if she was hoping that I was about to say, Actually, Trish, it's about you. And me. You see, I don't know how it happened so quickly but . . . but I'm nuts about you. (Fuck it, I can always make this speech later.)

'I probably shouldn't be saying this really, what with you being his father's housekeeper and all . . .'

She arches an eyebrow at me, a trick that I have always found fantastically attractive.

No, sorry. I'm helpless against a well-arched eyebrow. To me, the single arched female eyebrow speaks of sophistication, irony, a hint of physical playfulness, a degree of flirtation. It hangs up there, seeming to set a delicious question mark against things.

'You know something, Trish, I don't think I actually *like* Toby any more.'

She smiles knowingly. Then she says, 'Can you keep a secret?'

'Yes.' I know what's coming.

'I've *never* liked him, which is awful really, because I adore Digby. Everyone does. Despite, you know, everything.'

'What is it, do you think?' I ask. 'About Toby?'

She gazes at me rather seriously. 'I don't like the way he looks at me.'

'What do you mean?'

'He gives me the creeps.'

And what about the way that *I* look at you? 'Odd fellow all round, I reckon.'

'And he's really cold towards his dad. It's terribly sad, Alistair.'

The look of pain across her wide, open face fills my heart with longing. I can see the ridge marks in her black hair, still damp from yoga, where the comb dragged through it. I have a strong urge to tell her everything: about Toby's plan to steal the books; that I'm not Alistair, I'm Charles; not a doctor but a television producer; that I think she may be the loveliest woman I have ever laid eyes upon.

'The way he walked in through the door this morning. I mean, a smile doesn't cost anything, does it?'

Oh Christ. And it was all going so well.

11

Up at the bar, in a crush of young Totnes types, trying to get served, I'm able to check a peculiar phenomenon that I've just become aware of. I've been sneaking looks back to where Trish is sitting, on her own now, looking pleasantly off into space. Every time I glance over towards her, I confirm what I thought: that although she is *fantastically* attractive – she stands out here like a movie star fallen among goblins – no one else seems to have noticed. No lagered-up young men are giving her the leery once-over. No sad old bastards gaze resentfully over their light and bitters. Even the women haven't run the usual cold, hard stares across her bodywork. A smoky Balkan temptress sits in the midst of these people in her own little pool of light, and they simply don't see it.

Spooky, don't you think? Or perhaps it's me. Maybe she's really rather plain, and I'm the only one who's failed to recognise it. Fuck, maybe she's a ghost – she does look a little unearthly, bathed in the glow from a beam-mounted spotlight – and maybe I'm actually here on my own. Or how about this for a possibility: maybe I *died* in the arrivals hall at Heathrow, maybe the evil little fucker shot me, and everything that followed (Vic, the drive, Digby, Toby, Trish) is the afterlife. Or maybe . . . maybe I'm really on the operating table, a bullet in my brain, the life force ebbing away, and this is the weird shit my poor flickering synapses are coming up with.

Or maybe it's the heat and the noise and the strange zone of stillness round Trish. Or the booze. Whatever it is, I'm beginning to feel a little unwell.

'Forceps?'

'Sorry?'

'Fosters. Is Fosters OK? We've run out of Carlsberg.' The barman is looking at me like I'm stupid or something.

'Yes. Sure. Whatever.'

'What's the matter, Alistair? You've gone a bit pale.' I drop into a seat alongside Trish and put a hand to my brow. It feels cold, and slightly clammy. Now she does a wonderful thing. Almost in slow motion, she lifts her long hand, presses its fine warm fingers against my forehead and stares into my eyes. I have the instant urge to kiss her, ghost or no ghost.

'You do feel a bit chilly.' Her hand is still up there.

'It's the drink. That cocktail of Digby's would knock over a horse.'

'What do you mean?' The hand. Still at my head. Her eyes. Still peering into mine.

'It was a very big drink. He practically filled the glass.'

'What did you say about the horse?'

'Well, if a horse were to drink one, it would most probably fall over.'

'But horses don't drink. Not alcohol.'

'I know they don't. It's a turn of phrase.'

'Oh.' I can feel her fingers about to leave my forehead. I clamp my own over them, holding her hand in place.

'It's like . . . like . . . well, I can't think of another.'

'Water off a duck's back.'

'Yes. That's one. The cat's pyjamas, that's another.'

'Happy as a sandbag.'

'Sandboy, surely.'

'Is it?'

'It's sandboy, definitely. I'll be a monkey's uncle.'

'I don't think I know that one.'

'You must do. I'll be a monkey's uncle.'

'What does it mean?'

'It's an expression of surprise.'

'Why would you say it?'

'Probably to do with Darwin or something.'

She doesn't reply. Her breathing, I realise, has become rather heavy. Shit, it's arrived. The moment. Our faces are very close. Hers more or less fills my visual field. I can feel warm pulses radiating from her fingers into my head.

I do it.

I kiss her.

It was easy really.

She hasn't moved and she didn't resist.

So I do it again. This time, she even kisses me back a little.

Then a third time. She's somewhat tentative, but definitely answering.

'Sorry.' Why did I say that? I'm not a bit sorry.

'Well, Alistair,' she says, my hand still pressing hers against my head. 'I'll be a monkey's auntie.'

12

I laugh and it dissolves the spell. She settles back and picks up her drink. We're in a public place, and now we've got that embarrassing thing where we have to think of things to talk about instead of sinking joyously into each other's flesh. She takes a sip from her fresh pint.

'May I?' I ask. Slowly, I slide the tip of my little finger across her top lip, wiping away her froth moustache. Her lip *gives* slightly in the most intoxicating way. The spell is instantly recast. Never mind the whisky, the promising look she's giving me here could knock over a horse. A boy horse, I'm talking about.

'Don't go anywhere,' I tell her. Without breaking eye contact until the last possible moment, I get to my feet and head towards the gents.

Fuck, this is it. She's gone into that stunned, almost stupefied state some women go into when they are about to abandon themselves to you. Eyes widened, lips apart. As if they've just walked away from a car wreck.

I'm hosing a cigarette end along the porcelain canal when, horribly, the words of Toby Gulliver come back to me.

'Highly shaggable, don't you think?'

Shut up.

'Shaggable in both senses of the word.'

Please.

'Put in the spadework and you could definitely get into her knickers.'

Stop it.

But he's right. It *is* going to happen. My stomach lurches at the thought.

I couldn't tell you which I become aware of first. The wave of foul breath from somewhere over my shoulder. Or the sharp metallic point in the side of my neck.

In the end, perhaps it is the voice. The words that freeze my blood.

'You can come with me quietly. Or you can bleed to death in leth than two minitth. What'th it to be, cunt-faith?'

TEN

1

'You're pithing down your trouther leg, Charlth.'

I can't see him. He's behind me and to my right, to the side of my neck the point of the blade is digging into. I can tell he's been eating onions, though.

'W-w-w-w . . .'

I am having trouble speaking. For the second time in twelve hours, my legs have turned to custard. My heart is beating so hard I can hear it. If someone cuts your throat, do you really bleed to death in under two minutes? (Must look it up.)

'W-w-would you mind putting that knife away? It's rather putting me off. I won't . . . I won't make any sudden movements.'

He laughs, the Mutley *heh-heh-heh*. He chuckles to himself for an indecently long time.

'What's funny?'

'You are, Charlth. Thudden movementth. For a minute there, I thought you might have done a thudden movement in your pantth. You've gone awfully white.'

I'd laugh if I wasn't so frightened.

'Please, Luke.' Use the fucker's name. Get him to regard you as a human, not a tray of offal. 'Could you just take away the knife? I'll do whatever you say.'

I think of my friend Adele, exhausted mother of high-spirited toddlers Louis and Ben. Adele often talks about the folly of trying to reason with a two-year-old. How they simply don't get it. How it's not in their language. Does the same principle apply here, I wonder, attempting to reason with a psychopathic armed criminal?

I feel the blade withdraw.

'Thank you.'

Slowly I turn my head. And there it is. The great boulder of a skull, the shining greasy skin, the hair swept back, the arctic-blue eyes. The same horrible tooth round his neck. The same trench coat. He smiles and waggles an index finger in my direction. At the knuckle he's sporting some kind of Goth-style ring from which projects a short, sharp-looking blade. It flashes unpleasantly in the queasy lighting of the toilet.

'The body hath a number of extheedingly good entry pointth for a weapon of thith thort. The carotid artery, of courth, athending directly from the aorta, which, if you remember, ith the main blood vethel leading from the heart.'

'Yes.'

The same odd expression on his face as he talks, as if the words were sour or distasteful to him. As though his mouth was full of sores, and it was painful to speak.

'There'th the heart itthelf. Knife woundth to the heart are almost alwayth fatal, though you've got to make thertain you don't hit a rib.'

'No.'

'There'th the femoral artery, an increathingly popular target. Immortalithed by Dr Hannibal Lecter in *Hannibal*.' He pauses. 'If you've read the book.'

'Sorry, I haven't.'

'You should. I recommend it. Though now, of courth, there'th hardly any point . . .' He trails off alarmingly. 'I've made a thtudy of thith, you know.'

'I can tell.'

'Don't even think about running. You're not fartht enough.'

'I wasn't. Believe me.'

'We're going for a walk now.'

'Where?'

'To my car. It'th in the car park.'

'How . . . how are we going to get there?'

'Out of the toiletth, down the corridor, and inthtead of turning left into the bar, we're going to turn right out of the thervith door. I've taken the trouble to unlock it.'

He must see something in my face because he adds: 'Oh and, Charlth, believe me, you don't want to get any thilly ideath.'

He takes a step towards me, does something with his arm that's mostly a blur. The middle button of my jacket seems to be bouncing on the floor, a few sad strands of thread attached. It rolls into a corner under the condom machine.

'Good, ithn't it? Would you like to thee it again?' he asks.

'No, that's all right, thanks.'

'I can do it with shirt buttonth too.'

'I'm sure.'

'Right then, Charlth. If you're quite ready . . . ?'

2

It's something saloonish. Black and lived in. I guess I should
have clocked the car's plate, or the make and model and stuff.
I should be storing up details for the police, being massively
observant, logging clues that could get me out of this shit.
However, the only detail that really seems to have stuck in my
head is the menu from a takeaway curry house on the dashboard. That, and the shovel lying across the back seat. Two
questions are chasing each other round a tape loop in my brain.
The first is:

'How did you know I was here?'

And I'm too scared to ask the second.

'I've been watching you.' Luke drives with the *heel* of his
hand, with the brio of a cabbie or a stunt driver. Every time
he changes gear, I'm horribly aware of the blade riding along
the top of his index finger. We're out of Totnes in a matter of
minutes. Shit, I should be memorising this. Fuck, was that the
A385?

'How did you know I was in Devon? In Totnes?'

His face in profile is even more rock-like. The skin is
cratered with pockmarks, the legacy of childhood acne.
There's something crumbly too about the nose, the set of the
mouth. Since he's a short fucker, the driving seat is pushed
up close to the pedals. Somehow I think we both know I'm
not going to try anything.

'Can you gueth?' A small smile playing across the rubble.

'You followed me from the airport?'

'What airport?'

'Heathrow. Last Monday.'

'Have you been out of the country, Charlth?'

'You weren't there?'

'It'th my day of retht.'

'Well, now I'm stumped. Come on, how did you find me? I can see you're itching to tell.'

He slides me a look so chilly I feel it in my scrotum.

'Little tip. Never uthe a mobile telephone if you want your whereaboutth to thtay a thecret.'

'Oh shit, of course.'

'The poleeth are getting quite thophithticated at finding people through their mobileth. It'th to do with the transmitterth . . .'

'I read about it. As long as it's turned on, your mobile's sending out little signals which the transmitters can detect. And because you're always *somewhere* between any three transmitters, x miles from one and y miles from another and z miles from the third, they can, what's the word . . . ?'

'Triangulate.'

'. . . they can triangulate your position.'

'Thoon, they thay it'll be accurate to within a few feet. They'll know whether you're in the thitting room or the bedroom.'

'But still, how did you—?'

'I have friendth in the poleeth, Charlth. Doeth that thurprithe you?'

'It shouldn't, should it?'

We seem to have left habitation behind. A full moon rises over the black outlines of the hills. Moths dance before us in the car headlights. Every few minutes, one dashes its tiny brains against the windscreen, leaving a smear on the glass. What would they feel, I wonder? One moment, wheeling away in the brilliance, on the wing, full of mothy mothness, the next . . . *snap*.

It would be like flicking off a lamp.

'What are you thinking?' asks my kidnapper. 'You've gone quiet.'

'Moths.'

'Mothth?'

'What it would be like to be one.'

'That'th a funny thought.'

'What it would actually *feel* like to *be* a moth, with moth-thoughts instead of human ones.'

He thinks about it for a bit. 'Do you know what ith the latht thing to go through a moth'th head after it hitth the windthcreen?'

'What?'

'It'th bollockth.'

I can't help it. I laugh. It was boys like Luke Holderness who used to tell those sort of jokes at my school. I have a sudden urge to ask him: what's fishier than an anchovy? (An anchovy's cunt.) Maybe he'll find it so funny that he'll forgive me on the spot, and we'll become best buddies.

'Where are we going?' I enquire instead.

'You'll thee.'

Luke slows, and takes a right. The sign pointing in the direction of where we've just turned says 'Dartmoor'.

I feel ridiculously . . . well, I'm sorry, the word is *shit-scared*.

3

Fuck me, there are actual *sheep* out here. Their white faces loom from the darkness as we twist through the narrow lanes that Holderness seems to know like a local. We drive over tiny humpback bridges with room for only one vehicle, past remote cottages with a single light burning in a window. We slow to a crawl, and I realise dark eyes are peering in at us.

'Dartmoor ponies!' I squeal like a child. They're huddled

against the verges, a dozen of them, ridiculous sawn-off creatures, who I seem to recall have been roaming the moor since humankind was dragging its knuckles along the ground. 'Are they wild?' I ask.

'They are.'

'What do they do in winter?'

'Freethe their nutth off.'

'I bet they do!' My attempt to jolly up to the hardened criminal at the wheel does not come out as well as I hoped. He deals me a look of withering contempt and I feel myself shrivelling in the icy glare. Keep it up, though. Keep talking to the bastard. It's the only hope.

'You seem to know it quite well. The area.'

'Thpent a lot of time here ath a boy.'

Aha. 'With . . . ?'

'My granddad. Vithiting my dad. Would you care to thee where my dad uthed to live?'

'Er, if it's not . . .' Out of your way? Inconvenient? 'Yeah. Sure.'

The village of Princetown is a grim-looking settlement, workaday rather than picturesque. We pass barely a soul as we cruise its darkened streets. A pub. A chippy. A garage. Various industrial-looking buildings. Within moments we are driving past a sign reading 'Princetown' with a line going through it. Well, I guess that was Princetown. Blink and you miss it. We climb a hill, and then Luke slows to a stop. He gestures his thumb behind us. I turn and gasp.

Lit up in a grotesque sodium hue, the Victorian fortress of HMP Dartmoor rises out of the darkness like a bad dream. The phrase 'prison hulk' goes through my head. On this warm Devon night, I feel a *frisson* of horror at the thought of the hundreds of men occupying their little cells in the great factory of incarceration. I can make out their windows. From the topmost ones, I guess you'd be able to see out over the jail walls, across the huddled rooftops of Princetown, to the open fields and hills beyond. You'd witness the passing of the seasons. The baking hot summer days, buzzards circling. Winter's white wilderness. In all weathers, people in cars climbing this very hill, on their way someplace else.

Luke seems to be reading my thoughts because he says, 'It'th the sheep that get to you. Dad thaid you could forget you were living in the middle of a thite of outthanding natural beauty until the thodding sheep reminded you.'

'I can imagine.'

'I don't think you can, Charlth. Not really.'

We both stare at the prison for a while. Then he starts up again, and we drive on in silence.

Eventually I risk it. 'How long was your father in there, Luke?' Voice cranked round to maximum sympathy, same tone generally used for interviewing relatives of disaster victims. Eyebrows set to 'concerned' for good measure.

'Too long.'

'I see.'

'Do you know anything about thith part of the world?' he asks.

'Not a great deal.'

'Have you ever heard of a playth called Krapp'th Ring?'

'Krapp's Ring. I don't believe I have.'

'I uthed to go there with my granddad after we'd been . . .' he throws his rocky head back in the direction of the spooky penal settlement. 'Granddad thaid it wath a good playth for ghothtth.'

'Ghosts?'

'Lotth of ghothtth there, he uthed to thay. What with it being an ancient burial thite and all.'

4

Nothing moves across the moor tonight except our car. The criminal and the TV producer pass through the moonlit landscape without encountering another vehicle. Across fields, I make out the lights of a distant farm building. At the edge of the sky, a faint orange glow perhaps signifies a town, or maybe a city, but a very long way away. Small groups of absurd Dartmoor ponies eye us comically as we shoot past.

I do not feel like laughing.

We turn off the tarmac road, and on to a track between trees. A sign flashes by in the headlights. The only word I catch is 'Forestry'. Logs are piled in clearings. At the end of the track, Luke stops the car, kills the headlights and snaps on the reading lamp.

His smile sickens me to my boots.

'Luke, I don't know what you have in mind exactly, but do you think we might talk?'

'What do you want to talk about?' The tooth round his neck, I suddenly notice, has exceptionally long roots. In gangland, isn't there a long tradition of pulling teeth? Without recourse to anaesthetic. Or even appropriate dental qualifications.

I produce a heavy sigh, connoting, I very much hope, a mix of contrition, sincerity and grown men facing facts. 'The unfortunate circumstances surrounding your grandfather. What happened to him in connection with our . . .' *Don't call it a show.* '. . . our programme. I perfectly understand your wish for the facts to be . . . restricted.'

'Why would that be then?' – as if his words contain pieces of glass that he has to chew round carefully.

'That it's a matter of dignity in . . .' *Don't say death.* '. . . in mortality. I'm very aware of his status, of course. And how someone so . . .' *Don't say notorious.* '. . . so eminent within his particular community needs to . . . to pass away with, er . . . in the appropriate, dignified, manner. As befits a person of his standing. In that actual milieu.'

'Not becauth of a turkey then.'

'Exactly. And this is the point, Luke. No one knows what actually happened to your grandfather except you and Mrs Holderness. And me. And I only know because you told me. And I haven't told a soul. Everyone else is outside the loop. No one need ever know.'

It must have been quite an impassioned little speech, because there's a new expression bubbling around the surface of his face now.

'I'm imprethed with your grathp of the thituation, Charlth. Who'th in the loop and who ithn't. But there ith the matter of punishment.'

'Ah.'

'My granddad wath a thtrong believer in retribution.'

'He was?'

'If someone pitheth on your chipth, you go round to hith houth and shit in hith thoup. That wath hith motto.'

'I see.'

'Yeth.'

'He never made an exception to that, er . . . principle?'

'Never.'

'Not even if the chips were . . . were very elderly. Chips that maybe wouldn't have been so great to eat anyhow. On account of their great . . . age?'

He looks at me as if he's got a *very* bad taste in his mouth. I guess even a hardened crim (with a worrying expertise in the wielding of sharp blades as well as an almost reckless disregard for the free movement of television practitioners) can still spot a really stinking metaphor when he hears one.

'What I'm saying is, it could have happened at any time. It's just sheer bad luck that it was after the thing with . . . the, ah, bird.'

Why are my hands shaking? Luke gives me a long, hard stare.

'Yeth it wath bad luck.'

'I'm glad you're beginning to see it—'

'Your bad luck. It didn't happen *any* time. It happened after your thtupid, irrethponthible thick fucking joke. That man meant everything to me.'

'I understand—'

'You pithed on my chipth and now I'm going to have to shit in your thoup. It'th what he would have wanted.'

'Surely not. Surely—'

'It wath the code he lived by.'

'But what good would it do? What will you gain?' I wonder how fast I can run through this forest?

'I told you before. Thatisfaction.'

'You'd feel better for a minute, an hour maybe. Perhaps a day at the most. But then what do you have?' Has he noticed that my left hand is on the passenger door handle?

'No, Charlth. Another thing my granddad uthed to thay, revenge is the gift that goeth on giving. Every time I think of what happened to you, it will bring a little thmile to my lipth.'

'What do you mean, *what happened* to me?' Do it now. The crazy bastard means it.

'I wouldn't, Charlth.'

'Sorry?'

Suddenly I realise I'm staring down the barrel of what looks awfully like a Second World War Luger pistol. The sick fuck is reading my thoughts.

'Is it real?' Like I'm making pleasant conversation.

'Reconditioned. It fireth thoft-headed shellth. They make

an awful meth of your inthideth, tho pleathe don't make me uthe it.'

A bolt of anger arcs between my temples. How fucking dare you threaten me like that, you odious little freak. Who gave you permission to pollute my comfortable life with your horrible great head, like a talking fucking rock? What gives you the right to go around turning my bowels to water every time you open your repellent, twisted lips (apart from the gun, obviously, and the knife blade that seems to be growing out of your left hand like a sixth digit).

The squall passes. This is not yet the moment of Maximum Shit. When it arrives, please God, my body will know what to do.

Luke flings his door open and waggles the gun at me. 'Come on. And if you wouldn't mind, could you carry the thpade?'

5

The forest smells of pine resin. Luke's powerful torch beam probes the darkness as we tramp across its spongy floor, no shaft of moonlight able to penetrate the thick canopy over our heads. He's close behind me. I can hear his breathing as I follow the cone of light he plays through the maze of tree trunks. I'm thinking, He knows this place *very* well.

'You must have come here a lot as a child,' I venture by way of keeping open the dialogue, though I'm not sure Luke has heard of the human being versus tray of offal argument. I have a horrible feeling that this is what I think it is.

'We did. Thith wath our favourite thpot.'

The trees run out and I realise we've come upon a clearing. Luke snaps off the light, and the full moon reveals a circular site, maybe a couple of tennis courts in area. Groups of low, irregularly shaped boulders, some of them overgrown, stand at regular intervals round the perimeter.

'Krapp's Ring,' I find myself saying out loud.

'Yeth, Charlth.'

I have to say it's not the most impressive ancient site I've ever seen. The largest stones are only the size of a piece of luggage. And many have simply disappeared into the under-growth. Yet there is a certain *something* about it. An atmos-phere. Unconsciously or deliberately, I have walked into the centre of the circle. It's a perfectly clear night. The pitted cannonball of the monster's head gleams silver in the moon-light as he prowls about, kicking at the ground here and there, like he was looking for something. I can see the Plough. And, through my peripheral vision, the dusty streak across the sky of the Milky Way. With a sharp pang of regret, I realise this would be a fine, romantic spot to bring a woman in the right circumstances. We'd lie side by side on our backs, staring into the galaxies, and I'd do that old Mexican trick. The one where it helps to have tooted on a great fat J beforehand. Where you say, 'Look at those stars up there, way up there, they look so far up, don't they? So very high up and far away. But think about it . . . in space there *is* no up or down. So maybe they're not really above us; maybe they're really down below us. And we're really looking down, straight down below us. We're up here, looking down, deep down into the stars.' And then the universe drops away, and you find you have to grab on to each other for fear of falling off the earth.

'Krapp's Ring's, what . . . Neolithic?' I say as though Luke were an expert on mounds, barrows, cairns and whatnot. I guess the rationale is: if I *talk* to him normally, maybe he'll *behave* normally.

'I believe tho.'

'It's all to do with the alignment of the sun at certain feast days, I seem to remember.' Maybe we could join a fucking evening class and go on coach trips together to Stonehenge.

'OK, Charlth. Here'th a good playth.' He shines his flash-light on to the grass by his feet. 'Thtart digging.'

'Sorry?'

'I want you to dig a hole.'

'What do you mean?'

'A hole. You know what a hole ith, don't you?'

'What sort of hole?'

'A big hole.'

'You want me to dig a big hole.'

'You've got it, Charlth. A big hole. Just here.'

'I . . . I . . . I don't really understand, Luke.'

'What part of dig a big hole ith hard to underthtand?'

'Well, what do you call *big*, for example?'

'Big enough for a perthon to fit in.'

'A person.'

'Thomeone around your own thize.'

'Luke . . .'

'*Dig, Charlth.*' He does something with the gun that makes a scary ratchety noise.

I put the spade to the ground and manage to push it in about three inches. I turn up a sad clod of earth.

'That'th the idea. Keep doing that until you've dug a nithe big hole.'

'Luke, it'll take for ever . . .'

'I'm not in a hurry.'

'And besides . . .'

'Besides what, Charlth?'

'Besides . . .'

Besides, I can't dig. I don't know how. I don't really *do* manual labour. Yeah, maybe hump a few bags of old clothes down to Oxfam, or the hoovering if the cleaning lady doesn't show up. But nothing heavy duty like digging holes. For Christ's sake, I'm a television producer, not a builder. I'm good at making telephone calls, saying clever things over lunch, yawning with my mouth shut. I can do half an hour on what 'works' about *The Weakest Link* and what doesn't. I know fifteen ways of saying, I can't decide. A dozen versions of, that was fine, but could you do it again anyway? I'm trained to look at a piece of tape and calculate whether it's funnier if we cut *before* or *after* the angry fat man says, 'Actually, fuck you' (before). I've been trained to survive in the slithery world of TV politics. I can utter statements like, 'I'm really excited about this idea,' and not fall on the floor laughing. I can keep a straight face and tell someone, 'Everyone's *really* looking forward to working with you.' I can say nice things to horrid people, and horrid things to nice people.

But I can't fucking *dig*.

6

Actually, it turns out I was wrong about the digging thing.

You'd be surprised how big a hole one can produce with a sufficiently powerful incentive. As luck would have it, the soil here is quite light. Loamy, I think would be the technical term. And while I'm digging, I'm not dead, am I?

My hole is about three or four feet deep now, round rather than oblong (he didn't say anything about the shape, did he?). Luke is lolling on the grass beside me, lying on one elbow, fingering his Luger. And I've been speculating whether, in the course of excavating this hole, perhaps moving around the edge to attack another side of it, there wouldn't come a moment when I might have a fighting chance of smashing this spade against his appalling face. Stunning him enough with the first blow to be able to get another in. And then another and another. Hit him with the edge of the spade's blade, get a *thock* noise out of it, rather than a *clang*. Beat him insensible and then shoot him with his own gun.

As I say, I've been weighing up the chances, but have decided, for the moment at least, against. Stocky as he is, the fucker's as fast as a cat, and he's already displayed a disturbing ability to read my mind. Which isn't to say that later maybe, he won't get complacent. Believing that he's totally crushed my spirit, perhaps he'll turn his back on me for a few crucial seconds, and I'll take a lunge at him. Go for the *side* of the head, not the bit at the back where the skull is thickest. Behind the ear. That's the spot the professionals favour, isn't it? When they shoot you there, they call it giving you an OBE, don't they? One Behind the Ear. Keep digging and take a view.

In the meanwhile, well, the circs aren't the greatest, but it is a lovely warm night.

'I think I jutht thaw a shooting thtar, Charlth.'

'Make a wish.'

'A wish. What would I wish?'

'I know what I'd wish.'

'What?'

'If I tell you, it won't come true.'

'You didn't thee the thtar. You don't get a wish. I get to wish.'

'Go on then.'

'I'm thinking.'

I think he *is* thinking. His eyes in the moonlight have gone slightly strange. I stop digging and stare at him.

'Is it a woman?' I ask.

'I'm not telling.'

'It would be a woman with me.'

'Yeah? What'th her name?'

'Trish.'

'What'th she like?'

'Beautiful. Fantastic face, incredibly sexy. You just want to unzip her out of her jeans and . . .' Heavy sigh.

'And what?'

'You know.'

'What, Charlth?'

'You know . . .' I pick up the spade and drive the blade into the earth.

He giggles, a muted Mutley. 'That would be your thpecial wish?'

'I think it would, actually. What about you?'

'I'm thtill thinking.'

I can't imagine Luke doing it with a woman. Or rather, I can't imagine the woman who'd want to do it with Luke. Although thinking about it, actually there probably are women who would be attracted by his cold, hard demeanour. His uncompromising 'can do' approach. The undercurrent of menace. And that fancy trick with the shirt buttons. The ugliness wouldn't be a problem. Women don't really mind ugly, do they?

As I wait for Luke to think of a wish, his cold blue eyes silvered by the light of the full moon, I have another one of those what-am-I-doing-here? moments. I see the ridiculous tableau as if from a height. Midnight, a stone circle on Dartmoor, me in shirtsleeves, standing waist-deep in a hole, the strange criminal stretched out on the grass alongside, like some gone-wrong midsummer fucking picnic.

'I know what I wish, Charlth,' he says, looking at me oddly. 'I wish I didn't have to do thith.'

'Well, that's tremendous . . .' The words freeze on my lips.

If you tell, it doesn't come true, does it?

7

We go quiet for a bit after that and I dig, as slowly as I can without it becoming too obvious. But then the cunt starts humming. And now he's singing, quietly, as if he's embarrassed of his voice.

> 'Heartth of oak, are our shipth,
> Jolly tarth, are our men
> We alwayth are ready
> Thteady, boyth, thteady!
> We'll fight and we'll con-quer again and again.'

'We used to sing that at school,' I tell him softly.

'Really? Tho did we.'

'I always liked it when we came to that line . . .' I take a deep breath and bellow as loud as I can into the night, '"STEADEEEEE, BOYS, STEADEEEE."' My words find no echo. They are swallowed up by the darkness. Luke doesn't even flinch. Only owls and bats can hear me now, and they don't give a toss.

'Where did you go to school, Charlth?'

For some reason I find myself reluctant to name the smug comfortable suburb in question. 'North London,' I tell him. 'What about yourself?'

'White Thity.'

'They say there used to be a bloody good dog track there. Before they knocked it down and put up the BBC instead.'

'I know. My granddad uthed to take me.'

It feels like progress. The sharing of intimacies.

Luke must be immensely powerful, because with no visible effort, he suddenly springs to his feet. He circles my hole. Uncomfortably, I realise that it now comes up to my armpits.

'You've done an exthellent job,' he says. 'Thee what you can manage if you put your mind to it.'

And then he does a really not nice thing. My jacket, which I'd taken off and folded up neatly on the ground when I realised the digging was going to be a bit of a sticky job, he kicks it into the hole to join me.

'Hey!'

'Have you given any thought to your latht wordth?'

'Sorry?'

'Do you have any latht wordth? You don't want your latht wordth on earth to be "hey", do you? Or "thorry"?'

Absurdly, what comes to mind are the legendary last words of the Mexican freedom fighter Pancho Villa. Mortally wounded, he is said to have whispered into the ear of a *compadre*, 'Tell them I said something.' Somehow I feel this story would be wasted on fuck-nuts.

'Luke. You can't be serious. You can't mean to bury me here.'

'That's exthactly what I mean to do.'

'But . . .' That's just so hideously unfair. Most people, when they stuff up at their job, they don't get executed. This is grotesque. I'm too young to die. And it'll hurt. And it's illegal. And there are too many enigmatic women I haven't got to the bottom of. Trish. And Kate the copper. And by the way, where *is* Kate the copper when I need her?

'Luke. Please. We can get through this. Work with me.' Whoops. Another excursion into Oprah-speak.

'Work with you. How do you mean, *work* with you? Like on television?'

'Why not?' Fuck, anything.

'Could I have my own show?'

'Of course. Actually . . .' heavy sigh for emphasis, 'it's an odd time to be saying it, but you'd be a natural.'

I see it, even by moonlight: the subtle change in musculature that you get when a surgically aimed piece of flattery hits its target. Something in the shoulders and neck. Something too seems to soften in his brow. Fuck me, his head is cocking to one side, like he's *interested* or something. Go for an immediate second strike. Three, two, one, fire.

'Funnily enough, from the first moment we met – ignoring the actual, difficult circumstances, of course – but from the very outset I thought you had that . . . that *indefinable* quality. You don't see it very often. Maybe no more than once or twice in a career if you're lucky. That . . . that special magic that tells you that you're in the presence of . . . well, I'm sorry. The only word for it *is* star.'

His breathing has slowed down. Shit, have I overegged it? No. Remember the golden rule: you can never be too thin, too rich, or too highly flattered.

'Go on.'

'Do you mind if I get out of this hole? I'm getting a bit—'

'Thtay where you are. I'm lithening.'

'Luke, here's what I'm thinking. I'm thinking what we call a raft . . .'

Life is a pitch, as they've been known to say in this business. And it's always the same when you're pitching. The person you've come to pitch *to* will inevitably occupy the best chair in the room. You will find yourself squirming uncomfortably on some unit of foam-filled office furniture, *always* several inches lower, where you're in the position of supplicant, looking up. There are no exceptions to this rule. Whatever the actual physical geography of the setting, even if it *seems* equal (either end of a squashy sofa), it'll turn out that she's in the *up* position (she can see the telly), and you'll be in the other.

And so it is in Krapp's Ring. Unusual as it is to pitch from the bottom of a hole in the ground, the general scenario is familiar to me.

'I'm thinking factual, a completely fresh approach. We'll do a show called . . . *Luke at Life*. You know, one week it's supermodels, the next it's behind the scenes at the world's poshest restaurant or whatever. Or we could go frothier, we might think about you fronting some sort of peppy "things to do" format . . . *Luke Out!* You could do something on gambling, *Luke be a Lady Tonight*. You might actually be perfect for an adult education series, *Luke and Learn*. I can see you hosting one of those sadistic quizzes. You could make Anne Robinson look like Cinderella, right? Or what about one of those ensemble sorting-things-out shows, there'd be a team of you – we'll call it *Sending the Boys Round* – yes, that's it! Rough-and-ready solutions for tough problems. Rogue traders, cowboy builders, all that malarkey. ITV would commission it tomorrow. I think you could be really excellent in some sort of punitive entertainment environment, one of those formats where people get kicked out every week. And we haven't even *begun* to touch on what you're actually interested in. I mean, what is it? Cars? Gadgets? Foreign travel? I would *love* to see you doing the travel and holiday thing. It could be *so* refreshing. I think we could get you presenting the lottery – that always needs reinventing – and a *chat* show would be *fascinating*. I mean, we could go straight or ironic there, it doesn't matter. There's daytime confessional, I think you could be *super* at that. People would like, *tell* you stuff. Something with animals, maybe. Rottweilers and cockfighting, people who keep snakes and fucking Nile monitors. *Tough Critters*. That's the title. There's archive and clip – I could see you fronting a theme night around cop shows. Cookery . . . actually, maybe not cookery. But there's sport! There's *got* to be something for you in sport. *Nutter* sport. Throwing yourself off bridges and jumping out of helicopters.

We could go counter-intuitive and dream up a few ideas around religion and spirituality. *The fucking Gospel According to Luke!* You know, hard lessons in a hard world, sort of thing. And we haven't even *touched* on drama or comedy, where I have a suspicion – I wouldn't put it any stronger than that – a *suspicion* that you could really make a bit of a mark.'

It must have been quite an effective pitch, because Luke doesn't say anything after I finish.

'What do you reckon? Worth a shot? Worth giving it a whirl? I could introduce you to Erica Birkendale,' I throw in by way of an additional sweetener.

'Could I fuck her?'

'Why not? I don't see any reason at all why not.'

'Charlth, if you can fikth for me to fuck Erica, then we'll call our account thquared.'

'Luke, consider it a done deal. I know her terribly well. You can meet tomorrow. By tomorrow night, you'll be up to your apricots in lovely Erica Birkendale. She's a smashing lady, and I happen to know she's particularly attracted to your physical type.'

'I prefer it when women don't fanthy me. I like to see the look of dithgutht on their faith. I find it a turn-on.'

'Ah.'

'She'd be no good to me.'

'Actually I . . . I *exaggerated* when I said she was attracted to your physical type. I guess I have no direct evidence of that. But I think you should meet. I can see no reason at all why you couldn't fuck her.'

'Charlth, ith there *anything* you won't promith? Any lie you won't tell?'

'What do you mean?'

'All that bollockth about being on TV. Do you think I'm completely thtupid?'

'I was serious, Luke. I think you have the potential to be a major talent.'

'What about the voith, Charlth? Don't you think that could be a problem?'

'What about it?'

'The fucking *lithp*!'

'I hadn't noticed it, to be honest.'

'Charlth, thtop thquirming. I *dethpithe* television, and I dethpithe the people who make it. Apart from *EathtEnderth*, of courth. And *Have I Got Newth for You*.'

And now he does the horrible thing. He grips the Luger with two hands and points it at my head. I flinch instinctively.

'Luke, *don't*!'

'Although funnily enough, I don't dethpithe *you*, Charlth. I feel thorry for you.' A click, as he flicks off the safety or whatever.

'Wait, Luke. There's something I have to tell you.'

'What?'

'I need to tell you . . .' Tell him what? Fucking *think*, man!!! 'I need to tell you about . . . I need to tell you about Frank-out-the-back.'

A sigh. 'Go on then. And thith better be good.'

8

'Please. Please can you put down the gun for a moment? I can't concentrate with that thing pointing at me.'

He lowers it slowly, flicks the safety, jams it into the belt of his jeans. Thrusts his hands in his pockets, curls one ankle round the other. Stares down at me in my pit of destruction.

The full moon throbs. Oh Jesus. Oh Holy *Christ*. I sure hope he likes this one . . .

'There's a prospector, been up in the hills prospecting for gold. And he's been up there for a year prospecting away—'

'Charlth, thith ithn't a joke, ith it?'

'You'll love it, I promise. And this prospector, he's been prospecting all by himself for a year, when one day, he comes into town, all filthy, with a great big beard on him.' Fucker's listening, wants to hear the story, doesn't he. 'So he goes into the saloon, plonks this bag of gold nuggets on the counter and says to the barman, "Barkeep, give me two fingers of Red Eye and a woman." Barman pours the drink and says, "Here's your Red Eye, pilgrim, but there are no women in this town. Never have been. There, er, *is* always Frank out the back, though." Prospector downs his drink and replies, "Nope, I don't like the idea of that much." And he leaves.' He's hooked. His breathing's slowed down. 'Two years go by. And one day around sunset, the prospector comes into town again. Filthy. Beard's even longer. He walks into the bar, drops a bigger bag of gold on the counter and says, "Barkeep, give me three fingers of Red Eye and a woman." Barman pours the Red Eye and says, "Here's your drink, pilgrim, but it's like I told you: there are no women in this town, there never have been. But there is always Frank out the back." Prospector swallows his drink. Says, "Nope. I don't like the idea of that much," and walks out the door. Shall I carry on?'

The monster nods. You're not going to shoot a man while he's halfway through a joke, are you?

'Three more years go by. One day, in the late afternoon, the prospector comes into town again. Covered in dirt. Eyes peeking through this great mass of beard. Walks into the saloon. Bangs a huge bag of gold on the counter. "Barkeep, give me five fingers of Red Eye and a woman." Barman pours his drink. "There's your Red Eye, pilgrim, but there are still no woman in this town. Never have been. But, like I say, there is always Frank out the back."'

A chilly smile plays amid the loose rubble that is the Holderness countenance.

'Prospector downs his Red Eye. Calls for another. Downs that. Downs a third. Says, "Listen, barkeep. If I *did* go with Frank out the back . . ."' glance about stealthily for comic emphasis, '". . . how many people would know?" Barman thinks about it for a moment. "Seven," he replies. "Seven? Why seven?" asks the prospector. "Well," says the barman, "I'd know. You'd know. Frank would know."' Pause for timing. '"And the four people it takes to hold him down would know. See, Frank doesn't like the idea of that much either."'

Nothing.

Not a titter.

A terrible silence hangs over Krapp's Ring.

'That wath it?'

'You've heard it before.'

'I thought it wath going to be better than that.'

'You didn't find it funny?'

'Only thlightly.'

'Oh. Shame.'

It was one of my favourite jokes. My friend Andy Fineman loves to tell it. Andy has such an unreasonable affection for the Frank-out-the-back joke, that perhaps what I like about it is that *he* likes it so much. In fact, now I recall, no one else has ever found it particularly amusing. Still, you can't ever *insist* something is funny, can you?

Luke's hand comes out of his trouser pocket.

'Man walks into this bar—' I continue.

'Charlth, I think we've had enough.'

'Please. You've got to hear this. Man walks into a bar with a dog, a Jack Russell. And the man says, "I'll have a pint of lager please." And the dog says, "And I'll have a packet of crisps. What flavours have you got?"'

Holderness doesn't put his hand back in his pocket. But neither does he put it on his gun.

'The barman is absolutely stunned. "Fuck me, it's a talking dog," he says. "Oh yes," says the man, "little Bertie's a very clever animal. He can do all sorts of stuff. Ask him to do something for you." Barman thinks about it for a moment and says to the dog, "Could you nip round the corner and fetch me a copy of *Exchange and Mart* and a packet of Rolos?" "Sure," says the dog. The barman gives Bertie a five-pound note, and off he goes out the door. Have you heard it before . . . ?'

The monster shakes the cannonball sadly.

'Five minutes go by. Then ten. Then half an hour, and Bertie still hasn't come back. "That's odd," says the man. "He's normally incredibly obedient." So he goes off to look for him. And he's wandering around the streets near the pub, looking everywhere, when finally he glances down an alley, and he spots little Bertie, on top of this *gorgeous* white French poodle, giving her one. And the bloke says, "Oi! What do you think you're playing at? You've never done this before." And Bertie, on top of this poodle, still giving her one, turns his head and replies, "I've never had the *money* before."'

A chuckle. He *chuckled*. The Mutley *heh-heh-heh*. 'Very good, Charlth. I might tell that one mythelf.' And then the gun is in his hand. 'It'th a beautiful thought, that your final act wath to make thomeone laugh. Perhaps it'th what you would have wanted.' He levels the pistol at me.

'No, Luke. You don't understand. I told you those stories for a reason. I . . . I . . . I . . .' I'm losing it. I've run out of excuses. I can't stand in this hole telling jokes till the sun comes up. A bad smell is rising from the ground beneath my feet. Maybe it would be better for everyone if he just shoots me. How much can it hurt?

But a phone is ringing.

A mobile.

My mobile. In my jacket pocket.

I'm staring at him and he's staring back at me. His finger is on the trigger. An owl hoots. Maybe in reply to the song of the Nokia.

'Aren't you going to anthwer it? You never know, it might be important.' The evil fucker giggles.

I grab the phone and press the key.

'Hello? Hello?'

Silence.

'Oh Christ, you.' A deep weariness cloaks me like a shroud. I suddenly realise how *exhausting* all this having guns pointed at you and threats made against your life is.

'Sorry. Is it too late?'

'No. Not at all. Now's fine.'

'I can call back if you're busy. It's just that I did say I'd call you back this evening. And I've been out. Since we spoke.'

'That's OK. I've been quite busy myself.'

'It's just. Well I've had a chance to collect my thoughts. And now I think I'm ready to tell you who I am. And why I've been calling.'

'I'm pleased to hear it.'

Silence.

'Well, fire away then.' I throw an urgent glance up to Luke and jab a finger repeatedly at the mobile, just in case he were to think I was talking to him.

'Charles . . . this is . . .' A heavy sigh. A deep breath. 'Charles, you probably don't remember me. This is Simon, Simon Lowenstein.'

'From Fitzjohns . . . ?'

'You used to answer to my name at register.'

'Oh fuck. How funny. I was only thinking about you the other day. Seems an age ago now, though.'

'I saw your name at the end of a TV show. It's a bit of a long story really.' I picture the pleasant, freckled-faced boy staring straight ahead as I say, 'Here, miss,' on his behalf. The person I'm talking to sounds like a grown man. 'Do you think we might meet up?'

'Yes. Of course.'

'This week any good for you?'

'Er, a bit *difficult* to say when really. Can we leave it that I'll call you?'

'Fine. Look, I'm sorry for all the . . . the funny business.'

'Not at all.'

'I've been having a bit of a sticky time lately. I'll explain.'

'I'll look forward to it.'

When we hang up, Luke is looking at me with something close to pity on his face.

'Why didn't you tell them where you were? What wath happening?'

'I didn't feel like getting into a long conversation with him just then.'

'I would have shot you if you'd tried.'

'Luke, if you're trying to scare me, it's worked. I'm scared. But I seem to have been standing in this hole for days.'

'What, *get on with it*? Ith that what you're thaying?'

'Some sense of . . . of *closure* might be appropriate.'

'Have you got a latht requetht?'

'Yes. Don't shoot me.'

'Thorry, Charlth, but the ruleth are the ruleth.'

'Yeah, yeah. The chips and the soup thing.'

'It'th not even perthonal any more. I wath getting to quite enjoy your company.'

'Well, that's very fucking touching. A great consolation, I must say.'

The hand with the gun is hanging by his side. I have the peculiar feeling that he can't bring himself to do this. That my prevarication has played into his.

'Do you want to shut your eyeth or anything?'

'No, I'm fine thanks.'

I was wrong. He brings his arm up, sights along the barrel of the gun. I realise I'm sitting at the bottom of the hole. At some point, my legs must have given way.

It's not, as expected, a movie of my past life that flashes before my eyes – some corny reel of boy-to-man stuff, cameos of parents and lovers, bicycles, and first cars – it's one very specific scene. About fifteen years ago, staying over in a house in the Peak District, zipped into a single sleeping bag with a beloved girlfriend. Me on top, she with my face in her hands. We're kissing. And she's smiling and calling me her hairy beast. *My hairy beast.* I remember thinking at the time, this is the happiest moment of my life. And although it didn't last, and we went our separate ways, and all of us have passed a lot of water since then, I still think of that night, in the chilly upstairs bedroom in the old stone cottage near the reservoir, as the instant on earth that I was happiest.

Curious. That it's what I should think of in The Moment.

Lydia's lovely face dissolves into the monster's, one large, cold eye floating above his index finger, now curling round the trigger and beginning to squeeze.

In the hour of crisis, I knew I could trust my body to do something. And, sure enough, it doesn't let me down.

Put it this way. Now I know how the moment of Maximum Shit gets its name.

9

The explosion is much louder than I expected. And my first thought is, I don't believe it, the fucker's missed me. Actually, my *first* thought is, I'm still thinking, so he can't have snuffed me out like a candle. And then I hear the noise of leaves and branches being peppered with shot. When I open my eyes, I realise that Luke is staring off towards the darkness of the forest. And then with a surge of joy in my heart, I hear a voice. A deep, rather complex voice, full of separate notes and organ pipes. Slurred, but no mistaking its distinction. It bellows, 'Throw the gun down, and put your hands in the air. Drop the weapon, or you'll still be picking lead out of your arse next Christmas.' And then another voice, from somewhere else in the trees. Rougher, with the irritable urgency of the non-commissioned officer. 'Fucking *do* it! Fucking put it down *now*!'

Luke looks back at me. His eyebrows have advanced so far up his rocky face in surprise that I nearly laugh. I pull a *search me?* expression and shrug my shoulders. He tosses the gun on the grass, raises his hands, as requested, and turns to face my rescuers.

Cautiously, I lift my head clear of the edge of my hole. Moving out slowly from the cover of the forest, two elderly men bearing shotguns advance into the moonlit stone circle. One is tall and wide with a limp. The other is shorter and somewhat bow-legged. The latter, I notice, takes a step side-ways for each few paces forwards.

'Fuck me, it'th Dad'th Army,' says Luke to no one in particular. I see him tense subtly.

'Watch him,' I cry out. 'He's got a knife. Don't get too close. He's a tricksy fucker.'

'Tricksy'? Where did that come from? Luke glances back at me with a look of complete contempt.

The old soldiers stop about ten feet from the strange criminal. Digby is panting heavily. Even from here, I can detect the
waves of whisky coming off him. But his lopsided eyes are lit
with an intriguing new intensity.

Heart still hammering, I clamber out of my freshly dug grave.
(How often can you say that in your life, I wonder?) I'm very
aware of something cooling unpleasantly in my underpants.

Digby waggles the shotgun. 'Take off your clothes.'

'What?' says Luke.

'Take everything off. And the jewellery.'

Luke seems paralysed. There's a *very* unpleasant taste in his
mouth by the look of things. 'Why?' he asks.

'Because I'm pointing a bloody shotgun at you, man. Now
take off your clothes before I lose my temper.'

'Fucking just *do* it!' yells Vic.

Digby sways on his pins, eyes swivelling. His hair is all
messed up, and I notice he has got rather a lot of pine needles
stuck to his clothing. His cavalry twills are soaked below the
knees. 'Watch him for concealed weapons,' he growls.

The cornered crim assesses his situation. Under the full
moon, I see Luke Holderness wordlessly computing the
various possibilities of escape, murder, hostage-taking, mutila-
tion and Christ knows what other mayhem. But it's hopeless.
He may be facing two pissed and ancient relics of a bygone
age, but they're *armed* pissed and ancient relics.

Slowly, terribly sadly, Luke Holderness begins to undress.
I even begin to feel a bit sorry for the rock-headed gangster,
humbled by the two old crocks. Even while he was scaring
me half to death, there was something grotesquely magnificent about his performance as my lisping persecutor. It's the
Erica Birkendale phenomenon, the same with all monsters:
the moment they begin to act like human beings, they're
diminished.

Luke turns his back on us to discard his underpants (Y-fronts, very nasty) and finally the blue denim shirt. He cups himself in the time-honoured tradition, awaiting further instructions.

If anything, with no clothes on, he looks even more scary. His shoulders are powerfully muscled, as are the stocky little arms and legs. It feels like we've trapped a force of nature, some wild animal, a shark or a tiger, around whom one feels extremely uneasy in the absence of an intervening wall of bars.

'Turn round,' says Vic. Luke glares at him. 'I said turn *round*.'

He turns. And we all gasp.

Seeming to sprout from the roots of his pubic hair, rising over his stomach and spreading all the way across his chest, is a huge tattoo of a naked woman. I pick up Luke's torch and snap it on.

'Sorry, I've got to see *this*.'

It's a fabulously detailed piece of work. It must have taken ages and hurt like hell. To best fit into the space available, she's been contrived to fold back on herself, legs tucked up beneath her torso, face resting upon her arms. She's virtually squatting. The sort of shape one of those small, bendy women who collapse themselves into suitcases for magicians could assume. Striking the sort of cheesy pose a pocket Venus like Monroe might have been forced to strike in her early days. Except this is no Monroe. Under the blonde ringlets and the corny cartoon eyelashes, the face attached to this creature, the face staring back at our own shocked faces, belongs to none other than Luke Holderness himself.

10

I think we're all a bit embarrassed, to be honest. Digby and Vic have gone quiet. Luke looks like someone who's chewed a rotten Brazil nut.

'You, er . . . you want to tell us the history of that tattoo, Luke?' I ask sympathetically.

'Go fuck yourthelf,' he snarls.

I think we all see his muscles tense. 'Get in the hole,' booms Digby. 'You heard me. Get down that bloody hole.' He waves the barrel of the gun at him worryingly.

Luke pauses for a moment, then he scrambles down the sides of the freshly dug chamber. With the beast in his pit, we feel safe to draw nearer. Digby cracks open his shotgun and slips in another cartridge.

'Who is this bugger, Alistair?' he asks. 'Something to do with bad business out East?'

'It's a bit of a tale actually, Digby. But thanks for your, er, timely intervention. By the way, how did you know where to find me?'

'You've got Vic to thank for that. Thought we'd lost you for a minute back there. Oh, and I should do something about those trousers at some stage, if I were you.'

'Right. Yes, sorry.' I take a pace away.

'Shall I finish the fucker off?' He steps up to the edge of the hole. The gun wavers horribly in the general direction of Luke, who doesn't even flinch. He merely looks as miserable as I've ever seen anyone.

'*No!*' I cry.

'He was about to kill you,' says Digby. I can see a quarter-bottle of Famous Grouse peeking from the pocket of his tweed jacket.

'I know, but you can't.'

'Why not?'

'It's . . . it's not nice. Besides, it's illegal.'

Is Luke laughing or crying? It's hard to tell. His face is in his hands and his shoulders are shaking.

'Not *nice*? War isn't nice, Alistair. People get hurt in wars. Let me do it.'

He takes aim again, swaying precariously at the edge of the chasm.

I'm about to shout *no* again, but Vic grips my arm and shoots me a searching look. 'Leave it,' he whispers. 'He needs this.'

I shake off his hand. '*STOP!!*' I scream. 'Have you completely lost your marbles? It's *murder*. You go to jail and stuff for murder.'

'Let him do it, Charlth.' The mad fuck in the pit is staring out at us. He's struck a curious pose. Almost a ballet stance, arms stretched out behind him, fingers splayed, one foot sort of cocked forwards and sideways, head raised, like fucking Freddie Mercury or someone. 'Thith ith a good playth to thtay. I won't need to be angry or anything here.' He's gazing over our heads, beyond us. To the moon maybe. Or perhaps the stars.

Digby teeters on the edge of the chasm, eyes blinking, jowls wobbling. Slowly, he lowers the firearm. 'Why did he call you Charles, Alistair?' he asks, turning round to face me.

'Ah. Yes.' Heavy sigh. 'Interesting that you should latch on to that . . .'

'Yeth, Charlth, I wath meaning to athk. Why doeth he keep calling you Alithtair?'

'Good question. I'm glad you brought it up.'

Oh fuck. Here we go again.

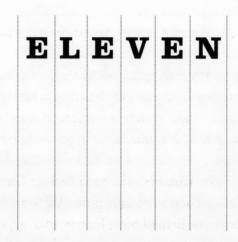

ELEVEN

1

Rose is squealing with excitement. She positively bounces up and down on my black leather sofa at the wickedness of it all.

'Oh my *God!*' She actually claps her hands together in sheer dark glee. 'So *then* what happened?'

'You have to absolutely *swear* to—'

'. . . never breathe a word to a living soul. Yeah yeah. *So?*'

The sexy hooded eyes are rimmed with red this evening. Geraldine, sitting alongside, chooses this moment to exhale a huge gust of cannabis fumes. The cloud settles over our heads like the weather.

I'm happy. I'm home.

The events of six weeks ago finally seem to have found their true perspective, although only this morning I once again had to drag myself awake, heart banging in my chest, lungs heaving like bellows, to shut out the vision of Luke's eyeball as it floated over the gun barrel at Krapp's Ring. His finger as it curled, squeezing round the trigger. Would the fucker really have done it? I must ask him again at the weekend.

R. and G. and I began this evening in TestTube, a sharp new bar/restaurant concept which has superseded Myxpqlncx, which itself, if you remember, was the renamed Zyplxqnk. It's clear that a frightening amount of money has been laid out on the design scheme, an extended fantasy in laboratory equipment. The woman behind the bar with many studs in her face has been replaced by a much more glamorous creature, with almost no studs to speak of. Her lovely eyes sparkle through anti-splash goggles. Under her loosely fastened white lab coat I notice she's wearing a red bikini. The entire place is lit by several hundred Bunsen burners, some flaming blue, others orange, others still, flaming – unaccountably – green. Drinks are served in those sensible Pyrex beakers we did chemistry experiments in at school. I go for a cocktail named Oxidising Agent; the girls plump for a pair of Funky Catalysts ('puts the fizz in any reaction').

I decide on the spot, I like it here – not for the silly drinks names (I deplore those) but for the dramatic low lighting, the chemical refinery glow, the sheer bloody *effort* that's been made, and the woman in the lab coat. Also, I got an A in Chemistry O level, and being here reminds me of early success.

A lot of the gossip has been about *The Uh-Oh Show*. And how – oh joy, oh thank you, God – the channel have decided not to recommission it for another series. Apparently, it's not that they think hidden camera shows have passed their sell-by date (although they have). It's not that they don't have the highest admiration for Erica Birkendale (although they haven't offered her anything else, tee-fucking-hee). The problem is that they don't believe the show is *cruel* enough for its slot. Peter Marcus went for a meeting with Electra Fuchs, the twelve-year-old at the channel in charge of the show. She says what they're into nowadays is angst. She wants *anguish*. She wants *distraught*. She wants shows where 'people *squirm*, Peter'. He said he'd see what he could do.

This, of course, is the best possible news. Particularly combined with the fact that Erica's crossover youth show, the one where she takes youth culture and pulls its teeth out – *Erica's Feeling Groovy* – has been an absolute turkey. Actually, a turkey is nowhere near big enough a beast to adequately convey the magnitude of the pile of cack she's landed in, to mix up the metaphors a bit. Think disaster. Think catastrophe. Think unmitigated fucking calamity. From the moment she first hove into vision, wearing a camouflage T-shirt and combat trousers for Christ's sake, you knew you were in the presence of an unfolding train wreck of a TV show. Her first 'interview', a succession of overlapping non sequiturs with a near-comatose young man who looked as if his hair had been styled with a shard of broken glass, will be played for years to come in compilations of TV's most hellish moments (high point: 'Sorry, luv, I'm fucking mashed, me'). From there, it went seriously downhill. Her constant use of the words 'kicking', 'wicked', and 'killer', the hysterically obvious lack of rapport between Erica and her guests; the way they'd take the piss, putting two fingers up behind her head; the bit when Darlene, the sexy Asian one from that girl band, said, 'Thanks, granny'; the sight of the arthritic old bitch actually *dancing* . . . well, I'm sorry. I can't remember ever watching a funnier forty-five minutes of live telly. Of course the viewing figures were an even bigger joke. And the reviewers set upon the whole ill-conceived confection with a savagery and a blood-lust to gladden the heart. Someone in the *Daily Mail* called it 'the single worst programme I have ever sat through in thirty years as a TV reviewer, and I write as someone who remembers *Club X*.' The second episode was a marginal improvement, though it didn't help that a hungover celebrity told her he was 'chuffed' to be appearing on 'the last show in your current series'.

The die had been cast. Badly rattled, you could read the fear in her eyeballs. One felt it could surely only be a matter of days before they pulled the proverbial plug.

They axed it the same evening.

Already, *Erica's Feeling Groovy* – both episodes – has achieved classic status. The show has become a byword for televisual meltdown. Nearly everyone associated with it, principally the luckless Robyn with a Y, has been sent into the countryside for retraining (got a job on *Kilroy*, hasn't she). Peter Marcus skilfully managed to decouple himself from the doomed loco just in time, somehow magically transferring the blame to the hapless executive at the channel who gave it the go-ahead.

And I'm so happy, I can barely wipe the big, fat grin off my face.

2

So there's a lot for us to celebrate tonight. I elect to try a sophisticated-looking brew called Dangerous Experiment. Rose goes for the TestTube Martini. Geraldine picks a Molecular Fission ('careful, this one will blow you away'). We all agree that the drink names are stupid, but we're prepared to sample them none the less.

I've decided to tell Rose and Geraldine the whole gruesome story of What I Did on my Trip to the Country. The industrial-strength cocktails have loosened my tongue. And I simply can't keep it to myself any longer. I have got all the way up to the scene at Krapp's Ring – '*No!* You made that up! It's not *really* called Krapp's Ring?' – when I realise that if I swallow one more ill-titled beverage, I may be sick. I suggest we cab it to mine and break out the recreational herbs. This meets with widespread approval.

Because I'm not in the mood for lachrymose Cubans this evening, I put on *Themeology* by John Barry. The television set plays silently. It's the news. Something about the latest fuck-up on the railways. A series of aggrieved passengers mouth their horror stories.

'So the drunken old fart couldn't bring himself to fire?' says Rose.

'He wanted to. You see, he'd—'

'. . . never killed anyone. He was terribly ashamed, being a soldier and everything.'

'Sorry. I've said that already. It's this stuff. It's rather strong.'

Under my new regime of stop lying, it's too confusing, honesty is the best policy, I'm giving Rose and Geraldine (almost) everything. How by the time we walked back through the trees to the Bentley, I was shaking. 'Delayed shock,' boomed Digby, and practically bottle-fed me Famous Grouse. How we set off across the moor to Totnes in the lovely old car, me up front with Vic, Digby dropping off in the back, the tattooed criminal naked and locked in the boot. (I spare them the details about my soiled trousers. Vic kindly swapped them for a pair of grimy garage overalls that he always carries on board. 'In case I need to get underneath for any reason. Oil leak or what-ever.')

En route, Vic revealed something I didn't know about Trish. It turns out he's actually her godfather – she's the daughter of his 'ladyfriend' in Torquay – and that he was 'not exactly spying, but shall we say keeping an eye' on Trish that evening.

Not because he had any worries about me, but because of rotten Roger, Trish's ex, who'd been making something a nuisance of himself, plaguing Trish with phone calls, turning up unannounced, and generally trying to reinsinuate himself into her skimpy white underwear. Vic decided that he should 'have a word with the bugger, pardon my French, man to man' as he put it. So he followed her from her yoga class to the pub, where to his surprise, he witnessed her assignation with me. Her hand against my forehead. The kiss. The next kiss. The wiping away her foam moustache with my little finger. An unexpected development from his point of view because, if you recall, I had stated publicly that I was going off to Paignton that evening to meet a friend of the family. Digby had been with him in the car. He'd come along to get a fresh case of Scotch from Victoria Wine.

'How did they see you and Trish, without you seeing them?' enquires Geraldine astutely.

'From the car park. They parked the Bentley there, and had a perfect view through the lounge bar window. While they were in the car park watching *us*, they also clocked lispy Luke in his car watching me, or watching someone, they didn't know who at that stage. Vic said straight away there was something not quite right about him. They can spot strangers in those silly little places.'

'They saw Luke go into the pub when you went to the loo,' says Rose.

'And they saw the two of you come out together,' says Geraldine, 'leaving Trish all by herself! It's just like *Inspector Morse*.'

According to Vic, something 'smelled funny' about the way we walked out through the pub's service door and got into Luke's car. Not saying goodbye to Trish or anything, after our . . . our tender scene. Even Digby agreed it was 'bloody rummy'. So they followed us out of town, at a discreet distance. When Luke turned on to Dartmoor, Vic killed his headlights and hung back a long way, so the big Bentley wouldn't show up in the moonlight. Army night manoeuvres drill or some such.

'It was like an adventure for the old chaps,' purrs Rose.

I explain how they had to hang back when Luke finally parked his car and we set off into the woods. How they got disorientated when they lost sight of his flashlight. 'Bloody dark in that forest,' Digby had said. 'Bloody trees everywhere.' How Digby had taken 'a tumble or two'. How Vic at one stage had to rescue him from 'a small gully or some such mantrap'. How it was only much later, when they heard someone singing 'steady, boys, steady' from 'Hearts of Oak', that they picked up our trail.

'Bloody plucky,' echoes Geraldine. 'And the guns?'

'I asked Vic about that. He said he always keeps a pair of shotguns in the car boot. Said it's normal in the country. Do you want to make another one of those? The last one was *so* perfect.'

Geraldine lays the final piece of vinyl I still own across her thighs – *Dare* by Human League – and starts rustling and folding and licking and crumbling, and all those other delicious precision movements.

'So what happened with Luke?'

'I'm coming to that. Look, you will keep this under your bonnets, won't you?'

'Char-*lee*!' they chorus.

3

Rose sews a wonderfully sexy furrow across her brow. 'At this point, they still think you're this Alistair Gough, do they?'

'I told them the truth on the car ride back to Totnes. Actually, they were incredibly good about it.'

I explained to the old soldiers it was going to be a tangled, and rather bizarre story, and that I wouldn't be in the least bit surprised if they didn't believe any of it. (I was finding it hard to believe myself, sitting in a pair of mechanic's overalls with 'Firestone' emblazoned across the top pocket.) I told them the entire tale from the beginning, that my real name was Charles Green, that I produced a TV show, that someone had collapsed and died after a scene involving a live turkey (explaining the turkey scam was a little uphill; actually, it didn't seem all that amusing in the retelling. Perhaps these gags date a little more quickly than we realise). I told them about the victim's grandson tracking me down and vowing to kill me (missed out the business with the Sainsbury's trout); that I'd fled the country, but had to return (didn't go into the business with Cheryl either); that I'd panicked at the airport on the way back, that I'd walked up to Vic and said, 'Car for Gough,' and that they knew the rest. That he'd driven me down to Devon. That I might have got out sooner, but I was enjoying the Elvis too much. I think the Elvis thing went down quite well. With Vic especially.

There was a long pause. Several whole minutes went by before two and two were successfully added to make four.

Warm whisky fumes assailed me from the back seat where Digby had been swigging away at the Famous G. 'So you *didn't* go to university with Toby?'

'No.'

'Aha.'

Another minute, maybe two passed.

'But just a sec. If you weren't at university with my son . . .'

'Yes?'

Vic remained silent. 'How do you two know each other?'

This was the sickener, the one I least wanted to answer. 'I guess we must have just . . . just bumped into one another, somewhere down the line, as it were. You know, in the way you do.'

'Ah.' I could hear Digby thinking about it for a while. Trying to pick his way through the verbiage. And then after a while, when he didn't reply, and after a further while when he *still* didn't reply, I looked round to see him asleep, head lolling against the seat back, lower lip hanging open like the mouth of a cavern in a cliff side.

'You want to run that last bit past me again,' said Vic humourlessly.

In a low voice, anxious not to wake the senior officer, I tell Vic about the son's treachery; how no one could have been more surprised than me when Toby said, 'Alistair mate. Great to see you. Where's your tan?' About the visit to the library. The plan to identify the precious volumes and spirit them away. That the *real* Alistair Gough – or rather the real book dealer playing the *part* of Alistair Gough (what was the bloke's name? Julian, that was it) – he must still be with his sister, waiting for the call from Toby.

'The fucking little shit-bird,' hissed Vic when I finished.

'Not nice, is it?' I agreed.

'If the old man ever found out, it would break him.'

'That's what I thought.'

'I'll fucking have the little cunt.'

'Maybe I should talk to him, Vic.'

'Maybe we *both* should.'

4

'Wait a minute,' croaks Rose, waving the spliff and trying to keep a lungful of smoke down at the same time. 'What happened to bathroom cleaner?'

'To Trish? I'm coming to her.'

'You haven't got anything to nibble, have you?' asks Geraldine. 'Any sort of chocolate. Maltesers would be good. Or cheese on toast. Or microwave chips and tomato ketchup. Or a toasted microwave bacon sandwich with HP Sauce. Actually, do you think it's too late to phone for a curry?'

It takes a full half-hour to collate the order and place the call (including a break to roll another J). Every time we can't decide between two dishes – I don't really care, but these two girls really know their Indian – we agree, fuck it, let's order both. Then there's a fair deal of negotiating about what sort of rice, what type of naan, plus the complicated multiple-choice pappadum and pickle options. Anyhow, when I get through and read it all over, they tell me the bill comes to £82.45, which means we've ordered a fuck of a lot of food, even though some of that is a couple of bottles of Chardonnay, just in case, you never know, sort of thing. I bring on a plate of cheese and water biscuits to tide us over while we wait.

'*So?*' says Rose, spitting crumbs. 'You get back to the house . . .'

We get back to the house. Vic puts Digby's arm over his shoulder and sort of sleepwalks him up to bed – he's obviously done it many times before. He returns and says, 'Now what are we going to do with this animal?' Meaning Luke. 'I suppose we should turn him over to the police.'

I agree. 'I suppose we should.'

'Though it might be better if we handled things ourselves.'

'How do you mean?'

Vic tosses me the car keys, nods his head towards the boot and does something metallic with the shotgun that leads me to believe it's loaded and ready for action. Cautiously, I slip the key in the lock, turn it, and fling open the lid. I step away in case the illustrated maniac inside should come at me with a tyre-iron or whatever.

The sight that greets our eyes is almost laughable. In an instant we see what's happened.

Perhaps to dissolve the humiliation, at some point on the journey back from Dartmoor, Luke Holderness has forced open Digby's case of whisky and helped himself. Naked, grotesquely tattooed, he now lies flat on his back in the Bentley's roomy boot, cradling a near-empty bottle of Famous Grouse, spark out to the world.

Vic laughs, and produces a Polaroid camera from the pocket of his grey car anorak. He fires off several shots; some from close to, highlighting the disturbing artwork so painstakingly created in the monster's flesh, others showing a more general view of the sleeping crim. He hands the pictures to me and recommends that I find a nice, safe place to keep them. Then he slams shut the boot lid and we drive to a deserted Totnes Station. There we transport Luke by his arms and feet on to the London-bound platform, laying him gently on a bench to await the arrival of the milk train to Paddington. Alongside, we leave his possessions (minus blade and Luger) and, as an act of kindness in a cruel universe, a fresh bottle of Grouse.

My conversation with Toby later that evening is a little strained, owing to the injury to his nose that he must have sustained some time between being awoken from his bed by Vic, and his subsequent appearance in the sitting room at close to three o'clock in the morning. The irritable veterinarian sits in an armchair, attempting to staunch the flow of blood.

'I think it's broken,' he moans.

'Bollocks,' growls Vic. 'I'll leave you to sort this fiasco out, Alistair. I mean Charles. I'm off to my cot.' The big man lumbers out.

After a good deal of snuffling and groaning, two hot, hurt eyes appear above the bloodied handkerchief and fix me in their gaze. 'So maybe you'd like to explain who the hell you are, if you're not Julian Woodhouse,' he says petulantly.

I explain myself once again, stripping the plot to its bare essentials. 'Sorry if I've spoiled your plans,' I add when I've done.

'Well, it's a bloody cheek,' he says, sounding close to tears. 'Sneaking in here, pretending to be someone you're not.'

'Looks more like a bloody nose from where I'm sitting.' Sorry, couldn't resist it.

'Everything's well and truly fucked now, isn't it?'

'Sounds like it. Although, look on the bright side, your father doesn't know about your . . . your plans for his library. And there's no reason why he should.'

'It's none of your fucking *business*,' he hisses at me, incensed. 'And anyway, why are you wearing those ridiculous overalls?' I think he must have started bleeding again, because there follows further groaning and sniffing. I make a discreet exit as dark blobs fall from the vet's shattered nose, blooming crimson on the legs of his striped pyjamas.

Dawn is peeking through the clouds by the time I reach my little cottage. A deep weariness pervades my bones. I fall on to the sofa in the tiny sitting room, shut my eyes and I feel that lovely whooshing gathering sensation you get just as you're about to drift away, when . . .

Tap tap tap. A fingernail against the window. I jerk awake, and for one horrible moment, it's the face of Luke Holderness that swims before my eyes.

But it's not Luke.

Far from it.

It's Trish.

5

She's wrapped in a nasty pink towelling dressing gown that carries that slightly sickening newly washed clothes smell. However, the coarseness of the material and the unpleasantness of its hue are counter-weighted by the idea that under it . . . under it, I strongly suspect we're talking nothing at all. She's curled herself up on the sofa, legs drawn beneath her, and she is listening to my tale with an expression of mounting amazement. I give her both barrels. About the only detail I leave out is Toby's book-larceny subplot. That, and her close physical resemblance to Magda, the chess-playing porn queen.

'What did you think had happened when I didn't come back from the loo?' I ask when she's digested the story.

'I didn't really know what to think. So you're not a doctor, then?'

''Fraid not.'

'You weren't at uni with Toby?'

'No, not really.' *Please* don't keep saying uni. It's *so* off-putting.

'But *he* thought you were. He *said* you were.'

'He was mistaken. It happens. It's what he *wanted* to think.'

'Those things you told me about your sister, your sister working for the television – you were really talking about you.'

'I was. I don't actually have a sister. Not as such.'

In her cheap towelling dressing gown, Trish is looking

wonderfully well scrubbed. A glow seems to rise out of her neck. Layers of shining black hair slide helplessly against other layers. I bet she washed it before turning in. But the sexy, stunned, accident-victim look that was on her face in the Totnes Tavern has vanished, replaced by a kind of anxious scepticism. Her eyeballs are dancing about, pinging into mine. I know what she's thinking. She's thinking: if everything I told her about myself was false, if my very reason for being under this roof was based on a lie, was I lying when I kissed her? When she kissed me back and said she was a monkey's auntie.

The happy atmosphere of, what, eight hours ago maybe, has been replaced with something different. There's still a tenderness, yes. But it's mixed with suspicion now. And confusion. Eight hours ago, when I drew my little finger across her lip, and the flesh tugged and sprang back in that delightfully spongy way, eight hours ago things were very clear.

But now, all sorts of mayhem have come between us. And much as I'd love to take hold of the dressing gown cord that she's twiddling between her fingers and give it a firm, insistent tug . . . waves of sleep are rolling in over my shoulders, making my eyelids droop and my brain trip out.

If I had the energy, I could remount the charm offensive, I could build the trust, develop the argument, make the case why nothing has changed since last night, and we should resume chewing at each other's faces without further delay. She's gazing at me, with those great, widely spaced eyes. But . . . *whoosh*, another wave of sleep comes in from behind, and I have to physically shake myself awake.

Fuck. It's all too fucking late in the day.

In love — as in deception comedy — timing is all.

'Look, Trish, I know everything's a bit mucked up between us. You don't really know who I am any more, and I don't blame you for that because I hardly know myself. But I tell you what I do know. I know that I think you're a great girl, and I know you deserve better than Rotten Roger, and I know that I'd feel terrible if we didn't get another chance to see. See if we. See if we like. If we like. Doing. *This*.'

Do I say the last speech out loud, or does it merely play in my head? Do I bring my mouth against hers? Do we kiss?

I have no way of definitively answering these questions. When I next wake up, I'm lying on the sofa, and my watch tells me it's ten past ten in the morning.

But when I wake again, an hour later, I notice that trapped in the links of my steel watchstrap, almost too fine to see, is a single long black hair.

6

'I'm full,' groans Rose. Her fork clatters on to the plate.

'I'm past full,' echoes Geraldine. 'I can feel the flesh bursting through my trousers.'

The delightful image of Geraldine's milky flesh popping through her blue velvet jeans fills my brain. 'I told you we didn't need the king prawn dopiaza,' I add limply. 'No one's touched it.'

The three of us lie on my floor, the remains of the mega-picnic spread across the carpet between us. I haven't shared with Rose and Geraldine *all* of the intimate details of my final hours in Devon. ('Did you snog her?' Rose asked. And, to cheering and general ribaldry, I confessed there 'may have been a tender little scene, yes.') Nor did I mention the business with the Polaroids. That can remain our nice little secret.

However, I do describe the fond goodbyes of later that day. Digby booming, 'Stay as long as you like, Alistair. Haven't had so much fun for years. Should have finished the bugger off, though.' Digby, who clearly never got his head round the various issues of identity at play under his roof. There is Vic, winking at me conspiratorially. Trish, blushing. Toby, glowering and bandaged, saying through gritted teeth how good it had been to see me – Toby, who'd told his father he'd walked into a door in the middle of the night. I tell the girls how the old soldiers drop me at the railway station in the Bentley, saluting as my train slips away from the platform.

'What was the present?' Rose suddenly exclaims. 'The one Luke posted through your letter box?'

'Oh, that. It was another trout.'

'Those fish were from *him*?'

'Real gangsters borrow a lot of their ideas from gangsters in film and TV, apparently. I guess it was a symbolic "getting closer, the net's drawing in" sort of motif. Fucking thing was lying on my doormat for days.'

For some reason, I don't mention the evening, about a fortnight after the events described above, when, safely reinstalled in London, the pizza delivery guy rings on my bell, and how, after I buzz him up to my door, standing there when I open it, brandishing a twelve-inch edgeless thin-crust jobby (with extra anchovies), is (in descending anatomical order) the heart-stopping, stomach-churning, bowel-loosening figure of Luke Holderness.

'Relakth, Charlth. Or ith it Alithtair tonight? I haven't come to kill you.'

The creature looks different. Gone are the ghastly trench coat, denim shirt and tooth-medallion. I realise with a bit of a shock that he's wearing a suit, with a shirt and tie. He's had a haircut too. Squatting atop the shiny great bowling ball this evening is a semi-fashionable Julius Caesar. His general air of menace is almost entirely absent. 'What are you doing here?' I stutter. 'All dressed up like that. With my dinner.'

'Have you been thmoking pot? There'th a funny thmell in here.'

'It's joss-sticks.'

'Yeth. And I'm Kate Moth. Are you going to invite me in?'

'Er. Well, to be honest, Luke, you aren't top of my list of favourite people right now.'

'I brought thome draw.' He produces a lump of hashish the size of a golf ball from his pocket, chucks it into the air and catches it. 'It'th good thtuff. Lebanethe.'

'Look. I'm sorry. I don't understand . . .'

'I'm jutht being friendly, Charlth. What do they thay, trying to mend fentheth.'

Is he taking the piss? Mind you, that lump of dope does look tempting. 'Oh fuck. Come on then.'

It's one of the odder evenings I've passed in recent years. He paces about the flat stockily, nodding appreciatively at the various modern lamps, and soft furnishings from Habitat. He gazes at the bookshelf in something like awe ('Have you read all of thothe?' 'Not even half, actually'). He spends a particularly long time flipping through my CD collection.

'Do you *like* Thteely Dan?'

'No, not really. Funny you should ask.'

He seems so utterly *un*threatening tonight, that I offer him a drink and half my pizza. He produces a little plastic dope pipe and crumbles some of the hash into the bowl. We pass it between us, and then we just sit for what seems a long while, blown away by the silky wondrousness of Karen Carpenter's singing voice (*The Carpenters Greatest Hits* – he picked it).

'I love that thong,' he says after 'Goodbye to Love'.

'I can't resist it,' I agree.

'And I love "Rainy Dayth and Mondayth" ath well.'

'Me too.'

'Have you heard Joe Cocker's version of "Whiter Shade of Pale"?'

'Actually, I think I have.'

'Do you love it?'

'I think I may do.'

It's rather unnerving. He's going to no particular effort to make proper conversation. He hasn't raised the subject of his grandfather, nor of the incident at Krapp's Ring, and I certainly haven't had the bad taste to bring up any of that business. He's not even curious about what I was *doing* down there in Devon in the first place, or who my ridiculous rescuers were. He seems content merely to sit in my flat, get wrecked and listen to music, which, as it happens, I too find a perfectly acceptable formula for a quiet weekday night in. So we're *hanging*, me and the rock-headed apparition who, a couple of weeks ago, had me digging my own grave.

Oddly, when I think about it, I find I bear him no ill-will (though it *is* hard to forget that, you know, *thing* stained into the flesh of his upper body).

He rests the great boulder against the back of my sofa, as I sit by the stereo and play us a few of my favourite tracks. 'Do What You Gotta Do', the version by Hazel O'Connor; 'In a Broken Dream' by Python Lee Jackson; 'Don't Think Twice, It's All Right', Dylan; 'You Don't Have to Say You Love Me', Dusty Springfield; 'She Came in through the Bathroom Window', Beatles.

Luke offers to spin the sounds for a bit. His playlist from the CDs available is slightly more sophisticated than mine, I'd say. 'Let's Get It On', Marvin Gaye; 'Down in the Valley', Solomon Burke (didn't even know I had that one); 'Behind a Painted Smile', Isley Brothers; 'Stop Your Sobbing', Pretenders; 'Walking in the Rain', Ronettes; 'Ain't No Love in the Heart of the City', Bobby Bland; 'The End', The Doors; 'Because The Night', Patti Smith.

He's lying on an elbow, working the CD. And then he does that stunt I first saw him pull in the stone circle on Dartmoor where he springs off the floor with one hand and is suddenly, alarmingly, upright; feet landing on the carpet with barely a sound, like a cat.

'That's quite a trick,' I tell him perfectly sincerely.

'I can do it the other way round too.'

Equally suddenly and silently, he's down on the floor, propped up on one elbow. 'It'th a Marine ectherthithe. I learned it from a man in prithon.'

'Ah. They say you can learn a lot in, er, places like that.'

'You can. It'th true.'

'Did you learn that thing with the coat buttons there?'

'No. My granddad taught me that one.'

You know that noise in quiz shows, that two-tone *wah-waaaah* with the dying fall that translates as 'Contestant, you are an ignorant worthless wanker. Take a bow, you have just completely fucked up'? That's the sound that's presently echoing through my brain cells.

But Luke seems unconcerned. I'd say he even looks mildly amused.

'Charlth, your faith.'

I guess I may have gone white or something.

'I wath upthet about Granddad. But I'm calmer about it now. You were right. It wathn't your fault. He could have gone at any time.'

'But what about all that business with the chips and the soup? The code?'

'Yeth, I thought about that. I dithcuthed it with my thera-pitht. In the end, we dethided it cometh down to what workth betht for *you*. By that, I mean me.'

'Your therapist?'

'Yeth, Charlth. Many people with my . . . my background, let'th thay, are now theeking professional help to deal with their issueth.'

'I guess everyone's seen *The Sopranos*.'

'*The Thopranoth* hath done a lot to dethtigmatithe thyco-therapy in the eyeth of thertain people on the marginth of conventhional thothiety.'

Christ, he's swallowed a fucking textbook.

'Well, I have to say, I'm very pleased to hear this, Luke.'

'I thaid to Diana, that'th my therapitht, I should in all con-scienth take the fucker out. No offenth. I thpeak my mind when I talk to her. But the thing ith, thomehow, I don't know how it happened, I got to quite like him.' He shoots me a sheepish look, quite a feat when you've got a face like his. 'Then she athked me, well, what do *you* really want to do? And I thought about it. And that'th when I knew.'

'I see.' Wonder if they talk about that tattoo.

'Anyway, I gave you a good fright, didn't I?'

'Fucking *right* you did.' A pause. 'You wouldn't have . . . ?' I tail off.

'Wouldn't have what, Charlth?'

'Wouldn't. Wouldn't have. Have pulled the actual. The trigger. As it were.'

An inscrutable smile bubbles through the rubble-strewn countenance.

'That'th for me to know, ithn't it?'

He enters another disc into the CD player. Reggae. 'Klu Klux Klan' by Steel Pulse. Treads back over to the sofa and refills the pipe. On we smoke.

Despite the somewhat sensitive subject just discussed, actu-ally, it's by no means an unpleasant evening we're having here. An empty pizza box lies on the glass-topped coffee table.

We've downed a couple of beers. The music selections have been never less than interesting. Not a hint of violence radiates off old boulder-head – if anything, the reverse. He looks, dare I say it, happy.

But still. What the fuck is this all about, do you suppose?

'Luke, I can take it that hostilities, as it were, have officially ceased between us?'

'Yeth, Charlth.'

'I mean, it is slightly odd, you sitting here in my flat, after . . . after everything that's happened. I'm having a perfectly nice time and all, don't get me wrong . . .'

'I think I told you. I enjoy your company. I don't really *know* anyone like you.'

'You don't?'

'I think I could learn thingth from you.'

'What? What could you possibly learn from me?'

'That thing where you yawn with your mouth shut. I'd like to learn how to do that.'

'You're not serious?'

'The way you wriggle.'

'*Wriggle?*'

'When you're in a spot. You know the Artful Dodger?'

'In Dickens?'

'You're the Artful Wriggler.'

'I'm flattered.' And you're fucking Bill Sikes, let's not forget. Or at least you were.

'When I'm in a thpot, I tend to . . . well, let'th thay there'th an art to it, but it'th not very polite.'

'Actually, Luke . . .' Oh *please*. No, sorry. I can't help myself. I have to say this. 'You've taught *me* something.'

'Really, Charlth?'

'About single-mindedness. About not ducking and diving the whole time, drifting with the tide, doing what's convenient, or politic. But sticking to your . . .' *Don't say guns.* '. . . sticking to your purpose. I suppose I'm saying I admire your sense of purpose. And your sense of when to *evolve* that purpose. Into another, er, different purpose.'

'Mental toughneth. The brain is a muthle. I learned that in prithon too.'

He puts on 'Alison' by Elvis Costello. And then he does a very uncool thing. He picks a biro off the table, and uses it as a 'microphone', singing along, swaying, doing all the gestures, the splayed fingers, the fist, the tortured facial bit. I feel embarrassed for him – this is secret stuff people should only do on their own – and it's quite tricky to keep the faint smile of amusement plastered on my face. Watching the bizarre performance, head thrown back, eyes closing, mouth drawn into a howl of pain, it occurs to me that the poor fucker may have no proper conception of what sensible people generally do in the context of other sensible people. Suddenly I feel his unknowability. What kind of twisted childhood could he have had? What could the inside of his house look like? Or the inside of his *head*? Thinking about it, maybe I seem just as exotic to him.

'By the way, Charlth,' he says at the door on his way out, 'your thecret'th thafe with me.'

'What secret?'

'I know you took some pictureth of me.' He jabs a thumb at his chest. 'I heard the camera.'

'Luke, don't worry. I won't tell anyone about your . . .' I can't bring myself to say the word. 'I won't tell anyone.'

'No, Charlth. And I won't tell anyone about the accident.'

'What accident?'

'In your troutherth.'

'Ah. That accident.'

'That thing you thaid that night about how you thought I

could have my own show — that wath all bollockth, wathn't it?'

Yes. 'Er, not entirely. Why do you ask?'

'No reason. Well, good night, Charlie. Thankth for a nithe evening.'

Charlie. He called me Charlie.

7

The two girls trip off into the night, heels clacking noisily on the parquet staircase of my building's common parts. On Monday morning, we all start work on our new programme. Actually it's what they call a broadcast pilot, a one-off that they'll transmit, and if it goes down OK, they'll fork out for a dozen more. The channel gave it the green light the day after they read the treatment, which I wrote the day after the visit from Luke that I've just described. The same afternoon that Peter Marcus told me we needed 'something *cruel*, Charles, something that *doesn't* feature Miss Birkendale, and urgently, please, or we'll all be out of a job.' Actually, what I dreamt up isn't that cruel, but it *is* quite nasty, though it stops short of actual unpleasant. Fortunately they were in the market for nasty, as well as for cruel.

It's an idea whose format, as I wrote, 'follows in the well-loved TV tradition of clever-clogs panel games. And whose zeitgeisty subject matter can be seen within the context of a popular culture in which the doings of gangsters, drug barons, bent coppers and associated lowlife are regularly celebrated in magazines, books and movies. The show — a cross between *Have I Got News for You* and *Lock, Stock and Two Smoking Barrels* — features two teams of "bad lads" from the demi-monde of underworld-meets-showbiz. Each week, they compete to answer questions on crime, criminals, and the authorities who try to bring them to justice – both in reality, and in fiction, television and cinema.'

We're calling it *Who's Been a Naughty Boy, Then?* and although we haven't quite found a host yet – Angus is thought to want too much money; ditto Anne Robinson – we think Luke Holderness would be perfect for one of the team captains. Peter Marcus believes his lisp could be developed into a national talking point. Like Cilla saying 'lorra, lorra'. Or that woman in *Big Brother* with the terrible laugh.

At this point, the end of the evening, guests gone home, instead of what I would normally do – fling myself on the sofa and wake up in the middle of the night with the lights on and the TV blaring – I exercise a bit of mental toughneth. I clear away the remains of the Indian, fire up the laptop and check my email.

There's one from Linds, to say that she and Prickface – sorry, must learn to call him Giles if they're really getting engaged, for fuck's sake – have booked themselves into a lovely country house hotel on Dartmoor for the weekend of Digby's summer fête. They – 'we' – very much look forward to seeing me down there.

There's another long message from Simon Lowenstein, once again twisting and agonising as he struggles to explain why 'for years', evidently, he let others speak for him 'both liter- ally and metaphorically'. At first in school ('when I abdicated my responsibility to answer to my own name'); then during his early failed marriage ('I came to realise that Helen was a seriously conflicted woman who had a great deal she needed to talk about'); finally throughout his 'absurd and undistin- guished' career as a professional ventriloquist. He too is embarking on therapy (for f's s.) and as part of 'the on-going struggle to find my own voice', he has been writing letters of 'apology and, hopefully, redemption' to everyone he has ever 'unconsciously manipulated' into spieling on his behalf. He's thinking of going into public relations . . .

I e him back to thank him for his frank and fulsome explanations. At the end I type: 'Couldn't have put it better myself.'

TWELVE

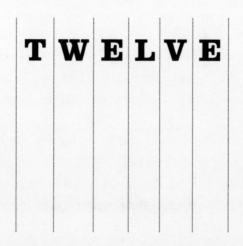

A tall, handsome woman, mid-fifties, bearing a striking facial resemblance to Trish, hands me a plastic cup of warm country cider.

'That's a pound, please, love.'

Digby's fête appears to be a great success. The general air of decrepitude hanging over the estate has vanished. The grass has been cut, the rusting tractor dragged out of sight. Now small stalls and tents dot the lawn opposite the big house. An impressive number of locals mill about, rummaging through trestle tables of old paperbacks, inspecting pieces of agricultural equipment, buying cakes, preserves, plants; guessing the weight of the tethered pig; digging deep into the bran tub for what turns out to be a wrapped bottle of Vosene. Across it all, a combo of four red-faced men blow jolly jazz tunes in the sunshine.

Rose sits at a little camping table, dressed in a flowery gown with a turban, hooped earrings and heavily darkened eyelids. The sign by her crystal ball reads, 'Madame Rose. Palmist and Seer.'

'How's business?' I ask cheerfully, dropping into the 'client's' chair.

'I think Psychic Geraldini is doing rather better.' She nods towards a stand nearby where a similarly comic version of Geraldine appears to be fingering a farmer's gold watch, her eyes shut, face pointed towards the sun, the better to receive the vibrations.

'Digby's awfully pleased you're doing this for him, Rose.'

'Odd-looking bod, isn't he?'

We watch as the lord of the manor makes his rounds, pausing to buy a ticket for the tombola here, receiving greetings from various well-wishers there. He's gone to a bit of an effort this afternoon. The brown cords have clearly come back from the dry-cleaners. They've been teamed with a fresh checked Viyella shirt, a knitted brown countryman's tie, a zippy green tweed jacket, and not an egg stain in sight. Amid the tragic ruins of his face, an unmistakable smile has come out to play. He's making his way towards the small stage, in time for the official opening of the festivities at 2 p.m.

'Care to have your future told? Cross my palm with silver, dearie, and Madame Rose will tell you all.'

I drop 50p in her dish. She takes my hand, tracing a sexy painted fingernail along its major cracks and crevices.

'Hmm,' she hmms. 'Interesting. I can tell immediately that you work with your hands. You're an artist. Or a sculptor. Am I right?' I give her an old-fashioned look. 'You have a very strong love line. In fact, I see that you are about to embark on a brand-new relationship. Is there someone you harbour thoughts about? Someone here today, perhaps?'

'You. You're a bloody shit-stirrer, you.'

'Actually, your palm *has* gone rather damp, Charles. Where is the bathroom cleaner this afternoon?'

A bright red sports car, expensive-looking, low on the ground and *thin* with it, noses under the banner reading 'Grand Summer Fête', slipping incongruously alongside the ancient Escorts, Datsuns, Toyotas and the odd Land Rover. The doors open upwards, like birds' wings; Linds and Prickface emerge like a pair of glamorous astronauts or something. She waves at me, and, as they approach, sickeningly they join hands.

'Hi!' I yell, perhaps a tad too enthusiastically to be taken seriously.

'Charles, this is Giles.'

'Hi, Giles.' Or may I call you cunt?

'Hello, Charles. I've heard a lot about you.'

'All bad, I assume.'

'On the contrary . . .'

It's true, the rather *over*-blue blue jeans have got a crease in them. The belt is somehow a few degrees off from what one would consider harmless (too wide, with the pointy silvered end dangling through the buckle, pointing down at you know what). The shirt – again with the fucking polo pony and rider, like blubber-chops in Yech – is a shade of pink not seen in nature. The hair is . . . well, I'm sorry, it *isn't* a thousand miles from Bay City Rollers. There's definitely some layering going on up there. Whether it amounts to full-blown feathering, I'm not qualified to say. Bottom line, in any case, is expensive poncy haircut. And the face. Well, dammit, it's tanned and handsome, relaxed, confident and smiling. The sort you immediately want to punch. I clock well manicured fingernails on the hand, when he extends it for a shake. A thin gold identity bracelet breaks cover from the shirt cuff. The squeeze is firmish and dry, manly without being aggressive. My own palm must feel like a warm kipper. Linds' eyes are glittering with pleasure and I feel dizzy.

'Giles has booked us into this most amazing place. You've got to come and see it. The rooms are incredible. They're all filled with this fabulous stuff the owners have collected on their travels. We've got one of those what-the-butler-saw machines in the bathroom. And there's one room with a huge stuffed ostrich!'

I can just picture the scene. The horrible wind-up gramophones. The ghastly old advertising posters. The displays of peacock feathers. The piles of junk masquerading as eccentricity.

'Is the owner, how can I put it, a bit of a *character*?'

Did that come out a bit sourly? Because Linds' face has fallen. Prickface deals me a searching expression, emphasising the clear, straight lines of his jaw.

'Actually,' he says, 'it's true, he can be a bit of a bore about his antiques.'

I warm to him slightly (P-face, not the owner).

And then a memory comes back, of a time that Linds and I were staying the weekend in some pretentious B and B in an English coastal town. There were loads of those nasty porcelain figurines in glass cases all over the shop. The proprietor and his wife radiated their disapproval of us. Everything about their house made it blindingly clear that they thought they were posher than us, that they didn't really need to be doing this B and B thing (except that they *were* doing it, *and* she tried to overcharge us). I remember we came to dislike them so much that in one of those promenade tat shops we bought a jolly ceramic of two pigs fucking. It was wittily captioned 'Makin' Bacon'. Before we checked out, we sneaked it into one of our hosts' glass display cases, amid all the fawns and pussycats, and top-hatted drunks lolling against lampposts and the like. I used to like to think it might still be there.

'Hey, congratulations, you guys,' I manage to crank out. 'Getting married and everything.'

'Thanks,' drawls Giles.

'It is rather grown up, isn't it?' squeals Linds.

'How did he propose?' Like I give a toss.

'Oh, Charlie, it was *so* romantic. He took me out to dinner at our favourite restaurant – didn't you? – and then the waiter comes with my starter, except it isn't a starter. It's a little blue box with a ribbon. And inside was a ring.'

She swizzles her left hand about. A diamond the size of a bird's egg roosts by a knuckle. It catches a ray of sunlight and sets fire to one of the smaller marquees.

'So when's the big day?' (Only two more obligatory questions now: Where are you doing it? Have you thought about a honeymoon?)

'Oh, not for a while. Not till Giles's divorce comes through.'

Whoops. 'Ah, I see.'

Cancel those last two obligatories.

'Still, a nice long engagement, eh?' I seem to have cheered up a bit. 'Plenty of time for everything.' Like going off each other.

'Bloody hell. Is that Erica Birkendale?' Linds asks suddenly.

'Yes. She's agreed to perform the opening ceremony. Seeing as how she's so pissed on her chips, career-wise.'

Giles returns my grin, but there's a note of something else in there. Disapproval, I expect.

Don't ask me why she agreed. I'm sure the hundred quid and her rail fare were neither here nor there. I guess in the end it's all about feeling that someone wants you; that you're still working. Though in this case, I feel with a depressing certainty that the temporary plunge in Ms Birkendale's share price will prove to be just that: temporary. Next year, or the year after, the terrible old bag will ride back triumphantly into the mainstream, fronting some new show about politics, or handbags, or sad children or sick animals (or sick children or sad animals). I guess she's one of those people about whom they'll never be able to do a *Where Are They Now?* . . . because she'll always still be *here*.

Anyway, her presence at the Gulliver Grand Summer Fête has caused a bit of a stir, prompting the appearance of a couple of photographers from the local papers, and even a TV crew from *Sheep Dip Tonight*, or whatever they call their regional news show (mustn't sneer though, must we?).

Right now, she's sitting on a collapsible wooden chair at the back of the little stage as Digby peers at his notes and taps on the microphone for a bit of hush. The musicians dribble to a halt.

'Brings me great pleasure,' he slurs. 'Really quite considerable pleasure to welcome you all to our house and gardens this afternoon. You know . . .' He takes a deep breath. His face becomes one of those sad Isle of Lewis chessmen. 'You know, there was a time when I didn't believe we'd ever be able to mount one of these little shindigs again. The old place got into a bit of a state, to be frank. Gone to seed, I believe is the expression. And for that, I can blame *no one but myself*.' The phrase hangs in the air, shuddering. Digby looks like he's playing King Lear. His face is a mask of sorrow, the eyes shining with remorse in their subsiding pouches. The crowd has become very quiet. Somewhere, a small child starts crying. Digby shakes his head, the loose sandpapery skin flapping to keep up. 'But we move forward, ladies and gentlemen. Boys and girls. Things change. That's the great secret: *things change*.'

Linds digs me in the ribs. 'Is he all right?' she whispers.

I shrug. Fucked if I know.

'So I urge you all to enjoy the afternoon. As I can remember my own father saying from this spot more than sixty years ago . . .' he blinks back a tear, 'what you lose on the tombola, you may well win back in the bran tub.' A smattering of embarrassed applause. 'And now, to officially get the proceedings under way, let me introduce our special celebrity guest. Of course you know her from the television, so please show your appreciation for . . .' his eyes swarm over his notes, '. . . she's a household name . . .' he can't seem to find his place, '. . . to the lovely, the, er, very talented . . .' a last panicky goggle at the script, '. . . Miss, er . . . Miss Ulrika Bermondsey.'

She comes back from this quite well, I must say, bounding off her seat, like she was fronting the Eurovision Song Contest. She bestows a pair of showbiz kisses on Digby. He looks as startled as if he'd been slapped round the face with a freshly landed salmon. Erica grabs the mike.

'Hello, Totnes!' she bellows. 'It's great to be with you.' The small child stops crying. 'We seem to be blessed with fine weather this afternoon, so I trust this won't turn out to be the proverbial fête worse than death.' She pulls her trademark teasy-weasy face. A camera shutter goes off; there are polite titters. 'Unaccustomed as I am to speaking to *lots* of people all at once . . .'

She holds the pause a terrifyingly long time. Several weak-spirited members of the crowd are browbeaten into laughing out of sheer embarrassment. You've got to hand it to the dreadful old trout, she's only playing to a couple of hundred distracted Devonians, but the way she's carrying on, you'd think it was Madison Square Garden. She's giving them her all. She's being The Star. Extra-impressive because I know that despite her public persona of being 'good at people', she actually loathes any contact with the general public ('if only they'd *wash* more often', is how she puts it).

'No, seriously. I've been in television a long time. When I started in this business, the day afterwards, one million TV sets were sold. It's true. The people who couldn't sell theirs gave them away.'

A single laugh.

'Thank you, sir. Nice to have an appreciative audience. Yesterday I had an audience who were with me all the way. No matter how fast I ran, I couldn't shake them off.'

The same man laughs again.

'My agent told me a story last week about a man he met. Said he had a terrific new job at the circus mucking out the elephants. Mucking out the elephants? asked my agent. How many of them? Twenty-five. Twenty-five elephants! How much do they pay you? Ten pounds a day. They pay you ten pounds a day for mucking out twenty-five elephants? If I were you, I'd chuck it in and get a decent office job. What, says the man . . . and leave show business?'

'Erica'th terrific, don't you think?'

Luke Holderness has crept up alongside.

'A terrific what?' I reply.

'I grew up watching that woman.'

'I grew old working with her.'

Rock-head gazes wistfully off into the crowd, where Erica is signing autographs and smothering babies. The celebrity gangster seems subtly different this afternoon. Maybe it's the smarter, sharper suit, a gorgeous deep purple that sheens blue or green depending which way the light strikes it. Perhaps it's the new hairdo, a hard core Grant Mitchell jobby that empha-sises his criminality. Or maybe it's merely the knowledge that the buzz about his pilot is getting very . . . er, buzzy. We haven't actually shot it yet, but several channels have expressed interest, and Luke's face has already appeared in a number of magazine articles about hoodlum chic. He introduces me to a well-dressed woman with blonde hair and wild eyes who turns out to be his agent.

'Luke says you discovered him,' she coos.

'We sort of discovered each other really.'

She looks at me as if I've disappointed her in some way. 'He's going to be very big, you know.'

'I don't doubt it.'

'Ridley Scott's casting people have already asked for a tape.'

'Great.' Just don't ask him to play any nude scenes.

'Do you think you *could* introduthe me?' says Luke.

'To Erica? Sure. How do you want me to describe you?'

'Admirer. The thuit will do the retht.'

Me and his agent look at one another. I'm thinking fucking cocky bastard. She's thinking, attitude. Mmm, excellent.

I walk Luke over to the little circle that has formed around Erica. She's wearing tight turquoise trousers, and a skimpy glittery top that shows off her bare brown arms. A Chanel handbag dangles off one shoulder.

'And this one is to . . . who is it, darling?'

'Cherie and Daryl,' says a blushing young mum.

Erica's felt-tip skates across her publicity photo.

'Erica, can I introduce an admirer, Luke Holderness?'

A slight skeletal crackle as she straightens and aligns herself in the direction of the newcomer. Her eyes widen, pupils flare. There's a flash of dazzling white teeth. 'Hi, I'm Erica,' she says, with sickening false modesty.

'Of courth you are.'

She laughs, like it's the first time anyone has ever said that.

'I uthed to watch you when I wath a kid.'

'Careful now, or you'll make me feel terribly old!'

'You were alwayth my favourite.'

'You preferred me to Graham, did you?'

'Graham wath a bloke.'

'I know. It was a joke.'

'I uthed to think about you a lot.'

'How nice. Would you like a picture?' She pulls another snap out of her handbag and, pen poised, cocks her eyebrows to *what name shall I put?*

'Actually, I wath hoping I could buy you a drink.' Luke skewers her with a look that could freeze running water. Without breaking eye contact, he takes the felt-tip out of her faltering hand, caps it, and slots it in his inside jacket pocket. Erica seems to sway slightly on her pencil heels. The fake smile has vanished. In its place is a sort of pained dismay. In a thin voice I've never heard her use before she replies, 'Actually, I am a bit thirsty.'

The bemused crowd parts as the stocky man in the colourful plumage steers the birdlike star towards the beer tent. As she teeters off, I see she's clinging tightly to his arm for fear of fainting dead away.

The afternoon sprawls onwards, the perfume of newly cut grass mingling pleasantly with frying onions. For the twentieth time, the jazz combo launch into 'When the Saints Go Marching In'. I run into Vic, arm in arm with the woman who sold me the glass of cider. It's his 'ladyfriend' from Torquay, Trish's mum.

'Good to see you again, Alistair,' he says. 'I mean Charles, of course. Everything all nicely sorted out between you and that odd feller, I see.'

'A misunderstanding, I think you could call it.'

'Have you said hello to Trish? You know she's back with rotten Roger?'

Trish's mum elbows him in the ribs playfully. '*Vi-ic.*'

'No. I didn't actually.'

'Everyone deserves a second chance, but only the one. If that little toerag stuffs up again . . .' Vic draws a finger across his throat.

'Go on with you,' says Mum.

'He's a very lucky chap,' I force myself to utter.

'She's a beautiful girl,' says Vic. 'Just like her mother.' He gives her a squeeze.

'*Vi-ic.* Go on with you.'

I begin to have a sense of where Trish gets her dazzling sense of wordplay from.

'Alistair. I mean Charles. This is Roger.'

Only by supreme effort of will do I stop myself from blurting out, You're joking? You can't be serious. This little . . . little speck is *Roger*? This . . . this *microbe* is the man who broke your heart and you've allowed back in for more?

'Hi, Roger.'

'Yeah, hi.'

Roger is as shifty-looking an individual as I've seen in a long time. Not particularly small, yet somehow slight. Dandruffy and insubstantial. One of those husk-like creatures you feel you could blow over with one powerful puff. He's obviously the living proof of Toby Gulliver's theory about the effectiveness of 'spadework'.

It's rude to ask, what the fuck do you see in him? So instead, I ignore him completely. Happily, after a minute of painful small talk, he slithers off to fetch refreshments.

'So you guys have patched things up?' I ask, marvelling once more at the way the skin of her face lies across its bones. The head atop the neck, the neck rising from the shoulders. Carrying on like that pretty much all the way down.

A surge tide of pink advances up her throat. 'Roger told me he couldn't live without me.'

'Jesus. That's quite a statement.'

'He's become ever so romantic since we got back together.' She smiles fondly at some memory, and I begin to feel a bit weak. 'He got down on one knee.'

'Christ, you're not going to marry . . .' the cunt.

'No. Not yet. I told him we need time to think.' About one and a half seconds should do it, I would have thought.

'But he's been such a . . .' shit. 'So difficult towards you. You told me all about it in the pub.'

'He couldn't help it. He's really sweet once you get to know him.'

'I don't. I mean, I hardly. He seems. Of course. There's no accounting.' Heavy sigh. 'Damn it, Trish. What has he got? Am I missing something here?'

'We just have this . . . this terrific rapport.'

'But you don't . . .' You can't *fancy* the horrendous little tick, can you? 'A sort of mental connection, is it?'

'We connect in lots of ways, Charles.'

Roger returns with three glasses of country cider, and I have to clink my plastic beaker sportingly against his when frankly I'd much rather dash it in his face.

'So what do *you* do, Roger?' I ask, trying to keep much of the poison out of my voice.

'I teach,' he replies, eyes flicking everywhere.

'What's your—'

'Divinity.'

'Div . . .'

'Yes.'

'Ah.'

'Are you going to the demonstration of agricultural machinery?' chirps Trish.

'Actually, I think I might give it a miss,' I reply.

'There's a new muck-spreader that everyone's very excited about.'

'I dare say.'

'Well, cheers anyway.'

We stand in a silent threesome drinking cider. I feel especially depressed, alone in a cold, uncaring universe sort of thing. Being as how I have just been handed the official, final, absolute *definitive* proof of the non-existence of God.

A strange thing has happened to Erica. I bump into her at the stall where punters are invited to take penalties against a goal-keeper from one of the local football teams, three kicks for a quid. She's holding Luke's jacket as the criminal takes several paces backwards, then buries a powerful left-footed drive into the top corner of the net. I can't help myself, I applaud. Luke walks back for the second.

'I *like* your friend,' she hisses at me from behind her hand. It's the most sincere, straightforward thing she has ever said to me.

'He's . . . he's quite a character.'

'I think he's a bit of a hunk.' And she giggles, a horrible girly giggle. I don't know whether to laugh or be ill.

The goalie manages to block Luke's next shot with his stomach. Winded, he sits in his goal mouth panting and eyeing the penalty-taker with suspicion.

'He says he's a criminologist; that he's making a show with you.' Her eyes are sparkling. I realise with slowly spreading shock that the awful gorgon is trying to be nice to me.

'He does know a lot about that sort of thing.'

'He looks dangerous. I *like* that.'

'I believe he has developed some considerable physical prowess.'

'Martial arts?'

'Of a kind, I guess.'

Erica turns to watch Luke take the third penalty, kneading her thumb unconsciously against the collar of his Hugo Boss jacket. He slots it away cleanly, bottom right-hand corner. The goalie offers him a choice of a stuffed toy or a coconut.

'Thith ith for you, darling.' He presents Erica with a bright blue elephant.

'My *hero*,' she gushes.

'Plenty more where that came from,' he adds a bit meaninglessly. But then sweethearts always talk rubbish, don't they?

'I had no idea you were such a gifted striker,' I flatter the rubble-faced felon.

'I only play well when I'm trying to impreth thomeone.'

Fuck me, the love-struck cow blushes. Or rather she *simulates* a blush, batting her eyelashes and putting a claw to her throat.

'Have you theen what I bought for Erica?'

'We found it in the sale of craft. Luke said I *had* to have it. Isn't it thrilling?'

From a Sainsbury's plastic bag, Luke removes a framed watercolour of a street scene in Vienna. The buildings are technically proficient, but the human figures are poorly rendered. Each seems curiously static and alone. The artist has initialled the work 'A.H.'

'Wath only five poundth. They think it'th by a local artitht.'

'I have just the spot for it in my dining room,' beams Erica.

'I hope it brings you years of pleasure.'

I am suddenly very happy. Perhaps there is a God after all.

On a whim, I wander into the big house. I pass the library door, which is open. Glancing inside, I see Digby Gulliver seated in one of the wing-backed armchairs, Scotch glass in hand, surveying the merry-making on the rolling lawns beyond the windows, a look of nostalgic contentment on his tragic features.

'I think it's quite a hit, your summer fête,' I venture.

'Alistair! Dear boy, come and join me.'

I thread my way through the tottering heaps of books and place myself in the chair opposite. Between us is the chess-board with the uncompleted game.

'I see you managed to offload your Hitler.' Confusion passes across his face like a cloud formation. 'I forget who told me you had one.'

'Oh yes,' he says at last. 'Bloody *horrible* thing. Must have been a present to my father. Should have chucked it years ago.'

'I believe it's found a deserving new owner.'

The eggy eyes drift away through the glass to the revellers outside. 'Good to see the old place with a bit of life about it again. Kiddies running around. Shame Toby couldn't make it down. Young Oliver and Josh . . .' He trails off, dimly aware, perhaps, of some unresolved difficulty as regards me and Toby.

'Hmm,' I hmm.

'I see that tattooed chap has shown his face again. Bit of a nerve, isn't it?'

'We've sort of mended our differences.'

'Glad to hear it. Doesn't do to bear grudges. Still wish I'd shot the bugger, though.' And he laughs. Or coughs, it's hard to tell.

'I'm glad you didn't. For all kinds of reasons.'

'Best sport I've had for years, that.'

'Has this chess game been . . . abandoned or something?'

Digby blinks a couple of times. 'Celia and I used to play. In the old days. Before she . . .' His eyes seem to roll into the bottom of their sockets and stare up at the ceiling. Like a cod, after receiving some particularly bad bit of news.

'. . . only I see black has mate in two.'

'This was our last game. We called it a draw. Never played again after that.'

'Black bishop takes king's pawn. White does whatever white does. Then rook to rook six. Mate.'

Digby stares at the board as though he's not seeing it. 'I was black.'

'You would have won.'

'I didn't see it. I offered the draw. Look here, are you sure . . . ?'

'Shall we play it?'

'If you're sure . . .'

Actually, I was wrong. It's not mate in two. Digby does the thing with his bishop. And then I, as white, suddenly spot a tasty knight move that dispels the danger. We bog ourselves down in fifteen minutes of mid-game skirmishing, Digby quietly humming to himself, his eyes oddly defocused over the chess pieces. After a spell of pointless harrying and parrying, I begin to see why he might have been tempted to offer a draw. For want of a better idea, I advance a pawn idly.

The humming stops. A long pause. And then a low rumble from the seat opposite. A rumble growing to a growl. Strange lights appear in the Gulliver eyeballs. The growl officially becomes a semi-howl.

'Got you, you treacherous bitch!' He slams down his black queen and yells, 'How do you like that, then? Fucking *mate*, matey!'

He's staring at me, but I think he may be seeing Celia.

'Well played, Mr Gulliver.'

Digby's panting slightly. His gaze readjusts to what passes for normal. 'I would have won.'

'Shouldn't have offered the draw.'

'Bloody silly of me, looking back.'

'Changing the subject, are you going to the demonstration of agricultural machinery?' I ask to change the subject. 'I believe it's in half an hour.'

'Am I expected to?'

'I don't think so.'

'Well, if it's all the same, I shan't bother. Bloody boring things, tractors.' He drains away the remains of his Scotch, the sad eyes widening momentarily as the Famous Grouse migrates south towards its nesting grounds. He shakes his head. 'Bloody stupid of me, looking back. Shouldn't have offered the draw, should I?'

Quite a large crowd has gathered to see the new muck-spreader. It turns out it's German, all gleaming black paint-work, sexy curves and styling, a real Mercedes Benz of a piece of farm equipment, radiating discreet mature power. Never mind spraying shit, this looks like a machine that could invade Poland. The man from the distributors says through the loud-speaker that the beast – he *calls* it a beast – can spread more manure over a wider area more evenly in a faster time than any other machine on the market. Thus the manuring process itself becomes quicker (therefore cheaper) *and* more efficient, and how many things can you claim that about these days? In addition, crop yields in some German place with a long name where the beast was tested were found to have increased significantly. It's shortly going to be his privilege to provide the first demonstration in the United Kingdom of its awesome muck-spreading power.

The beast stands in a little roped-off corner section of lawn, its business end, like a giant Hoover attachment, pointing omin-ously across the fence into the neighbouring field, where a series of coloured flags have been planted at intervals, like markers on a golf driving range. Various red-faced farming types in tweed jackets and wellies stand behind the cordon, arms folded, waiting to be impressed. Rose and Geraldine have abandoned their posts for the event, nudging one another and wisecracking out of the corners of their mouths, no doubt at the rural comedy of it all ('What did you get up to in the country then?' 'Went to a really cracking muck-spreading demonstration'). I clock Trish and repellent Roger in the crowd. Vic and his ladyfriend. Even Luke Holderness has been drawn to the occasion.

'And now,' announces the man with the microphone, 'it's my pleasure to ask this afternoon's special guest celebrity to fire up the beast and show you what she's capable of. Ladies and gentlemen, Miss Erica Birkendale!'

The crowd applaud as Erica waves from the vehicle's cab. A big cheesy grin for the photographers and the film crew.

'You all know I've had quite a bit of c.r.a.p. flung at me over the years,' she quips, 'so it's very nice to be able to throw some back for a change. Here goes. Green button, is it?'

A powerful engine thrum. The machine starts to vibrate on its wheel base. A murmur of excitement runs through the crowd. The giant vacuum cleaner attachment shudders and swings round worryingly, threatening sections of the audience who instinctively flinch and duck in alarm. Unless this is all part of the shtick, something's gone wrong. The man with the mic yells 'Press the *red* button! The *red* one!' He's waving his arms. Erica can't hear him; doesn't know what to do. I am suddenly very aware of what lurks within the beast's great tank. Is it German horse shit, I wonder foolishly, as the huge nozzle swings round towards my section of spectators. We shy away like a gun's been trained on us. Now a grinding noise, followed by a really worrying *clanking*. The nozzle is swinging from side to side, out of control. A wave of anxiety emanates from the crowd, and people start to move away. The vehicle bounces up and down on its great wheels, its curvy flanks shaking in paroxysms of frustration.

And then the awful thing.

The manure spreader's great muzzle swings around slowly and comes to a halt. I realise I'm staring straight into it when, with a nicely understated Germanic *vroom* noise – like a BMW revving its engine at the lights – it discharges a huge plume of shit straight at me.

I go down like a skittle, upended as though caught by a jet from a water cannon. I'm winded and there's a powerfully horrible smell in my nostrils. I lie there panting for a few moments, then, palms and knees skidding on the slippery grass, I try to haul myself to my feet. The apparatus shudders, and releases a second muscular gout which catches me squarely amidships. Someone in the crowd laughs. I'm lying in a pool of ordure, fighting for breath. With a deeply disturbing sureness of action, the hellish German contraption now points its barrel almost straight up at the sky, and projectile-vents a third great fountain of droppings.

All the fight has gone out of me. All I can do is look on helplessly as the brown cloud hangs momentarily at the top of its arc . . . and commences its inevitable descent. I try to cover my head as it lands, stinging, slapping and splatting like some biblical plague.

The beast rattles, gives a final clank, and dies.

I rest stupefied in my personal pool of degradation. The last time I can recall seeing anything as comprehensively covered in cack was in a wildlife programme, and I'm almost certain it had four legs, and like, *feelers*.

A buzz goes through the onlookers. Smear and Stain materialise, tiptoeing towards me, speculatively waving their tails. Resisting an urge to sob, I close my eyes, as the two dogs gently begin to lick my face.

When I open them again, I realise I am looking into the dark, puzzled and . . . yes, ticking eyeballs of Kate the copper.

EPILOGUE

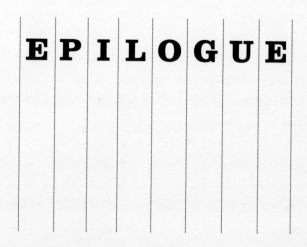

It's not Café Rouge – the scene, if you recall, of our first somewhat duplicitous encounter – it's the bar of the chintzy Totnes hotel that she's booked into. None the less, Kate sways in through the door like a perfect replay of the original event. Same checked trousers. Same leather jacket and serious glasses. Same dark hair swinging across her face like a curtain.

My same instant sense of . . . yes, excitement. Her same ants-in-her-pants twitchiness.

She hops on to the bar stool alongside mine.

'Matthew! I mean Charles.'

'Please. It's not funny any more. Shall I order a bottle?'

'You managed to get cleaned up OK then?'

'It went up my *nose*, Kate. I've had German horse . . . horse filth in my *ears*. That can't be good for you.'

'I doubt it very much. I think a bottle would be a fine idea.'

'You can't . . . can't *smell* anything, can you?'

She leans up close and sniffs a cartoon sniff. 'Only after-shave. Is that Eau Sauvage?'

'Sorry, I may have overdone it. I find I prefer it to *Merde de cheval*.'

She actually giggles.

Kate had called me about a week ago, out of the blue. Explained that she still felt a bit bad about creeping away after I'd fallen asleep over the alco-chess, leaving that note: 'Match suspended.' I'd said, not at all, on the contrary, all my fault, sort of thing, I shouldn't have nodded off. Oh, and by the way, you don't fancy going out for a drink one evening this week, do you? She'd said she'd like to, but it was a bit difficult on account of how she'd been seeing 'something of someone lately'. Bit of a sickener that, naturally. But then she asked, was I free perhaps for lunch on Saturday? I explained about Digby's summer fête – didn't go into the *whole* story, obvi-ously – but she was more than welcome to come down to Totnes; it was going to be a lot of fun, daft country folk to laugh at, guess the weight of the pig, all that sort of carry-on. She didn't think she could really, what with one thing and another, although 'they' had been talking about having a weekend away together. Come down to Devon then, I'd insisted like some tourist brochure, although, in truth, the idea of seeing her with a bloke in tow made me feel slightly sick.

Anyhow, I'd thought no more about it. That it was just talk. That I'd probably never see her again. But it turns out that they *did* book a weekend away. *He* badly needed a break, and she'd had a few childhood holidays in Torquay, so she knew this part of the world. However, at the last minute, he couldn't come due to – you'll never guess – due to 'urgent govern-ment business'. Yes, the someone she'd been seeing something of was Matthew, the guy she was meant to be meeting the first time round – the suit standing at the bar in Café Rouge, who stared at us quizzically. New Labour policy wonk. Gordon Brown's tennis partner. Something about her manner suggested she wasn't entirely disappointed to have left him in London.

She told me all this in the aftermath of the muck-spreading disaster, in the confusing, not to say humiliating interval between scraping off the worst of the immediate cack, and squelching up to the big house for an intensive programme of baths, showers, and strong whiskies.

'So, are you free tonight?' I enquired.

Afterwards I realised it was the first time I've ever asked anyone for a date whilst combing shit out of my eyebrows.

'So what was he like?' I say 'was' because if he was Mr Bleeding Marvellous, she wouldn't have come down without him, right? I hope there is an amused twinkle in my eye.

'A very good chap. But ultimately,' sigh, 'I think he may be a bit too serious for me.'

'Ah.' One of those. Excellent.

'I mean, I'm not uninterested in P.S.B.R.'

'It can be fascinating, I expect.'

'Although after a while, one does long to . . .'

'. . . talk about something silly?'

She smiles. Oh good. If it's light and frivolous she's after, she's come to the right place. I order a bottle of house white. Saves mucking around with single glasses, doesn't it?

'So how's life in the old police laboratory, then?' I ask brightly.

She gives me a funny look. Eyes doing that ticking thing again, as if she can't decide which one of mine to peer into.

'Confession, Charles.'

'Oh yes?'

'I'm not actually a police forensic scientist.'

'You're not?' Oh fuck. Where's the hidden camera?

'No.'

'Why did you say you were? Not that I'm claiming any moral high ground or anything.'

'I didn't actually. You did.'

'But you *agreed*.'

'You seemed so certain.'

'What *do* you do, then?'

'Twenty questions?'

'Oh fuck, don't start all that again!'

'I'm reluctant to say.'

'Why?'

'Well, it might put you off.' She stops fidgeting for a few seconds. Then she begins to scratch at her knee, allowing the curtain of hair to swish across her features. I do believe she may be concealing a blush.

'Kate, I know you're very smart. You've got a phenomenal memory. You can beat the pants off me at chess. You can drink me under the table. You've seen me covered in horse manure, for Christ's sake. And. And. And. You look great in those checked trousers.'

The curtain hangs in place for a few seconds. Then she lifts her head slowly, and it falls away.

'Really?'

'Really.'

She takes a deep breath. 'I teach Philosophy. And study it.'

I knew it. 'What branch?' Hope it's one I've heard of.

'Existentialism, chiefly. It's a bit out of fashion now.'

'I tried to read *Being and Nothingness* once. I got about halfway down the first page and decided I'd wait for the movie.'

She's sweet enough to laugh.

'You know, you would have won that chess game, Charles.'

'Sorry?'

'The chess game we played at your flat. You had mate in three moves. Before you . . . resigned, shall we say.'

'Really? That is so weird.' Not to say maddening.

She smiles. 'We should do it again some time.'

'We definitely should.'

On impulse, I ask: 'Is Kate your real name?'

'Actually, it isn't.'

It isn't? 'Why not?'

'You've got to be a bit cautious when you answer those ads, haven't you? You don't want to give too much away at first.'

'All that stuff about living in Ealing. *Captain Corelli's Mandolin. Four Weddings and a Funeral*?'

'Men don't like it if they feel threatened, do they?'

'This one does. I love feeling . . . *challenged*, shall we say.'

We drink in silence for a bit, thinking our separate thoughts. Mine largely revolve round the checked trousers. The ants-in-your-pants motif.

'What's your real name, then?' I ask eventually.

'Fabienne.'

'Christ!'

'It's French. I'm half-French.'

'Well, it just shows, doesn't it?'

'What?'

'Appearances needn't be deceptive. Oddly enough, when I first clapped eyes on you, I thought French. I even thought Philosophy.'

'In dreams, an umbrella can be a phallic symbol. But sometimes it's just an umbrella. Can't remember who said that.'

'Absolutely.' Phallic symbols, eh? Prom-is-ing.

'Do you know what I thought when I first saw *you*?'

'No, what?'

'He looks fun.'

'*Fun*?!'

'Fun.'

'Not intelligent, sensitive, charming . . .'

'What's wrong with fun?'

'Bit superficial, isn't it?'

'Someone once said, if a thing's worth being serious about, it's worth being funny about.'

'Is that profound?'

'All I'm saying is that I have a lot of respect for Fun.'

We stare at one another. Her face is flushed from the wine. The eyes tick about, then slow down to a steady gaze. I have a powerful feeling that at some point during the next bottle of wine, I shall feel compelled to suggest we relocate. Maybe try another game of . . . what's it called? That memory game? Fuck, what *is* it called? I cast my mind back to that evening in my flat, sitting side by side on the black leather sofa. The sexy indentation she left in it, I realise, still occupies storage space in my brain tissue.

Fun she wants, is it? If a thing's worth being serious about, it's worth being funny about, is it?

I take a deep swallow of Chardonnay. Then another, just to be on the safe side. 'Kate. Sorry . . . *Fabienne*. Can I ask? Do you ever think about death at all?'

'Death?'

'The fact of extinction. Mortality. The end of days. The big sleep.'

'You asked me that once before. I have thought about it, yes.'

'Doesn't it give you the shivers? When you're lying awake in the middle of the night. The idea that it doesn't go on for ever. That one day it all just *stops*.' I pull a solemn expression, and as spookily as I can manage, I intone the magic words.

'The truly awful thought of everything carrying on regardless. *After we've gone.*'

'Actually, I find it rather exhilarating,' she replies. 'The principle that whatever there is, is solely contained in the here and now. I think of life as like surfing. Rushing forward at the cutting edge of a perpetual present.'

'It doesn't bother you about the wave collapsing eventually?' This death thing isn't playing nearly as well as I'd hoped. 'Or falling off before your time? Or not being allowed to get back on?'

'The joy is all in the ride.'

'Or the misery, presumably.'

'Absolutely.'

'You could get on a really shitty wave.'

'Who promised life would be fair?' My sentiments exactly.

'Or even interesting.'

'The past is history. The future, a mystery. The present is a *gift*. That's why it's called the present.'

'Jean-Paul Sartre?'

'Joan Collins, I think.'

'Ah.'

'So tell me about deception comedy.'

'What?'

'I'm curious.'

'Can't we talk about death instead? I find it more cheerful.'

'You've asked me all these questions about myself. Let's talk about *you* for a change.'

Me? 'What about me?'

'Apart from the obsession with mortality, who is the real Charles Green?'

'The real Charles Green. Hmm. Golly. Interesting.' Heavy sigh. 'Where on earth to begin . . . ?'

Kate refills both our glasses, until they're very full indeed.

'I've got plenty of time,' she says with a small, particular smile. 'Why don't you start at the beginning?'

'Really . . . ?' Christ, I think she's serious.

Oh, fuck it then. Here we go.